THESE VENGEFUL GODS

ALSO BY GABE COLE NOVOA

The Wicked Bargain

The Diablo's Curse

THESE VENGEFUL GODS

GABE COLE NOVOA

RANDOM HOUSE · NEW YORK

Random House Books for Young Readers
An imprint of Random House Children's Books
A division of Penguin Random House LLC
1745 Broadway, New York, NY 10019
penguinrandomhouse.com
GetUnderlined.com.

Text copyright © 2025 by Gabe Cole Novoa
Jacket illustration © 2025 by Leo Nickolls based on art copyright © 2025 by
Marcos Mesa Sam Wordley/Shutterstock (girl) and Redcollegiya/
Shutterstock (title lettering) • Cover design by Leo Nickolls © 2025
Old vintage paper background by detshana/stock.adobe.com

Penguin Random House values and supports copyright. Copyright fuels creativity, encourages diverse voices, promotes free speech, and creates a vibrant culture. Thank you for buying an authorized edition of this book and for complying with copyright laws by not reproducing, scanning, or distributing any part of it in any form without permission. You are supporting writers and allowing Penguin Random House to continue to publish books for every reader. Please note that no part of this book may be used or reproduced in any manner for the purpose of training artificial intelligence technologies or systems.

Random House and the colophon are registered trademarks of Penguin Random House LLC.

Editor: Jenna Lettice
Associate Editor: Jasmine Hodge
Jacket Designer: Angela G. Carlino
Interior Designer: Michelle Canoni
Production Editor: Clare Perret
Managing Editor: Rebecca Vitkus
Production Manager: CJ Han

Library of Congress Cataloging-in-Publication Data is available upon request.
ISBN 978-0-593-89812-3 (trade)—ISBN 978-0-593-89813-0 (ebook)

The text of this book is set in 11.75-point Carre Noir Pro.

Manufactured in the United States of America
10 9 8 7 6 5 4 3 2 1

The authorized representative in the EU for product safety and
compliance is Penguin Random House Ireland, Morrison Chambers,
32 Nassau Street, Dublin D02 YH68, Ireland, https://eu-contact.penguin.ie.

Random House Children's Books supports the First Amendment
and celebrates the right to read.

To my disabled comrades:
We get to be heroes too.

THESE VENGEFUL GODS

An excerpt from The Book of Deities, *second edition*

THE GODS

Creators of godmagics. Ancestors of all. Keepers of civilization.

Glamor (he/him): the benevolent god of influence; the father of Charisma, Beauty, Love, and Lust

Architect (he/him): the sculptor of the world; the father of Space, Earth, Skies, Ocean, Textiles, and Industry

Mind (she/her): the strategic thinker; the mother of Logic, Empathy, Foresight, Telepathy, Illusion, and Telekinesis

Flora (she/her) and **Fauna** (they/them): the twin gods; the parents of Animalia, Vegetation, Harvest, and Hunt

Discord (he/they): the unknowable god; the father of Flame, War, Disaster, Panic, Deception, Destruction, and Chaos

Life/Death (he/him): the god of the beginning and the end; the father of Herald, Medic, Malady, and Shade

An excerpt from The Book of Deities, *second edition*
Transcribed session of Godcouncil meeting A62DL7

It is known that Death and his children were godkillers.

"They will kill us all if we do not act," said Glamor.

"It is logical," said Mind, "to remove the threat."

"I do not wish to die," Architect said.

"Nor do we," said Flora and Fauna. ████████

██████████████

"You are forgetting," drawled Discord, "that Death cannot be killed."

"But his descendants can be," said Mind.

"Then it is settled," said Glamor. "The Deathchildren must be removed."

████████████████████████████
████████████
██████████████████
████████████████████
████████████████████████████████
████████████████████████████████
████████████████████████████████
██████████████████
████████████████████████████
████████████████████
██████████████
████████████████████████

██████████████
██████████████
███████████████
███████████████
██████████

"The Council has decided to remove your children," Discord said to Death.

"So be it," replied the eldest god, ████████
████████

So it was.

I

THE SHALLOWS

CHAPTER 1

You call it the worst night of your life, and child, it is also mine.

You're six years old when you wake to the sound of arguing just outside your bedroom window. Perhaps, on another night, you might have rolled over and gone back to sleep, but tonight your dreams are plagued with smoke and flame and blood.

(It is the first time, but it will not be the last.)

So instead you sit up and roll out of bed. Your bare feet pad on the cool slate floor. You stand on the tips of your toes to peer out the window. The darkness is complete, and the arguing figures are illuminated by the light of your neighbor's open door.

Who is arguing outside Lark's house? you think, and even though you don't get along with Lark, that recognition of her home is enough to spark your interest.

No one notices as you step outside and slip soundlessly into the shadow of the near-full moon. The arid earth is hard and dusty beneath your toes as you move toward the arguing adults. The cool air of the desert night makes you shiver, but you don't turn back. With a start, you recognize the voices: Your mother and Lark's mother are arguing in a poor attempt at hushed voices.

"Have you lost your godsdamned mind?" Lark's mother hisses. "If you think I'll let you leave Homestead with my daughter—"

"Then come with me," Cara says urgently. "Bring the family. If we hurry—"

"If it's such an emergency, why aren't you leaving with your child and Falcon?" Lark's mother responds. "Shouldn't you be prioritizing your family over mine?"

Cara shakes her head. "Those with Deathmagic don't have a chance—"

"Mom?" The word bursts out of you before you can stop it. Your mere curiosity has twisted into something sharper, something more urgent. It twists in the center of your chest, ratcheting your pulse to discomfiting levels.

Lark's mother and yours both jump. Lark's mother covers her mouth with her hand while Cara spins around to face you, wide-eyed. But the shock on her face disappears in a blink, so quickly you question whether you imagined it altogether. Her expression smooths into something placid and placating. She smiles at you, and it's a balm to the buzzing energy gathering in your stomach.

"Dear," she says softly, "what are you doing out of bed? It's late, my sweet."

The pet names are . . . odd. It's been well over a year since your mother has called you *dear* or her *sweet*. But if she doesn't seem concerned, then maybe you have nothing to worry about. If she's smiling at you and being kind, then maybe that's all you need to breathe in the cool night air.

"I had a bad dream," you say. "And then I heard you arguing."

"Oh, sweetie." Cara laughs lightly and crosses the space between you, placing her hands on your shoulders and turning you gently back toward the house. "We aren't arguing, we're just having a discussion. Come, let's get you back to bed."

As your mother steers you toward the house, you glance over your shoulder at Lark's mother, who is standing stricken and pale in the doorway of her own home. When she meets your gaze, she frowns, then retreats inside, closing the door.

In your room, as your mother tucks you into bed (which is odd, isn't it? She never tucks you in, not anymore), you bite your lip and ask, "Are you leaving Homestead with Lark?"

Cara arches an eyebrow. "Leaving Homestead with Lark? Why would I do that?"

You don't know. It's no secret to you, even at six, that your mother likes Lark more than she likes you, that Lark is the daughter your mother expected *you* to be, but that doesn't explain why Cara would *leave* with Lark.

Cara runs her fingers through your hair, pushing your fringe out of your face. "You must have dreamed that. I'm sure you're very tired; it's late and you should be asleep. Go to sleep, dear one. I'll see you in the morning."

You're quite sure you didn't dream it, but this—your mother being sweet and gentle and lulling you to sleep—this must be a dream. It's a warmth you crave, a kindness you need. So when your eyes drift closed, you don't fight it. And when your mother presses her soft lips to your forehead, you smile.

It's a beautiful dream you don't want to wake from.

But you do. And when you wake, it is to smoke, and flame, and blood.

CHAPTER 2

The bell rings and the hulking fortress of a man who is my opponent does exactly what you'd expect from someone who calls himself the Great Rhinoceros: He charges. I slip out of the way, letting his arm graze mine as his momentum carries him past me. The contact isn't strictly necessary for what I do, but it makes it a hell of a lot easier.

Because the moment his skin touches mine, magic sparks invisibly between us, scanning his body from head to toe. A picture of energy flashes in my mind, outlining his every tendon, every nerve, in a perfect representation of his body. In the space of a blink, red bursts through the represented nerves in my mind, like drops of neon dye bleeding into a glass of water. The red highlights a bad left ankle and some bruising around his right rib cage. His fingers are weak from breaking too many times, and his footwork is sloppy.

So this won't take long.

Rhino man's sheer mass has carried him to the other side of the ring. He turns around, glowering at me. "This isn't a dance. *Fight me!*" he screeches.

I keep my stance wide and beckon him forward. His eyes narrow. The Rhino charges again, roaring as he rages toward me.

One, two, three steps toward me and he's closed the distance between us in half. I don't move, not until he's within arm's reach. He swings. I duck out of the way, pivot, and slam the side of my foot into his weak left ankle.

He screams. The combination of the momentum of his missed punch and the crumpling of his ankle sends him sprawling onto the floor. I take three large steps back, out of reach, and wait. I need him on his feet, where his bulk—and now his screaming ankle—will make him clumsy. Engaging him while he's still on the ground, where his weight could crush me, would only give him the advantage.

Rhino man scrambles back to his feet, chest heaving, his face contorted into an ugly grimace, which I can see because, unlike most of us down here, he isn't wearing a filtration mask. His ankle is pulsing a deeper red in my mind's eye, so the pain must be pretty bad, even if he tries not to show it. His eyes glint with malice. He growls—literally *growls* like some animal—before charging forward again.

This time he leads with his right side, presumably to make it harder for me to target his ankle again. His bruised ribs would be more easily accessible, except he has his arm and elbow covering them, ready to ram me, so that's not going to work—at least, not from the front.

I slip out of the way when he gets close again, but this time he's ready for my dodge. He pivots on his right foot, spins back, and swings his left elbow out for a jab. I duck beneath his arm and twist to face his rib cage. I make a quick set of punches, my wrapped knuckles connecting with his now-unprotected ribs. I land three jabs, then twist out of the way.

His side pulses with red pain in my mind, but the deepest throbbing still comes from his ankle. If I could hit it one more time . . .

"Fight me, godsdammit!" he screams, spittle flying from his mouth. I suppose he's used to people trying to outmuscle him, but that's never been my style. And anyway, he's probably three times my weight, so that would never work.

"But we're having so much fun," I respond with a smirk he can't see beneath my mask.

"You're going to wish you were never born, boy," Rhino growls. Then he's moving forward. This time he isn't charging, but his steps are long and steady even despite the continued pulsing of his ankle. Still, it seems he's done racing past me like a bull. His punches come quick. I slip back, light on my feet, the *whoosh* of warm air against my cheek as his fists barely miss. So that's a little worrying.

Then he does something weird—his right arm comes swinging out from the side with his fingers extending flat, palm down. He's aiming for my torso with the side of his hand. A well-aimed chop like that between the ribs would *hurt*. I shift back, throwing both of my hands out to block. I catch the hit right at my side, which jams my thumb knuckles into my ribs with bruising force.

But now I have his fingers in my hands, so the pain is worth it. I grip his fingers hard and yank back with the full force of both of my arms. His fingers give way with an off-putting crunch. The scream that rips out of him is pure agony. He yanks his arm back, and I let him pull me forward with the motion, just close enough for me to slam the blade of my foot against his bad ankle once more.

He screams again as he crumples, trying to pull me down with him, but his broken fingers don't have much grip. I slip out of his hold as he hits the floor, then stomp on his bad ankle yet again for good measure.

This time it snaps beneath my foot. His howls fill the arena as I take several steps back, arms up in case he manages to somehow get up on just one foot. It's an unnecessary precaution, though. He doesn't even try to get up again. Instead, he curls up into a ball as he cradles his ankle and hand.

The crowd begins the countdown from ten. And even though it's obvious he's not getting up again without help, I don't lower my arms until the bell signals the end of the match. The crowd roars. The host bounds into the ring, grabbing my hand and holding my arm up.

"Let's hear it for tonight's winner, Murder of Crows!"

With the cheers of the crowd ringing in my ears and the buzz of latent adrenaline in my veins, I let myself enjoy this victory. Just a minute to breathe in the high of a win, the corners of my lips tilting up into a small smile.

Just for a minute.

CHAPTER 3

Now this is the part that sucks.

In the men's locker room, I sit on a bench, my rune-chilled canteen beside me as I grip the edge of the fabric wrapped around my knuckles.

In the ring, there are few rules: No weapons. No spelled defensive objects. No spelled offensive objects. That's basically it. You can use godmagic if you have it and mundane magic—runes—if you know it. Where godmagic is limited by heritage, runemagic is available to anyone with the opportunity to learn it. And my uncles made sure I had the instruction I needed.

In the interest of fairness, however, there are certain spelled objects that are allowed for everyone—one being knuckle wrappings spelled with numbing runes; another being face masks spelled with filtration runes, like the one I wear.

There is a danger to using numbing wrappings, of course, especially over your knuckles. Without the pain, it's easy to punch too hard and break your own fingers—and not even realize it until you take the wrappings off and the pain floods in.

Still, you don't have much choice if you fight for a living

and have an autoimmune disease that makes your joints swell painfully.

The irony is, as a Deathchild with access to Deathmagic, I have the ability to heal—it's how I've survived this long fighting for a living every night. Healing scrapes, cuts, bruises—even sprained limbs and broken bones are all easy. It's also how I remind my body to produce elevated levels of testosterone every week, and how I began reshaping my chest when I was thirteen to get the flat shape that feels right on my body today. But I have limits—and convincing my immune system to stop attacking my joints all day, every day, is one of them. I can temporarily ease the pain when it comes, but as much as I wish otherwise, I can't make my immune system stop creating the problem to begin with.

I unwrap the black cloth carefully, clenching my jaw in anticipation of the throbbing that's sure to meet me. I've never actually punched anyone hard enough to break my own fingers, but that doesn't much matter, because my finger joints are some of the worst in my body. Without the wrappings, punching anything at all—with any amount of force—would be absolute agony. The wrappings don't really save me from the pain—they just make it possible to ignore until after the match is over.

Taking a deep breath, I pull off the cloth. The pain is intense, overwhelming, and instant. It throbs from my knuckles, so strong that I feel it in my fingertips and all the way to my wrist. I close my eyes, breathing through gritted teeth, already dreading doing this again for my left hand. But I can't treat the inflammation without removing the wrappings, so I have to do it if I don't want to permanently screw up my hands.

I gingerly grab one of my spelled fingerless gloves and slide it onto my right hand. The smooth black leather is cooling. Once it's on, I trace the runes etched into the leather over each knuckle, activating the anti-inflammatory magic. The relief is instant. It starts in my knuckles and slowly spills over to the rest of my hand. The pain melts away like butter on a hot pan—not completely gone, but much more bearable.

I close my eyes with a sigh, slowly flexing my fingers and working the stiffness out of my joints. Once the pain has dissipated fully and my fingers are flexible again, I repeat the process on my other hand. I've just finished and stretched out my left hand when loud voices burst into the room.

The loudest of them is, unfortunately, familiar. "Where is he?"

I don't look up, though I'm pretty sure the *he* in question is me. Instead, I pack my wrappings, towel, water, and the sweaty clothes I changed out of into my bag. As my most recent opponent's voice nears, I swing my bag over my shoulder and stand.

Rhino man rounds the corner and spots me. He still isn't wearing a mask. His face is red, eyes narrowed and boiling over with fury. His ankle is wrapped, probably with a runed bandage, judging by the fact that he's actually standing. There hasn't been anywhere near enough time for his ankle to be healed, though—while healing runemagic exists, it's slow— so his gait is unsteady. He's probably making it worse putting his weight on it like that so quickly, but the murder in his glare tells me he doesn't care.

"You," he growls out. "Give me my godsdamned money."

I arch an eyebrow. "*Your* money?"

He steps toward me, towering over me but wobbling on his

bad ankle. "There's no way you could have beat me fairly—you're a cheater. And you cheated me out of my win. I want those winnings. *Now.*"

I snort, barely resisting the urge to roll my eyes. I start to walk around him, but he shifts directly into my path. I stop and meet his gaze coolly. "I suggest you get out of my way if you don't want me to ruin your ankle for good."

His face reddens. "Who told you about my ankle? There's no way you could have—"

"Noticed that you favor your right foot? Yeah, impossible that I would have picked up on that." Strictly speaking, that isn't how I figured it out, but he doesn't need to know that.

"I *know* you cheated," he seethes.

To be clear, I didn't cheat. Again, it isn't against the rules to use godmagic if you have it, which I do. Technically speaking, using *Deathmagic* is illegal *anywhere* in Escal—because *being* a Deathchild is illegal—but seeing as this entire underground fighting ring is illegal, my being a Deathchild is just one more taboo to add to the list.

So is using Deathmagic to scan his body and learn his weak spots illegal? Yes. But cheating? Not even a little.

"Whatever helps you sleep at night," I say, sidestepping him.

He swings. I duck and jam my boot into his bad ankle. My heel scrapes the wrapping off in the process.

This time the crack of his bones is so loud, I'm pretty sure everyone in the room hears it.

The healing magic fails and the Great Rhinoceros screams as he hits the floor. I step over him and walk past some snickering bystanders as the man's shrieks devolve into sobs.

I reach the door to the locker room, but it swings open

before I can grab it. A boy with light brown skin and black hair, wearing a hot-pink beanie, a black filtration mask, and mismatched black and white boots, is holding the door open. I step to the side to let him in, but his eyes light up and he steps back to let *me* through.

I'm nowhere near polite enough to make this awkward, so I step through the door and turn toward the exit.

"You're Crow, right?" the boy says behind me.

I pause. "Who's asking?"

The boy lets the door close without entering the locker room, muffling Rhino man's screams. Instead, the boy jogs to catch up with me. "I'm a big fan of your work."

Oh, great. A *groupie*.

"Thanks," I say. I'm trying not to be a dick, but I'm tired and beyond ready to go home.

"You *humiliated* that meathead. It was glorious." He grins so widely it reaches his eyes—which are two different shades of blue. And there's something . . . vaguely familiar about him. I shake the feeling—I probably saw his face in the crowd.

"Guys like him rely too much on brawn," I say. "Anyway, I'm headed home, so . . ."

"Oh, no problem," he says, not budging. "This won't take long. I actually have an offer for you."

I frown, looking him over again. He seems about my age, and his odd, mismatched outfit is loud but doesn't scream wealthy. I suppose that could be a deliberate choice—and a smart one—given that we're in the Shallows.

Still, now I'm curious. So, fine, I bite. "What . . . kind of offer?"

He straightens, radiating confidence. His eyes gleam with

something like excitement. "I'd like to sponsor you for Tournament of the Gods."

I snort and turn away. "Yeah, okay."

The Tournament of the Gods is a biannual televised competition. It's a traditional thing—nearly as old as Escal itself—and supposedly meant to promote the coming together of all godchildren and celebrate magic. And maybe it started that way, who knows, but it's definitely not like that now.

The Tournament is for people who don't value their lives or privacy. People obsessed with fame. Rich people, really, because no Shallows-born has ever made it past the Opening Trial of the Tournament, let alone come anywhere near winning. Gods, most winners aren't even just Midlevelers, they're Uppercity folk—as rich as you can get without being a Godleveler yourself.

I think it's how some bored rich people get their kicks. *Their* real lives aren't dangerous or at risk—not like the lives the rest of us in the Shallows struggle through just to make it to tomorrow. So they enter the Tournament, where they face a real chance of death for the first time in their lives. For the adrenaline hit, I guess.

Or, if they're not into gambling with their own lives, they sponsor someone else to do the job, for the chance to get even richer.

Even if my privacy wasn't literally the only reason I'm still alive, I still wouldn't be willing to risk my life for the nonexistent chance of getting fuck-you money. Because the Tournament may not *necessarily* be to the death, but killing is not exactly discouraged, and people die in it all the time. And anyway, even if it wasn't essential to my survival that people don't know I exist,

I'm really uninterested in being famous. The way the media and people salivate over every damn thing famous people do could not be less appealing.

"Wait!" The boy keeps pace with me. "I'm serious—I think you'd be a real contender."

"Shallows-born can't win," I say.

"Just because no one from the Shallows has won yet doesn't mean they *can't*."

"Pass."

"But—"

I turn on him, not bothering to hide my distaste anymore. "What are you, like, some trust-fund kid playing a poverty tourist down here? Sponsoring is expensive as fuck and most Midlevelers aren't even eligible."

I don't say it, but I also have no idea why anyone would gamble their sponsorship on someone nearly guaranteed to lose. It's not like they can sponsor more than one person—they have to throw their weight behind *one* person per Tournament year. So why pick someone from the Shallows—someone with virtually no chance of winning?

The boy blinks and tilts his head. "Wait, you really don't recognize me?"

"Should I?"

"Huh. Maybe it's the mask." his eyes light up. "Well, that's a nice change of pace, I suppose. Does the name Chaos ring a bell?"

Oh. Oh *fuck* no.

Everyone's descended from the gods—we're all godchildren of some kind or another. But the gods often have flings with mortals, and the resulting offspring are minor gods themselves. Where the rest of us have access to diminishing godmagic as it drips down family lines—to the point where half of Escal's population doesn't have access to godmagic at all—minor gods are incredibly powerful. And basically celebrities.

This time when I turn around, I don't stop walking even when he keeps pace with me. "Pass," I say, louder this time.

Chaos laughs. "So you *do* recognize me."

"I *recognize* that I couldn't be less interested in messing around with the gods, so yeah, I'm out. Find some other sucker to sponsor."

"Why would I do that when you're clearly the best fighter down here?"

"Good thing you're not required to pick someone from the Shallows. And anyway, I'm not the only one here who knows how to throw a punch."

"I think we both know there's more to a good fighter than knowing how to throw a punch."

He's right, of course, but that's beside the point. I push the exit door open and waltz out into the rain. Unfortunately, Chaos follows me.

"Just think about it," Chaos says. "I'll be down here for a little while longer—the deadline for entrants is in four days. Whatever you want, you could get it if you win. Money? Easy. A home on Midlevel? Make it far enough in the Tournament and I could make it happen. Hell, even if you *don't* win, the notoriety alone—"

"Is exactly why I'm not interested."

Chaos blinks, his puppy-dog excitement melting into something like confusion. It's almost adorable, like it never occurred to him that someone might not *want* to be famous.

Then again, for a minor god who's been treated like a celebrity since birth, I suppose that might come as a surprise.

"Just—forget it," I say, shaking my head. "I'm not interested, but it's nothing personal." (That's a lie, it became kind of personal the moment I realized he's a god.) "Good luck finding your Champion or whatever."

"Just take my card," he blurts out, holding out his phone.

I hesitate. I don't want to give him the impression I'm actually considering this on any level, but having the direct line to a minor god could come in handy one day.

So, reluctantly, I pull my phone out of my pocket and tap it against his. Our phones buzz and his card appears on my screen before I lock it and shove it back in my pocket again.

"Cool," he says. "If you change your mind, you know how to contact me."

I nod and walk away.

"Good to meet you, Crow!" he calls out somewhere behind me.

I don't respond.

CHAPTER 4

⋈

As I step into the street, my boot sinks into ankle-deep flood-water. The waterproofing runes carved into the leather glow white for a second as the protective magic activates, repelling the water and keeping my foot dry. By the time I get home, it'll be the only part of me that's dry. The drizzle that started on my way to the Underground has evolved into an outright down-pour. The gray-brown floodwater ripples with it, cans and bottles and random garbage dancing with hundreds of impacts.

Pulling my hood over my head, I slog forward, grimacing at the resistance against my feet. It's going to take me twice as long to get home if all the streets are this flooded, but so what else is new?

I've taken all of three steps when a tiny familiar squeak stops me. I glance around and find the source of the noise immediately—a small gray dust mote of a cat sitting on a dumpster, watching me with her head tilted. Mouse's gaze is fixed on me, expectant—this has become a nightly occurrence. She squeaks again, louder this time, earning the name I've given her.

I sigh and wade forward, unzipping the front of my hoodie

halfway down. I pull it forward to make space so she can climb into the large pocket I sewed into the lining for exactly this purpose. As soon as I'm close enough for her to reach, she stands and slips into my sweatshirt, purring as I zip it up. I really shouldn't be indulging her like this—it's entirely my fault that she's become this attached. But I can't say no to her.

I slip out of the alley and onto the sidewalk, which is barely distinguishable from the street thanks to the floods. Still, the raised pathway means the water is only ankle-deep instead of shin-deep, so it's some improvement.

The downpour has sent most people inside, so the streets are fairly empty. That, and the late hour—people typically try to avoid getting caught out after dark, especially during flood season.

The rain helps dull the usual garbage smell, at least, which my mask doesn't filter out. I probably could change that if I tinkered with the runes on my mask. It's been spelled to filter out air pollution, mold, and viruses—something that became necessary after the explosion of airborne illnesses that hit us ten years ago.

The pollution and mold deaths were bad enough before the Silencing a decade back. No one knows for sure exactly what it was about slaughtering Deathchildren and minor Death gods that has caused constant outbreaks of disease ever since (though personally, I think murdering the minor god in charge of disease was a shit idea). Honestly, the why matters less than the reality of the dozens upon dozens of outbreaks that have killed so many of us. I'll never forget the way the worst wave three years ago led to corpses crowding the streets for weeks, bloating with floodwater before it became bad enough that the upper levels had to stop ignoring us for once and send in health officials to dispose of the bodies safely.

The ghosts, visible only to Deathchildren with access to Deathmagic like me, never really left after that.

Neon lights flashing off storefronts and too-bright billboards reflect off the water in a chaotic mix of colors. I pass a couple of guys who have pushed their masks down their chins so they can make out under the world's smallest awning, and a group of masked teens sitting on top of a long-abandoned rusty car, chatting casually.

A food cart crowded beneath a too-small umbrella advertises freshly fried savory hand pies. Three kids sit on the curb nearby, nearly up to their knees in floodwater, huddled beneath a single raincoat held above their heads as they hungrily eye the cart. A small, gray-tinted ghost joins them on the curb, staring at the food cart with a longing that makes my heart hurt. I slow to a stop in front of the cart and check the listed prices. It's not overpriced—my winnings tonight cover the gap in this month's rent, but I have a little extra. I can afford this.

"What can I get you?" the vendor asks, adjusting his mask with gloved hands.

"Three chicken, please."

Ten minutes and a quick payment later, the vendor passes me three individually wrapped steaming hot pies. I approach the kids, who have been watching me in wide-eyed silence this whole time, crouch, and offer them each a pie. I don't look at the ghost-kid—as far as I can tell, the ghosts don't know that I can see them, and I'd rather keep it that way.

"Be careful," I say. "It's really hot."

The kids on either side take the pies without hesitation.

The one in the middle looks at me thoughtfully instead of taking it, tilting their head slightly. "Are you Murder of Crows?" they ask. "The Underground fighter?"

I blink. I hadn't thought these kids were old enough to attend Underground matches—they don't look like they could be older than ten—but then again, malnourishment can stunt growth pretty badly, so who knows?

I hand them the remaining pie. "Yeah. That's me."

The kid takes the pie and breaks off a corner, smiling as steam releases from the inside. They pop the crispy dough into their mouth. "You bought some food for my friend Jessa last week. She was telling everyone about it."

I try to smile, but it comes out thin and forced. There are way too many people who can't afford food down here, and my winnings aren't anywhere near enough to help everyone.

Fifteen minutes later my calves are burning and I'm not even a quarter of the way home, so once I turn the corner around the block, I pause to take a break.

It's a bad move. There's a livestream playing directly ahead of me, the volume up so high that the politician's booming voice reverberates in my chest. My eyes snap up to the billboard playing the feed, remembering her voice like you might remember touching a red-hot stove. Wishing more than anything that the recognition didn't wind me like a kick to the gut.

(Wishing more than anything that I could purge her voice from my memory entirely.)

President Cara looks exactly the way she does in my childhood memories. Though it's been ten years since I've seen my mother in person, her face hasn't aged a day, probably thanks to some hired Glamorchild's magic. Her skin is pale, her hair black, her eyes a piercing blue so bright they almost look unnatural. Her voice makes me want to puke, but I can't move. I hate that she has this power over me, but even a decade later it's hard to shake off your mother's claws.

"Citizens of Escal will always be my first priority, no matter where they live or what profession they have. It is our responsibility as citizens of this great land to keep each other safe, and my responsibility as your president to give you the resources you need to do just that."

Someone snorts next to me and I jump. I hadn't even noticed the bearded man who'd stepped next to me, his tired eyes still on the screen.

"She means she's sending more Enforcers down here," he says, wiping rain off his mask. "Damned Glamorchildren. Barely leaves the Manor to see Midlevel, let alone look at us down here."

He's probably right about the Enforcers. He's definitely right about how little she leaves the guarded Manor, where she has every possible luxury. I shake my head. The interruption was enough to pull me out of her grip, so it's time to go before I get pulled back in. I grunt in response, shove my hands into my pockets, and trudge forward. Her voice chases me all the way down the block, but I refuse to catch the words. Instead I focus on Mouse's steady vibrating purr against my chest, on the splash of my boots in the water, on the static-like endless patter of rain.

Technically, the bearded man was right about the Glamorchild thing too. Like nearly all politicians, my mother is a Glamorchild—but so distantly it's practically irrelevant. Like most people these days, she doesn't have access to her godly ancestor's godmagic.

Sometimes I think the world would be better off without the gods. A world where people could decide their own fate without relying on *one* person to represent us in a council of gods oblivious about what life is like out here. A council that gets to decide what we lowly godchildren need without deigning to come see for themselves.

Of course, without the occasional new minor god to create new godchildren with access to godmagic, I guess all godmagic would die out eventually. Still, it's hardly a surprise that Glamor—the god of influence and father of Charisma—ended up leading the Godcouncil. Or that nearly all our presidents have been his descendants.

Finally my mother's voice becomes a murmur somewhere far behind me; then that too fades, and I pause to slow my racing heart, resting my forehead against the cold wet brick of a closed storefront.

"She's not here," I whisper. "She doesn't know you're here, or that you've changed your name. She thinks you're dead."

And it's for the best. It's necessary. It's safe.

But repeating the mantra does little to ease the ache deep in my chest.

CHAPTER 5

⨉⨉⨉

Mouse pops her tiny head out of my sweater and rubs her cheek against my jaw. She's soft and warm, and the gesture is so sweet, I can't help but smile, just a little. I gently rub behind her ear. She squeaks indignantly at my wet hand and hides back into my hoodie.

Pushing off the wall, I blink rain out of my eyes as I take in the grungy brick buildings around me. The neon lights and flashy advertisements of a few blocks back have disappeared; we're deep in the Shallows now, too far from the border wall to attract any tourists. Which means, finally, I'm almost home.

Water sloshes against my soaked pant legs as I push on forward. I pass the butcher shop my uncles and I sometimes go to when we can afford it, the hum of security runes buzzing loudly as I pass it, warning potential thieves away. A few crows are sitting on the shop's awning, and they caw at me as I walk by. I've just gotten far enough from the drone of the security runes to escape the constant buzzing in my ears when a gangly boy lurches out of an alley in front of me, plowing right off the curb and into the knee-deep water of the empty street. He swings his arms, straining to move quickly through what has basically become a shallow river, when a distorted voice sets the hairs on the back of my neck on end.

"Halt, citizen!"

I move without thinking, stepping into a patch of shadow under the shop's awning and crouching. I close my eyes, sensing the darkness around me like a cool blanket. Inhaling deeply, I pull the night's shade toward me, until the air is thick and cold and shadow sits tangibly on my shoulders.

The weight of the cool shadows is a familiar comfort. No one can tell just by looking at me that I'm a Deathchild, but the last thing I need is Enforcers investigating me or my family. I may be only distantly descended from the god Death, but my access to Deathmagic has been as natural and easy as breathing since I was five years old. And one of the very first things I learned to do was become shadow.

Using Deathmagic like this is also extremely illegal. If I get caught, I'm dead. So I move fast, melting into shadow before anyone spots me.

When I open my eyes, the world is draped in gray. Out of the alley come two Enforcers revving their sleek black hover bikes, zipping over the water and ramming right into the kid. He falls into the water, submerged for just a second before he comes up, spluttering. The Enforcers cut him off, one in front of him and the other behind, and the boy stands, shoulders sagging as he wipes his drenched hair out of his face. He looks young, maybe twelve or thirteen, and the thought of what these Enforcers might do to him makes me nauseous.

"Leave me alone!" the boy yells. "I haven't broken any laws!"

The sounds that reach me beneath the shadows are

muted—almost like I'm underwater. But I'm still close enough to make out what they're saying.

The man in front of him steps off the hover bike, pulling a baton off his belt. "You disrespected two Enforcers. You need to learn a lesson."

With a flick of his wrist the baton extends to about a foot long. The shaft hisses with cords of red, dripping magic. My heart punches my chest so hard it hurts. I shouldn't get involved. I *can't* get involved. I should turn around and walk away, slip my puddle of shadow into the darkness of the night and disappear.

But even muted, the hissing crackle of the batons is impossible to ignore. One hit from one of those won't kill you, but it is *agony*. Multiple hits can absolutely kill an adult.

I don't know how many hits it'd take to kill a gangly preteen, but I'm not about to find out.

I let the shadows fall off my shoulders and step into the light. "Hey! Is that what all our tax money is paying you for? To pick on kids in the Shallows?"

Both men jerk to attention and turn to me. One Enforcer is dressed in their usual uniform: all pure white from head to toe, with a helmet that completely covers their face. The front part of the helmet has a glass screen so the Enforcer's face is still visible—although it's not uncommon for them to tint the glass black to prevent even that.

I've been told that even though it'd be ridiculously easy to do so, their helmets are *not* rune-spelled to filter out air pollution *or* viruses, which would make the Enforcers down here the only ones who consistently ignore the ever-present dangers that have killed so many of us.

The other Enforcer—the one nearest me—has an identical

uniform, but in bright red, indicating he's the commanding officer. The second Enforcer has pulled out a baton of his own, the red light glinting on the petrified kid. The boy looks at me, wide-eyed, and I keep my gaze on the Enforcers to avoid drawing any more attention to him. I gesture with my hand at my side for him to run; but I'm not sure if he gets it, because he doesn't move.

"Move along," the red-clad commander says through his tinny voice distorter. "This is Enforcer business."

"It's really not," I say. "What crime did he commit?"

The commander steps toward me, close enough that the putrid smell of burning and metal cuts through the fresh rain. "I *said* move along."

"Why do you need two adults to beat on some kid anyway?" I ask, proud of the way my voice doesn't shake though my insides are quivering. I want nothing more than to turn on my heel and run, but I have both Enforcers' attention now. They've started moving toward me, leaving the kid behind them.

"If you don't turn around and leave right now," the commander says, taking another waterlogged step toward me, "I'll have you arrested for Interfering with Justice."

I snort. "The justice of beating a preteen for *disrespecting* you? What does that even mean? He say a bad word?"

Now both Enforcers have fully turned their backs on the kid, who finally seems to understand what I'm doing. He mouths *Thank you* before slinking backward until he reaches the curb and makes a run for it. Both Enforcers are so focused on me, they don't even notice.

Which is great. Except for the part where I now have two angry Enforcers just an arm's length in front of me.

"What he did is irrelevant," the commander says. The smell of the burning magic is so strong, the taste of metal coats my teeth with a gritty film. "And unlike him, you're old enough to know better."

I opt not to comment on his acknowledgment that the kid *wasn't* old enough to know better and he was ready to beat the shit out of him anyway. Instead I say, "Yeah, that's true. Guess you showed me. I'll just be on my way now."

I step back, my heel hitting the curb behind me. The commander squints like he doesn't fully believe my retreat, but the other Enforcer is smarter than that, I guess, because he looks back over his shoulder to where the kid used to be and swears loudly.

"The kid is gone!"

The commander goes rigid, but he doesn't look back. His eyes narrow on me and he points the baton at me. My mouth goes dry. The thing is so close to me now, the ripples of power buzz against my skin. "Where did the kid go?" he barks.

"I dunno. I wasn't watching him. I was watching you and your glow stick."

The other Enforcer makes a sound somewhere between a cough and a scoff.

"Don't think I won't use this on you," the commander says.

"Oh, I don't doubt that" comes out of my mouth before I can stop it, but it's the truth. Enforcers have always loved pushing us Shallowsfolk around, but it's gotten a lot worse in recent years. Just in the last few months there have been more *Enforcer-involved fatalities,* aka fights between Enforcers and Shallowsfolk that ended with dead civilians, than there were in the whole past year.

Oddly, killing the Shallows-born only seems to cause more confrontation and aggression between us and them. Go figure.

"For what it's worth," I add, "you can hit me with that all you want, but I really wasn't watching where the kid went. You'll just be wasting your time."

I'm not sure I really expected him to consider that seriously, but what I *didn't* expect was him to smile. "On the contrary. I came down here to remind some of you of your place. It doesn't matter to me if it's some moody teenager instead of a mouthy kid."

Well. Shit.

"My bad," I say, since my fate is sealed either way. "I thought you were here to pretend to stop crime."

He raises the baton. I tense, shifting my shoulders and raising my arms to protect Mouse—

The crackle of an Enforcer comm module rips through the air. "ALL UNITS IN ZONE SIX TO COMMAND. REPORT IN, ZONE SIX UNITS."

The following silence is thicker than midsummer humidity. The Enforcers glance at each other, the commander scowling before he stands up straight and lowers the baton. "Get out of here before I change my mind."

He didn't, of course, change his mind as much as get summoned elsewhere, but I know better than to mouth off when I've just gotten an unexpected lifeline. Without another word, I step back onto the curb until I'm out of reach before turning on my heel and hurrying down the street. My heart is in my throat, my head light, fingers cold and shaking, but I'm alive, and so is that kid.

I breathe deeply through my nose, grateful for the cool

filtered air my mask is blowing gently on my lips. My stomach roils with waves of anxiety, even with the danger of the Enforcers well behind me.

"It's okay," I breathe into my mask. "You're okay."

Mouse chirps and rubs her head against my chest.

Gods. I can't wait for this night to be over.

CHAPTER 6

The moment I've opened the door to our small home a wall of smoke wafts past me. My mask filters out the worst of it, but my eyes water with the sting immediately. I blink hard, stepping inside even as panicked heat bursts from my chest.

"Hello?" I call, squinting into the smoky space. The door opens into a small living space where a run-down sofa and handmade coffee table sit crammed into the corner beside a small end table where Uncle Orin's sketchbooks are stacked. The smoke is wafting out of the kitchen directly ahead, so I continue forward, still blinking hard to clear my watering eyes.

Here, the source of the smoke is immediately obvious. Uncle Alecks is at the counter, throwing papers and notebooks into a fire in the metal sink. The windows are open, but it's not letting out nearly enough of the smoke. Uncle Orin rushes into the room, arms full of notebooks that he tosses into the sink as well.

"Is that the last of it?" Uncle Alecks asks.

"I think so," Uncle Orin pants. "Unless—"

"What's going on?" I interrupt.

Both of my uncles spin to face me, their faces pale. Alecks's blond hair is sticking up at odd angles. Orin has one hand on his thick black beard, stroking it from stress. I don't know why either of them should be surprised to see me—if anything, I expected them to be worried about how late I was coming home.

"Crow!" Uncle Orin exclaims. "Oh good, you're home. Are you back early? Unless—what time is it?"

"Shit, it's after eleven," Uncle Alecks breathes, turning to his husband. "Or, we need to hurry."

"What's going on?" I repeat. "What are you burning? Why are you even awake?"

Uncle Orin picks up a black backpack I hadn't noticed that was sitting on the floor by his feet. He passes the bag to me—it's heavy and packed so full the sides are bulging. "I've already packed your things. We need you to get out of here—just for a few days maybe. Ravenna should be expecting you—"

"I— What?" I stutter. "What do you mean? Go where?"

"To Ravenna's," Uncle Alecks says. "She's going to take care of you for a few days while your uncle and I lie low."

"Lie low?" My voice croaks. "Why?"

"There's no time—"

A squawking noise blurts through the air, and a red light flashes twice. Both of my uncles stiffen.

"That's the perimeter alarm," Uncle Alecks says in a low voice.

Perimeter alarm?! Since when do we have a perimeter alarm? *How* do we have a perimeter alarm?

Uncle Orin takes my shoulders and gently but firmly steers me toward a small closet where we keep cleaning supplies and extra linens. He pulls open the door, steps inside, and crouches, pushing piles of neatly folded linens to the side. Once it's cleared, he grabs a water bottle shoved into one of the outer pockets of my backpack and squirts water onto his hands before returning it to the bag. With wet fingers, he traces a large square on the floor, then what must be a rune in the center. Finally, he presses his hand flat over it.

I open my mouth to ask him what on earth is going on when the square he's traced glows bright white. Then, within the confines of the glowing square, the floor disappears, revealing a staircase descending deep beneath our home.

I gape. "What— How long has this been here?"

"We'll explain later, I promise," Uncle Alecks says behind me.

Orin stands and pulls me into a hug and Alecks joins in from behind, enveloping me in their warm embrace.

"I'm sorry we don't have time to explain right now," Orin says softly.

A booming noise startles me—someone is pounding on the front door. Neither of my uncles seems surprised; they just hold me a little tighter. Mouse squeaks in my sweater and my uncles laugh, albeit weakly.

"We love you," Alecks says. "Never forget that."

"I love you too, but—"

"The stairs lead to a tunnel," Orin says. "Follow it all the way to the end. Go straight—don't take any turns. It leads to the outskirts by the shore. You'll recognize where you are— find your way to Ravenna's immediately. Avoid the pier as much as possible—the flooding is sure to be especially bad there. Do not stop anywhere else. Do you understand?"

"No, I don't," I say, tightness crawling up my throat. The

pounding on the door has gotten louder. Someone is yelling outside, and I can't make out their words, but the squawk of Enforcer voice distortion is far too familiar.

My uncles release me. Orin nods toward the staircase in the ground. "We're out of time. You need to go. Now."

A loud crack makes us all flinch—the Enforcers are starting to break down the door. I don't understand any of this. Why are the Enforcers here? What were my uncles burning? Why is this tunnel here? None of it makes sense, but when Alecks gently pushes me forward, I descend the stairs in a haze.

Once I've fully entered the stairwell, Orin crouches on the floor above. "Remember Crow, don't stop anywhere until you get to Ravenna's. We love you."

A crash signals the Enforcers have broken through the front door. Orin makes a large circular gesture and the floor reappears, closing me in darkness.

CHAPTER 7

"Pigeon," Lark says when she opens the door, continuing a long-held tradition of refusing to use my name. Instead, she swaps it out for the names of other, less dignified-sounding birds.

I am drenched to my clammy golden-brown skin. Shivering with adrenaline. My hair drips onto my face like tears I'm too numb to shed.

"Shitface," I answer, with an oddly comforting familiarity.

She gives me a once-over, her precisely shaped eyebrows rising with something like amusement. Her long black hair is thrown back into a messy bun that somehow looks professionally done, and her pale skin is annoyingly blemish-free. She's also a solid six inches taller than my barely five-foot-three stature, which has never made me jealous at all.

"You look like a drowned rat." She tuts. "It's an improvement."

"Succumb to a mold infection," I say, but my heart isn't in it, and she can tell. Lark is the only person I know from Homestead who survived the Silencing, which means we've known each other for way too long. She frowns as I step past her and onto the drying mat inside. She closes the door behind me and crosses her arms as the rune-spelled mat sucks all the rain off me. Once I'm no longer dripping, I barely hold in a contented sigh. I've been rain-soaked for so long tonight, I almost forgot what it was like to be dry. Inside my hoodie, Mouse purrs against my chest, warm and soothing.

"So?" Lark says. "What's got you looking like the last puppy at the pound?"

"Lark," says a welcoming, warbly voice. "Be kind to our guest." Ravenna steps into the entryway, face wrinkling with a kind smile. She's short—shorter than me, even—and her cropped hair is pure white.

Lark snorts. "Not sure you can call them a guest when he's here every day for class."

"I'm sorry, dear," Ravenna says to me. "I've made you some tea. Come, let's have a chat." She rests her soft hand on my back, and my shoulders relax. I didn't even realize I had them tensed. I follow in a daze. With the danger behind me, everything feels detached. Distant. Like I'm not in my body, like I'm watching myself move through the narrow hallway into the small kitchen, where two steaming mugs of tea are waiting for us at a tiny table.

Ravenna pulls a chair out for me, and I sit automatically. The kitchen smells like pan-fried garlic and spices. The familiarity should be comforting, but I don't feel anything at all. I don't really understand it—I should be feeling *something*, shouldn't I? I should be devastated. Or terrified. But all I feel is emptiness.

I stare into my mug, where pale green liquid waits for me.

Ravenna places a jar of honey in front of me with a spoon. She even opens the jar for me and places the spoon inside.

"Honey, dear?" she asks, prompting me.

I take the spoon and scoop a large, sticky spoonful with a mumbled *Thank you*. As I stir the honey into my tea, the heat of the steam caressing my nose and lips and cheeks, I slowly come back to myself. Everything still feels strange and disjointed, but I pull the mug to my lips and close my eyes as I take a small sip. The tea is clear and faintly sweet, and the heat pours down my throat and blossoms in my chest.

It's nice. A sigh slips out of my lips. I didn't realize how much I needed this.

"Thank you," I say a little louder this time.

Lark mumbles something behind me that I don't catch and shuffles out of the room. Ravenna sips her tea, her warm dark eyes settling on me. There's pain in that gaze, and a deep sadness. It's like she already knows what happened. Like I don't need to explain anything at all because it's already written all over my face. Like she expected all of this, somehow.

"How . . ." My voice comes out weak at first, scratchy. I take another sip of tea and try again. "How did you know I was coming?"

"Your uncles contacted me a couple hours ago. They were worried they might be arrested tonight. I'm presuming since you're here that they were right."

Oh. I nod and nod and nod, unprepared for the wave of emotion that rolls over me. The pain awakening in my chest. The numbness is fading, and I'm not sure I'm ready for it. I don't know how anyone could be ready for this, for this soul-deep ache that will build into agony. My uncles—

This is my fault. I am the only law my uncles have broken.

My vision blurs. I wipe at my eyes, swearing under my breath. Ravenna doesn't even flinch.

"It's okay if you need to cry, dear," she says softly. "You've been through so much in your short life. I'm so very sorry. You don't deserve any of it."

I expect her words to break the dam, but for some reason they don't. I just find myself nodding endlessly as I take another sip of hot tea.

"Do you . . . know what happened?" I ask.

She grimaces. "I don't know the details of what you experienced tonight, but I know what your uncles told me before their arrest." She lifts her mug and takes a long, slow sip, as if gathering her thoughts. I trace the rim of my mug with my forefinger, smothering the impatience rising in my chest.

After a moment, she lowers the mug again and sighs wearily. "For nine or so years now, your uncles have been working covertly to help locate Deathchildren in hiding and get them out of Escal. I don't know the details of how, or where they go, but your uncles have saved countless Deathchildren."

I hear her words, but they feel like rain on my skin—not penetrating. "My uncles . . ." I frown, shake my head and start over. "Wait. Other Deathchildren? I thought—you, Lark, and me . . ."

Ravenna doesn't interrupt as I try to process.

Even before the Silencing—the genocide ten years ago that wiped most of us out—we Deathchildren were a minority. Pushed to Escal's outskirts. Living in Deathchild towns like Homestead, where I grew up. Treated with unwarranted wariness, like strangers if we dared to step foot beyond Deathchild borders.

So a lot of us didn't.

But they came for us anyway. Glamor led the charge, turning the Godcouncil—and the larger populace—against us. Said we were too dangerous to be left alive. Then he formulated a plan with Mind and Architect to be rid of us for good. Architect armed the Enforcers with neutralizing agents to take out the minor Death gods. And Mind used her magic to literally silence Deathchildren towns the night of the attack so we couldn't warn each other. Now, after the Silencing, our numbers are nearly nonexistent.

Ravenna is the only surviving Deathchild elder I know—and she probably only survived because she can't do Deathmagic herself and hasn't lived in a Deathchild community in thirty-some-odd years. But since she's the only Deathchild elder who survived the Silencing, she's also the only one who can teach me about my heritage—our religion, our culture, and what life was like before the gods took it all away from us. And she has. Information that not even my uncles—who are neither, technically, my literal uncles nor Deathchildren themselves, but were close friends with my dad, Falcon—could teach me.

I've known *some* other Deathchildren still survived, of course—I'm one of them, and so is Lark. I've also figured most of the survivors would be like Lark and Ravenna—unable to access Deathmagic, and therefore more difficult to identify. I've assumed if there were any others out there, there'd be a few dozen scattered across Escal at most.

It's so much to take in. And not remotely what I expected. But somehow, it's a comfort, because if my uncles were helping Deathchildren escape the city, then their arrest wasn't my fault.

It wasn't my fault.

I close my eyes and take a deep, steadying breath. "How . . . many?" I finally ask, opening my eyes. "Did my uncles help?"

"Oh, several hundred easily," Ravenna says.

My mouth drops open. "Several *hundred*?" I fall back in my seat, my head light and buzzy. "I didn't think there were nearly that many of us left."

Ravenna smiles weakly. "I'm sorry I didn't tell you sooner. I hope you can realize your uncles and I were trying to protect you and Lark both. We'd discussed letting both of you in on it soon, once you became adults, but . . ." Her smile slips into a grimace. "Well. Our plans changed tonight."

I have so many questions, I don't even know where to begin. Where did my uncles take the Deathchildren? How did they get them out of Escal safely? How did they hide all of this from me for so long? Why did they risk their lives? And why didn't they ever get *me* out of Escal?

"I can see in your face you have much to ask, but I'm afraid I won't have most of the answers for you. I knew of what your uncles were doing in case something happened to them, but they never shared the details with me and I never asked. I know they were working with others, but I wasn't involved. That was part of the plan to keep both you and Lark safe."

"Do you know where my uncles were sending the refugees?"

Ravenna hesitates, then shakes her head. "Not exactly. All I know is it's somewhere outside the city."

I grimace. Most of Escal's population lives in the massive metropolis we know as Escal City, which is made up of three parts: the Shallows, Midlevel, and Godlevel. There was a time when more of us lived out in the Wilds, but extreme weather, difficult terrain, and frequent natural disasters made it increasingly hard to survive. Too many settlements to count were destroyed in wildfires, earthquakes, tornados, droughts, and famines.

Now, as far as I know, the only people who live in the Wilds are small sects of Florachildren and Faunachildren, who prefer to stay connected to nature, but even they're a tiny minority. There are so few people left out there.

Escal City is supposed to keep us safe and insulated from the dangerous Wilds. But maybe it makes sense that Deathchildren would start over out there. When the city has become hostile to us, risking the turbulent environment isn't unthinkable anymore.

I bite my lip, my gaze slipping back to my half-full cup of tea. If Ravenna doesn't know anything, then the only way I'm going to get any details is through my uncles. But knowing what the government does to "traitors" who aid Deathchildren, it's unlikely that I'll ever see them again.

My throat aches at the thought. Is that it, then? They've been arrested, and I just have to accept that soon they'll be dead? I close my eyes and press my face into my palms. They risked everything for me, for people like me. I can't just move on. I can't just leave them to their fates. I've lost too much already. I can't lose them too.

"Child," Ravenna says softly. "You've been through so much tonight. You should try to rest. Drink the rest of your tea— it will help."

I finish the tea in a quick gulp that goes down in a burst of heat. And when Ravenna helps me out of my chair and down the hall to the bedrooms, I don't protest.

CHAPTER 8

I want so desperately to close my eyes and drift away, but every time I start to slip into shadow, a jolt in my chest startles me awake. It happens again. And again. And again.

Your uncles are in prison. I wake.

You don't have money for a lawyer. I wake.

They'll have an unfair trial. I wake.

They'll be executed. I wake, tears blurring the room and my chest aching fiercely. I can't do this. I can't pretend this is a normal night. I can't sleep. Even if I wanted to pretend, my body won't let me. The dread in my stomach has built to a knot, tight and heavy and full of swarming energy with nowhere to go. My fingers tap on my chest, my toes squirm, desperate to be moving.

I sit up and stretch my arms over my head, trying to ease the discomfort in my torso, but even the sensation of stretching barely scratches the itch. I stand, throwing my pants on and inhaling deeply, my hands pressed against my flat chest. I push gently against my rib cage as it inflates and close my eyes—but that's a mistake. The moment my eyes are closed, my uncle flashes across my vision. A snippet of Orin closing the entrance to the tunnel. The last time I saw him.

Is that the last time I'll ever see him? The thought fills me with heat and my breaths come quick. My eyes snap open in the darkness. I can't do this. I can't stay here. I can't do nothing and accept that I've lost my uncles forever. I already lost an entire community and my dad to the Silencing. And I lost my mother to her abandonment. I can't just sit back and wait for my uncles to die. They're all I have left.

I stand, grab my shirt, and shrug into it, then grope around blindly for my hoodie. My hand lands on a soft and warm ball of fur—I gasp as Mouse squeaks in protest. Gods above, I completely forgot she'd been through this entire nightmarish evening with me. Now with my hand on her, Mouse purrs and rubs her soft cheek against my palm. I can't help it—I smile, just a little. It should be a little worrying, maybe, how this cat makes me melt every damn time, but right now she's a comfort I need. I carefully pull her into my arms, hoodie and all, and her soft body against my chest is such a relief. I close my eyes, taking in the vibrating hum of her contented purrs.

Slowly, my racing pulse returns to something closer to normal. Slowly, I pet her, breathing deeply, soaking in every second of the warm happiness radiating off her.

"I have to save them," I whisper into her fur. "If I go tonight, before they're moved to the Uppercity, maybe I have a chance."

What time is it? I don't even know, but it's still the kind of pure darkness that only comes in the ungodly hours of the night, so I must still have time. I just don't know how much.

"I have to go," I whisper to Mouse. "Stay here and be good.

I'll come back with my uncles, and then we can figure out where to go from there."

"Gods above and below, will you shut *up*?"

Lark's voice very nearly makes me jump out of my skin. The bedroom light flashes on, blinding me, and I squint blearily through the brightness. Lark is sitting up in her bed, hair ruffled and glare murderous.

"You are so godsdamned annoying," she says. "You know it's, like, three in the morning, right? And who are you even talking to? Is that a—" She squints. "A . . . wait. Is that a cat?"

"Her name is Mouse," I mumble.

Lark's face scrunches in confusion. "You named your cat . . . *Mouse*?" Mouse squeaks. Lark's eyebrows shoot up and her face softens. "Oh. Does she not meow?"

"Sometimes." I shrug and gently place Mouse on the bed, then carefully disentangle her from my hoodie. She squeaks in protest and bats at my hands, but when I've freed her from my sweatshirt she makes a new nest in the crumpled bedsheets beneath her.

Lark watches in silence as I slip my hoodie on, her gaze raking slowly over me. She doesn't say anything until I start shoving my boots on.

"You realize my nan will kill me if I let you take a walk at three in the morning, right?" She frowns. "I mean, personally I'd throw a party if someone stabbed you to death while I was sleeping, but then Nan might give me the cold shoulder, and I wouldn't enjoy that."

I almost smile as I lace up my boots. "Die in a fire."

"Choke on your own blood," she responds warmly. "But seriously, where are you going?"

"I'm not sitting here while my uncles wait to be executed."

"Buzzard," Lark says, sounding exasperated. "What are you even going to do?"

"If I can get them out of prison—"

"You do realize that they would have taken Orin and Alecks directly to Midlevel, right?"

I pause. "They'd be held at the station down here for processing first."

Lark shakes her head. "Yeah, but Deathchild-related charges are high priority. Their processing would have been fast-tracked so the Enforcers could transfer them to Midlevel prison ASAP. There's no way your uncles are still in the Shallows—it's been too long already."

I stare at my boots, suddenly cold. I don't want to believe Lark, but she's right that Deathchildren-related charges are fast-tracked. If my uncles have already been moved . . . I don't even know how to get to Midlevel so I can *try* to save them. You need a visa to go up a level, but they don't process visas in the Shallows, so it's impossible for us to leave unless we know someone in the Uppercity.

"For what it's worth, I'm sorry," Lark says. "*You* may be an asshole, but your uncles have always been decent people. They deserve better."

I close my eyes and press the heels of my palms against my eyelids, shivering with a scream trapped inside my lungs and the reality that I don't know how to fix this.

CHAPTER 9

A cabin door creaking open. In the woods, a path blanketed in fallen pine needles, soft beneath my feet. Ahead, a campfire, crackling in the night. A raven bristles its black wings as I approach. Its gaze meets mine and—

I wake to a scratchy dry tongue licking my nose. I blink hard, my face crinkling as Mouse stares directly into my eyes. As soon as I make eye contact, she squeaks and resumes licking my nose.

I smile softly and pick her up off my chest, placing her gently next to me. She's probably hungry. I rub my eyes and sit up, disorienting bright light streaming in through an unfamiliar window. The dream is already fading, but its familiarity runs bone-deep. It's not the first time I've dreamed of a night path in the woods.

My phone buzzes with a weekly reminder: It's time for me to adjust my hormone levels. I close my eyes as I allow my focus to settle on my godmagic. I've been doing this ritual every week since I was fourteen—and it's become one of my favorite times of the week. It's a moment for me to pause, to let everything else fall away and use the magic of my birthright. The godmagic buzzing through my veins is a gentle presence—a familiar comfort intimately tied with shaping my body in a way that feels like home. I don't even have to think to find the hormone receptors I need and push my testosterone levels higher. Not too much—not so much that it'll remetabolize into estrogen again—but enough to settle the unease within me.

It only takes minutes. It's meditative, a grounding breath that calms me like nothing else. A full-body hug, a quiet embracing of my birthright in a way I could never do aloud. Not in a world determined to stamp Deathchildren out.

When I open my eyes, I'm reminded again of how grateful I am to have this magic—without it, I'd have to rely on synthetic testosterone, which doesn't come cheap down here in the Shallows. Most trans folks can't get access to the mediation they need to feel whole. I'm privileged to be able to handle my own care.

I bet no one has this problem on Midlevel.

All at once, the memory of last night comes flooding back: My uncles are on Midlevel. They'll be executed. I can't hire a lawyer or leave the Shallows. I'll never see them again, because it's not like I know a Midleveler who could—

Wait.

Wait. I *did* meet someone from the Uppercity recently—that minor god who wanted to sponsor me for the Tournament of the Gods. It's impossible to enter the competition without a sponsor, but if I accept Chaos's offer, the border guards will *have* to let me through to Midlevel so I can compete.

My heart pounds hard, my pulse aroar. Of course, accepting would mean I'd have to compete.

I bite my lip and pick at my nails. Shallowsfolk have never

made it past the Opening Trial, let alone won. But maybe I don't have to win. Maybe I just have to survive long enough to get my uncles out of prison.

I unlock my phone and navigate to Chaos's contact card, my mind racing. Maybe I'm thinking about this the wrong way. If there's one thing I know how to do, it's fight. Sure, no Shallows-born has ever won the Tournament, but the winner gets a prize you can't get anywhere else: an audience with the gods, who grant the winner a single request. A boon.

If I won, I could ask the gods to pardon my uncles. I wouldn't have to break them out. They'd be free—they wouldn't even have to hide. And with the money I'd win as Champion, we wouldn't have to come back to the Shallows. We could make a new life on Midlevel.

If I don't win, at least I'll be on Midlevel. One step closer to figuring out how to break them out of jail.

My fingers are tapping the contact card open to a new message before I even register what I'm doing.

If I accept your offer, what's in it for you?

The notification that Chaos is typing appears instantly.

You mean besides the sponsor prize pool and lifelong bragging rights?

I roll my eyes, but I don't respond. He types again.

Maybe I just love the idea of an underdog from the Shallows making the gods and Midlevelers alike sit up and pay attention to people they like to pretend don't exist.

I won't admit it, not to him. But maybe I like that too.

I accept.

I hit send before I can change my mind. Once the message is out, my insides twist in nauseating waves, but I press my hands against my belly hard and take a long, deep breath. Agreeing to do a public, televised competition—one that the media fucking *loves*—is the antithesis of everything I've done to keep under the radar. To stay unnoticed so no one realizes who I am. My uncles will be furious, but at least they'll be alive.

My phone buzzes and I jump, ripped out of my thoughts. Chaos has already responded.

Amazing. Pack a bag and meet me at the wall at sunset.

My heart thrums, my stomach swarming with bees. Holy shit. I'm actually doing it. This is happening.

My phone buzzes with another message.

You won't regret this.

The kitchen smells like eggs, bacon, and fresh tortillas when I walk into the room, and even though I'm vibrating with unwanted energy, the warm, salty scent instantly reminds me how long it's been since I've had a proper meal. Ravenna smiles at me when I enter and gestures to the table, where she's set out a plate for me and a small bowl of chopped bacon for Mouse.

"Your timing is perfect. I just finished cooking, so your plate is still hot."

"Thank you," I say, sitting at the table. Lark is already halfway through her meal of eggs wrapped in a thin flour tortilla, and she doesn't even glance up at me, which is for the best. I grab a tortilla from the stack and can't help a smile—the flatbread is fresh from the stove, still hot. I pile on some scrambled eggs and shredded cheese, then wrap it up. It's warm and savory and familiar. It tastes like home.

For a short while, the delicious food is enough to distract me from what I've just done. But once my stomach is full and my plate is empty, there's nothing left to distract me from reality.

Now that I've had time to process, the whole idea seems even riskier than I originally thought. What if someone realizes I'm a Deathchild? I've never slipped up and used obvious Deathmagic in a match, but my life has never been at stake before. What if something slips out in self-defense? Or if I have no choice but to use Deathmagic to survive and it's obvious to everyone?

Or what if none of that happens because I don't even make it that far in the competition? What if I don't even make it past the Opening Trial, like every other Shallows-born who has tried? It's not like I'm the first Shallowsfolk entering who knows how to fight.

I might be the first Deathchild, though.

Much good that does me if I can't use Deathmagic.

"Don't think too hard, Shoebill," Lark says. "You might just self-combust."

It's exactly what I need to hear to yank me out of my doom-spiraling thoughts. I scowl at her.

"Lark," Ravenna chastises. "Be kind."

Lark just lifts a shoulder. "Given that I'm pretty sure they were thinking their way into a panic attack, I think I *am* being kind."

It irritates me to no end that Lark is right.

I ignore her and look at Ravenna. "Thank you for your hospitality. I'll be heading out this evening, but I really appreciate all of this."

Ravenna arches an eyebrow. "Where do you plan to go, child?"

I open and close my mouth. It's not so much that I take issue with telling Ravenna the truth, but maybe I should have started this conversation in private, instead of right in front of Lark, who will certainly be a huge bitch about everything.

I guess it's too late for that now.

"Last night before . . . everything happened, I was approached by a sponsor. For the Tournament of the Gods."

The silence that follows is so complete, I'm certain everyone must be able to hear my heavy heartbeat. Ravenna's expression is thoughtful, her warm eyes examining me not unkindly. A small frown crinkles her brow just as Lark bursts out laughing behind me.

"*You?*" Lark exclaims. "For *the Tournament?* Have you lost your godsdamned mind?"

It's not, to be fair, an unreasonable response. Lark knows I fight in the Underground, of course, but she also knows what it would mean for me to be found out as a Deathchild on a world stage.

Ravenna, who has some tact, says, "Are you sure that's wise?"

"No," I answer bluntly. "But I don't have a choice. It's the only way I can get a visa to Midlevel so I can even have a chance at saving my uncles."

Lark groans. "Not this again."

"Lark," Ravenna says, her usually kind tone laced with steel. "Do not make me reprimand you again."

Lark's mouth snaps shut. It's so satisfying I almost smile.

Ravenna turns to me, her face full of warmth and concern. "I understand you want to help your uncles, Crow—that's perfectly reasonable. But do you think your uncles would want you risking your life to help them?"

I happen to know that's the exact opposite of what they want; they told me as much last night. But I can deal with disappointing them if it means saving their lives.

"I can't sit around and wait for them to be killed," I say instead. "That's not who I am."

Ravenna purses her lips and nods. "I don't have to remind you of the risks—you know them already. I hope you know you don't have to do this, though. You could stay here with us. Lark and I are more than happy to welcome you into our home."

Lark does absolutely nothing to hide how utterly appalled she is by that idea. She speaks up anyway. "Just to be clear, you do realize if anyone discovers you're a Deathchild with access to Deathmagic, you'll be killed, right?"

"Obviously," I say icily.

"You're also aware they don't *let* Shallowsfolk win."

I glance at her. "Just because it hasn't happened yet doesn't mean it's impossible."

"Sure, but—"

"To be honest, Lark, I'd think you'd be happy to see me go. I'm sure watching me die on live television would be a dream come true for you."

"It would be the highlight of my life," Lark says without missing a beat. "But I suspect it'd make Nan upset."

Ravenna grimaces at her granddaughter with disapproval, but she just shakes her head. With a sigh, she crosses the room and wraps her arms around me. "I'll pray to the god who is the beginning and the end for your safety."

It's an old way of referring to the god Death (who is also the god Life, though most people who aren't Deathchildren like to forget that tidbit), and it's oddly comforting to hear. I'm not sure I believe that the gods give a shit about our prayers—in fact, I'm pretty certain they don't. But I'll take any chance I get at tilting the scales in my favor.

"Thank you," I say. "I'll need someone to take care of Mouse while I'm up there, if that's okay."

"Of course," Ravenna says, smiling as my little gray fluff ball looks up from her bowl and wanders over. With a flop onto the floor, Mouse squeaks at my feet, sending a pang through my chest at the thought of leaving her behind. But I know Ravenna will take good care of her. She's going to be spoiled with bacon breakfasts and a soft place to sleep. And anyway, I'll probably be back when I lose.

"And I'll put down a big bet in your honor," Lark says, grabbing a rolled-up tortilla with a self-satisfied smile. "Against you, of course."

CHAPTER 10

The border wall separating the Shallows from Midlevel is an impressive—if ugly—thing. Made of thick black metal, the wall towers over everything else in the Shallows, standing so high, you can't see the top of it when you're at the bottom. Floodlights shine down from the top, illuminating the base of the wall at all hours of the day and night, which seems unnecessary given the impossibility of climbing the sleek surface.

The space between the wall and the city falling away behind me is barren. After you pass the final building on the outskirts, with some ravens perched on the roof, there's a hundred-foot gap of just empty, muddy ground laid with uneven stones. The border station up ahead is simple: a heavily guarded long black gate with barbed wire at the top, and behind that the elevator to carry people up and down the wall. The border station is the only place you can cross from the Shallows to Midlevel—the latter of which sits on elevated land that overlooks the Shallows. A dozen guards—each wearing all white except for the one red guard—stand in front of the gate blocking off the elevator. A couple of them look my way as I approach, but Chaos isn't here yet, so I slow to a stop and pull out my phone, trying to look casual.

To Deathchildren, ravens and crows are good omens. I glance up at the ravens perched nearby, who seem to be watching me with their shiny black eyes. I'll take that as a positive sign.

Looking back at my phone, I bite my lip. No messages. The sun has started setting, but only just barely, so it's not unreasonable that Chaos isn't here yet. Still, I couldn't stand waiting around under Ravenna's watchful gaze and Lark's incredulous mockery. Of course, waiting here under the increasingly suspicious stares of Enforcers isn't exactly an improvement. At least it's finally stopped raining.

Movement in the corner of my eye makes me do a double take—the gray, translucent image of a too-thin man wandering aimlessly across the muddy ground. Another ghost. I grimace and turn my attention back to my phone.

Maybe I should turn around and come back in ten or fifteen minutes. But then again, what if Chaos arrives and thinks I'm a no-show? I can't risk missing out on this opportunity. It's literally the first time since I moved here ten years ago that leaving the Shallows has even been an option.

If I don't take it, I may never get another opportunity to leave. And I certainly won't get the chance in time to save my uncles.

Maybe I should send Chaos a message, just to let him know I'm he—

"You there!" The mechanical distortion of the Enforcer's voice turns my blood to ice. My gaze jerks up from my phone, and though I'd like to look nonchalant, I can't stop the blood from draining from my face as three Enforcers approach me: one red, two white, batons out.

They're already preparing to attack me just for standing here. "Yes?" I ask.

"What are you doing here? This is a restricted area."

That isn't technically true—anyone is allowed to walk around near the border wall as long as they don't try to force their way past the gate. But it *is* a high-security area and Enforcers are naturally suspicious of any Shallowsfolk, so best not to argue with them.

"Oh," I say, trying to keep my tone casual. "Sorry about that; I'm waiting for my sponsor. He told me to meet him here."

The red Enforcer frowns. "You really expect us to believe *you* have a sponsor?"

It takes everything in me not to roll my eyes. "For the Tournament of the Gods."

All three Enforcers look me over like they're examining a piece of meat. It's gross, to be honest, but I stand there, breathing deeply, forcing myself to stay calm. The moment I look agitated is the moment they get aggressive, so the best thing I can do is pretend that none of this is out of the ordinary and that I'm not bothered getting the third degree from a bunch of bored Enforcers.

"Bit puny for the ring, aren't you?" one of the guards in white finally says.

Puny?! My mouth opens in outrage before I snap it shut. I've been adjusting my testosterone levels long enough that I generally pass for an androgynous boy unless I go out of my way to balance it out with some makeup or something, which suits me well enough. However, I'm also short, which for whatever reason seems to make people—especially grown cis men—think I'm not capable of holding my own.

As I swallow every insult and challenge that I want to hurl, my eye twitches. Instead, I say, "Not everyone in the ring relies on physical strength."

Now it's the red Enforcer's turn to look skeptical. "You don't look rune educated either."

I want to ask what "rune educated" *looks* like, but I know the answer: wealthy. Most Shallowsfolk can't afford much of an education, so Midlevelers as a whole tend to be better practiced in runemagic, even though runemagic was always intended to be accessible to everyone.

"Then I suppose I won't last very long in the competition," I say icily.

"I think you'll do just fine," says a voice behind me.

I spin around as a lanky boy approaches. Chaos is dressed even more bizarrely than he was the first time around. His shirt and pants are all black, but his white boots have been doodled all over in what looks like some kind of colored ink, and instead of the pink beanie he had on before, he now has an oversized rainbow-colored one. But what really makes his whole outfit stand out is the enormous, chunky hot-pink knitted scarf he has wrapped around his neck at least three times.

As odd as it is to see him now for the second time in two days, I can't hide my relief. The Enforcers might not want to let *me* through, but they'll have no problem letting Chaos through. And anyway, it doesn't matter what the Enforcers think if Chaos says he's sponsoring me.

"Lord Chaos," the red Enforcer says, his voice thick with reverence even through the distortion of his mask. "Welcome back to the wall. Are you ready to return to the Uppercity?"

"I am," Chaos says cheerily. "And my friend Crow here will

be joining me. I'm sponsoring them for the contest, as they mentioned to you."

This time when the Enforcers look at me again, I smile.

"I—see," the red Enforcer says haltingly. "Do they have a visa?"

"They do not. My understanding is visas aren't issued down here, so we'll need to fill that out at the top of the wall."

All three Enforcers look at each other uncomfortably before the lead Enforcer clears his throat. "You're more than welcome to pass through the gate, of course, Lord Chaos, but your . . . friend can't pass through without a visa."

Chaos tilts his head. "That's interesting, because when I tried to get a visa preemptively, I was told that the person I was sponsoring had to be there in order for the visa to be issued."

"That's true," the Enforcer responds.

"But you don't issue visas in the Shallows."

"Correct."

Chaos stares at the Enforcers, who stare back at him blankly. The minor god is clearly trying to make a point, but his efforts are wasted on them. Enforcers aren't known for their critical-thinking skills—the entire purpose of their job is to enforce the laws, even when the laws are wholly contradictory.

"It would seem," Chaos says slowly, "that there's a breakdown in the system here if you won't allow me to get a visa for my chosen competitor. Which is fascinating, because I was under the impression the contest is open to all." He taps his chin. "I suppose I may have to mention this to my father. Of course, Discord has never been a fan of bureaucracy, but they *do* have a soft spot for the Shallows, so I'm sure he'll appreciate the opportunity to come down here themself and take a closer look."

The Enforcers go utterly silent, and it takes some effort not to laugh. Being a minor god, Chaos is a god's literal child—in his case, Discord's son. Of all the gods except Death, Discord is the most feared—not because they're evil or anything, but because he thrives on all the things that scare the shit out of people. Natural disasters, fire, war, fear—he can do it all, which makes them someone you don't want to fuck with.

I couldn't tell you if Discord actually gives a single shit about the Shallows, but if it's a bluff, it's working. The lead Enforcer clears his throat and steps to the side, clearing a path for us. "That won't be necessary. You two can pass—just make sure to fill out the visa at the station at the top of the wall."

"I'll be sure to do that," Chaos says with a grin. He starts forward, then pauses and looks at the lead Enforcer again. "I'm sure Crow here won't be the only Shallowsfolk sponsored for the contest. It would be a shame if I heard from the others that they ran into any difficulty getting visas for their contestants."

The red Enforcer's throat bobs. "I'll personally make sure the sponsors don't run into any difficulty with getting visas."

"Excellent," Chaos says. "I'll hold you to that."

And with that, he strolls forward with all the confidence of a monarch. I follow, half expecting the Enforcers to change their minds, but no one so much as moves. As the black gate nears ahead of us, I can hardly believe this is happening. It feels impossible, like I must be dreaming, but it's real.

I'm leaving the Shallows.

II

MIDLEVEL

CHAPTER 11

When we arrive at Midlevel, I'm furious.

There isn't a single fucking puddle up here.

It's the first thing I notice when we get through the border station with my new visa, but not the last. Standing just feet from the border wall, I should be on the outskirts of the Midlevel city sprawl, but it looks nothing like I imagined. The outskirts of the Shallows is a barren marshland. The ground is spongy at its driest, but usually buried in at least an inch of rain. The buildings are sparse, moldy, and falling apart. And sure, I expected Midlevel to be better maintained—I *knew* it would be wealthier, the conditions improved—but I didn't expect . . . this.

The Midlevel outskirts is bustling with activity and shiny, bright buildings with fresh paint and well-stocked storefronts. The ground is dry, the foliage green. A neat little walkway paved with gray stones leads us directly into town. It's brighter up here too—still evening, but there are streetlights every fifty feet or so with actual functioning lightbulbs.

And the people. Even out here in the outskirts, at night, there are people milling about casually and totally carefree. Their clothes look new and fit them properly. They aren't wearing hand-me-downs that they outgrew two seasons ago. Their clothes aren't stained and muddy, patched over and holey. And while there's a decent number of people out, they aren't crowded on top of each other like in the Shallows.

I thought I knew what life was like up here, but it is obvious to me, just minutes after stepping foot on Midlevel, that I could not have been more wrong.

"I have to admit," Chaos says, "I expected a lot of reactions from you coming up here, but silent fury wasn't one of them."

"This is . . . the city *outskirts*?" I try to keep my voice calm, but my outrage leaks in at the end, and honestly, I can't be bothered to care. If this is the *less* wealthy part of town, what is the city center going to be like? Or the Uppercity, where the wealthiest of Midlevelers live?

Gods above, what is *Godlevel*—where the gods and megarich live—like?

"Yes . . ." Chaos says, glancing around uncertainly like he's trying to spot what it is about up here that has me so furious.

"You realize this is nicer than literally anywhere in the Shallows."

Chaos stares at me like it might be a trick question. "And that's . . . a bad thing," he says slowly.

"Do you not think it's a little fucked up that the *least* wealthy part of Midlevel is several levels of magnitude wealthier than the *wealthiest* part of the Shallows?"

Chaos's eyes widen and his lips form an O, so I guess he finally got it. I shake my head, stalking forward. There's something odd about the sound of my boots on the cobblestones—or maybe I'm just not used to the lack of a *splash*. Chaos follows quickly, as I anticipated. People stare at us as we walk by, and for a second I think they're staring at Chaos because he's a celebrity or whatever, and maybe there is some of that, but then I spot a couple people openly staring at *me*.

"What?" I snarl. There's some lady who is literally gaping at me like I'm a creature that just crawled out of the frothing abyss. "Never seen someone from the Shallows before?"

Her mouth snaps shut with an audible click as Chaos steps between us, chuckling, perhaps nervously. "She probably hasn't," he says, throwing the lady an apologetic smile.

Somehow, that reality isn't comforting.

Chaos keeps pace with me as I walk, and a *lot* of people keep looking at me. I guess my clothes give me away. In the Shallows my black, muddy pants, mud-stained boots, and black jacket and tee are fairly normal, since nothing stays white for long down there. Up here, though, I stick out like a sentient stain in a parade of creamy pinks and whites and blues and yellows— I swear to the gods it's like a fucking storybook up here. It's honestly unbelievable. How do people afford all of this?

"Can't imagine what the rent must be," I mumble as we pass a row of cookie-cutter homes, perfect brick next to perfect identical brick, each with different pastel shades of shutters, front door, and roof, and some variety of potted flowers.

"Wouldn't know," Chaos says with a shrug. "No one rents up here."

I stop so abruptly that someone behind me bumps into me, then hurries around me, muttering an apology without looking at me. I ignore them and look again at the copy-and-paste homes, with their identically manicured lawns and perfect white fences.

"*No one* rents?" I ask, disbelieving. "As in *everyone* can afford to *buy* and *own* a home?"

Chaos grimaces. "Yeah."

"*Everyone.*"

"Well, yeah." He hesitates. "Anyone who can't afford a home ends up in the Shallows."

Now *I'm* gaping. "And what happens to their home if they can no longer afford it?"

"It gets repossessed, then sold for cheap to a new home-owner, or someone looking for their second or third home or something."

Second or third home?!

The notion that Midlevelers kick their unhoused population out, banishing them to the Shallows, is so repulsive, I can't help but be disgusted with absolutely everyone living up here. I knew the city levels were based on economic class, of course—the Shallows, Midlevel, and Godlevel have existed since the founding of the city—but I don't think I'd really processed how stark the difference was until now. My uncles and I were lucky—between Alecks's nursing job, Orin's craftwork, and my fighting, we could afford rent and food.

But there are a *lot* of people in the Shallows who can't, and the population of unhoused folks only seems to be growing. We have some free housing but no money to maintain the homes and nowhere near enough apartments to hold everyone.

Meanwhile, up here some people have two or three homes just for fun.

"You do realize how fucked up that is, right?" I finally manage to say.

Chaos nods, his lips pressed flat. "I'll admit I didn't realize how bad the inequality was at first, but now that I've spent some time in the Shallows . . . yeah. I do."

Gods. No wonder they don't want any of us getting up here. If people in the Shallows knew just how wide the gap between Midlevelers and Shallowsfolk has become, they'd fucking riot.

<hr />

A shiny black car that looks more expensive than my home picks us up to drive us the rest of the way. The deeper we travel into Midlevel, the more opulent it becomes.

Identical rows of attached homes become full-sized single houses, each with its own fenced-in yard. These give way to houses big enough to be apartment buildings, but Chaos informs me are not, in fact, inhabited by multiple families. *Those* give way to monstrosities that are far too large for any one family to live in, with sprawling yard space, enormous driveways, and gated-off property complete with Enforcers standing guard at the entrance.

Beyond that, the landscape transforms from alternating neighborhoods and small patches of local commerce to full-on commercial complexes. The buildings grow taller the deeper we go, complete with parks and public pools and gyms, museums, and picturesque walkways that wind around the city and border a huge, shockingly clean, man-made lake. When we've reached a strip of giant buildings reaching into the clouds with large flashing billboards advertising the wares of too many stores to count, the car stops, and Chaos tells me it'll be more fun to walk the rest of the way.

The crowds are thick, and something about the denser population and the neon lights of the advertisements *almost* reminds me of home. Except even here there are still fewer people than on most streets in the Shallows. And it's bone-dry. All the buildings are shiny and well maintained, and everyone is dressed in clothes that probably cost more than a month's rent back home. No one is wearing a mask either. It's like an upside-down version of the Shallows, where half the people sneer at me simply for existing and the other half apparently don't see me at all for the number of times they ram into my shoulder when passing me by.

(I'm pretty sure no one is trying to pickpocket me, if only because of where we are, but even if they were, they'd find quite literally nothing in my pockets.)

"Have they gotten rid of the viruses up here or something?" I ask.

"Hmm?" Chaos glances back over his shoulder. "Oh. You mean because of the mask thing? No. Airborne diseases have been eliminated on Godlevel with high-level filtration in all indoor public spaces, but not here."

I frown. "Is illness . . . less common on Midlevel than in the Shallows, at least?"

"Not really," he answers. "Which is why *I* wear a mask here."

This information is all so baffling I don't know what to do with it. There's clearly less pollution up here, so maybe that's part of it—when the wave of illnesses hit the Shallows, most of us were used to wearing filtration masks because of all the smog and mold everywhere.

"And there aren't any outbreaks?" I finally ask.

"There are." Chaos lifts a shoulder. "But it doesn't get talked about much. I think people here would prefer to just pretend nothing has changed."

I don't understand that at all. I might as well be on a different planet for all the differences between the Shallows and Midlevel.

Chaos hesitates, then adds, "We do have access to largely successful treatments, though. And hospitals up here aren't overcrowded like I hear they are in the Shallows."

I grimace. With my healing ability I haven't had need for a hospital myself, despite my autoimmune disease, but Alecks has told me plenty of stories of working long shifts in overcrowded corridors. Too few doctors, too few beds, and too many patients. And most of those patients can't even afford the care they need.

I follow Chaos through the crowd, weaving between people and turning abrupt corners as advertisements flash at us from all sides. We pass a square where some musicians are playing for people sitting at outdoor tables chatting and drinking coffee. We walk past too many subway entrances, tram lines, and shiny new cars to count, and beyond a massive regal-looking building labeled Public Media Center. Then we cut through a park where people perform flashy mundane magic for tips while others picnic nearby.

The thing that gets me is how clean and new and *maintained* everything is. No matter where I look, there isn't a single wrapper or trash bag on the ground. The air smells clean and fresh, and though it's warm out, there's a breeze. The topiary and flowers set up in the park are meticulously manicured, and there isn't a single run-down building that I can spot.

Maybe this should all be nice, but instead it just awakens something ugly inside me. Because now that I'm here, it's obvious that our government, our city, knows *how* to maintain a public space. The city has the resources to keep a city habitable and safe and godsdamned *picturesque*.

They just don't share those resources or infrastructure with the Shallows. They ignore us and leave us to rot, to drown, in our constantly flooded streets. They don't send us maintenance workers to keep the trash off the streets or prevent buildings from crumbling. They don't care.

As nice as it would be to just enjoy myself up here, how am I supposed to enjoy anything when I know the reality everyone is ignoring? When there are people just a car trip away who are unhoused and dying in the streets? How is any of this okay?

"Here we go." Chaos stops short in front of a storefront and opens the door, nodding at me. "Let's get you some new clothes."

I hesitate for only a second—I don't have any money, and the thought of Chaos buying me new clothes is, well, weird. But there's no sense in pretending I won't need them if I don't want to be stared at everywhere I go. I step inside, blinking as a wall of cold air slams into me, wicking the sweat off my face. The door closes behind me, and I take in the massive space.

Standing here, at the entrance of what is a truly monstrously sized store, I'm certain this is the largest building I've ever entered.

The space is so large I can't see where it ends from where I'm standing. Directly ahead is a set of moving staircases to an upper floor. To the left, a bunch of small self-checkout counters where people are paying for their stuff. To the right, rows upon rows of clothes.

"C'mon," Chaos says, sauntering confidently forward. "It's all old-people shit down here; what we want is upstairs."

I follow numbly, stepping onto the moving staircase. Even though the staircase is moving, you could easily climb it and go up twice as fast, but Chaos leans casually against the banister and there are people standing ahead of us, so I guess no one does that here.

When the staircase deposits us at the top, I literally don't know where to look first, let alone which direction to head. There are signs and displays everywhere—a screen advertising spelled objects like headbands that change your hair color and perfumes that temporarily make you more likable; a sign advertising coats that are embroidered with runes to keep you warm no matter the temperature and T-shirts that keep you cool on hot days; a whole section of what just looks like belts, of all things—

"Crow?"

I startle. Chaos is watching me with a little worried frown creasing his brow. "This floor has the clothes we want. You ready?" he asks.

I thought I was. But I'm starting to think nothing could have prepared me for any of this.

CHAPTER 12

×

Forget what I said about the clothing store being the largest building I've ever been in.

The hotel Chaos brings me to is massive. The lobby itself is probably half the size of the clothing store, with shiny marble floors, a waterfall pouring over the back wall, three different lounging areas, a bar, and an entrance to a sizable restaurant. After checking in at the front desk, we get into the gold-plated elevator, where the buttons indicate there are seventy floors.

Chaos punches the button for the sixty-ninth floor, with a spark in his eyes that tells me that isn't a coincidence. I roll my eyes. Once the elevator stops, Chaos gestures like a perfect gentleman for me to go first.

"Welcome to our temporary abode," he says cheerily.

Stepping into the huge suite, I don't know what to feel. The suite is easily four times the size of my home in the Shallows, complete with a full-sized kitchen, a large lounging area with a huge sectional and a TV half the size of the wall, four bedrooms, and two bathrooms. Everything is shiny and new, from the hardwood floors to the kitchen appliances and furniture. Even the air is lightly perfumed with something sweet and spicy.

This is pure luxury, and I wish I could just enjoy it. But why do the two of us need so much space? It feels wasteful to take up a suite that could house many more people.

But of course, the reality is if we weren't in here, some other rich person would be—and the space still wouldn't be utilized to its fullest capacity. It wasn't made to be practical. It was made to make rich people feel like royalty.

"What do you think?" Chaos asks, plopping the bags on the floor.

I hesitate. I'd assumed Chaos lives on Godlevel, but the luxury of this place is making me second-guess that. "Do you live here?"

"Oh, absolutely not," he says with a laugh. "I have an apartment downtown, but this is more comfortable and a lot closer to the arena."

Huh. So he doesn't live here *or* on Godlevel. Interesting.

Chaos reaches for his mask, then pauses. "Do you mind if I take this off while we're inside? This suite does have good air filtration installed—I checked."

That's a relief to hear, at least. I nod. "Thanks for asking."

"Sure."

Chaos takes his mask off and so do I. Back in the Shallows I wear it anytime I'm not home, so removing the slight weight from my face somewhere decidedly *not* home feels weird. The prickle of being watched washes over me, and I glance up to find Chaos looking at me with a soft smile. Now that the lower half of his face is uncovered, I can confirm what I suspected was true: Chaos is, unfortunately, nice to look at.

And he's still smiling at me.

"What?" I finally ask.

He grins and my stomach swoops in a way I did *not* sign up for. "Nothing, nothing, you're just a good-looking guy."

My face bursts with heat, but there's nothing I can do to stop the blush. I cover my face with a groan and Chaos laughs.

"Sorry, I didn't mean to embarrass you. Actually, while we're on the topic, is *guy* okay for you? How do you like to be referred to?"

With a sigh, I let my hands fall from my face. "Guy, boy, person, anything neutral or masculine is fine. I prefer to be referred to with *they* or *he.*"

"Got it," Chaos says. "*He* and *him* for me."

I nod and lower my backpack to the floor, taking in this monstrosity of a room. The wall next to the lounging area is just floor-to-ceiling pristinely clean windows. From this high up, the view is mesmerizing, and I find myself nearing the windows without really meaning to.

Nearly seventy stories up, the city looks so small, the people and cars and buses and trains like ants. Midlevel is sprawling and huge—definitely several sizes larger than the Shallows, which I can't see from here—with patches of well-lit green parks and sparkling lakes interspersed between neat rows of buildings. It's night, and the lights from the buildings all around us glitter like multicolored stars that have come down to earth.

It's breathtakingly beautiful. And somewhere in this enormous, beautiful city my uncles are prisoners, waiting to be sentenced to die.

Chaos gasps so loudly, for so long, it sounds like he's deflating. I spin around, heart in my throat as he points at my bag on the floor, his eyes as wide as the moon. "Is that a *cat?*"

"What?" I blink and look down at my bag, where a tiny gray head has pushed out of the top. Mouse blinks up at me with her large blue eyes and squeaks. My mouth drops open. "Mouse?"

I crouch and pull my bag open, carefully lifting the tiny ball of fluff out. Mouse purrs and rubs her head against my chest, and a choked squeaky noise that *isn't* Mouse reminds me I'm not alone. I glance up to find Chaos covering his mouth with his hands, grinning so widely it reaches his eyes.

"You didn't tell me you brought your cat!" he exclaims. "And you named her Mouse? Amazing. Can I pet her?"

I shrug. "Sure."

Chaos crosses the space between us and tentatively reaches out, offering his hand to Mouse for investigation. She sniffs his fingers, then rubs her cheek against his hand.

"Ohhh," he coos, "she's so soft!"

I smile, then shake my head at her satisfied purrs. "For the record, I didn't bring her intentionally. She must have snuck into my bag before I left."

"That's not a problem," Chaos says, still petting her with a huge grin on his face. "What does she need? A litter box, food, a cat bed? Toys? Oh, and those cat tree things. Whatever she needs, she can have."

I can't help it, I laugh a little. Chaos looks up at me and blinks. "What?"

"Nothing," I say with a smile. "She just has this effect on people."

"She's perfect and I would die for her," Chaos declares. "Now let's get her whatever she needs."

CHAPTER 13

Once we get back to the hotel suite loaded with more bags and boxes of cat stuff than Mouse has ever had access to, it's beyond late. By the time we get the new cat tree, three new cat beds, food, water fountain, and litter boxes all set up with the help of a masked porter, it's well into the ungodly hours of the morning.

I did tell Chaos that we didn't need most of this stuff—Mouse has never had a cat bed, or a cat tree, or a water fountain for that matter—but Chaos declared Mouse a princess who will get every ounce of pampering she deserves, and I couldn't argue with that.

If a minor god wants to blow his money on spoiling my cat, who am I to stop him?

When I finally crawl into the softest bed I've ever touched, I can't help but think that Mouse made an incredibly strategic move sneaking into my bag.

I sleep in fits and starts. My dreams are plagued by my final moments with my uncles and my worst fears of what may happen to them. It feels as though every time I close my eyes, I jolt awake with images of their pending executions.

So when I jerk awake for the umpteenth time at six in the morning, I don't bother trying to go back to sleep. Instead, I roll myself out of bed, take a shower, and get dressed. Chaos is still asleep when I emerge from my room, but Mouse immediately trots over and rubs against my legs. I pet her back and she flops over, showing me her fluffy belly. Many minutes of belly rubs and chin scritches later, I grab my bag and head to the door.

Mouse races ahead of me and sits directly in front of the door. She blinks up at me with an inquisitive *brrp?* noise, so with a sigh I crouch down and open my bag. She climbs in and curls up at the bottom of the bag, content, and then I'm out the door.

Stepping outside, you wouldn't know it's not even seven in the morning yet. The streets are just as full of cars and people as they were last night, and the smell of freshly baked goods filters through my mask. My stomach growls, but I ignore it and turn toward the media center we walked past yesterday.

Being on Midlevel has been a pretty major distraction—and I've certainly kept busy over the last day—but my sleepless night has refocused me on what's important: saving my uncles. The problem is I don't know anything about how the justice system works up here, except that it's never favorable for people accused of helping Deathchildren.

Still, I can't begin to figure out how to help my uncles without information, so I guess the media center is as good a place as any to start.

It occurs to me once I arrive that most places are probably

not open this early in the morning, but when I reach the front doors, I'm relieved to find the media center's self-services are open twenty-four seven, even if the staff aren't in yet. Which works for me, since I didn't really want to talk to anyone about this anyway.

As soon as we cross the threshold inside, Mouse hops out of my bag and *bolts*. I gasp as she darts around the empty welcome desk in the center of the large space and up a huge staircase.

"Mouse!"

I race after her, but she doesn't so much as hesitate, and she is *fast*. I've never had to chase her before (if I had, I probably would have known how futile it is), and it doesn't take long for her to race so far ahead that I lose track of her. I reach the top of the stairs, breathing heavily, turning in circles trying to spot her. The landing branches out into an enormous space filled with bookshelves and empty tables, and I don't know where to even begin to look for this damn cat.

"Mouse!" I call again, and a tiny squeak responds somewhere way ahead. I start forward, my heart throbbing in my chest as I take deep, slow breaths, trying to calm myself. *Mouse is fine,* I tell myself. *It's a library; it's not like it's dangerous in here. You'll find her. She's fine.*

I continue forward, past countless rows of bookshelves to a space in the back of the room where there are rows of tables and chairs set out, each table with a tablet embedded in it. In the far corner to the right, near the very back of the room, I spot a girl somewhere around my age with dark hair cut in a bob and bright red glasses. She's looking down at her lap with a confused smile, where a ball of gray fur has curled up.

"Gods above and below," I mutter, stalking forward.

The girl looks up and smiles. "Is this your cat?"

"Yes," I say. "Sorry about that. She just took off as soon as we arrived."

"That's okay." The girl pets her, and she purrs so loudly I can hear it from several feet away. "She's cute."

"I'm starting to think she's a little too aware of how cute she is," I answer, and she laughs.

"I'm Jimena," she says, pushing her glasses up the bridge of her nose.

"Crow," I answer. "And that manipulative ball of fluff in your lap is Mouse."

"Hello, Mouse." Jimena scratches just behind her ear. "Good to meet you, Crow."

Mouse hops off her lap and walks around my legs, rubbing against my pants. She's not really apologizing as much as she's buttering me up so I forget to be annoyed at her. It is, unfortunately, effective, and I pick her up, sighing as she purrs against my chest.

"You're already making me regret letting you come with me," I say to her, even as I pet her cheek. She just stares innocently at me in response.

"Did you come here looking for something specific?" Jimena asks.

I look at her. Her dark hair is ruffled in a way that looks like she just ran her hand through it, possibly a couple times.

"You a librarian?" I ask. She looks the part.

"Journalist," she answers. "But I spend so much time in here, I might as well be. I've never seen you here before—though of course, that doesn't mean much—"

"It's my first time," I admit. "I'm looking for . . . public records, I guess."

Jimena nods and taps the tablet in the table she's sitting at. It props up at an angle toward her, making it easier to use and she starts tapping on the screen with both hands. "What kind of public records?"

I hesitate, but I guess it doesn't really matter if she knows what I'm looking for as long as she doesn't know the exact details of why, so I go with the truth. "Arrest records. And upcoming trial dates."

Jimena doesn't even blink at the request—she just nods and keeps typing, the reflection of the text on the screen scrolling across the lenses of her glasses. "Recent?"

"The arrest was two days ago. In the Shallows."

At this she pauses, but when she looks up at me, it isn't judgmentally. Instead, she looks thoughtful. "Do you know if the person you're looking for has been processed up here? Or are they still in the Shallows?"

I'm honestly a bit taken aback at how casual she is about all this. Granted, I haven't really talked to any Midlevelers about the Shallows before, but judging by the way people reacted to me when it was obvious I wasn't from around here—and from what I've heard—I'd assumed most Midlevelers would freak at the mere mention of the Shallows. But Jimena seems totally at ease with all this. Maybe it's because she's a journalist?

"They're up here," I say. "I don't know if they've been processed yet."

She nods and leans back in her seat, rhythmically tapping her purple-painted nails on the table. "Well. The Tournament of the Gods starts today, so all trial dates are delayed until after the competition is over. If the arrest was that recent, they'll be waiting until after the competition for their trial."

My eyes widen. "Trials don't happen during the competition?"

Jimena shakes her head. "A lot of government responsibilities are put on hold until after the Tournament. The competition is basically all that the media will focus on for the next few weeks. Once it's over, though, everything goes quickly back to normal."

For the first time in two days, I can breathe deeply. This is better news than I dared to hope for. The Tournament runs for twenty-two days, which isn't a lot of time, but it's more than I thought I'd have.

I just hope it'll be enough time to figure out how to free them in the likely event that I don't win the Tournament.

CHAPTER 14

After I pass out on the sofa upon my return, with Mouse curled up on my chest, Chaos wakes me up with a huge plate of fresh waffles before pulling me into the whirlwind of preparations for the Opening Ceremony today. It's the first of many televised Tournament events, where the viewers get to meet the contestants and celebrate the start of the competition. It's a big deal, since the Tournament happens only once every other year. The thought of being on TV is so nauseating I can barely finish half my waffles.

After I try on three different outfits, we compromise on a color-blocked dark-green-and-navy T-shirt, black skinny jeans, and black leather boots. It's a simple outfit, but the clothes fit me better than anything I've ever worn, and the fabric is surprisingly soft.

Looking in the mirror, I have to smile at the way the fitted shirt accentuates my flat chest and toned arms. And though I never would have imagined I'd squeeze myself into a pair of skinny jeans, I have to admit they *do* make my legs look good.

"What do you think?" Chaos asks with a glimmer in his eye that says he already knows the answer.

"It'll do," I answer.

A meal and many hours later, Chaos and I are standing in an overcrowded room waiting to be allowed entrance into the arena. Though the doors are closed, the room we're in is situated partially beneath the stands, so the muffled roar of the crowd above us feels like thunder in my chest. I'm instantly glad we left Mouse safely in her palace of a hotel suite, because losing track of her here would have been a nightmare. The room is huge, but there are so many people crammed in here it's standing room only.

And once again, Chaos and I are among the few wearing masks.

"Whoa," someone says near me. "Oh my gods, are you, like, lost?"

I turn to the speaker—a tall, blond girl in a purple tank top, white shorts, and very tall white sandals—outright sneering at me.

"No," I say flatly. "Are you?"

The girl blinks, appearing so taken aback, you'd think she didn't expect me to be capable of speaking at all. "Do I *look* lost?"

I'm opening my mouth to tell her exactly what she looks like when Chaos steps between us.

"Shouldn't you be with your sponsor?" he asks the girl with a smile that's all teeth.

"My sponsor is *very* busy," she says. Then her lip-gloss-painted lips part in an O before snapping shut. Her perfectly manicured hand flies to her mouth. "Wait, oh my gods, you're Chaos!"

"I am," Chaos says coolly.

"I'm Astrid," the girl says. "My sponsor—"

"Isn't important," Chaos cuts in. "And my friend here and I are going now."

He pulls me deeper into the crowd, and I can't help but smile as we leave her stunned face behind.

The doors to the arena open, and we all move forward like a river current. There are so many of us, it takes several minutes of walking to actually get to the doors, but when we do . . . whoa.

The crowd roars as we enter, so loud that I can't even hear the thundering of my own pulse. The cheers vibrate in my chest: a low, steady thrumming along the pulsing beat of the music blasting through the arena.

The stands are all elevated twenty feet above the arena floor, leaving me with the disconcerting sensation of being one of many ants streaming into a dead end. The lights are so bright I can barely make out any of the audience, which is probably for the best. Enormous screens show a live feed of us as we enter, the camera view zooming in on our faces as we take everything in.

The arena is decorated in gold and silver: from the dancing lights racing around the stands to the shiny ribbons and banners welcoming us in. Bursts of gold and silver confetti dance in the glittering air. Even the track we're walking on has been altered to look like shiny molten gold bordered by silver.

And even though this whole thing feels unreal, I can't help the awe that creeps through me. I'm here, in the Midlevel arena, surrounded by thousands of people, in a live televised event. I'm somewhere I never imagined I'd be—and truthfully, never wanted to be. But I have to admit being here is exhilarating. Sure, the crowd isn't cheering for *me,* but their excitement is catching. The buzzing energy is similar to what I love in the Underground—but magnified several times over.

I can't believe this is real.

"Wow," Chaos says next to me, speaking directly in my ear so I can hear him over the roar of the crowd. "This is . . . pretty cool."

I look at him. It's an odd thing to say, since sponsors always enter the arena with their chosen competitors. "You sound like you've never done this before."

"I haven't." Chaos smiles slightly. "I don't know how old you think I am, but you have to be at least eighteen to sponsor, and I wasn't last time around."

Even though Chaos looks to be around my age, this is a surprise—it's near impossible to guess a minor god's age, since after adolescence, their aging slows to a crawl. I knew he was the youngest of the minor gods, but I didn't realize he was *that* young.

"Oh," I say. "Well, is it the way you imagined?"

"Better." He grins; then, his face softening, he adds, "I hope you're enjoying yourself too."

I wouldn't say *enjoy* specifically, but I don't hate it. "Honestly, everything since leaving the Shallows has felt . . . unreal. This isn't any different."

Chaos nods and starts saying something, but I don't hear him because that's the moment my gaze falls on an all-too-familiar face. A tall woman towers over the competitors ahead, her short black hair gelled up in a big swoop, lines shaved into the buzzed sides of her head. She wears a deep purple suit with a silver cravat, of all things, and her ears glitter with half a dozen earrings.

As she begins taking the bend of the oval track we're on, I spot her face—and my blood runs cold. I know this woman, because she, like me, is from the Shallows—where everyone knows to stay away from her. Dez is the only notoriously wealthy person in the Shallows—there's no way she would have lowered herself to *competing*.

"Holy shit," I whisper. "Who did *Dez* sponsor?"

Chaos blinks. "Dez?"

I nod at the woman up ahead. "I feel bad for whoever accepted her sponsorship—there's no way it's going to end well for them if they don't win. She's a notorious Shallows crime lord."

"Oh, I know who she is," Chaos says with a grimace.

I arch an eyebrow. "Midlevelers know about her?"

"Some probably, but I would know her regardless. She's my sister."

I stare at him for so long that I nearly walk into the person in front of me. "*Dez* is a minor god?"

Chaos nods. "Does that really surprise you?"

I almost say yes, but then I think about it. The most surprising part is a minor god taking up residence in the Shallows— why do that when you have access to Godlevel? But then again, Dez practically owns the Shallows. I guess if any minor god would opt to make themselves the feared ruler of the poor and desperate, it'd be the daughter of Discord.

Still . . .

"Dez is an unusual name for a minor god," I finally say.

Chaos laughs. "That's because it's a nickname. Her name is Destruction."

"Oh," I say, feeling a little ridiculous for not thinking of that.

Chaos nods. "In any case, just stay away from her and whoever she's sponsoring as much as possible and you'll be fine."

That should be easy enough—I have no desire to be near Dez at all. But then I spot the person walking next to her, who, in that moment, glances back and catches me staring.

We make eye contact for only a second before Lark smirks at me and waves.

CHAPTER 15

Gods above and below, what is she thinking?

I cannot for the life of me get over that *Lark* is here and *she accepted a sponsorship from Dez.* Everyone in the Shallows knows only the truly desperate work with Dez—and Lark isn't desperate. She has a warm, dry home. She has reliable access to food. She even has an aboveboard job as a tailor! There is literally no reason for her to get into a risky partnership with the biggest crime lord of the Shallows. That never ends well for anyone but Dez.

The Opening Ceremony doesn't take long: Hundreds of competitors and their sponsors walk the long length of the track a couple times while some announcer hypes the crowd up, announcing favorite sponsors and candidates by name and ignoring the rest of us. Then there are fireworks that in any other circumstance I might have enjoyed, but . . .

I don't get it. What is Lark *thinking?*

When we exit the arena, we're led into a huge hall where people start mingling. Ordinarily this would be a hell I'd avoid by leaving immediately, but I have to find Lark. It only takes me a few minutes to spot her leaning against a wall twenty feet away. I barely hear Chaos mutter something about talking to his sister before he wanders off. I'm on a mission—I push through the crowd, weaving along the edges until I'm in front of the last person I thought I'd see up here.

"The fuck are you doing here?" I hiss.

Lark arches an eyebrow. "What does it look like I'm doing, Bushtit? I entered the Tournament."

"*You* told me I was out of my godsdamned mind for entering!"

"You are," she responds.

"But *you* aren't?"

Lark glances around, then—I suppose satisfied that no one near us is listening—leans in toward me and lowers her voice. "Unlike *someone* I know, *I* don't have *that.*"

It's so cryptic that even if someone *did* hear her, it's impossible that they'd know what we were talking about. I, however, do. She means that even though we're both Deathchildren, only I have access to Deathmagic—the thing that would surely give me away.

It's also dangerous for Lark to be here, of course—it's technically illegal for her to be alive too. But now that we don't live in communities together anymore, identifying a Deathchild who doesn't have access to Deathmagic is damned near impossible. Someone could accuse Lark, sure, but they'd never be able to prove it.

In some ways, she's lucky that her ancestry is removed enough from Death that Deathmagic is unavailable to her.

"Okay, but you came here with Dez. *Why?*" I shoot a glance at the crime lord in question, who is on the other side of the room, talking to Chaos. "What could she have *possibly* offered you—"

"You're assuming," Lark interrupts, "that she approached *me* about sponsorship."

My mouth drops open. If Lark asked Dez to sponsor her, that means she now owes the most notorious crime lord in the Shallows a debt. "You *asked Dez* to sponsor you?"

"Who else was I supposed to ask?" Lark snaps. "Not like anyone else in the Shallows has the capital to enter."

"You weren't supposed to enter at all!" I exclaim. "Why would you risk so much? For what? Money?"

Lark looks at me incredulously. "What, it's only reasonable for you to risk your life to change it?"

"I'm risking my life for my uncles—"

"Like you won't keep the prize money if you win."

I bristle. "Obviously, but that's not why I entered."

"Then congratulations, you're more noble than the rest of us."

"I'm not saying that. I just—You don't have any reason to risk everything. You have Ravenna and—"

Lark actually laughs. "Is that what you think? Gods above and below, Pheasant, you really don't know anything." I frown and open my mouth to answer, but Lark cuts me off. "How about you mind your own damn business and leave me the fuck alone? I'm a big girl. I can take care of myself."

"This seems like a bad time to interrupt," a voice near us says.

I jump, expecting it to be Dez, but it isn't. Instead, a tall boy with dark brown skin and long locs pulled back into a thick ponytail is smiling at us through a clear mask. He looks vaguely familiar.

Lark stares at him. "And yet here you are. Interrupting."

The boy flashes a bright smile. "Guilty as charged. You two are Shallowsfolk, right?" He gestures to our masks.

Lark's eyes narrow, and I step in before she bites his head off. "Yeah. What of it?"

"I thought so. I am too." He beams. "I'm pretty sure the three of us are the only Shallowsfolk who entered this time around."

My eyes widen. "Oh! You've worked on my uncles' boat." The connection comes so fast, I can't stop it from spilling out.

The boy's eyebrows raise. "That's possible—I'm a mechanic back home and I've worked on a lot of boats . . ."

"Orin and Alecks?" I prompt.

He blinks, and all at once that magnetic smile is back. "Oh yeah! Wait, then you must be Murder of Crows, right? The Underground fighter?"

It's so unexpected to be recognized up here that I can't help my smile. "That's me."

"Your uncles brag about you a lot." The boy smiles. "Actually, that's even better. Because I was thinking—none of us have ever made it past the Opening Trial before, so it might help if we form an alliance. Plus, I mean, if you're the infamous Murder of Crows, then I'm even more motivated to try to ally with you."

I'm not sure where I expected this conversation to go, but this has been a genuinely nice surprise. Alliances are rare in the Tournament, but they happen occasionally, especially in the Opening Trial, where the entire point is eliminating the bulk of the entrants. Contestants with allies have a better chance of surviving the Opening Trial, but Midlevelers as a whole tend to prioritize looking out for themselves. It never occurred to me that someone would know who I am, let alone want to ally with me.

He must interpret our hesitation as confusion, because his eyes widen. "Oh! Where are my manners? I never introduced myself. I'm Maddox."

"You know my name, I guess," I say, "but this perpetually scowling person is Lark."

Lark glowers at me, which only proves my point. Maddox laughs. "Good to meet you both. So what do you think? Allies?"

"I'm in," I say with a shrug. "Why not?"

Lark huffs, crossing her arms over her chest. "Sure, whatever."

"Amazing." Maddox's grin is magnetic, and I find myself smiling in return without meaning to.

⌒⸺⟶

Some time and too many introductions later, Chaos has invited Lark and Maddox to stay with us in our suite. Maddox—who was sponsored by a Midleveler cousin who is completely uninterested in the actual details of the Tournament—happily agrees. Lark is less enthused by the idea, but since the alternative is sharing a suite with Dez, she reluctantly joins us.

Which is how, hours later, we all end up lounging on the too-big sectional in the massive suite. Or most of us do, anyway—Lark claimed a bedroom and disappeared into it pretty much immediately. Chaos got the rest of us cold drinks and sat next to Maddox, his arm slung over the back of the sofa. Maddox got comfortable pretty quickly and began talking animatedly about his experience on Midlevel so far, while shooting Chaos little smiles all the way. Chaos has responded to the smiles by scooching closer to him and—most recently—grazing his hand on Maddox's shoulder.

I've been sitting a few feet away from them both, sipping my drink quietly with Mouse curled up in my lap, wondering how I already managed to become the third wheel. I'm not even mad about it—why would I be? If anything, watching them not so subtly flirt is kind of cute, I just don't know why I'm still sitting here.

"I got my sponsorship on a favor," Maddox is saying now. "I'm a mechanic back home, and my cousin James—the Midleveler I mentioned—paid me to give his car some upgrades. Well, he was so happy with the job I did, he offered me a favor, and when the Tournament came around, I took it." He grins, crossing his arms behind his head. "James's only done the bare minimum—you know, registering as my sponsor, paying the entry fee, and being here to do the mandatory stuff, but he could not care less about any of this, which is fine by me. He was thrilled when I told him I'd be staying here instead, because it means he gets the suite to himself."

"So am I," Chaos says with a smile.

Maddox's grin turns sheepish in a way that's purely adorable. Chaos asks him about his home back in the Shallows, and Maddox talks about his enormous family (he has four younger sisters and a baby brother) and how the Tournament winnings alone would lift his family out of poverty.

Eventually, their conversation falls away. My head is reeling from the events of the past two days. I keep waiting for the moment that it all sinks in—that it feels real that I'm here in some fancy hotel on Midlevel—but it hasn't happened yet. It still feels like when I blink, it'll all dissolve into a dream.

It still feels like at any moment someone will reveal who I am—a Deathchild with access to Deathmagic—and have me dragged into the dungeons alongside my uncles.

The thought of them sends a sharp pang through my chest. Their trial may have been delayed for over three weeks, but that doesn't get me any closer to figuring out how to break them out if I don't win the Tournament. Realistically, I need a backup plan—because if I'm being honest, my chances of actually winning the Championship are depressingly low.

I need better than relying on bad odds.

My gaze falls on Chaos, who is now so close to Maddox that he might as well be sitting on his lap. The two of them seem to have completely forgotten I'm here, and as I sip my sweet, fizzy drink, an idea begins forming in my mind.

I'm on a first-name basis with a literal minor god. Maybe I don't need to rely on bad odds at all.

I clear my throat and both boys jump, confirming my suspicion that they forgot I'm here. Chaos blinks at me repeatedly, like he's waking from a daydream as I carefully move Mouse to the sofa cushion beside me and stand.

"Sorry to interrupt," I say. "Chaos, I have to talk to you about something. In private."

"Actually," Maddox says, "it's getting late. I should head to bed anyway." He stands and stretches his arms over his head, making his shirt ride up a bit. Chaos's gaze lands squarely on the strip of Maddox's now-visible waist, and he bites his lip.

"Sure," Chaos says slowly. "Night, Maddox."

Maddox grins. "Good night, Chaos." He turns and walks down the hall to the bedrooms. When the door has closed behind him, Chaos sighs heavily and flops back into the sofa.

"This better be important," he grumbles.

"Sorry," I say again, sitting next to him. Mouse glowers at me from the sofa cushion I left her on, mortally offended that I moved her off my lap.

Chaos waves away my apology. "It's fine—it *is* getting late. What did you want to talk about?"

I swallow hard, anxiety already churning in my stomach. I take a deep breath and press my shaking palms against my thighs, hard.

Chaos frowns and sits up straighter. "You okay?"

"Yes. No. I don't know." I run my hand through my hair and meet his gaze, which is now filled with concern. "I . . . never explained why I changed my mind about accepting your sponsorship."

Chaos pauses, then nods. "True. I just assumed you decided it was a good idea after giving it more thought."

I laugh despite myself. "Not exactly. I still think it's a terrible idea, if I'm being honest."

Chaos smiles slightly. "Okay. So what changed your mind?"

I pause. I have to be careful about this part. Chaos may be the son of Discord, and he may—so far, at least—have proven to be a decent person. But I can't assume that means he thinks favorably of Deathchildren, so I can't let on that I am one.

"I need to know something first," I say at last. "Why did you pick me, of all people, to sponsor?"

Chaos's eyebrows rise, but then he nods and leans back on

the sofa, crossing his arms behind his head. "When I decided I was going to sponsor someone, I knew I didn't want to pick some Midleveler or Godleveler. So it was suggested to me that I check out the Underground for the best Shallows fighter. From there it was pretty easy—you realize you have the longest-running Underground win streak, right?"

My face warms a little, though it shouldn't. I know I'm damn good at what I do. I guess I'm just not really used to people outside the Underground acknowledging that.

I take a deep breath. "The night that you offered the sponsorship, Enforcers raided my home and arrested my uncles. For . . . supposedly . . . harboring Deathchildren."

Chaos's eyes go wide. "Shit."

I smile thinly. "Yeah. Shit."

"Are you okay? No, forget that, of course you aren't." He shakes his head. "The laws around Deathchildren are beyond fucked up. What happened ten years ago . . ." He grimaces. "It was genocide."

The room blurs and my eyes fill with tears before I can stop them. I've heard my uncles, and Ravenna and Lark, say the same, but Ravenna and Lark are Deathchildren themselves and my uncles were raising *me,* so of course I expected as much from them. But never have I heard anyone not directly involved with Deathchildren admit that what happened to us—what's *still* happening to us—is wrong.

"Sorry," I say, frantically wiping at my face. "I'm just . . . really worried about my uncles."

Chaos leans toward me and gently places his hand on my shoulder. "You don't have to apologize. Of course you're worried—I'd be more concerned if you *weren't* worried, to be honest."

I try to smile a bit, but it's too hard, so instead I take a deep breath, trying to steady my shivering insides.

Chaos hesitates, then, so gently, says, "I don't think I'm making the connection to the Tournament yet. Are you trying to say that you changed your mind about accepting the sponsorship because you need the winnings to survive without your uncles?"

I shake my head. "I make enough from my fights in the Underground to get by."

Chaos looks instantly relieved, and I almost feel bad because I know what I'm about to say next is going to evaporate that relief like a drop of water in the desert.

"I accepted your sponsorship because it was my only way to get to Midlevel. And I . . . can't save my uncles from the Shallows."

Chaos frowns, evidently not understanding where I'm going with this. "I don't see why being on Midlevel would affect your ability to help them . . . unless you're referring to the Champion's audience with the gods?"

"That's one option," I say, "but I can't rely on the small chance of winning." I hesitate, but if I'm going to ask for his help, he needs to know exactly what I need help with. "All trials are postponed until after the Tournament, so I have just over three weeks to figure out how to free my uncles before they're executed."

Chaos's eyes go wide. "Crow—"

"Just hear me out," I say quickly. "You know their trial will be meaningless. Everyone knows what they do to anyone who is so much as *accused* of helping Deathchildren. It won't be fair. If I don't do something, they're going to die."

Chaos's eyes look sad in a way that makes my stomach flop. He looks like someone who knows he has terrible news to share.

"Crow . . ." he says softly.

"Chaos, please." I'm not above begging. I'm desperate, and I don't care if he knows it. "You're a child of Discord. You and your siblings have access to so much godmagic . . ."

"It's not that," Chaos says. "You're right—the power is there. But you don't understand. I don't have the kind of political sway needed to convince the Godcouncil to pardon them. And even if I considered the illegal route—Discordmagic is *not* subtle. If I used godmagic to break your uncles out of prison, *everyone* would know it was me who did it. I'm a child of Discord, not Death—which means I *can* die, even if I am a minor god. And the gods will absolutely kill me if I abuse my access to Discordmagic like that."

I want to take the rejection gracefully, but I am a beacon of pain. And he's not being unreasonable—he just doesn't want to die. I can't ask him to give his life up for two men he doesn't even know.

"Crow . . ." I've never heard Chaos sound so small, and for some reason it hurts. "I'm sorry. Say something."

I stand. "I need to take a walk."

Before he can stop me, I turn around and walk out the door.

CHAPTER 16

I've taken all of two steps out of the hotel before I realize venturing into the city of Midlevel is a bad idea—because it's absolutely pouring. I stand beneath the long overhang protecting several feet of space in front of the hotel's entrance from the rain, closing my eyes with a sigh as the misty damp air settles on my cheeks and hair. My mask protects my mouth and chin from getting wet, but the cool, clean smell of the rain is so surprisingly pleasant that I can't help but stand there for a couple of minutes, just breathing it in.

It's not like this in the Shallows when it rains.

The rain helps with the smell, of course, but it's never enough to completely wash away the scent of garbage and sewage that follows you everywhere in the warmer months—it really only goes away completely when we get heavy snow.

Then there's the more obvious difference.

I open my eyes, confirming what I already know: My boots are dry. There isn't so much as an inch of flooding anywhere. I step to the edge of the overhang, peering into the torrential downpour dumping out of the sky. The bright neon lights of the ads and storefronts are all blurred in a smear of bright color, reflecting off the streets and sidewalks, like glints of mirrored color bouncing off shattered glass sprinkled everywhere. It's beautiful in a way I'd like to appreciate, but I can't turn off the voice in the back of my head that says if it's raining this hard, it is *absolutely* flooding in the Shallows.

For just a split second I hope my uncles are okay before I remember they aren't in the Shallows at all—and they aren't okay. The pang of pain spears through my chest, and I rub my torso with my palm. My uncles may not be in the Shallows right now, but a lot of people are, including Ravenna. And this time Ravenna doesn't have Lark there to look after her. I want her to be okay. I want everyone in the Shallows to be okay.

But I know better than that. Most of us in the Shallows haven't been okay in a long time.

The patter of rain on concrete and asphalt reminds me what drew my attention to begin with: the lack of flooding. The water has to be going *somewhere*, doesn't it? How are they keeping the streets so dry up here, even in a rainstorm?

I head back into the hotel and beeline it for the elevator, where I punch the number for the top floor. Fortunately, no one gets on with me, and I get an uninterrupted straight shot to the top floor while soothing music pipes into the rising box. The elevator dings and I step off, looking around for the nearest window. I'm standing in the middle of a windowless hallway that extends to the left and right with no other options. I pick left and start walking, my boots silent on the lushly carpeted floor.

The hallway turns right, then opens into a large lounging area with a dozen sectionals creating a generous amount of seating, a huge two-level keyboard pushed against the left wall near an oversized TV, an indoor waterfall on the right wall behind a currently unoccupied bar, and, most important, floor-to-ceiling windows. I walk right past everything to get to what I need, peering out through the glass—but the reflection from the light inside makes it impossible to see anything outside.

I turn around and start scanning the walls for a light switch. After ten minutes of searching fruitlessly, I actually seriously consider using Deathmagic to call on the shadows, but if anyone walked by, I'd be absolutely caught.

And I didn't survive this long by taking unnecessary risks.

Frustrated, I trudge back to the elevators. Someone is waiting there, and I make a point of not looking at them to avoid conversation, focusing instead on the numbers above the three elevator doors indicating what floor they're each on. Two of them are already going down and the only one coming up has just left the lobby. I barely avoid groaning aloud—we're going to be waiting here awhile. Maybe I should try to find the stairs—

"Crow, right?"

I start at my name, turning to the speaker. It's her red glasses that jog my memory first. "Oh," I say. "You're the journalist."

She smiles. "Jimena, yeah. I didn't realize you were staying here."

"Sponsor's choice." I shrug.

"Sure." She nods with a smile. She has kind, dark eyes. "You know, I'm actually glad I ran into you. I was looking at the roster of registered entrants for the Championship and I recognized your name. I'd love to interview you about your hopes for the Tournament, if you're up for it."

I am, decidedly, *not* up for anything to do with the media. Jimena seems nice, but media coverage has historically been unkind to Shallows-born and Shallowsfolk, to say the least. And even if that weren't true, the last thing I need is to draw media attention to myself. Of course, the whole Tournament is televised, so I won't be able to avoid it entirely, but a one-on-one interview with a journalist *is* avoidable.

"That's a—nice offer," I say haltingly. My overwhelming instinct to say *Absolutely the fuck not* wars with my desire not to be an asshole to someone who, so far, has been nice to me. "I have to pass, though. Sorry."

The elevator dings and I step inside, relieved to have an excuse to leave until I remember Jimena was also waiting for an elevator, and there's nowhere to go but down. She steps on with me and the door closes, leaving us in the most painfully awkward silence of my life. Jimena hits the L for the lobby while I hit the button for the floor below us.

"It's all right," Jimena says, breaking the awkwardness with forced cheer. "Can I leave you my contact info in case you change your mind?" She holds her phone out, and I tap mine against hers to accept her contact card.

The elevator doors open to my floor and I step out.

"Good luck with the Opening Trial," she says.

"Thanks, you too," I say automatically as the doors close. Then I stare at my reflection in the closed doors and groan aloud. *"You too"? She isn't competing, genius!*

Face burning, I waltz into our suite, refocusing on the task that brought me back here. Inside, I find Chaos pacing while Maddox—who apparently *didn't* go to bed after all—is watching him uncertainly. Mouse, who evidently thinks this is a great game, keeps pouncing on Chaos's feet—which, to be fair, are in giant fluffy slippers.

Both boys turn to me the moment I walk in. Chaos's mouth actually drops open as the door closes behind me.

"I— *What?*" Chaos splutters. "Holy shit, Crow, I thought you left the hotel! I was freaking out!"

I slap off the lights and walk past him to the window wall. Chaos stares. "What are you doing?"

"And why are we standing in the dark?" Maddox adds.

"Keep the lights off," I say, blinking hard as my eyes adjust to the darkness. It doesn't take long for me to make out the city in crystal-clear detail. I press my forehead against the glass as I look down below.

The ground is dizzyingly far from where I'm standing, and the glass is so perfectly clean, it's easy to forget it's there at all. As the rain races toward the ground below, I scan the buildings beneath us—rows of restaurants across the street, nearby hotels, and a variety of retail stores. From up here it's clear that it isn't just this street that isn't flooding—every street that I can see from up here has a system redirecting the water to keep the ground level clear.

Chaos steps next to me, squinting out into the rainy night. "What are you looking at?"

"There isn't any flooding," I say. "Where is all the water going?"

"The pumps keep the streets clear." Chaos points to the top of a low building next to the hotel we're in, where a large tank is sitting on the roof. A thick pipe runs from the tank down the side of the building to the ground. From here I can see the string of faintly glowing runes etched on the side of the tank. They look familiar—like I may have seen this combination of runes before—but I couldn't tell you where or what the rune equation does.

Maddox approaches the window with a frown. "How many pumps are there?"

Chaos shrugs. "Loads. Hundreds, I'd guess."

"We could use those in the Shallows," I say.

Maddox nods. "Probably expensive to install and maintain, though." His face darkens. "And Midlevelers aren't going to volunteer to help us Shallowsfolk."

I grimace, but he's right. If the Midlevelers wanted to help us, they wouldn't have shut us away on a piece of land slowly sinking into the sea where they don't have to look at us while we drown.

Still, there's something weird about the tanks that doesn't sit right with me. "Those tanks can't possibly hold all the water coming down right now," I say.

Chaos shakes his head. "The tanks don't hold any water at all—that's just the pump mechanism. I think the pumps evaporate the water or something."

I squint harder out the window. I don't see any mist or anything coming off the pumps, but then again it's raining so hard that everything looks like a wet smear anyway.

"What are you thinking?" Maddox asks.

I shake my head. "I don't know," I admit. "Something about the whole thing just puts me on edge."

"Tell me about it." Maddox leans against the glass next to

me, peering out into the rain-drenched night, his eyes sad. "It feels wrong being safe and dry while my neighborhood back home is likely underwater again. My moms are probably spending half the night reinforcing the runes at the windows and doors again to keep the water out of our home."

Maybe that's it. Maybe safety feels like a betrayal when my neighbors in the Shallows are fighting for survival again tonight.

But I still can't shake the feeling that I'm missing something.

CHAPTER 17

The next morning Chaos wakes us with iced coffee and individually packed bags full of more pastries, bagels, donuts, and muffins than I could possibly eat in a day, let alone for a single meal.

"I didn't know what everyone likes, so I got everything," Chaos says by way of explanation. "Mads, I don't know about your sponsor, but Lark, I expect my sister will want to touch base with you before the Opening Trial."

I arch an eyebrow at *Mads*—are they already on nickname basis?—but I don't comment. Lark grabs an iced coffee and bag, thanks Chaos for the food, then heads out to meet with Dez.

"James doesn't care. I don't think he's even nearby," Maddox says, pulling a chocolate muffin out of his bag and taking a huge bite. "This is delicious—thanks, Chay."

I swear my eyebrows must disappear into my hairline at *Chay*. Chaos grins; then he must spot my look, because he blushes and clears his throat. "Good news. We're all assigned to the same bus. I packed everything into to-go bags because we don't want to miss the bus. We'll be eating on the road. The rules for the Opening Trial will be explained on the way. Any questions?"

I break off a piece of plain bagel to give to Mouse. "Just one, *Chay*," I say, absolutely relishing the delicious way his face reddens anew at my use of the nickname. "When do we leave?"

We don't have public transportation in the Shallows. With all the flooding, most people have abandoned using cars or anything else that can't travel in water. When flooding is especially bad, people who have them will break out boats and motorized rafts, but the only vehicles that can reliably take both dry and flooded streets are hover bikes, which aren't cheap. My uncles and I mostly relied on walking, with the occasional use of a rickety old boat in desperate times. I was saving up for a hover bike—a good one that would last us a long time—before everything went to shit.

This is all to say I have never been on a bus, or given much thought to what a bus might be like, for that matter. Given my extremely limited experience with transportation options, it's not a surprise that the vehicle we all pile into is the nicest I've ever stepped into—and it's clearly not made to be luxurious. The cabin is long and double-decked, with plush seats in two-by-two rows on both levels.

Chaos leads us upstairs to the very back of the bus, where there's a row of six seats put together. There the four of us have space to sit comfortably without being on top of each other.

"There are fifteen buses," Chaos says, "so there will be plenty of room for everyone. We shouldn't have to crowd in."

Despite that, the bus gets full, and once again Chaos, Maddox, Lark, and I are the only ones masking. And Dez, actually—though she's sitting a couple of rows away from us. At this point I assume the only people I'm going to see wearing masks are either medical professionals or Shallowsfolk—and Chaos, apparently.

"I didn't expect you to sit with us," Maddox says cheerily as Lark plops down against the window. "I'm glad you've joined us."

Lark pulls a wooden hoop stretching out a square of black fabric, a pack of neon thread, and a small tube of embroidery needles from her backpack. "Believe it or not, most of you are better company than my sponsor," Lark says, turning her gaze outside.

I choose to ignore that *most of you* almost certainly excludes me.

The bus whirs, and a low hum vibrates the entire bus as it rises a foot off the ground. My heart leaps into my throat at the motion, but I quickly adjust. I wasn't expecting the bus to be a hover vehicle—mostly because it doesn't really seem like hover vehicles are *necessary* up here, with the pump system keeping the streets dry—but that was naive thinking. Just because Midlevel doesn't *need* a piece of technology doesn't mean they won't use it.

"So where are we going?" Maddox asks as the bus slips forward.

Chaos brightens and pulls a tablet out of his bag. "I actually couldn't open the info packet before ten-thirty a.m.—it's to ensure none of us have an advantage or more time to prepare than others—but now that the bus is moving, it should be time." He slides his fingers over the tablet's glass surface, tapping until his face bursts into a grin.

"It's unlocked! Okay, let's see." He's quiet for a moment while his fingers dance across the glass. Then he pauses. "Oh. Interesting."

When he doesn't elaborate further, Maddox clears his throat. "What's interesting?"

"Right! Sorry. So it looks like we're headed to the Drylands."

I frown, and even Lark has glanced over from the window. The Drylands are on the very outskirts of Midlevel, the last section of land before you reach the Wilds. They're west of the city, on the opposite side of Midlevel from the Shallows. It's there that most of the Deathchild towns were before the Godcouncil ordered Enforcers to destroy them all.

It's where Homestead, the town I was born in, was until Glamor, Architect, and Mind orchestrated our ruin.

"Have they hosted a trial there before?" I ask, racking my brain for a recent example. The Opening Trial is always somewhere on Midlevel, but I can't recall a time any part of the Tournament was hosted in the Drylands.

Chaos shakes his head, confirming what I was already coming to guess. "No, this'll be a first. Hope none of you mind the heat."

None of us says anything. It's been a long time—ten years, to be exact—since I've experienced the dry desert heat of my homeland. A warning thrums inside me at the thought of going back—could it really be a coincidence that the very year there are actual Deathchildren competing, they're bringing us to the Drylands, of all places? But there's literally no way anyone could know who we are—the only reporter I've spoken to is Jimena, and that was explicitly to decline an interview. Unless Lark let something slip? But I can't imagine Lark willingly *speaking* to a journo, let alone spilling her most dangerous secrets to one.

I glance at Lark and nearly startle—she's already eyeing me, her piercing gaze practically screaming *You didn't spill, did you?* I frown and shake my head a little, trying to ask *Should we be worried?* with just my eyebrows. Lark watches me a moment longer, her face unreadable beneath her mask.

I bite my lip. It's just a coincidence. It has to be.

But that doesn't mean I have to like it.

"Hope someone packed sunglasses," Lark mumbles.

Chaos brightens. "Actually, I got us all matching sunglasses."

I laugh, because surely he must be joking, but then he reaches into his bag and I realize he's serious. Out comes a handful of shiny sunglasses, which he begins passing out to each of us. Maddox immediately put his on with a huge grin while I stare at mine, somewhat incredulously.

"Aviators?" I say, holding back a laugh. "Seriously?"

"Aviators are cool," Chaos says, putting his on. "And now we all match! Like a team."

Lark puts hers on without comment before turning back to the window. Wearing matching sunglasses—let alone matching reflective aviators—feels silly, but it's already getting pretty bright, so I put them on.

"All right, so it's in the Drylands," Maddox says. "What else do we know?"

"Right, right." Chaos picks up his tablet again. "The other interesting part is they've broken up all the entrants into three groups. Each group will go to one of three different arenas. I guess this year they've received a record-breaking number of entrants, so it would be too crowded if they put you all in one unless they made a truly enormous arena."

I'm sure they haven't done that before. I frown. "How did they decide who goes to what arena?"

Chaos shrugs. "They don't say."

We take that in silently. I don't know if anyone else is thinking it, but I for one find it *interesting* that all three Shallowsfolk entrants ended up in the same arena. Somehow, I don't think the choice was random.

Chaos continues scrolling on his tablet. "Okay, rules—here we go. Other than splitting up the field, the setup is the same as most Opening Trials: a free-for-all fight with thirty-two tickets hidden in caches throughout the arenas. Note that killing in the Opening Trial is allowed, and there will probably be weapons placed sporadically around the arena.

"You need a ticket to move on to the individual fights— and there's thirty-two *total,* across all three arenas. The tickets are spelled to bind to the first competitor who touches them, and you can only claim one. Once a ticket is bound to you, it stays on unless you die or are eliminated from the Tournament, until a Champion is crowned. Everyone who doesn't get a ticket when the last one is claimed gets sent home.

"You'll hear a klaxon at the start of the trial and when the trial is over. And this is important: If you attack anyone *after* the closing sound, you'll be automatically disqualified. There is absolutely no tolerance for fighting outside of the Tournament rounds. Understood?"

We all nod mutely. Maddox pauses, then asks, "What

happens in the individual fights if your competitor is disqualified before your match?"

"You automatically move on to the next round," Chaos answers. "So there's plenty of motive for someone to goad you into disqualifying yourself between rounds. Don't fall for it. I bet on all three of you to advance, so don't let me down."

I'd heard that sponsors can place bets on the competitors, but it feels oddly reassuring to know that Chaos has not only bet on me by choosing me, but also put money down on all three of us advancing. Granted, for a minor god, throwing money around probably isn't much of a risk, but still.

"Do I even want to know what they've placed our odds as?" Lark asks, leaning back in her seat.

Chaos laughs slightly. "Let's just say if all three of you make it through the trial, I'm ordering us a feast to celebrate."

We sit with that for a while before Chaos, seemingly satisfied, puts his tablet back into his bag and pulls out a small black case. Inside are what appear to be four coin-sized black plugs. He hands each of us one and then pops the last one in his ear.

"These will allow us to communicate when you're in the arena. Since I'm a sponsor, I can't go in with you, but I'll be watching live."

I take the plug and squish it between my fingers. It's soft, like foam, but when I put it into my ear, it doesn't block any sound.

"Tap it once to turn it on," Chaos says. "It'll be on at all times from there until you take it off."

"Easy enough," Maddox says cheerily. "Any tips you can share with us?"

Chaos pauses, looking thoughtful as he mulls the question over. "Well, the idea is to try to find as many caches as possible, because not every cache has a ticket. But most of the caches are trapped in some way, so be careful."

Lark arches an eyebrow. "Trapped?"

Chaos blinks. "Have you never watched an Opening Trial of the Tournament before?"

"No," she says bluntly.

Chaos could not have looked more surprised if she'd slapped him across the face with no provocation. He turns to Maddox, wide-eyed. "Have *you*?"

Maddox grins sheepishly. "No, actually."

"I have," I say helpfully, "though it was . . . several years ago, so I don't really remember the details."

Chaos groans and runs his hands down his face. "I guess the Tournament is more popular up here than in the Shallows. All right, *yes*, there are traps all around the arena—not just around caches, though you can almost guarantee there will be one at every cache. Remember what I said earlier about killing in the Opening Trial being allowed?"

I frown, not liking the direction this is taking. "Yeah . . ."

"Right, well, it's also not uncommon for the *traps* to be lethal. Most of the time when people die in the Opening Trial, it's because of the traps or fighting over the tickets. Any questions?"

Part of me wants to ask what percentage of people who've died in the Opening Trial are Shallowsfolk, but I suspect the statistic won't do me any favors, so I keep my mouth closed.

When no one else asks anything, Chaos reaches back into his bag and this time pulls out a set of small knitting needles connected with a cord. The ring of a partially done project in thick black yarn speckled with neon colors is stretched over them.

"You're all welcome to watch me knit my beanie," he says, "but this isn't going to be a short bus ride, so you might as well get comfortable."

CHAPTER 18

By the time we get off the bus over an hour later, my neck is aching from sitting still for so long. Five other buses have stopped in the same area as us, and people come pouring out into the hot sun—mostly competitors, but I spot a couple minor gods I've seen on TV, like Mind's child Illusion, a wispy androgynous person wearing a glittery powder-blue suit; and Fauna's daughter Hunt, a stocky woman with bronze skin and silky black hair pulled into a ponytail who looks like she could break me in half with one hand tied behind her back.

I stretch my arms over my head and massage my neck, closing my eyes as the beacon of red inflammation pulses in my mind's eye. It's the same inflammation that makes my hands hurt, thanks to my body's overreactive immune system. Ordinarily I'd take a nap, or loosely wrap a spelled compress to lessen the inflammation, but that's not an option out here in the middle of the Drylands.

Instead, I pop a couple painkillers from a stash in my bag before handing that over to Chaos, since we're not allowed to bring anything into the arena with us.

If you can call it an arena, anyway.

"Maybe it's a misnomer," Maddox says next to me. "But I'd expected the arena to be more . . . arena-like."

We're standing at the very edge of what appears to be an old, abandoned town, in a small clearing between two buildings that leads deeper into the town. I can only assume this was built to look old for the purpose of the competition, but I can't shake off how much it reminds me of Homestead.

The town is in the middle of the desert—nothing but flat, sunbaked rock, dirt, and dust for miles in every direction. The sun is hot on my skin in a way I haven't felt in years, and the air is so dry, I know my lips will be chapped to a paperlike consistency before the day is over. I'm already regretting my choice of long black pants. In my defense, I didn't know this morning that we were going into the literal desert.

The buildings ahead of us are made of brick, mud, and thatch. Their roofs are flat, and the tallest building I can see seems to be a tower way to our left. Other than the tower, most buildings seem to be single story, save for a couple of two-story buildings here and there.

It's so similar to Homestead, I can't help but think this place was modeled after a Deathchild town. Long before the Silencing, most Deathchildren were pushed out of the city proper and into the Drylands as the general population became more hostile to us. The Drylands were only marginally more hospitable than the Wilds, so few others built towns out here—but Deathchildren found a way to not only survive the desert but flourish in it.

But why would a Tournament arena be modeled after a Deathchild town? The only ones who would even know *are*

Deathchildren, since Deathchild culture hasn't been taught in schools since before I was born, and we're all supposed to be dead.

Still, I can't think of a better way to torment Deathchildren than making them play a fucking game in a town made to look like the home they can never return to.

"Turkey!"

The only thing that annoys me more than Lark's refusal to use my name is that fucking *Turkey* actually pulls me out of my thoughts. I glower at Lark, who smiles smugly while Maddox and Chaos look at the two of us incredulously.

"Did you seriously just respond to *Turkey?*" Chaos asks, barely suppressing a laugh.

"You do realize," I say to Lark, "that you're named after a bird too."

Lark does not seem bothered by this incongruous reality. "Chaos was trying to get your attention."

Oh. I turn to the minor god, who is laughing now. "Shut up," I say. "What is it?"

"I was *trying* to remind you to turn your earpiece on," Chaos says.

I tap the plug in my ear and it beeps. "Done."

"Good." Chaos touches his ear. "Do you all hear me?"

His voice comes through so close that I actually jump. It sounds like he's speaking directly against my ear, which I suppose he is. It's disconcerting.

Lark grimaces. "Unfortunately."

"Loud and clear, boss," Maddox says, somehow still smiling. I'm starting to think he never *stops* smiling, to be honest. Which is also disconcerting.

"Oh my *gods*," a gratingly familiar voice says, because apparently the gods hate me. "It's that lowtowner *again.*"

I grit my teeth at the slur but keep my face blank when I turn to face Astrid, the stuck-up girl from the Opening Ceremony.

"It's so embarrassing that they think there's a chance they'll make it past the Opening Trial," she says to a tall femme competitor standing near her.

"*So* embarrassing," the competitor deadpans while filing their nails into sharp points. I honestly can't tell whether they're agreeing with Astrid, humoring her, or making fun of her.

"What do you think they did to get Chaos's attention?" Astrid asks, staring at me but clearly not speaking to me.

The femme competitor continues filing their nails until a blond boy next to them nudges them. "Mae," he mutters.

Mae doesn't look up from their nails. "I don't think she actually wants an answer," they respond flatly.

Astrid rolls her eyes and turns around to face the other competitors. "It was a rhetorical question. We all know the only thing a lowtowner's good for is jumping into bed."

I'm contemplating whether being disqualified would be worth the look on Astrid's face when I break her nose so badly it'll never be straight again. To Astrid's luck, a rail-thin woman with long silver hair steps in front of us, clapping her hands over her head. "Contestants!"

Five different drone cameras—small fist-sized black boxes— all converge on her while a sixth pans above our heads, scanning the gathering crowd of contestants and sponsors.

All eyes are officially on us.

"The time has come to separate the contestants from the sponsors," the woman says. "Sponsors, please say goodbye to your contestants. You'll see them again after the Opening Trial is complete. Contestants, please stay behind the red line."

It takes me a moment to spot the line she's referring to—a line painted on the baked earth creating a huge semicircle around the entrance between the two buildings ahead, just a couple of feet behind her.

"Remember the strategy," Chaos says.

"Find tickets for everyone and look out for traps," I say. "Which is probably everyone else's strategy too."

Chaos shrugs with a small smile. "There are only so many ways to survive the arena. I'll see you all on the other side."

He nods to the three of us, turns around, and heads back to the buses, where the other sponsors are gathering.

As we make our way to the starting line, someone bumps my shoulder—hard—and I'm zero percent surprised to find that it's Astrid. Adorably, the contact barely makes me budge, but I won't pretend my shoulder doesn't throb.

Maybe she'll trigger a trap and something will eat her.

Then Lark sticks her foot out and Astrid trips, planting onto the hard-packed earth on her hands and knees. It's so beautiful, it's physically painful for me not to laugh. I bite back a grin, but I'm pretty sure my lips twitch into a smirk anyway.

"Oh my *gods!*" Lark mimics with an exaggerated gasp. "I'm *so* sorry. Are you okay?" Lark's voice is absolutely dripping with mockery—I'd know, because she's used that tone on me more times than I can count—but of course Astrid can't really know that for sure.

Astrid glowers daggers at both of us as she stands and brushes herself off. She's fine, unfortunately, but she turns and pushes through the crowd to the front.

Lark sighs happily.

"You know," Chaos says in our ear, his voice tight with laughter, *"I may be sponsoring Crow, but I'd actually be sad to see any of you disqualified before the Tournament even starts—I meant what I said about betting on all three of you."*

"I'm innocent," Maddox says.

"So am I," Lark says lightly. "It was *completely* accidental."

"Uh-huh," Chaos laughs. *"Just keep an eye out. I wouldn't be surprised if she goes after you in there."*

Lark cracks her knuckles. "Don't threaten me with a good time."

It is extremely weird for me to agree with Lark, but here she is, tripping one of the worst people I've ever met and all but salivating over the thought of fighting Astrid. So maybe we can agree on this one thing.

I'm not the only one who knows how to fight. If I don't get to wipe that smug smile off Astrid's face, I could be satisfied with Lark doing it instead.

"Contestants!" The crowd has gotten so thick at the starting line that I can no longer see the woman speaking, but her voice rings out clearly nonetheless. "On my mark!"

Blue light flashes over us in a shape I can't quite make out. "FIVE" a deep robotic voice booms over us. The light changes to green with a new shape. "FOUR."

My heart trills in my chest and I take a steadying breath. Here we go.

"Whatever happens," I say, as the light turns yellow and "THREE" blasts over us, "we make it through the trial. All of us."

Shallowsfolk have never made it through the Opening Trial. We will.

"That's the idea," Lark says as Maddox says, "You know it" with a grin.

The light turns orange. "TWO."

I am ready to run. I am ready to fight. I am ready to make a name for myself in a world determined to grind me to dust.

Red light.

"ONE."

CHAPTER 19

The crowd surges ahead of us, and we let them as the three of us jog forward between the two dusty buildings. There are only two ways to go: left or right. Most everyone turns right, with maybe a quarter of the crowd going left, which is where we go. Everyone continues forward, but to the left there's a break between buildings and I turn that way. We haven't really spoken about our strategy navigating the town, but Maddox and Lark follow my lead.

The alley opens up into a small clearing. Behind us and reaching around to the right is a long strip of attached buildings. Dead ahead is a single squat mud-brick building. To our left another strip of attached buildings curves around us, but one small building sticks out at the end. There's a red X painted on the rusted steel door, and a raven is perched on the roof. It tilts its head at me as I spot it. A good omen.

"Huh," I say as we slow to a stop in front of it. "Did they mark the caches?"

Maddox frowns and Lark shakes her head. "Too easy. It's probably a trap."

"Chaos said all the caches are traps," I say. "So its being a trap doesn't mean it isn't a cache."

Lark rolls her eyes. "Why would they mark the doors of the ticket caches? They aren't trying to make this easier for us."

"There are probably hundreds of buildings in this town," I argue. "Don't you think it'd be boring to watch people comb through hundreds of empty buildings to find the dozen that actually have shit in them—"

"Gods above and below, Ostrich, are you really so juvenile that you think—"

Maddox gives the door a swift kick—it slams open with a thud. "Are you two, like, exes or something? You sound like my sister and her ex-girlfriend."

I've done well so far to keep the bulk of my reactions to myself, but *that* throws me. My face wrinkles with disgust as Lark's mouth actually drops open.

"*What?*" we say at the same time, which, given the circumstances, somehow only makes all of this worse. My face is definitely red, and I'm relieved that none of the drones thought it important to follow Team Shallows, because at least this mortifying conversation isn't being broadcast to all of Escal.

"No," I say.

"*Gods*, no," Lark spits.

Maddox shrugs and gestures to the now-open door. "Who wants to go in first?"

It's obvious that the answer is none of us, and we stand in awkward silence for a second. Then Lark says, "Fuck it," and waltzes into the room. It's too dark inside for Maddox and me to see from where we're standing out in the sun, so when Lark disappears in the shadows, we both tense.

Then Lark calls out, "I'm not dead—come in!"

Maddox and I look at each other. He shrugs and strides in breezily. I follow. Once inside, I blink rapidly, willing my eyes to adjust. The relief from the hot sun is instant, and the ten-degree temperature drop is heavenly. As the shadows slowly recede to something I can make out shapes in, the room around us starts to make sense.

The building is small, longer than it is wide, with a counter Lark is standing behind taking up three-quarters of the length of the far side of the room. Shelves built into the wall are full of half-empty stoppered glass bottles, each labeled, though the labels faded long ago. Bits of wood litter the slate floor, and some collapsed crates are huddled together in the corner. There are hooks on the ceiling, but all of them are empty save for a couple of hanging baskets made of woven dried grass.

The more I take in, the lower my stomach sinks. I approach a shelf of jars, something thrumming a warning inside me. A vibration in my bones, twisting around my torso and making my teeth chatter in my clenched jaw.

You know what this is, a small voice whispers, and I want so badly, so desperately to be wrong. I pick up a bottle with a dried black substance inside that has painted the bottom third of the container. The back of my throat burns as I pull the cork stopper out, dumping the desiccated contents onto my palm. Flakes of black fall out of the jar onto my fingers. When I rub them together, the black stuff smears smoothly, exactly like I knew it would.

It's charcoal paint. Or it was, before it completely dried out.

Charcoal paint, used in every Deathchild ritual I participated in as a child.

The memory rushes toward me, unstoppable.

I'm five years old, and my father is dipping his fingers into a jar of fresh charcoal paint. He crouches in front of me, his fingers dripping in black, and he smiles so warmly, so genuinely. Mom doesn't smile at me like that, I think, but it doesn't matter because Dad does, and he is here. He runs his paint-drenched index finger from the center of my forehead down the ridge of my nose, over my lips to my chin, and down my neck to my collar. The paint is cool and thick, and though I can't see the line he's painted on my skin, I can feel it.

"There," he says softly, his voice deep and resonant. "Now you mark me." He tips the jar toward me, the paint sloshing a little inside.

My eyes go wide. "Really?"

His smile widens. "Go on."

I reach toward the jar, then hesitate. "What if I mess it up?"

"There's no way to mess it up," he says. "You should mark my face the way your spirit leads you."

I bite my lip, dipping two fingers into the jar. The paint is silky around my fingers, and it drips onto the slate floor when I pull my hand out. With shaking hands, I draw a line from the center of my father's forehead all the way down his neck, mirroring what he painted on me. Then I dab each of his cheeks just once and step back with a grin.

"I did it," I say proudly.

"Of course you did," he says, like he never doubted me for a second. "You're a Deathchild. This is your heritage. All of this is

yours, like your ancestors before you, and your descendants after you. It will always be yours."

I don't realize I'm crying until Maddox is suddenly standing in front of me, peering into my face. "Hey," he says, his voice ripping me out of my reverie. "What's wrong? Are you hurt?"

I quickly return the bottle to the shelf, shaking my head and wiping at my face furiously. "No," I croak. "I'm not hurt— I'm just . . . Fuck."

Maddox's frown deepens, but then Lark says what I couldn't. "This is an apothecary shop." She hesitates. "A Deathchild apothecary shop."

Maddox's eyes go wide, and I take a moment to close my own and breathe deeply. Can it really be coincidence that they sent two Deathchildren to an abandoned Deathchild town? There are three arenas, so there's only a one-third chance I'd end up here, and an even smaller chance for both Lark and me to end up here, assuming the arena assignments were random.

The notion that the arena assignments might *not* have been random makes me sick to my stomach. Heat flashes through my chest at the thought, and I grit my teeth. I need to pull myself together. A camera drone may not have followed us in here, but one could show up at any time. And crying in a Deathchild apothecary shop is not a good look for someone hiding their Deathchild heritage.

"Do you mean . . ." Maddox hesitates. "Do you mean they made it *look* like a Deathchild apothecary shop? Or . . ."

Clearing my throat, I manage, "If it's a reproduction, it's very convincing."

If Maddox is wondering how Lark and I know this, he

doesn't ask. Instead, he just nods with a grimace and steps to the back of the room where the broken crates are.

"Anyway." Lark lifts a metal box from behind the counter and places it on top with a hollow *thunk*. "Ta-da," she says flatly.

Maddox and I step up to the counter, peering down at the container. The box has a large red X painted on it.

"This has to be it, right?" Maddox says.

"Either that or it's a trap," Lark says. Then she opens it. Maddox and I flinch back, but inside is a stub of shiny gold paper with big black text that reads "TOURNAMENT ENTRY." A ticket. My shoulders relax as my eyes widen. Lark actually found a ticket.

We stare at it in silence for a minute, none of us reaching for it. Chaos said it'll bind to the first person who touches it, but we never figured out how we were going to determine who gets the first ticket.

Still, the answer seems clear here. "You found it," I say to Lark. "You should claim it."

Maddox nods, and so, with a shrug, Lark reaches in and grabs it. The moment her fingers touch the ticket, it jerks up. We all jump. Lark watches, eyes narrowed, as the ticket slithers over her hand, wrapping around her wrist. Then it *melts*, disappearing into her pale skin and leaving a band of three swirling golden threads forming a triple helix like a metal tattoo on her wrist.

Lark runs her finger over the smooth band, then snaps the box shut and vaults over the counter, landing smoothly next to us. "Well, I'd rather leave before we find the trap. Let's go."

I'm halfway to the door before it occurs to me that Lark is next to me but Maddox isn't. When I turn back, he's looking down at his foot, paused midstep. For a moment it looks like he's just frozen for no reason, but when I squint at his foot, the source of his hesitation becomes obvious: The toe of his boot has caught on a translucent wire.

"Shit," he mutters as growling fills the room.

It's so loud I can feel it in my chest. I look up and find two hulking bear hounds emerge. They're huge. Standing on all fours, they're both nearly as tall as I am. Drool drips off their jowls in thick strings as they bare their sharp yellow teeth. They look ready to pounce at any moment.

"Don't make eye contact," Lark says in a low voice. "Just back slowly toward the door."

Sweat drips down my temples as I follow Lark's advice and step backward toward the door.

There's a wooden shelf behind the counter that has tilted a little to the right. It's still full of glass jars. I keep my gaze steady on the shelf as I slowly trace the disruption rune in the air at my side, followed by the gravity rune.

"Get ready to run," I say.

With the mundane magic buzzing at my fingertips, I focus on the wobbly end of the shelf, then yank my hand down, releasing the magic.

The shelf groans, then collapses, the jars sliding off and hitting the ground with a thunderous crash. The bear hounds jump and twist around to face the noise, their growling intensifying. The three of us bolt for the door. I'm the last one out, and I've barely made it over the threshold before the bear hounds begin howling behind us.

With Lark in the lead, we race back through the alley we came from and turn left, our boots kicking up dust as we run around a building and past another alley. I dare a glance back and regret it—the dogs are gaining on us.

Lark turns right into an alley, then right again, and skids to a stop in front of a building with a rope ladder slung over the side. She begins climbing, and the two of us climb up after her. Once again I'm last, and I'm only partially up the ladder when the dogs skid into the alley and spot us. Bursts of purple and red mundane magic race over my head as Maddox and Lark throw energy spells at the bear hounds. I scramble to the top, gasping but unscathed.

A camera drone has found us interesting, following us as we catch our breath, the dogs barking and growling furiously below. One of the hounds jumps, snapping a few times at us, but his claws can't find purchase on the side of the building and he slides back down. The animals can't get up here and they know it, so eventually they slink away.

I fall back on the mud-brick roof, drenched in sweat as I slow my racing heart with measured breaths. Apparently bored with us, the camera drone zips off to gods know where. Probably to record some other contestants having near-death experiences.

Maybe, if I'm lucky, they'll terrorize Astrid.

"Well," Chaos's voice says through our earpieces. *"I'm glad none of you were mauled to death by rabid bear hounds—that would have been hard to watch."*

"Thanks for the concern," I respond with a groan.

When I sit up, Maddox is peering over the far edge of the roof. I step next to him and find an open courtyard below, surrounded by flat-roofed buildings on all sides. There actually doesn't seem to be any way to get into the courtyard without going through—or, in our case, *over*—one of the buildings.

Like most of the town we've seen so far, the courtyard looks like it's been abandoned for years. A completely dry fountain sits in the center, with dusty stone benches around it. Shrubs and dry weeds are scattered across the cracked ground.

And on the building across from us, a ledge six feet off the ground holds a large white box with a red X on it.

"That has to be a cache," Maddox says, pointing to the box. Lark and I nod.

"We could get to that roof pretty easily," he says, and he's right. All the buildings between here and there are connected in one big rectangle, so we can walk around the perimeter of the courtyard to get to the other roof without ever going into the courtyard. Reaching down to the ledge and getting back up—let alone with the cache—would be a challenge, though.

"We'd need a rope or a ladder or something," I start. "Oh! A ladder!"

The rope ladder we climbed up to get to the roof is anchored with two big metal spikes that I suspect weren't here originally. It doesn't matter, though—it's rope, so it shouldn't be too difficult to untie it from these anchors and retie it . . . somewhere else. I don't know where yet, but this is a necessary first step.

I crouch in front of the first anchor, find the rope end, and begin untying. Maddox's eyes light up, and he kneels in front of the second anchor to help.

"This is perfect," he says. "Even if we don't find an anchor, there are three of us, so two of us could hold it while the third lowers down to the cache. Then—"

"I think," Lark interrupts, still looking down into the courtyard, "there's going to be a hiccup with that plan."

Four people have walked out of one of the buildings and are strolling into the courtyard, led by a tall, broad-shouldered boy. Two of their group—a pale-skinned girl with pink-striped hair and a guy with a beard—follow directly behind him, while the last—a short person looking around the courtyard—trails after them. The team has clearly spotted the cache, and since they're cutting *through* the courtyard, there's no question who's going to get to it first.

"Godsdammit," Maddox mutters.

We watch them near the cache. As they get closer, the large cracks in the ground begin to glow bright orange and red. The team below doesn't notice it at first—or if they do, they don't react.

Then lava begins seeping out of the cracked ground.

The three of us watch in stunned silence. The group has made it only a third of the way to the cache when the lava begins to spread. The short person shouts, "Run!" before sprinting back to the door they entered from. The pink-haired girl screams—the fissures in the ground are everywhere. She runs for the exit, vaulting over overflowing cracks and springing between rapidly shrinking islands of untouched ground as her two team members follow on her heels. With an enormous jump she launches herself over a moat of lava into the open doorway, just seconds before the simmering lava covers the entire ground. The bearded guy abandons his flaming, melting boots and leaps for the door.

The broad-shouldered boy isn't so lucky. He's too far from the door when the lava coats the entire courtyard, swallowing his boots up to his ankles. He collapses near the center of the courtyard, far from the walls, with a long, gut-wrenching scream. He shrieks in agony as the lava coats his legs and stomach, setting his clothes on fire. As the molten earth swallows him whole.

We can't reach him to even try to help. It's one of the worst things I've ever witnessed.

When the screaming mercifully ends, the quiet feels unnaturally loud. The lava doesn't stop spreading until the entire courtyard is covered in over a foot of the sizzling molten rock. The heat is so intense, it burns my face even up on the roof. Once the lava's growth slows to a stop, Maddox clears his throat.

"Well, I still think our plan of rappelling down from the roof is the best bet. Any volunteers?"

Lark and I look at him incredulously.

"Pass," Lark says.

I shake my head. "I'm good."

Maddox smiles grimly. "That's fine—I'll do it."

We slowly make our way around the perimeter of the broiling-hot courtyard, careful to look out for anything suspicious about our surroundings—we don't want to end up like the other team. Once we've reached the building with the ledge holding the cache, we look around for a place to anchor the ladder. Maddox spots a pair of hooks exactly where we need the ladder to go, which makes me think this is the strategy the Tournament designers wanted us to use. We attach the rope ladder and carefully lower it to the ledge.

Maddox climbs down and picks up the box. He hoists it over his head to hand it to me and Lark. We reach over the edge and pull the box up onto the roof. It's smooth and cool, with only a simple latch. We've just opened it when Maddox climbs over the edge of the roof.

"What's in it?"

There's only one item: another ticket.

My fingers itch to grab it, but I ball them into fists at my sides instead. Clearing my throat, I look at Maddox. "You're the one who climbed down to get it. You should have it."

His eyes go wide. "We worked together to get it—"

"I agree," Lark says. "Maddox should have it." Maddox still hesitates, and Lark rolls her eyes. "Don't think I won't force you to take it."

With a short laugh, Maddox nods. "Okay," he says, rubbing his hands together. "Okay." He takes a deep breath. And reaches into the box. Like Lark's, the ticket melts into his skin, leaving a swirling gold band behind.

Two tickets down. One more to go.

CHAPTER 20

Maddox has just run his fingers over his new ticket tattoo when a distant explosion rocks the building we're standing on. I crouch instinctively as Lark and Maddox freeze before I turn to the source of the sound. A plume of thick black smoke has formed in the southwest portion of the town. I feel ill at the thought of the buildings this Tournament is destroying. The history.

People lived in this town, probably for centuries, before Glamor, Mind, and Architect wiped them out. And now the Tournament designers are treating these ruins like a playground that's theirs to destroy.

"They aren't messing around," Maddox says grimly. "It'll be a miracle if that explosion didn't kill anyone."

"I think watching someone drown in lava made it clear they're not against killing us," Lark says.

I grimace.

A much closer blast makes me jump, and the dirt kicks up just a couple of feet from my boot. A deep, smoking gouge in the roof turns my blood cold.

Someone is shooting at us.

I jump to my feet and spin around. On the roof of the building behind us stands an infuriatingly familiar contestant with a camera drone hovering above her. Astrid grins so widely at me, I can see it from here before she raises the rifle a second time.

"If she kills Maddox or Lark, she can take their ticket." Chaos reminds us through our earpieces, his voice strained.

The thought is nauseating. "Run!" I shout.

We race across the rooftops and find another ladder to climb down. Back on the street level I turn left, then right down a nearby alley with Maddox and Lark on my heels. This opens up into a small clearing with a single huge mud-brick tower—the one I spotted earlier before they released us into the town. We burst through the door and slam it shut behind us, panting hard.

"Is there a lock?" Maddox asks.

I examine the steel door and shake my head. "No. We'll need to blockade it if we want to keep everyone else out."

The circular room we've entered has the start of a staircase winding up the perimeter of the tower on the far side of the room. About five feet to the right of that is a long-abandoned dusty desk, followed by multiple three-shelved bookcases, made of sturdy-looking wood. All of them are completely packed with yellowed books, some with books stacked on top of each other and even on top of the bookcases.

I approach the one closest to the door and pull the books off the top, coughing as the motion kicks up dust in the air. Maddox gets the idea and rushes over to join me in clearing off the top, before positioning himself to push the other end of the bookcase while I pull. Lark gets in the middle to help lift it, and the three of us shuffle it over to block the door, pushing it tight against the wall. We pile a bunch of books on top, then do the same with the second bookcase, positioning it against the left corner of the first, then finally repeat the process a third time with the last bookcase against the right corner.

Once we're finished, we're dripping sweat and panting, but the work is done and there's no way someone is going to brute force their way in.

It occurs to me only then that we could have just sealed the door closed with runemagic. I opt not to mention that to the rest of the team.

After we take a couple minutes to catch our breath, Maddox says, "Hope there's another way out of here in case this place burns down."

"Mud brick doesn't burn," I say.

"Flood?"

"In the desert?"

"Earthquake?"

"How about instead of imagining ways to die, we see what's in the rest of this godsdamned tower?" Lark interrupts.

As we move toward the stairs, a quiet skittering noise stops me cold. I whirl around, but the only thing behind me is Maddox, who is looking at me with a perplexed expression.

"What?" he asks. "Lark is right. We should—"

"I thought I heard something," I say. "Like . . ." But I'm not sure what it is. The noise was enough to prompt a deep instinctual fear that sets my heart racing, but I can't place what it is. I only heard it for a moment and now it's gone.

I shake my head. "Maybe I misheard. Forget it."

When I turn back to the stairs, Lark is frowning at me. She doesn't say anything, though, and instead starts toward the stairs. Maddox and I begin to follow just as a pale boy descends the stairs and pauses midstride upon seeing us.

The boy has the palest skin I've ever seen on someone living—so light it looks almost translucent. His short hair is white-blond and his arms are tattooed from shoulders to fingertips with a collection of runes too numerous to count. The biggest rune on his left shoulder is the rune for *multitudes* or *swarm,* which isn't concerning at all. He's a mage. But it's his eyes that stop me.

They're pure black.

Lark swears and takes several steps back until she's next to the two of us. And right about now I'm severely regretting not using runemagic to blockade ourselves in—that would be a lot easier to undo than the three bookcases we heaved in front of the door.

"Maybe he's friendly?" Maddox says with a note of alarm.

That skin-crawling *skittering* noise rolls through the room, making me shiver. The boy doesn't speak, but he continues his descent down the stairs, then walks toward us. We all keep our distance from him as he edges around the circular room while we walk through the center until he's standing in front of the barricaded door—and the only exit.

Then he opens his mouth so wide, I can almost feel my jaw ache. For a moment he just stands there silently with his mouth open, and the three of us glance at each other uncertainly.

Until two large iridescent blue-green pincers wriggle out of his mouth.

The pincers are followed by a small shiny-shelled body, eight legs, and a long, curving tail dripping with saliva and venom. We watch in horrified fascination as the shiny jeweled scorpion beetle crawls over his tongue and his lips, then down his chin and neck. A second one follows, then a third, each one emerging a little more quickly than the next, which is about the moment I realize the scorpion beetles are racing *toward* us and none of us have moved.

"Run!" I yell, spinning around. This seems to snap Maddox out of his frozen state, and he begins sprinting up the stairs. Lark, however, doesn't move. She stands there, wide-eyed and pale, until I grab her arm and yank her up a stair with me.

"Go!" I scream, and this time she seems to hear me. She races ahead and I follow on her heels as the skittering grows louder, louder, *louder*. I run up the stairs taking them two at a time. Nothing has touched me, not yet, but my skin is absolutely crawling with the horror of it all. Daring a glance back, I have instant regrets—there is a *wave* of multicolored scorpion beetles racing up the stairs behind us, climbing on the walls, inching closer to us.

I push my legs harder, pounding up the long staircase until we burst through a door at the top landing, slamming it shut behind us.

This time I remember runemagic and immediately begin sealing it by tracing runes in the center of the door. The space around the edges of the door glows white, but the seal is weak—I need to mark the door somehow, and fast, if I really want a stable seal. Carving it would be ideal, but that would take way too long given the circumstances.

Shiny beetle legs and pincers begin pushing at the space around the door, testing the weak seal. Maddox shrieks when a full pincer reaches through the crack under the door.

"I need to mark the door!" I trace the runes again and

again, sweating and shaking so hard my teeth clatter. "Find paint! Or water! Anything!"

"*Paint?*" Lark asks incredulously.

"Just look!" I scream, unable to keep the desperation out of my voice. The light barrier filling in the cracks around the door pulses every time I complete tracing the runes, but my arm is getting tired and I can't keep retracing these forever.

"How's ink?" Maddox calls. "There's no brush or pens or anything, though—"

Lark must grab the inkpot from him, because a second later she's holding the unstoppered pot and tracing runes of her own along the tall edge of the door. I dip my fingers in the pot and trace my runes more deliberately, aiming for precision now that I'm actually marking the door. The light barrier sealing the door glows bright orange, like looking directly into a forge, before the steel door *expands,* filling in the crack around the doorframe with molten metal and rapidly cooling into a solid form.

When it's done, I look down at my trembling hands. They're covered in long stripes and drips of black ink. Lark's expansion runes combined with my sealing barrier runes, and the door is no longer a door. It's just a flat sheet of steel embedded deeply into the mud-brick walls.

"Holy shit," Maddox says. "*Holy shit*—we were just almost devoured by an ocean of scorpion beetles!"

Lark shudders visibly, and honestly? Same.

Maddox steps up to the door, examining our combined runes, now dripping black as they dry. "Will that mage be able to undo these? I'm assuming he knows runemagic too, given the state of his arms."

Lark shakes her head. "He'd have to be inordinately power-ful to get through combined magic. You can add your own if you want to be sure."

Maddox smiles sheepishly. "I was never any good at rune-magic. I'm just as likely to set the door on fire as I am to strengthen the seal."

Lark doesn't comment. I lean against the wall and let my head fall back, closing my eyes, suddenly exhausted. My finger joints are throbbing from all the exerted effort, and I rub them carefully, slowly stretching out each painful joint.

When I open my eyes, Lark is sitting on the floor about ten feet to my left, meticulously cracking her knuckles, one by one, while Maddox shuffles through the drawers in a beauti-fully carved desk of black wood. Ahead of us is a long row of built-in shelving, with loads of what look like hand-bound manuscripts and long rolls of paper. Like everything else in this abandoned town, it's long out of use.

Ten years long, I'd guess.

Maddox suddenly sits up straight, grinning widely as he holds up—"Look! Another cache!"

My mouth drops open as Maddox crouches in front of me and opens the box. The gold ticket inside gleams in the light.

Lark and Maddox look at me expectantly. "Well?" Lark asks. "What are you waiting for?"

I hesitate. It feels weird just taking it when Lark and Maddox found their own tickets. But when I say as much, Lark snorts. "No, you just led us to this tower and saved us from a night-marish death by keeping the door sealed. You've more than earned it, Bananaquit."

Maddox blinks at her, but Lark doesn't offer him an

explanation. Instead, she raises her eyebrows at me as if to say, *Are you going to take it? Or am I going to make you?*

With a deep breath, I grab the ticket. Watching it slither over my arm somehow isn't less disconcerting even though it's the third time I've seen it. When it melds into my wrist, it leaves a warm, tingling sensation.

I let out a shaky breath. And then that's it. As long as no one kills us, we're in.

A blast like a burst from a horn fills the room, making us all jump. The silence that follows envelops us as my startled heart rams against my chest.

Then, slowly, Lark says, "Was that . . . the closing sound?"

"THE LAST TICKET HAS BEEN CLAIMED," a robotic voice booms over us. "CONGRATULATIONS TO THE TICKET HOLDERS."

Maddox drops the box, leaping to his feet. "Holy shit! We did it!"

CHAPTER 21

By the time we get back to our hotel, I never want to move again.

I collapse on the sofa, sighing as my aching body sinks into the soft cushions. Mouse immediately hops onto my lap and begins kneading my thighs, purring loudly. Sitting here was a mistake, because there's no way I'm going to want to get up now. Still, I take a moment to rest, massaging my aching hands, then my neck.

Despite the pain, I find myself smiling as I run my thumb over the golden ticket etched into my skin, because *we did it:* For the first time in history, someone from the Shallows made it through the Tournament's Opening Trial. And not just one of us—*three* of us.

Chaos has already pulled his tablet out to begin ordering the previously promised *celebration feast*. He hasn't stopped grinning since we stepped out of the arena.

"We'll be moved to the official accommodations tomorrow," Chaos is saying as the four of us settle on the sectional.

"Since you're all officially finalists, you'll have access to all the same resources as the rest of the contestants. There's food, lodging, a hospital, even shops all on the premises."

"Sounds nice," Maddox says.

Lark wordlessly turns on the TV and starts flipping through the channels.

"I've heard it is," Chaos says. "This is my first time sponsoring, though, so I've never been. I hope it lives up to the hype."

"If it's a third as nice as this place, I'm sure we'll all be happy," I say.

Chaos's smile finally fades. "Well, I don't want them to think that because you're all Shallowsfolk, you don't need accommodations as nice as everyone else's."

He has a point, even if benefiting from this kind of luxury still feels wrong. It isn't so much that I think we deserve less than the standard of living everyone else gets—it's more that I don't think *anyone* deserves this kind of excessive wealth.

Then again, this isn't anywhere near the luxury that God-levelers presumably enjoy. So maybe I'm looking at this wrong. If we have the resources, then *everyone* deserves to live this comfortably.

Lark shatters my thoughts with a triumphant announcement: "Beetle boy didn't get a ticket!" She's paused the TV on a channel with pundits currently discussing the results of the Opening Trial. A small graphic shows a blank bracket-style Tournament with thirty-two slots, which will presumably be filled in with our names once the first matches have been determined. Below the graphic is the table of the contestants who made it through the opening round, each name paired with a picture of a face.

Maddox snorts. *"Beetle boy?"*

Lark lifts a shoulder and changes the channel. "He *did* try to kill us with a flood of carnivorous beetles."

An image on the screen catches my eye: an overview of the Shallows.

"Lark, hold on," I say, sitting up. Lark pauses and glances over at me. I lean forward as the footage cuts to what looks like a huge brawl in the street, with Enforcers arresting bruised and bloodied people. My stomach churns. "Raise the volume."

"A mob of Shallowsfolk attacked a group of Enforcers this morning, triggering a violent brawl. Several Enforcers were seriously injured, and mass arrests have continued throughout the day. Enforcers have declared a strict curfew for all Shallowsfolk for the foreseeable future—"

"A curfew?" Maddox exclaims. "What about the night workers?"

I grimace, the news doing little to ease my rapidly worsening headache. Probably a third of Shallowsfolk all work at night—like me. A strict curfew would make it impossible for those people to work, which would be immediately devastating for so many.

Too many of us down there live paycheck to paycheck. Missing even a couple of days of work could be enough for some people to lose their homes or be unable to afford food.

Not that the Enforcers care about that.

"This brawl is another escalation in the increased incidents of fighting between Enforcers and Shallowsfolk. Enforcer Chief Davies says they're currently discussing further measures to suppress the violence . . ."

We sit in grim silence until the report ends and Lark turns off the TV. After a long moment she says, "So are we not going to talk about how they used a real Deathchild town as an arena?"

Chaos blanches. "They did *what?*"

Maddox grimaces and I nod, my stomach twisting as I recall the apothecary shop. "I really don't think it was a reproduction."

Chaos frowns. "How do you know?"

"I've read books about what life was like for Deathchildren," Lark says smoothly. "And the place felt too old to be created just for the Tournament. I know the Architects are experts and can easily make something feel old, but . . ."

"It did feel . . . off," Maddox confirms.

Chaos shakes his head, a bit pale and his expression twisted. "If you're right, that's . . . vile. They've never done anything like that before, to my knowledge, but I suppose that doesn't matter. Gods."

Maddox clears his throat. "Do we think it means anything that they sent all three Shallowsfolk to a Deathchild town? If there were two other arenas we could have ended up in . . ."

We fall into a quiet as smothering as a lead blanket. No one has an answer. And none of us feel like celebrating after that.

The next morning we pack up our stuff—including Mouse's mountain of cat supplies—and leave the hotel. Lark separates from the group to go meet up with her sponsor while Chaos,

Maddox, and I head outside, where a long black car is waiting. A man in a suit stands on the curb next to the car. As soon as he sees us, the chauffeur opens the back doors and gestures politely inside.

Chaos waltzes in confidently, so I follow, picking up my bag.

"I can load your bags in the trunk," the driver says. "Please leave them here."

Feeling oddly chastised, I put my bag down and pull Mouse out before I slip inside next to Chaos. And stare.

I don't know what I was expecting entering a luxury vehicle, but this isn't it. Instead of rows, the seats are placed along the long rectangular perimeter of the car's back cabin. There's enough space to stand, which I wasn't expecting based on the outside of the vehicle, so this must be Architect made— and the cabin is large enough that twenty people could fit comfortably.

Floating along the center of the cabin, there are trays of drinks and finger food set out on large circular trays. One tray is full of cheeses, fruits, small selections of meats and crackers; another has small pastries, cookies, glazed breads. Chaos is already eating a donut with a satisfied smile, a glass of some kind of fizzy clear beverage in his other hand.

"What do you think?" he asks between bites as Maddox climbs in after us and the suited man closes the door behind him.

Maddox's mouth drops open. "It's bigger on the inside."

"Yeah, this is definitely Architect made," Chaos confirms. "Pretty great, isn't it? Personally, I'm a fan of anything that gives me food."

The food is, undeniably, a draw. I place Mouse on the seat

next to me and pick up a small cheese Danish drizzled with raspberry jam and icing. The pastry is flaky and sweet and the cream cheese and jam combination is smooth and tart. It might actually be one of the best things I've ever tasted.

"Isn't this . . . a bit much?" Maddox frowns as he looks around the luxurious cabin. Mouse rubs against his leg and his face softens a little. He plucks a cheese square off the tray and offers it to her. "Do all the contestants travel like this?"

"The top thirty-two, yeah. As long as you stay in the competition, you'll all get a taste of luxury."

Maddox doesn't look thrilled to hear it, and I'm honestly not sure how to feel about it either. I'm not doing any of this for the sake of luxury.

I'm here to save my uncles. I just haven't figured out a way to do that without relying on winning the Tournament.

The reminder of why I'm here sours my stomach a bit, but I still try to eat some cheeses and meat. If I'm going to win this competition, I need to keep up my energy.

"It just . . . feels wrong," Maddox says after a pause, "to not be able to share this with my family."

Chaos nods slowly, his face serious, for once. "You're right. It's not fair. I'm sorry."

Maddox just nods.

A few minutes later, Chaos clears his throat, breaking the heavy quiet. "I should mention, since you two and Lark are the first Shallowsfolk to ever make it this far in the competition, I'd expect some media attention to follow you going forward."

I grimace. "What kind of media attention?"

Chaos lifts a shoulder. "Interview requests, some paparazzi from time to time. The usual."

I suppose for a minor god, that *would* be the usual. Chaos must notice my lack of enthusiasm, because he adds, "It's not a bad thing. If the media are paying attention to you three, then the Tournament runners can't as easily cheat to knock you out early."

Maddox blinks. "Is that something we should be worried about? Cheating?"

Chaos pulls a big roll of fluffy white yarn speckled with rainbow colors out of his bag and begins attaching it to one of his knitting needles, wrapping the yarn around the needle with a dizzying hand motion. Mouse sits at his feet, staring at the moving yarn with rapt attention. "I wouldn't *worry* about it as much as I'd look out for it. I expect the showrunners aren't thrilled that the three of you have made it this far, but they can't be obvious about it or viewers will get pissed off that the illusion of fairness is broken."

Neither Maddox nor I has to ask why the Tournament showrunners wouldn't be thrilled about our advancing. No one may say it explicitly, but it's obvious Midlevelers—and, I'd presume, Godlevelers—see Shallowsfolk as beneath them. After all, they're perfectly happy to let us starve and drown while they look away and live in luxury.

But the three of us making it this far means they can't look away. They have to acknowledge that we're here. And I intend to keep it that way.

CHAPTER 22

The moment we step out of the car, I realize Chaos was not exaggerating about the media thing. Camera drones swarm us, the rapid-fire flash of photography blinding. I'm immediately glad I closed Mouse into the safety of my bag as Chaos shepherds us past a crowd of journalists.

"Chaos! Why did you choose to sponsor a Shallows-born fighter?"

"Crow! What do you have to say to your friends and family back home now that you've made it past the Opening Trial?"

"Maddox! How did you all survive the Opening Trial?"

"Are you three Shallows-born fighters working together?"

I can barely process the flurry of questions before Chaos has pushed us through the hotel's entrance and into the lobby, enveloping us in quiet.

In contrast to the chaos outside, the lobby is shockingly peaceful. I can only assume the journalists aren't allowed to follow us inside, which is a relief. Chaos deposits the two of us in a lounging area far from the doors and windows while he goes to the front desk to check in.

I wonder if Lark has made it here yet.

Sitting in comfortable chairs in the quiet, Maddox distracts himself on his phone while I take in what just happened. The jumble of questions and voices and cameras churns deep in my chest uneasily.

What do you have to say to your friends and family back home now that you've made it past the Opening Trial?

I close my eyes and lean back in the seat, trying to push the question from my mind, but it sticks precisely because I don't want to think about it. I don't want to think about how the only family I have left back home is Ravenna. And even so, I didn't enter this competition to become some kind of spokesperson for the Shallows-born. Gods, I'm technically not even Shallows-born, not that I can admit that to anyone if I want to keep breathing.

I'm here for my uncles. That's it. That's all that matters.

"Look who's joined us."

My eyes snap open at the voice. Chaos and Lark are standing in front of us, Chaos with an oddly forced smile and Lark looking bored.

"Our room's ready," Chaos adds. "Let's go before some journo tries to sneak in."

⌣══⌐

Our new hotel suite makes the last one look small in comparison.

This one is essentially a house—complete with a full kitchen, five bedrooms, three full bathrooms, and a living room. Everything from the pristine wooden floors to the shiny stainless steel kitchen appliances is equipped with self-cleaning and self-healing runes, to keep everything looking as new as the day it was installed. Framed paintings decorate the walls between floor-to-ceiling windows, and every room has a variety of plants and sculptures.

As I release Mouse from my bag and we take in the gleaming spectacle that is our new living quarters, Chaos is frowning.

"What is it?" I ask. "Is this place really not up to your standards?"

Chaos grimaces and shakes his head. "The suite is nice, but each of you is supposed to have your own, like the rest of the contestants, and the sponsors are supposed to have their own suites as well. No one else is being asked to share quarters like this, but when I pointed that out, they told me they'd run out of rooms, which is obviously bullshit."

I can't imagine why any one person would need a suite with three bathrooms and five bedrooms, but I get what he means.

"I know it's not the point, but I kind of prefer this," Maddox says. "Having all this space to myself would be . . . uncomfortable. Honestly, it's gross that every contestant and sponsor is supposed to get essentially their own multi-bedroom house.'''"

"I agree," I say.

Chaos looks at Lark, who just shrugs. "Better this than sharing a suite with Dez. She was pissed when they told her she was expected to share with me."

"What a coincidence that only the Shallowsfolk sponsors are affected by the shortage," Chaos grumbles. He takes a deep breath and sighs heavily. "Fine. I don't mind sharing with all of you either, of course, so if you're all okay with it, I won't fight this one. Take a few minutes to settle in and choose your rooms and whatnot, but we don't actually have a lot of time. We have to prepare for your first media appearance."

Lark drops her duffel bag with a *thump.* "Our first *what?*"

Once we're settled, we join Chaos in the main room, where he is setting out clothes for each of us to wear at the interview.

"The top thirty-two contestants all do media appearances together," he says, smoothing a few wrinkles from the shirt he's just laid out on the sofa. "The first one is a way to introduce you to the rest of Escal and let the media get to know you a bit. They'll probably ask you the same kinds of questions they asked outside, so be prepared to answer. You're also not obligated to respond, if you feel uncomfortable, but I'd save your passes for especially egregious questions. People tend not to like it when competitors refuse to answer."

I'm not sure when I was supposed to begin caring what people think about me.

Chaos steps back from the three outfits and touches his chin, thinking. "You *are* all Shallowsfolk, though, and I expect some journos are going to try to make that salacious. Don't rise to the bait. If someone asks a rude question, better to pass than say something rude back."

"Why?" Lark asks bluntly. "It's not like people vote on which of us move forward. What does it matter if we piss someone off?"

Chaos hesitates. "I'd be less worried about pissing audience members off than pissing off the president. Or someone else in government. The Tournament designers are supposed to be fair and all, but I wouldn't count on that."

The ruins of the Deathchild village rise in my mind, sending a fresh wave of nausea through my gut. Combined with mention of my mother, even just in passing, the thought makes me somehow hot and cold at the same time. I bite my lip and shake it off.

But what Chaos said about not pissing off anyone in government resonates more than I'd like to admit. Especially with my uncles in custody.

"Why did you get *me* clothes?" Lark asks, nodding at the third outfit. "I get you're Frogmouth's sponsor and have basically adopted Maddox, but I have a sponsor."

"Frogmouth?" I blurt before I can stop myself as Maddox lets out a booming laugh. "Is that even a bird?"

"It is," she says, still looking at Chaos, who is clearly struggling not to laugh himself.

"I'm a simple man who enjoys playing the role of stylist," Chaos says. "You don't have to wear it if you'd prefer not to, but it'd irritate my sister *spectacularly* if you did, and nothing would make me happier."

With a shrug, she grabs the clothes and disappears into her bedroom to change.

We've barely gotten into our new outfits before Chaos whisks us away to a large auditorium on another floor in this massive building. The room is packed with people, most with cameras, and camera drones zip through the air, recording us as we enter. A low buzz begins in my stomach as we walk to the stage down the long aisle alongside the rows of seats.

It's not so much that I've never been on a stage—after all, until I came up here, I was fighting most nights in front of crowds that were sometimes bigger than this one. But that was *fighting*. I never had to *speak* to them.

When we reach the stage, we're directed to sit at the far end of the first row. Other contestants have already taken their seats. Most of their faces I don't recognize, and when I don't spot Astrid, I can't help but smile, just a little, as Chaos leads us to our seats.

Then that awful voice comes from behind me. "You can't be serious. All *three* of them made it through?"

I suppose getting rid of her in the Opening Trial would have been too good to be true. I suppress a groan and refuse to look back. I don't know who Astrid is speaking to, but she's doing it loudly enough to ensure that everyone onstage can hear her.

"They *do* realize this isn't a game, right? This is a serious competition, and now there are three fewer *genuine* competitors because of them."

Lark, who until now has appeared completely unbothered by everything, mumbles, "Would it really be against the rules if I set her hair on fire?"

"Yes," Chaos says quickly, though he's smirking. "One of you will just have to eliminate her in the matchups. It would make my entire year to see her lose to any of you."

I smile. That *is* a nice thought.

Chaos sees us seated, then goes to join the other sponsors in the seats below. Astrid glares daggers at us. We ignore her—at the very least, it's satisfying to not give her the reaction she's looking for. The longer we ignore her, the more agitated she seems to get until she huffs and looks away from us.

Eventually the seats are all taken and the auditorium is completely full of people. The journalists seem to be seated in the first three rows, followed by two rows of sponsors, both of which are separated from the rest of the audience. I don't know who everyone else is—just curious people who paid to be here, I guess.

A woman with buzzed curly hair comes down the row with some kind of clear marker, drawing what I presume is a rune on every contestant's throat. When she reaches me, I gesture to the marker. "What is that?"

The woman blinks. "Oh, I'm drawing amplification runes on everyone. It will amplify *everything* you say, including whispers and mumbles, so be careful. Once the press conference is over, everyone will get wipes to remove them."

I nod and she presses the cold marker tip to my neck, quickly scribbling the rune in invisible ink before she moves on to Lark, then Maddox.

Once the woman has finished and steps off the stage, a willowy person in a glittery bright blue tailored suit and silver stilettos glides ethereally in front of us, facing the crowd. Their platinum-blond hair is styled in an undercut, and their bold eye makeup matches their suit. I recognize their face instantly—Charisma, Glamor's eldest child. "Thank you all for joining us today to welcome our top thirty-two contestants!"

They pause and clap politely with a smile as the room fills with cheers. The lights are so bright on the stage, I can barely see the audience below, which is probably for the best. The heat from the light blazes on my face, and sweat is already dripping down my back. At least my dark clothes will make it less obvious that I'm a sweaty, anxious mess.

"Our contestants will be paired off with each other for individual matches, beginning tomorrow," Charisma continues. "But today they're here so all of Escal may get to know them before the matches begin. For the sake of organization, every journalist will be given the opportunity to ask *one* question, beginning at the start of the row here and ending there." They gesture to the rows.

Every journalist? I bite my lip, holding back a cringe. There must be close to fifty journalists here. If every one of them gets to ask a question, we're going to be here awhile.

"If you have any follow-up questions for any of the contestants, you may, of course, submit an interview request to their sponsor," Charisma continues. "With that out of the way . . . shall we begin?"

The first journalist, a woman with sleek black hair and light skin, stands. "Sakura from EEW. I have a question for the three Shallows-born contestants."

I bite my lip harder. Of course she does.

"I'd love to hear how they're feeling as the first contestants from the Shallows to make it to the top thirty-two."

That one's not so bad. Maddox gives some long-winded bubbly response about how excited he is, and it's so endearing I almost forget where we are. When he's done, Lark says, "Sure. Same."

Then she looks at me, so I guess that's the entirety of her answer.

"I'm proud to be among the first of the Shallowsfolk to make it this far," I say. "But I'm sure we won't be the last."

Astrid snorts. It's not subtle.

The next journalist, a man with bright orange hair, stands. "Arthur from *Escal News Today*. I'm curious if any of the Shallows-born contestants have a response to the rumors that the only way all three of them could have made it through the Opening Trial was through cheating."

The accusation lands in the room with a silence so thick it's oppressive.

Cheating? What would cheating even *look* like? I suppose maybe someone could smuggle something in, but none of us did. Gods, I didn't even use illegal Deathmagic.

"Excuse me?" Lark says, her eyes narrowing dangerously.

Arthur pauses. "Should I . . . repeat the question?"

"I think we heard you the first time," Maddox cuts in before Lark can speak. "But I think I can speak for the three of us when I say it's insulting to imply the only way the three of us could have survived the Opening Trial is through cheating simply because we're Shallowsfolk. We made it through because we worked as a team and watched each other's backs. That's all there is to it."

Lark still looks like she'd personally like to break the nose of anyone accusing us of cheating (which, same), but Maddox, it turns out, is pretty good at this media stuff.

The next hour is a blur of questions—many of which, thankfully, are not directed at us. As my anxiety around being in front of a large crowd fades to boredom, I struggle to keep focused.

That is, until Astrid starts bashing us.

"It's a shame to see three spots lost to unserious competitors," she's saying in response to a question I missed. "It would have been better for those slots to go to competitors who actually have a chance of advancing, but I suppose it was inevitable that some of them would get lucky eventually."

My eye twitches with the strain of keeping my expression neutral. Before any of us can respond to the insult, another journalist stands.

"Lenari, ELN. I'm curious if any of the Shallows-born competitors care to share their reaction to Maddox and Crow being selected to fight each other in the first round."

For a second I'm sure I heard wrong. Sure, I expected that the three of us might have to face off eventually, but the first round? And why does the press get the matchup order before the rest of us?

When neither Maddox nor Lark speak up, I say, "I don't think any of us were aware of that."

The journalist's eyes light up with excitement. "Oh! Well, in that case, could you share your initial thoughts?"

My *initial thoughts* are the kind that would definitely piss off government officials—like how it sure seems awfully coincidental that they've guaranteed eliminating one of the three Shallows-born contestants in the first round. Thankfully, I don't have to figure out a diplomatic response, because Maddox responds for me.

"May the best fighter win."

CHAPTER 23

The mood is glum when we return to our shared suite. For a long, uncomfortable moment the silence is tense between us after the door closes. I don't know what to feel, let alone what to say. Chaos checked the schedule after the media appearance and confirmed Maddox and I are scheduled to fight on the last day of the first round, with Lark's match immediately after ours—four days from now. Of course, I knew it was possible I'd have to fight Lark or Maddox eventually—but there are five total rounds. The shock of being matched against Maddox in the very first round still stings, now with an aftertaste of resignation.

At least we have half a week to process the bad news.

Mouse hops down from her cat tree and rubs against our legs, purring. Lark mumbles something about using up all of her *people energy* and goes directly to her room.

Maddox sighs and looks at me. "Well, I'm not going to go easy on you, but if you agree not to use lethal force, then I'm happy to agree the same."

My stomach lurches at the thought of killing him. I haven't known Maddox that long, but I've known him long enough to not want to seriously injure him if I can avoid it. "Agreed. No lethal force."

"Well, that's a relief," Chaos says. "Would've sucked to watch either of you die, especially so soon."

"Yeah, I'm sure that would have been hard for you," I deadpan.

Chaos blushes and Maddox laughs. "I guess I should ask—what happens when one of us loses? Assuming we don't die, I mean."

The minor god brightens, probably glad for the subject change. "Well, there are two options. Most of the time people just go home, but you also have the option of joining another competitor's team for the remainder of the Tournament, if you so desire. You don't get to fight for them or anything, but you can help support them behind the scenes, like with training, or media events, or gear—stuff like that. The contestant has to agree too, of course, since they'll be sharing a portion of their winnings in return, but it can be beneficial for both sides as long as the contestant can trust you not to sabotage them."

I arch an eyebrow. "Does sabotage happen often?"

"I wouldn't say *often* . . ." Chaos shrugs. "But it has happened, yeah."

"Of course it has." Maddox sighs. "Well, I don't know about everyone else, but I'm exhausted. I'm going to call my folks and relax in my room for a while."

Now that he mentions it, relaxing actually sounds nice. I nod and stand as Maddox turns toward his room.

"Crow, before you go, can I talk to you in private for a minute?" Chaos asks.

My eyebrows raise at the question, but I don't protest.

Once Maddox has disappeared into his room, Chaos takes a deep breath and smiles softly at me.

"I looked into what's going on with your uncles, and I still can't help you free them. However, I *can* get you in to see them, if you'd like."

My eyes go wide. The thought of seeing them again awakens a longing so strong it hurts. "I can see them?" My voice cracks with emotion and I can't be bothered to care. "Are they okay?"

"They're doing as well as can be expected given the circumstances," Chaos says. "I can't do this often, but I did arrange for a visit tonight. But this has to stay between us, understand?"

"Yes," I say immediately, my pulse pounding. Suddenly, all thoughts of sleep have evaporated entirely, replaced with the jittery need to move. "Thank you. This means everything to me—I won't forget it."

Chaos just smiles.

Seven impatient hours later a prison guard is escorting us down a long set of stairs. We descend deep beneath the ground, where the air feels damp and heavy. We follow winding corridors lined with steel windowless doors. The corridors are lit with long strips of cool blue light, and our steps echo on the stone floor, the only sound breaking the silence.

It's uncomfortably quiet down here. There's little to distract me from the anxiety buzzing in my stomach, or the jittery thoughts bouncing around my skull. It's been only four days since I last saw them, but that panicked night feels like an age ago. And I can't help but suspect my uncles aren't going to be thrilled to learn I'm competing in the Tournament.

The guard stops at a door and quickly traces some pattern I don't catch on a metal panel beside the door. The panel beeps and flashes green, and the guard turns to us.

"You have fifteen minutes, after which I'll be coming in to retrieve you. The two of you will enter the cell, then the door will be locked behind you. If you need to leave early, knock on the door."

"Oh," Chaos says, "I was planning to wait out here in the hall if that's okay. To give Crow some privacy with his uncles."

The guard stares at him for a long, uncomfortable minute. Then, slowly, he says, "The two of you will enter the cell, then the door will be locked behind you."

Chaos grimaces. "Got it."

The guard nods and steps aside as the door slides open. The two of us enter, and the door slips closed behind us with a quiet *snick*. A wave of something like static dancing on my skin rolls over me, and Chaos touches my shoulder.

"I've set up a disruption field, so you can talk freely in here. The cameras won't pick up any audio."

I nod, my heart in my throat. The room is a small concrete box with the same blue striplights running along the floor and ceiling. A bunk bed is set up on the right wall, taking up half the width of the room. A toilet is in the far left corner, beside the world's smallest sink.

And sitting on the bottom bed are both of my uncles, whose jaws drop when Chaos and I walk in.

"Holy shit," Alecks says. *"Crow?"*

Orin hops off the bed and envelops me in a hug, Alecks

right behind him. I thought I was fine before I stepped in here, but the moment they pull me into their arms, I'm sobbing—full-on, shoulder-heaving uncontrollable sobs. The flood of emotion catches me off guard, but I don't fight it. I press my face into Orin's chest and take in both my uncles' warmth and softness.

In their arms, I'm seven years old again, crying as they hold me after yet another nightmare. I'm ten, sobbing because it's my dad's birthday and I miss him. I'm twelve, furious and wailing because my mother is on TV, advocating for people like me to die.

Orin's and Alecks's arms have been my home for so long. I didn't realize just how badly I missed them until now.

"It's okay," Orin says gently as I cry. "Your uncle and I are okay."

After several minutes of weeping I finally manage to pull myself together enough to form coherent words and look at my uncles. Orin is smiling sadly at me, while Alecks is frowning at something behind me—which is when I remember Chaos is still here with us.

"Oh," I say, wiping at my eyes. "Sorry, Uncle Orin, Uncle Alecks, this is Chaos. He helped me get onto Midlevel and arranged this visit."

Chaos smiles weakly and gives an awkward little wave.

"And what does the son of Discord want in return?" Alecks asks coolly.

Chaos and I exchange a glance.

"It . . . wasn't like that," I say haltingly.

Alecks arches an eyebrow. "He brought you to Midlevel and arranged a visit with us out of the *kindness of his heart*?"

I blink, taken aback by the hostility. But if my uncles' suspicion bothers Chaos, he doesn't show it.

"I didn't bring Crow to Midlevel just to visit you two, no. Before you two were arrested, I met him at the fighting ring in the Shallows, where I offered them my sponsorship for the Tournament of the Gods. Crow initially refused, but after you two were arrested, he accepted my offer. And now they're in the top thirty-two."

Orin has gone even paler in the blue light. "The Tournament?" he says softly. "Oh, Crow . . ."

"And you let him enter knowing what they'd just been through?" Alecks yells at Chaos.

"I didn't know about the arrest when they accepted," Chaos says with a shrug. "Though frankly, Crow is more than capable of making his own decisions."

Alecks's face darkens, which is the moment I step between them. "Okay, that's enough," I say. "I didn't come here for you to yell at Chaos about *my* decisions. I need to talk to you."

"Crow . . . why would you do such a thing?" Orin says.

The room goes quiet as my uncles turn their attention back to me, and all at once I realize I wasn't prepared for this. I was ready for anger. I was ready for fear.

I wasn't ready for the utter devastation painting my uncles' faces.

"I couldn't just wait around for you to die," I say, and though I try to stop it, my voice shakes. "I had to do something. And I know the odds are against me, but if I win, I could save you both."

"And risk your life in the process?" Orin lowers his voice to just above a whisper. "Crow, even if you *do* win, have you considered what that kind of media attention could mean for you?"

"Of course I've considered it," I hiss. "But as long as I don't do anything obvious—"

"What if she recognizes you?" Alecks cuts in.

Neither of them has to clarify who *she* is. The specter of my mother slams into me, an icy punch to the gut that leaves me breathless. "It's been a long time," I say softly, unable to hide the tremor in my voice. "She won't recognize me."

"Really," Alecks says flatly. "You don't think she'll recognize a Shallowsfolk competitor with a striking resemblance—"

"As far as she knows, I'm dead," I whisper. "And I've changed my name since then. She won't recognize me." The name part is true—my mother was resistant to my social transition when I was a kid, but once she was gone, my uncles let me choose my name. Still, my argument sounds weak even to me. The truth is I've worked hard to avoid thinking of my mother. Of course I'm aware of the risk, but I'm willing to risk my safety to save my uncles.

"Have you had your first media appearance?" Alecks finally asks.

I grimace. "Unfortunately."

Alecks closes his eyes for a moment, then, with a deep breath, opens them. "The damage is already done. There's no going back now, so I think we should focus the rest of our limited time with the *other* important thing we needed to talk about." He looks meaningfully at Orin, who purses his lips but nods.

"Crow," Orin says carefully, "I'm sure you've heard why we were arrested."

I swallow hard and nod. Helping Deathchildren escape a

government trying to kill them shouldn't be illegal, but here we are.

Orin glances at Chaos, who has retreated next to the door, as far from us as he can get, and lowers his voice to just barely a whisper. "There are more Deathchildren," he says. "Here."

I frown. "On Midlevel?"

Orin shakes his head. "In this prison. And your uncle and I—we don't know for sure, but we think the minor Death gods are being held here too."

I blink. Death has only four direct children: Herald, Medic, Malady, and Shade. They're purveyors of Deathchildren culture and power and experts in their abilities. Medic and Malady together can diagnose and cure just about any ailment. Herald is the bridge between life and death, the one who brought us to this world and leads us out of it. And Shade can manipulate darkness and light in ways that would make the little bit of shadow magic I can do look like child's play.

All of them disappeared after the Silencing, but I never thought . . .

"How do you know?" I ask. "I assumed the minor Death gods were killed or . . . I don't know, went to wherever Death's realm is or something."

Orin shakes his head. "The minor Death gods can't die. They're Death's direct children—the only truly immortal beings. Deathless."

I'm all too aware that most Deathchildren can and do die, but I suppose it makes sense that Death's direct children would be immortal. Apparently they can't pass that immortality down to the rest of us.

"How many Deathchildren?" I ask, changing the topic.

"A couple dozen," Alecks says. "They'll be executed after the Tournament like us. We heard the guards talking about it."

I'm not sure what to do with any of this information, but if minor Death gods are being held here, it changes everything. All this time I thought the minor Death gods were gone, but instead they've been trapped here. If they were free . . . maybe the Deathchildren who survived wouldn't be so powerless. Maybe we could actually fight back.

Before I can think about it any further, the door opens behind me. "It's time," the guard says, and dread chills me from the inside out. The reality that I don't know if I'll get to see them again makes me tremble.

"It's okay, Crow," Orin says gently.

"We love you," Alecks says.

"I love you too," I whisper, my voice breaking.

Chaos must see the dread in my face, because he gently takes my shoulder and says, "I'll see if I can get you another visit in the future. C'mon."

I cling hard to that possibility as I turn around and walk out the door.

CHAPTER 24

I'm standing in the Underground fighting ring, bouncing on my toes as the crowd roars around me. The rhythmic thumping bass of the music resonates in my chest as I wait for my opponent to enter the ring. But though the energy of the animated crowd and the heat of the lights on me is usually energizing, a cold sense of foreboding sits heavily in my gut. Something is off, but I can't name what.

All at once the cheering crowd goes quiet. I squint through the stage lights to the eerily silent audience, and my stomach plummets to my toes. Where audience members once sat, now Enforcers—hundreds of them—take their place. All watching in complete silence. All waiting.

Then my mother steps into the ring.

My blood is ice. I can't breathe. "You can't be here," I croak.

"Oh, ▆▆▆▆*" My mother laughs. "Did you really think you could hide from me?"*

My eyes snap open as a gasp rips through me. My heart is absolutely galloping in my chest, and I've kicked the sheets completely off the bed. I sit up, pressing my palms against my closed eyes, but I can't shake the stubborn image of my mother's malicious smile. My body is trembling, my hands are cold, and I feel like I'm going to puke. I stumble out of bed, my head light; hot and cold roll through me in shuddering waves.

It was just a dream. It was just a dream, but I can't shake the tremor in my core or the bone-deep panic clawing at my skull. I push open my bedroom door, waving around blindly for the light switch, when my hand hits something cold and hard. It gives way beneath my palm and hits the floor with a crash that sends my racing pulse rocketing.

I just broke something. I just broke something that's probably expensive. I sink into a crouch, furious at the tears blurring my vision and my breaths coming in tiny gasps. *Pull yourself together, Crow, gods above and below—*

The light flashes on.

"Crow?" Chaos's groggy voice for some reason only makes the tears slip down my cheeks faster. I wipe at my face, blinking hard to try to clear my vision and adjust to the sudden light.

When I look up, Chaos is crouching in front of me. He isn't wearing a shirt. Just hot-pink-and-purple pj pants. His mismatched eyes are full of concern, and I want to tell him I'm fine, but I'm pretty sure I can't pull off faking fine right now.

"Hey," he says softly as Maddox and Lark enter the hallway behind him. "Don't worry about the vase—they're not even going to notice it's gone." He waves his hand and the broken pieces of the vase I knocked over gather in a spiky, trembling ball before falling into a nearby trash can.

"Sorry for waking all of you," I say.

Chaos shakes his head. "It's no problem. How are you feeling?"

Awful. I'm a wreck, and for what? A bad dream? My stomach is full of bees, and I can't stop shaking no matter how hard I wrap my arms around my midsection, and my heart is tripping over itself in my chest. I'm hot and cold all over, and Lark and Chaos and Maddox are all watching me, and I'm not even distracted enough by my haywire brain to not be embarrassed.

I want to crawl into a small dark hole and never come out again.

"Not great," I finally say.

"What can I do to help?" Chaos asks, but my mind is static and I don't know what to ask for.

"Move." Lark crouches next to Chaos, pushing him aside with her shoulder. Then all at once she's in front of me, her gray eyes boring into mine. "Extend your arms."

I don't know why, but I obey. Before I can question what she's doing, her hands clasp around my forearms, right beneath my elbows, her arms pressed against mine. She squeezes lightly, then slides her hands down half an inch and squeezes again, continuing down my forearms until she reaches my wrists, then moves up my arms again. She works silently, her gaze focused on the movement of her hands, and something about the gentle pulsing up and down my arms is grounding. Soothing. I'm here, and Lark's warm, soft hands are running over my arms, and slowly, slowly, my heart returns to something like normal.

It is godsdamned *hard* masking my shock at Lark, of all people, comforting me.

Warmth presses against my shoulder as Chaos sits next to me, his weight an added balm. Maddox does the same on my other side, and I close my eyes, taking in their warmth as Lark continues working my arms.

I don't know how long I sit there between Chaos and Maddox with Lark crouched in front of me, holding my arms, the three of them grounding me in the moment. Eventually, the bees in my stomach lighten to something closer to butterflies, and the trembling in the center of my chest releases with a sigh. Eventually, I open my eyes and meet Lark's gaze, and the rhythm of her hands falters.

"Better?" she asks.

I nod, and it's true.

"Good." She gives me one last squeeze, then stands, stretching her arms over her head before she turns and walks back to her room without so much as a backward glance.

Then it's just me and Chaos and Maddox. For a long, soft moment, no one moves. Then Maddox says, "Do you want us to go?" and I find myself shaking my head before I can stop myself.

Chaos nods and stands, then offers me his hand. "C'mon."

He helps me up and leads me over to the huge sectional, where he sits and pats the cushion next to him. I sit, and Chaos pulls me into a one-armed hug while Maddox settles on my other side, draping his arm over us both. I need the comfort, and between them it's soothing. Safe.

"Do you ever think about what life might be like without the gods?" Maddox asks.

The question is so unexpected, it grinds my swirling thoughts to a halt. And maybe that's the point. Maybe that's what Maddox intended.

The truth is, I *have* thought about it. A lot. But I don't know how to say that in a way that doesn't sound *concerning,* so I just say, "Yeah."

"Should I be worried?" Chaos asks with a slight laugh.

Maddox chuckles. "I don't mean minor gods. Just the original gods."

"Just our parents, you mean," Chaos says, though his voice is teasing. Are they flirting again?

"I . . . guess when you put it that way it sounds bad," Maddox hedges.

"It's fine," Chaos says. With my head pressed against his chest I can't see his face, but I can hear his smirk. He's definitely teasing. "I hadn't thought about it, but it's an interesting question. What do you think it'd be like, Crow?"

I take a beat to gather my thoughts. To feel Chaos's heart beating within his chest. To breathe. "Well . . . it'd probably be chaotic at first, since our whole government is structured around gods as rulers. So the government would need restructuring. And there'd probably be some initial disagreements between minor gods and different kinds of godchildren, which could get messy." I frown, thinking. "I imagine people would be worried about godmagic dying out over the generations, which . . . it would. But maybe that's not a bad thing. Maybe, after all the dust settled, it'd be better if we were on more even ground."

"Hmm," Chaos says, the hum reverberating so loudly in his chest, it feels like a purr.

"I think people will always find a way to establish classes of people," Maddox says. "Like the Shallows, Midlevel, and Godlevel aren't based on godmagic, they're based on income."

I nod. "That's true, but maybe we'd finally be able to change how Escal is structured if we weren't ruled by ancient beings who are so completely divorced from what life is like for us."

"Maybe," Maddox says.

"Maybe," Chaos echoes.

It's a question without an answer. We let the uncertainty hang like fog. Eventually I close my eyes, cocooned in their warmth, in the press of their bodies against mine.

***

I don't remember falling asleep, but when I wake in a sun-washed room, it's in a tangle of arms and legs, squeezed between Maddox and Chaos on the sectional just wide enough for the three of us to lie side by side. A pleasant familiar weight sits on my chest, where Mouse is curled up, asleep. Maddox's arm is tossed over my belly and Chaos's chin is on my shoulder, his breath on my neck. I'm utterly buried in heat and it should be suffocating, but it's a welcome gentle pressure, like a weighted blanket.

For a few minutes, I just enjoy it and breathe.

I'm due for my testosterone adjustment today, so I close my eyes again and sink into the magic flowing through my body. This kind of Deathmagic isn't visible, so I don't have to worry about Chaos or Maddox noticing if they wake up. If anything, it's kind of nice doing my favorite calming ritual surrounded by the comforting presence of my friends pressed against me.

I've just finished adjusting my hormones when Lark opens her bedroom door. My eyes snap open as she walks past the sectional. She does a double take and stops in her tracks. I don't even have the luxury of pretending to be asleep, because she catches me with my wide-eyed gaze. My face instantly warms at her arched eyebrow.

"*Seagull,*" she says, drawing out my not-name in a tone somewhere between sounding impressed and like she's caught me doing something lewd.

"I just woke up like this," I say, which somehow only makes this worse. My face grows hotter by the second, but the triumphant grin on her face tells me I am never, *ever* going to live this down. It occurs to me only then that neither Chaos nor Maddox has a shirt on, and though I'm fully clothed, I can't pretend I wasn't enjoying their nearness.

Then Chaos rolls over and promptly falls on the floor with a *thunk.* He groans, rubbing his head and blinking blearily in the light as he sits up. "Oh," he says, his gaze landing on me and Maddox still squished on the sectional. "Morning."

"Five more minutes," Maddox mumbles, pressing his face into the sofa cushion.

"Personally," Lark says, opening the fridge way on the other side of the room and peering inside, "I'm going to be spending the morning preparing for our first matches."

The reminder sits like a lump of cold coals in the pit of my stomach. With all three of us scheduled on the fourth and final day of Round 1, we've spent the last three days training separately and watching some matches. Before I knew I'd be fighting Maddox, I'd been looking forward to my first match—after all, fighting is what I do. Now, as I glance back at the sleeping boy who helped comfort me through a hard night, the thought of having to fight him—and soon—makes me vaguely queasy.

We won't use lethal force, I remind myself. *No matter what, we'll be fine.*

But will we? I can't go back to the Shallows, not without saving my uncles. And winning the Tournament would mean lifting Maddox's family out of poverty.

We all have our reasons for doing this. Both Maddox and I have our families depending on us. And it sucks knowing that in a matter of hours, it'll be over for one of us. One way or the other.

CHAPTER 25

I have never dreaded a fight like I do this one.

The backstage portion of the arena is, more accurately, the *under*stage. The roar of the crowd above us shakes the building in thundering waves as the emcee riles the attendees. Our guide—a man with a sparse beard—greets us when we arrive. Chaos, Maddox, and I follow him through the huge underground complex in glum silence. The guide brings us to a large empty room that echoes with the shouts of the crowd above us. In the center of the room a huge blue circle is drawn on the shiny white-tiled floor, with a red line running along its diameter.

"Crow will begin on this side," the guide says, pointing to the side closest to us, "Maddox on the other. In this first round, no weapons are permitted, so the platform won't rise until you're both fully disarmed. Once you're both in position and the emcee is ready, the platform will rise into the arena. You will both wait until the emcee declares the match has begun and the siren goes off. Once you hear the siren, you can begin. The match is over when one of you cannot continue fighting. Any questions?"

Chaos told us this morning about the no-weapons rule, so Maddox and I left our stuff back at the suite. I run my fingers over the rune-spelled wrappings protecting my knuckles and make sure my oil flask is ready at my hip.

As Maddox crosses to the other side of the circle, Chaos turns to me, his face serious. "Maddox may not have the fighting experience you do, but don't underestimate him. I have no doubt that he'll be able to hold his own up there."

I arch an eyebrow. "Are you giving me tips on how to beat your boyfriend?"

Chaos smiles, just slightly. "He's not the one I chose to sponsor—you are. At the end of the day, I have your back. He knows that."

It's oddly comforting, knowing Chaos is looking out for me. Of course, sponsors get prizes—money and luxury things, mostly—if their chosen fighter wins, so Chaos has extra motivation to help me pull ahead, but still.

"Thanks," I say, and Chaos nods and gives me a firm pat on the back.

"Kick his ass."

I smile and step into my side of the ring.

He's just another opponent, I remind myself as Maddox steps inside the circle on the opposite side of the ring. *He's just another opponent . . . who fell asleep holding you last night.*

The platform begins to rise beneath us, floating above the ground. The ceiling that had been muffling the noise of the crowd opens up, and the sound floods in like a crashing wave. Long before I can see the people, their voices thunder in my ears, drowning out the hammering of my pulse. The platform rises smoothly, and it doesn't take long for us to pass what was once the ceiling.

And then we're in the arena.

I expected the platform to stop once we reached ground level. Instead, we continue rising. There are tens of thousands of people in the arena—more than I've ever seen in one place. Four huge screens float in the air, facing each cardinal direction, so everyone in the stadium can see the action. With a start, I catch a close-up of my face on the nearest one. They're livestreaming the match, which is expected, even though I'd temporarily forgotten about that. All at once I find myself doubly glad that my mask covers the lower half of my face— hopefully my mother won't recognize me.

I shake my head; I can worry about that later. Right now the only thing that matters is the match.

The platform finally comes to a stop, and with a *whoosh* of magic, water floods the bottom of the arena far below us, stopping just a foot from the lowest of the elevated bleachers. It's still a long drop from the platform to the water's edge.

With the thunder of the crowd humming in my chest, I turn my attention to Maddox standing on the other side of the platform. His gaze is washing over the crowd, a grin on his face visible beneath his clear mask as he takes it all in. It's unfortunately endearing, so I close my eyes and take a deep breath, allowing the rumble of the crowd to roll through me.

It's just another fight. I know how to fight.

I open my eyes as a loud beep rings through the arena and the crowd chants "Three!"

Maddox turns his attention to me and smiles grimly.

"Two!"

Anticipation ripples through me, a familiar sensation that travels down my spine like lightning. The arena is bigger than the Underground, but the electric hum of a match about to begin is the same. I can do this. I will do this.

"For Alecks and Orin," I whisper.

"One!"

The siren blares.

CHAPTER 26

Maddox races toward me, splaying his fingers about a foot from his chest. I hold my ground. Then his jacket starts moving—it rips open on its own, and the silver buttons shoot off the garment and into his hand.

Which is how I learn Maddox is an Architect.

I swear under my breath and trace a shield rune on the back of my glove. Maddox throws his arm out—I raise my shielded hand—six sharp metal studs ram into the invisible shield, just a foot from my chest.

Maddox said he wasn't going to use lethal force, so I can only assume he didn't intend to impale me with those. But it still would have been a bitch to dislodge from my skin.

I don't have much time to think about it, though, because the metal rips out of my shield and melts over Maddox's hand, coating his entire fist and hardening just before he swings for my face.

I duck and ram my entire body weight into just below his center. We both hit the polished white tiles hard, but I'm on top and he's winded, so I have about ten seconds to figure out how to remove his godmagic advantage.

The reach of my Deathmagic at the moment of contact is so habitual, I don't have time to stop it even if I wanted to. Before I've even processed what I'm doing, the Deathmagic has scanned through him, drawing a map in my mind's eye. Unlike the meathead I last fought in the Underground, Maddox doesn't have any glaring-red badly healed old injuries, which is lucky for him. Maddox's Architectmagic circles through his body in endless motion, rivers of swirling silver particulate magic.

The problem with metal is there isn't really an easy way to destroy it. Fire won't burn it, just melt it—and Maddox will still be able to manipulate that. Disintegrate it and it'll turn to dust, but it'll still be metal—and frankly I don't want to see what an Architect can do with metal dust, at least not applied to me.

Which means if I want to remove his advantage, I need to remove the metal entirely.

The oil flask is in my hand, uncapped, and my fingertips are oiled all in one fluid movement. Shoving the flask back into my pocket, I grab Maddox's metal hand and press it hard into the ground with my dry hand. He struggles, still trying to catch his breath. I draw three runes on the metal in quick, precise movements.

Wood. Apply to. Metal.

I've barely finished before the metal shifts, like a stone dropped in a liquid metal pool. A pale brown spot appears in the center of the meat of his palm, like a bit of tarnish. Then it spreads rapidly, racing across his palm and up his fingers and down to his wrist, where the metal ends.

Which is when Maddox's hips jerk up beneath me, throwing me off center before he twists hard. I roll as I hit the floor, creating some distance between us before I jump back to my feet, double-checking for the edge of the platform, hand outstretched in case I need to defend myself. It isn't necessary, though, because when I stand, Maddox has staggered to his feet and is staring at his wood-covered fist. He shakes his fist, trying to dislodge it; then when that doesn't work, he grabs it with his other hand and pulls.

Nothing.

Maddox looks up at me. "Bro."

I quirk an apologetic smile, but I'd be lying if I said I wasn't enjoying every second of this. While I was grappling with Maddox on the cold tiles, the roar of the crowd fell away, but now it all comes back, filling me with energy. I bounce on my toes, fists up, and beckon him forward.

Maddox shakes his head, but he's smiling too. And then he slams his foot on the floor and the tile beneath his sole crumples like crushed paper. My stomach drops out from under me as the realization hits me like a physical blow.

The tiles.

They're metal beneath the white coating.

Maddox flicks the ball of crumpled metal up into the air with his foot, then kicks it. It races toward me like a bullet. I dive out of the way, but a second and a third follow, the last one grazing my shoulder and throwing me off-balance as I skid too close to the edge of the platform. I switch direction to get back toward the center, but the three balls of metal curve in the air, homing in on me.

Shit.

As long as I keep away from Maddox he's going to keep throwing these metal tiles at me. I pivot to run toward him, and the tile beneath my foot flies up. I sprawl on the floor hard, barely catching myself on my forearms. The impact vibrates painfully up my arms. I get my right foot under me; then metal slaps my forearms, melding into the tile. Cold tile slams into my left leg and wraps around my right foot. And just like that, I can't move.

He's just cuffed me to the floor.

I stare, examining the cuffs, but there isn't even a seam where the metal wrapped around my forearms, leg, and foot melts into the floor. I'm stuck to the floor, my right leg bent where I was about to stand but now stuck in this half-crouched position, which is really godsdamned uncomfortable.

This is where my existence being illegal is really godsdamned inconvenient. If I could use Deathmagic, it would be so *easy* to melt into shadow and slip out of these restraints. Instead I'm stuck here, furious that I have to ignore the obvious solution.

Looking up, I find Maddox walking toward me, a victorious grin spread across his face, his wood-gloved fist at his side. He walks casually, enjoying the cheers of the crowd as he slowly approaches me. He even throws his arms up in a *Louder* motion, and the crowd obliges. Gods, he takes his sweet-ass time getting over here. When he finally crouches a foot ahead of me, he's smiling so wide his cheeks are dimpled.

"Yield," he says. I laugh. He laughs too, his eyebrow quirked in a question. "C'mon, Crow. Don't make me knock you out. Yield."

"It's cute that you think you've won," I say.

"It's cute that you think you haven't lost," he shoots back. "You literally can't move. What are you going to do?"

I smile, even though he can't see it. I lift my hands, showing him the oily runes hidden on the floor beneath my palms. His eyes go wide. Then I slam my hands down, activating the command I wrote into the metal.

Flip.

The platform jerks beneath us, rising on my left side like a ship dipping violently sideways into the sea. If I weren't attached so securely to the platform, I would go flying.

Maddox isn't so lucky.

The platform flips fully upside down. And he drops like a rock into the water below.

CHAPTER 27

✕

I find Chaos and Maddox backstage after the match, the latter still dripping wet and grinning despite his loss.

"That was *incredible*," Chaos says, utterly beaming with pride. "When you flipped the platform, I lost my entire mind!"

"You definitely got me," Maddox says with a laugh, rubbing at his wrist where his gold ticket tattoo has disappeared. "I was *sure* I had you. Damn. You earned that win."

"You were amazing," I say to Maddox. "Also—" I punch him in the shoulder.

"Ow!" He laughs again. "What, throwing me into the pool wasn't enough punishment?"

"No. That was for not sealing the door with your Architect-magic when those scorpion beetles were trying to eat us."

Maddox grins guiltily. "All right, I deserve that. In my defense, you and Lark had it under control!"

"Uh-huh." I shake my head and look at Chaos. "How's Lark's match going?"

"Ended about a minute before you walked over," Chaos

says. "Lark won. I think the whole match was, like, two minutes long."

I smirk. "So what now?"

"Well, there's a two-day break after each of the five rounds, so we have a little downtime. Mads has graciously offered to join Team Crow as a weapons and armor master, if you're open to it."

I arch an eyebrow at Maddox. "Weapons and armor master?"

Maddox grins. "The first round was no-weapons, so I couldn't really show off my skills, but yeah, that's my Architect specialty."

"Sounds useful," I say. "You seem awfully cheery given the circumstances."

Maddox's smile softens, but only a little. "It would have been nice to win, obviously, but helping someone else from the Shallows win would be a pretty great consolation prize, if you'll have me." He pauses. "I mean, the money would also be a big help for my family. And my moms were so worried about me getting hurt or worse in the fights, so I think maybe . . . they might prefer this."

It's not even a question. I smile. "Welcome to Team Crow."

Unlike godmagic, runemagic is like a muscle, in that the more you practice using it, the more you can use it in the future. Unfortunately, it's also like a muscle in that if you overdo it, you'll eventually hit muscle failure and regret your choices the next morning.

I wouldn't say I overdid it fighting Maddox in the arena

yesterday, but I've certainly used it more in the last couple of days than I have in a while, and today as I walk to the complex training grounds in the unholy hours of the early morning, my immune system is working overtime to attack the joints in my fingers and the back of my neck. I massage my neck as I walk, grimacing as I send pulses of numbing Deathmagic into it. That dulls the pain but isn't enough to wipe it out entirely. It'll have to do, though.

I grit my teeth. This never happens with Deathmagic.

The indoor gym is empty except for Lark. I knew she would be here, which isn't to say I came *looking* for her, but since she's here, I might as well make use of the sparring partner.

Lark grimaces when I enter. "Goose."

"Larky," I respond, using her least favorite variation of her name.

"Larkness sounds like darkness. I like that," she said when we were kids. Then her nose wrinkled. "But Larky sounds like baby talk, and I'm not a baby."

Eleven years later and it still has the same nose-wrinkling effect.

I've just turned to the weapons rack when Lark says, "Ten people have already died in the first round of matches."

I pause, the words filling my stomach like lead weights. *Ten* people? That's nearly a third of the competitors! Maddox and I of course agreed not to use lethal force, but it sure sounds like most of the others don't have any qualms about killing. And that shouldn't be a surprise—after all, part of the reason I didn't want to enter this godsdamned Tournament to begin with is because even if I *didn't* get caught, I'd be putting my life at risk. But still. The reminder that people are dying in this competition every round is sobering.

I glance back at Lark and she narrows her eyes at me. "No," she says, answering my unspoken question. "I didn't kill anyone."

I nod, more relieved than I'd like to admit. I approach the weapons rack and look over my options. Lark's weapon of choice is the staff, which is unfortunate for me since I tend to prefer close contact fighting. Still, since we've sparred together hundreds of times, I've learned a thing or two. I'll probably never excel at it like she does, but I can hold my own.

I grab a staff off the weapons rack to meet her on the mats. She rolls her eyes. "Gods above and below, you really can't stand that I'm better than you at something."

I blink and look at the staff in my hand. "What?"

"Out of *all* the weapons you could have picked, you chose the staff."

I frown. "If I had the choice, I'd pick no weapon or knives. Neither of those is a great strategy against a staff, though. So yeah, I'm opting to practice with a long-range weapon so I can improve."

Lark scoffs. "Whatever you say."

I step onto the mat, bristling with irritation. "I've never denied that you're better than me with the staff."

"Because it's undeniable."

I shift into a starting stance, holding the staff out in front of me, ready to strike. "Does it really bother you so much that I'd like to improve a weapons skill?"

"Yes!" she screams, slashing with the staff.

It whips toward me, so fast I hear the metallic whirring *whoosh* as I just barely move my head out of the way. I parry. The impact of our metal staffs crashing against each other reverberates down all the way to my shoulders. I've barely registered the impact before she swipes at my legs, forcing me to jump back. The blows come fast and hard, keeping me on the defensive as I counter for my life.

"Why?" I shout.

"You have to be better than me at *everything!*" Lark moves fast, and metal crashes into the backs of my knees. My back hits the mat hard, the air *whoosh*ing out of my lungs. She brings the staff down and stops just inches from my nose. I lie there for a minute, catching my breath, processing what she just said as she scowls over me.

"You've always thought you were better than me," Lark says bitterly. "That's why we could never be friends, because you couldn't see me as your equal." She crouches over me, her voice seething but barely above a whisper. "Because *you* have god-magic and I don't."

Then she stands and turns her back, marching to the other side of the gym.

There are few times I can say I've truly been rendered speechless, but as I lie there on my back, staring up at the fluorescent gym lights, I honestly don't know what to say. Not because it's true. Because the *opposite* is.

I laugh.

Lark whirls on her feet, glowering back at me. *"What,"* she seethes, "is so funny about that?"

I sit up, shaking my head as I meet her scowl. "My mother tried to save you that night, you know. She told *me* to go back to bed, but she tried to convince your parents to take you and run."

Lark stares at me, confusion fracturing the anger in her expression. I won't risk being any more explicit about what night I'm talking about. But after a moment, Lark's eyes widen in understanding.

"Yeah," I say, at the change in her expression. "You were the perfect daughter my mother wished she had. Instead she got me." I stand, rolling the ache out of my shoulders as I turn to the door. "Anyway, it doesn't matter. It was a long time ago. I don't think I'm better than you, Lark. Because I know you're better than me."

CHAPTER 28

"You've got an interview request."

I've barely stepped into the suite, still achy from my perilously quick sparring match with Lark, when Chaos accosts me with the news. He's lying sprawled out on the sectional in pastel-pink sweatpants and a black hand-knitted tee speckled with bright neon colors. His black metal knitting needles *snick* softly against each other as he works, a long hot pink, purple, gray, and black tube dangling from the cord connecting the needles. Mouse is curled up on his legs, eyeing the moving yarn with rapt attention.

"Pass." I sit next to him, barely suppressing a groan as my achy muscles sink into the soft sofa cushions. I press my hands over the back of my neck, where the effort of the match is already starting to flare from distant pain to a full-on headache, and focus my Deathmagic. I imagine the inflammation cooling, the pain dripping away like hot butter on a stove, and sigh into the warm, numbing magic. Once the pain has dulled to a simmer, I do the same with my hands.

Chaos's feet wiggle just six inches from me—adorably, his toenails are painted neon blue, purple, yellow, green, and pink. Mouse looks at me and squeaks in greeting, then turns her gaze back on the yarn, her pupils dilated into huge black discs.

Chaos's gaze flicks up at me over his knitting project. "As your sponsor, I'd recommend taking it. Public perception may not factor into whether you win or lose, but you and Lark represent all Shallowsfolk right now, and it could be a good opportunity to remind Midlevelers that Shallowsfolk are people too."

I grimace, guilt gnawing at my insides. He's not wrong, but the last thing I need are journalists digging into my past.

"If it helps, Jimena seems like a decent person," Chaos adds. "She's done some really great pieces on the Shallows before. She seems genuinely invested in bringing attention to the inequality between the city levels."

If I were anyone else from the Shallows, someone who wasn't a Deathchild in hiding, someone whose mother wasn't *the literal president,* this would be an amazing opportunity. A chance to bring what's happening in the Shallows to the attention of Midlevelers, whether they like it or not.

"She should talk to Maddox," I say.

Chaos frowns. "Maddox has been eliminated from the competition; he's no longer interesting to the press."

"Well, that's too bad, because I don't want any more attention than is absolutely necessary."

Slowly, Chaos puts his knitting project down on the coffee table next to us. Mouse stands and stretches her back. "Is it because you're worried about how it'll affect your uncles' case?"

Truthfully, that thought hadn't even occurred to me. Here

I am, worried about someone noticing *I'm* a Deathchild, not even thinking how speaking out about the inequality between city levels could piss off the wrong people, who may take it out on my uncles.

I don't answer and reach instead to pet Mouse. She accepts my affection with a rumbling purr while she casually steps onto the coffee table and curls up directly on top of Chaos's project.

"What are you working on?" I ask, nodding at the bundle of fabric now squished beneath a very contented cat.

"Infinity cowl," Chaos says without missing a beat. "Like the scarf but shorter."

I nod; then my eye catches on a bit of fabric sticking out from beneath Mouse's paw. I tilt my head a little—I hadn't noticed it before, but the colors on the cowl Chaos is working on aren't random. They make out tiny repeated images like . . .

I squint. "Is that Mouse?"

Chaos grins and gently moves Mouse's paw out of the way to uncover the image. A small cartoon-style gray cat face stares out at me over a purple background. I make a truly undignified noise at the adorable motif.

Chaos laughs. "I'm glad you like it. The yarn is a yak-paca blend, so it's super soft."

I run my fingers over the material, marveling at how cozy it feels.

"By the way, I know you changed the subject, but we should discuss your media plan going forward. The more you advance in this competition, the more journalists are going to want to talk to you—and not all of them will be as scrupulous as Jimena seems to be."

I knew I'd have to confront this reality eventually, even though I've been ignoring it thus far. But he's right. I just don't know how to explain my reticence to Chaos without telling him the truth. And as much as I want to believe I can trust him, I've known Chaos for, what, a week? How am I supposed to know whether he could keep the secret that will literally get me killed?

Chaos must see my thoughts warring on my face, because his expression softens. "Crow . . ." he starts.

Whatever he was about to say is lost, because Maddox bursts in, holding up a tablet. "Hey, have you two seen what's going on in the Shallows? It's all over the news."

My heart immediately pounds harder.

"Put it on," Chaos says, nodding to the massive screen in front of us.

Maddox swipes his full hand over the tablet, as if swiping the image on the screen toward the TV. The huge screen blinks on as a news report shows footage of another brawl between Enforcers and Shallowsfolk. It takes me a minute to place the location—it's dark around the edges, and stark floodlights cast harsh shadows and bleach everything else of color—but there's a moldy gray brick building that I'd recognize anywhere: the Underground.

There's something odd about it, though. A huge flock of crows has been spray-painted on the side of the building since I last saw it. A *murder of crows,* one might say.

"Tension between the Enforcers and the Shallowsfolk is at an all-time high," the reporter says. *"Incidents like these have been increasing for a week, but especially in the last couple of days."*

"I need to call my moms," Maddox says, his eyes full of concern. "Make sure everyone's okay."

Chaos frowns. "Do you think it likely they got caught up in that fight?"

"No," Maddox says. "But this means there'll be more Enforcers out. And they'll be jumpy and looking for trouble."

Chaos's frown deepens.

"He's right," I say. "On-edge Enforcers make the Shallows more dangerous for everyone."

"I didn't think of that," Chaos says softly.

"Why would you?" Maddox asks, suddenly sounding exhausted. "You've never had to deal with it before."

Chaos grimaces. "You're right. I'm sorry. Let us know what your family says."

Maddox nods and disappears back into his room.

"Lark and I should check on Ravenna too." I stand.

Chaos nods, his face heavy with sadness as he watches the rest of the news coverage. But even as I walk away, one image sticks in my mind above everything else: the mural.

After all, everyone in the Underground knew me as Murder of Crows.

CHAPTER 29

Maddox's family is shaken, but safe. Still, his moms made him swear he'd do everything possible to stay out of the Shallows until things calm down.

Ravenna told Lark and me not to worry about her. "I'm just an old lady," she'd said with a mischievous smile. "I'm practically invisible to those armored bullies."

The next fight comes so soon that if I weren't a Deathchild, I would still be sore from battling Maddox. Somehow, I think it's not a coincidence that I was scheduled on the last day of the first round and the first day of the second round, giving me the smallest possible break. But even with just two days between the matches, my new weapons expert doesn't disappoint.

"I didn't have enough time to do anything major," Maddox says, passing me a pair of black leather gloves and my knives. "But since you'll be allowed weapons this round, I sharpened your knives. I also upgraded a basic pair of mage gloves."

I put them on, smiling at the smooth slide of cool soft leather. Mage gloves look almost like archer's gloves, with only the thumb, index, and middle fingers covered. Maddox points to a disc of extra cushioning on each palm.

"This is a reservoir of oil—though you can also fill it with ink if you prefer. You press on the reservoir to push the oil into your fingertips, here." He points to my leather-covered index and middle finger, which have tiny perforations at the fingertips. "In addition to the numbing runes you requested, I added multiplying and direction runes to the inner lining of the fingers for a smoother flow, and to ensure you don't run out of oil in the middle of a fight. But the multiplying runes are powerful, so you don't need much. One press of the palm should be enough for a couple spells, assuming you use oil."

I arch an eyebrow at him. "So much for being bad at rune-magic."

He smiles sheepishly. "I have better luck with runes when I'm not under pressure."

A Florachild named Oak is my next opponent. They watch me with a dagger-like stare. Beneath their shaved head, white flower tattoos are etched on their scalp, reaching around their ears and down either side of their neck. The white ink tattoos are stunning to look at and gleam on their deep brown skin.

As we rise into the arena, their gaze remains, unsettlingly, on me. Soon the roar of the crowd washes over me, the ceiling of the understage closing beneath us before the arena begins filling with water. The platform comes to a stop, level with the first tier of the audience but high above the deepening pool below. I bounce on my toes, ready to move, to burn the anxious energy skittering through my torso and legs.

Then a *thunk* sounds throughout the arena, and four circles running down the center of the platform, maybe twenty feet in diameter each, glow bright white. The one I'm standing on marks the farthest northern edge, and the one Oak is standing on marks the farthest southern end, with two more circles in between us.

The rest of the platform—the platform that is *not* in one of the four glowing circles—descends into the pool.

I stare, processing the new arena we'll have to fight in. The circles aren't touching—there's about five feet of space between them, which shouldn't be hard to clear. I'm going to have to keep track of where the circles end at all times to avoid getting knocked into the pool.

The crowd begins the countdown.

As I work to keep any expression of surprise off my face, Oak looks calm as a lake on a windless day.

Okay, I think. *You've got this.*

A single black raven perches on the giant viewing screen nearest me and cocks its head, looking directly at me. I'll take the good omen.

The siren blares. The round begins.

Oak races forward, grabbing a handful of seeds from the small burlap bag tied at their waist. They throw the seeds out in front of them, and before they hit the ground, tangles of vines burst toward me. I watched the replay of Oak's first fight, and this is exactly how they started that fight too, so I've somewhat expected this. This time, instead of creating a forest, the vines race forward and fill the space between their starting platform and the one directly ahead of them, creating a bridge.

Convenient.

The vines don't stop there, however. They bridge the gaps between all the circular platforms, giving Oak a straight shot to my platform. I don't trust that the vines will maintain a bridge for me, so as I run forward, pressing on the oil reservoirs in my gloves, I leap over the first gap, ignoring the vine bridge altogether.

Something snags my left ankle, jerking my momentum to a halt just as I clear the gap.

As the vine cinches tight around my ankle, a map of green energy explodes in my mind's eye. Oak's green Florachild energy courses through every inch of vine bridging the gaps between the platforms, leading right back to them. It's all connected, the godpower feeding the vines and racing through Oak. I haven't touched Oak, but I can see them like I see any other opponent I've ever made contact with, and though I don't see any obvious immediate weaknesses, it *does* give me an idea.

Then my body hits the platform—hard. I groan, my forearms and hip throbbing.

I was right not to trust the vines. But it was a mistake to ignore them, even just for a moment.

A sharp tug backward sends my heart lurching. The vine wrapped around my ankle drags me toward the edge of the platform. There's nothing for me to hold on to, so I move fast, grabbing a knife from the sheath at my side and slashing through the thick vine in one quick stroke. The recently sharpened blade slices through with frictionless ease, and I make a mental note to thank Maddox.

With the vine wrapped around my ankle cut off from Oak's godmagic, it goes limp and falls off as I jump to my feet.

Oak and I are on the same platform now. I start toward them, knife in each hand, and they reach into their pouch and throw another handful of seeds. A thick fifteen-foot-high wall of vines bursts up between us, and I skid to a stop. For a split second I wonder how hiding behind a plant wall is going to lead to a win, but the question is answered before it's fully formed in my mind. Tiny tendrils of vine reach out about an inch, and the entire wall *crawls* forward. It's slow, and unsettling as anything to watch, but it doesn't have to be fast to inch me off the platform.

I could blast through it, but Oak still has that seed pouch, so they could repair it easily. And after the way it grabbed my ankle, I don't really want to risk touching it if I can avoid it. Which means I need to either somehow get the seed pouch away from them—unlikely, since it's on the other side of the wall with them—or . . . I need to remove the option of using plants at all.

I turn and race to the far side of the platform—which, admittedly, is only about ten feet from the wall. Skidding to a stop at the edge, I crouch and draw a large circle around myself in oil, about as large as my arm span. I glance up at the wall and regret it—it's still crawling forward, but it's not slow anymore. The thing is outright *skittering* forward on dozens of tiny vine feet in a way that makes all the hairs on the back of my neck stand on end.

Swearing under my breath, I reach outside the circle I outlined and scribble the runes. When I'm done, I slam my hand over the runes to activate them so hard my wrist aches.

Only then do I dare look up.

The wall is far closer than I'd like—it's already crossed half the distance and is still moving steadily toward me on those creepy tiny vine legs, like a crab-walking plant centipede wall.

But something is already happening. The metal tiles outside

the protective circle I drew are glowing a faint orange, and though the heat isn't unbearable yet, the warmth coming from the tiles is undeniable.

Then the faint glow becomes a searing deep orange, the tiles emitting so much heat the air above them shimmers. And the tiny vine feet curl up and begin to brown.

Then they catch fire.

I grin as the rune spell takes hold, turning the tiles outside the circle so hot that it hurts to look at them. And it isn't just the platform we're standing on—the other circular platforms are also glowing as well. I've just started wondering what Oak is doing to stay unburned on the other side of the wall when they climb over the top and sit there, glaring daggers at me. The bottom of the wall is in a full burn now, but the plants making up the wall are green, so the spread is slow. Still, the burn is steady, and Oak can't very well repair it by throwing down more seeds—they'll just be incinerated by the heat.

I won't lie—I'm feeling pretty good about winning this fight. Oak can hang out at the top of the wall for now, but their haven won't last. The bottom half of the wall is burning already. Soon the fire will spread to the top and they'll have to jump into the pool below to escape the flames. It's just a matter of time. And I'm more than happy to wait and watch it happen.

Satisfied with my work, I smile at them and wave.

Which is when a thick vine from the still-unburned top of the wall shoots out and wraps tightly around my wrist. It yanks me forward so hard it nearly pulls me clean out of the protective circle, but I grab the vine with my free hand and pull with my entire body weight. If it successfully pulls me out of the circle, I'll burn along with it.

There's no time to think. No time to reach for my knives. My boots are sliding against the smooth metal tile and I have seconds to figure out how to get this godsforsaken vine off my wrist. I tighten my grip with my free hand around the vine and *pull*.

Then something strange happens: In my mind's eye, the green Floramagic coursing through the vine turns white beneath my grip.

White like Deathmagic.

The white magic spreads from my grip and shoots up the vine, devouring the green Floramagic along the way. As the white magic spreads, the vine turns brown, brittle, and limp, the power behind it gone. I tug, and the vine snaps off the wall and hits the ground, burning up the moment it hits the superheated tile.

I don't know what just happened.

Standing in my protected circle, panting, sweat dripping down my temples from the rising heat all around me, I barely register the flames reaching the top of the wall. As Oak leaps off the wall into the water below, the arena feels distant. I've won. I should be elated.

But all I can think is that I may have just used Deathmagic in a televised event. And I don't even know how I did it.

CHAPTER 30

I stumble backstage in a haze, vaguely aware I might be having a panic attack.

I just used Deathmagic. On national television. In front of a massive crowd. I'm certain of it, even though I'm not sure *how*. I mean, yes, I know how to use Deathmagic, but never like *that*. There are categories of things I can do: seeing the spirits of the dead, calling on and manipulating light and shadow, and healing, which includes the sight I use in the ring. I've *heard* of other categories of Deathmagic I've never tried, like making someone ill, or using Deathmagic to break a bone or flesh, or necromancy. But what happened in the arena was none of that.

And yet . . . it *felt* like Deathmagic. It *looked* like Deathmagic.

I move numbly through the crowd of sponsors and competitors understage. I should be trying to find Chaos and Maddox, but everything feels distant and I can barely focus on not running into anyone, let alone figuring out a direction to walk in.

Someone grabs my shoulder and I jerk to a stop, my heart tripping in my chest as I spin to face—

Lark. She's frowning, and her grip on my shoulder is gentle but firm. "Hey," she says softly. "You with me, Cockatoo?"

"You're gonna run out of birds eventually," I mutter.

"I don't know about that," Lark says. "There are a *lot* of birds out there." She smirks, and for some reason I find myself smiling along with her, albeit just a little. Still, something about the pressure of her hand on my shoulder, of having her here with me, is grounding.

"I think I messed up," I whisper.

Lark frowns. "What do you mean?"

"That sure was an *interesting* use of magic," a new voice interrupts.

The boy who's approached us is only vaguely familiar, but something about his spiked-up black hair rings a bell. I think I must have seen him in the Opening Ceremony.

"Thank you," I say coolly.

"It wasn't a compliment," he snaps. "What in the gods' name kind of magic was that?"

My insides have gone cold and hot at the same time, but masking my emotions is a skill I honed in the Shallows. I keep my face blank, but before I can think of a response, Lark arches an eyebrow and says, "That can't possibly be the first time you saw runemagic." She turns to me. "Don't Uppercity kids learn runemagic in school?"

The boy's face goes red. "That *wasn't* runemagic!" he sputters. "The thing with the vine around your wrist—the way it just *withered*. That wasn't any kind of runemagic or godmagic that I've seen before."

Internally, I'm swearing endlessly and kicking myself for

letting my godmagic slip like that. Externally, my face is a placid mask while I race to come up with a plausible explanation.

And then Lark laughs. "Wait," she says through her laughter. "Are you implying they used some kind of *sinister magic* because it didn't occur to you that a vine stretched over *super-hot metal tiles* would dry up and burn? Gods above and below, did you skip basic biology?"

The boy's eyes go wide, his face reddening by the second. "It didn't just—"

"You know, Sergio," Lark interrupts, apparently recognizing him, "it's okay to be nervous about facing Crow in the ring—they're a godsdamned *excellent* fighter. But it's pretty fucking cowardly to throw out baseless accusations to try to get him disqualified before you have to fight them. *Embarrassing*, really. Somehow, I don't think your father would approve."

It is an unexpected relief to see Lark defending me. Lark, who knows I am a Deathchild who can access Deathmagic. Who, out of everyone here, would have the most reason to believe I did actually use Deathmagic.

Lark, who knows exactly what being found out for using Deathmagic would mean. Who has seen it herself, because like me, she is old enough to remember the Silencing.

Sergio's face has gone fully red at this point. "I'm not— *scared*," he splutters.

"Convincing," Lark deadpans.

Sergio scowls and turns away, storming off into the crowd. Once he's gone and my heart slowly stutters back to a more normal pace, I turn to Lark.

There are many things I could say. Things I *should* say. Like

Thank you. Like *You didn't have to do that.* Like *I'm so relieved you did.*

But Lark and I have always had an understanding. We dislike each other *and* we would never turn on another Deathchild.

Out of all the things I could say, I go with: "So you *can* say my name."

Lark rolls her eyes and says, "Fall into a pit of acid, Stork," but it sounds like *You're welcome.*

"Drown in a boggy marsh," I respond. But the words taste like *Thank you.* Then, before silence settles over us both, I ask, "Do you think he's going to be a problem?"

Lark frowns. "If he publicly accuses you without proof, it'd be embarrassing for his sponsor."

"His sponsor?" Now I'm frowning. "Why would his sponsor care?"

"Sergio's father is his sponsor," Lark answers. "He's a politician. Not as high up as your—as the president, of course, but he's rumored to be preparing to run against her next term, so appearances matter. If Sergio accused you and then couldn't prove it, it'd look bad on them both."

That explains the comment about Sergio's dad. I don't know if that will be enough, but for now it'll have to do. I thought I was being careful before, but I can't slip up again. Not as long as I know Sergio is watching.

⸺

The next day Chaos asks if I want to visit my uncles again tonight, and the timing couldn't be more perfect.

As a prison guard escorts us once again down a long set of stairs, my mind is miles away. I can't shake the feeling that I'm in trouble. That at any moment the safety I briefly enjoyed is over. That it was just an illusion to begin with.

Like last time, the guard stops in front of a steel windowless door and gestures the password into a metal sheet embedded in the wall. Like last time, he instructs us both to enter the cell and tells us we have fifteen minutes. And like last time, when the door seals shut behind us with a *clunk,* Chaos sets up a disruption field to give us some privacy.

It's been only thirteen days since my life flipped upside down, but my uncles look undeniably thinner already. And haggard. Orin has always had a beard, but it's thicker now than I've ever seen it, the edges uneven. Alecks's unshaven blond beard looks prickly in the blue light, and the shadows under his eyes make his face look gaunt.

It scares me, seeing how much they've changed in just under two weeks.

My uncles pull me into a group hug, and when I close my eyes—my face pressed against Orin's soft, broad chest, Alecks's body curved over me like a protective shield—I feel safe. Truly safe. Just for a few moments.

"How are you?" Orin asks, his dark eyes glinting in the cool light.

"Are you still in the Tournament?" Alecks adds.

"I am." I laugh slightly, hardly believing my own reality. "I won my second match yesterday, so I'm almost halfway there."

Alecks grins. "Of course you did."

Orin ruffles my hair and pats me on the back. "Good," he says. "Good."

I arch an eyebrow. "I thought you didn't want me in the Tournament at all."

"We don't," Alecks says without missing a beat. "But since we can't change the fact that you're in it, best we can hope for is that you make it through unscathed."

I'm not sure *unscathed* is accurate.

Orin must see the hesitation on my face, because his expression darkens. *"Are* you okay?"

"I am," I say quickly, even before I can consider whether that's true. "At least, as okay as can be expected. But something *did* happen in my last match, and now I think . . . I don't know."

I tell them everything. Or at least, the condensed version, as I'm all too aware of the ticking clock.

My uncles exchange a glance I can't read; then Orin says, "That was good of Lark to back you up. Do you think he bought her explanation?"

I grimace. "I'm really not sure. He didn't seem convinced to me."

"If he publicly accuses you, say you're a Discordchild."

The voice is so unexpected I actually spin around. I'm sure my uncles hadn't, but I'd completely forgotten Chaos was in here with us. And none of us has said it aloud, but it's obvious what we're all implying, isn't it?

Orin frowns. "Would that . . . work? Wouldn't you or one of your siblings or even your father deny it?"

Chaos's mouth scrunches together like he's chewing on his lip, but finally he shakes his head. "I could vouch for Crow if needed, say they're a distant cousin some generations down or something. My dad won't contradict me in public, and my siblings would just assume I'm living up to my name." He smiles.

"What Crow is describing isn't any known type of Discord-magic, though," Alecks says.

Chaos lifts a shoulder. "The public doesn't really understand Discordmagic, not well anyway. Any unexplained disruption is blamed on us—which is fair a lot of the time. I think the public will believe it, especially if I vouch for them."

"Why would you do that?" I ask.

Chaos blinks. "Why would I vouch for you?"

I nod. "You know I'm not a Discordchild."

He hesitates. "No, but . . ." He sighs and runs his hand through his hair, pushing his beanie nearly off his head. "Look, I was too young to understand more than superficially what the Silencing meant, but my dad and my siblings stood with Death that night. And we Discordchildren may not agree on much, but if there's one thing we do agree on, it's that what happened to the Deathchildren—what's *still* happening to them—is a fucking atrocity. It's genocide. And I may not be able to do too much about it, but if you need an extra shield, you have me."

It's more than I ever could have hoped for. More than I ever would have thought of asking for. And the relief of having a backup plan, a safety net, washes over me in a cooling wave.

"Thank you, Chaos," Orin says.

Alecks nods. "That's an enormous help." He turns to me. "And if your mother suspects . . . that could throw her off."

"Maybe," I say.

At Chaos's blank look, Orin's brow furrows. He looks at me. "Haven't you told him?"

Now everyone is looking at me. I shift uncomfortably. "I don't really make a habit of speaking about her, so . . . no."

"At this stage, don't you think you should?" Alecks asks.

I bite my lip, but they aren't wrong. And with the distortion field Chaos has set up, this is probably the safest place to do it. I turn to the patiently waiting minor god with a sigh. "The president is my mother," I blurt out before I can overthink it.

Chaos's eyes go huge. "The *president?*" he hisses. "But I thought she hated Deathchildren!"

I grimace. "Yeah. Well. Surprise."

"Your uncle and I have actually discussed that," Orin says. "I don't think she hates Deathchildren as much as she decided it was politically useful to her to capitalize on fear of Death-children."

Chaos scowls. "That might actually be worse."

No one argues with that.

Alecks turns to me, his gaze heavy with something unsaid. "Before we run out of time, there's something Or and I have to talk to you about. You remember what we were arrested for?"

I blink, thrown by the sudden change in topic. "Obviously."

"Did Ravenna tell you the truth of it?" Orin asks.

I nod, Ravenna's revelation—that my uncles *were* in fact helping Deathchildren leave Escal in secret—coming back to me all at once.

Alecks takes a deep breath. "If it comes down to it, if you need to run, you need to know how to find them. So that you can find safety too."

"Why didn't you send me there years ago?" I ask.

Orin frowns. "The journey there is long and dangerous. And you know how hard life is outside of Escal. They don't have the same kind of protection from the elements, or access to food and medication as we do here in the city."

I open my mouth to argue that the Shallows was lacking in many of those protections too, but Orin lifts his hand. "I know, the Shallows has really deteriorated over the last few years, and your uncle and I discussed leaving at times. But we thought we could keep you safe in the city."

Alecks grimaces. "We were wrong. And for that we're sorry." He takes my face in his hands, his soft fingers warm on my skin, the tips of his middle fingers pressed gently against my temples. I smile at him uncertainly as he meets my gaze, his eyes strangely luminescent in the pale blue light.

Then my mind flashes white. A gasp rises in my chest as the white fills my vision. I have just enough time to think *This is impossible.* To think *But Alecks is mundane* before images flood my mind.

I'm back in the Shallows, staring at the back of Ravenna's home, smushed between a run-down grocery store and a now-defunct library overflowing with mold. My view races inside her home fluidly, like in flight. It races past her kitchen, past Lark's bedroom and the bathroom, into what I can only assume is Ravenna's bedroom. It stops before a tall five-shelf wooden bookcase. Five different books—one from each shelf—are pulled out and returned in sequence; then the bookshelf swings out like a door, revealing a tunnel.

A tunnel like the one that was beneath my home.

My view races into the tunnel, through dark, damp labyrinthine halls. There are more twists and turns than I should be able to remember, but somehow I know I won't forget the route. I can feel it embedding into my mind, encoding a core memory that will stay with me forever. The view moves faster and faster, far quicker than anyone could run, the blur of motion settling into my bones.

At last—a white lantern. Outside. On a hilltop I've never been, overlooking the city. Escal is a riot of colorful lights and winking stars in the night. From my vantage point, the tower prison sitting at the edge of a cliff is a lone, dark sentry in a splash of color.

The trail leads away from there. It turns its back on the city that has birthed and hurt me, the capital that has spit on and crushed my people. My family. Instead, the path leads away and away and away, through waist-high grass and past shimmering lakes, then at last up a long winding path carved into the side of a mountain and into a community nestled in a mountain range far from home.

I break out of the vision with the same gasp that started when the vision pulled me in. It all happened in the span of less than a second, and I stumble out of Alecks's grip and into Orin's thick chest.

"Wh-what was that?" My hand slaps over my chest, pressing hard against my racing heart. Alecks is looking at me with something like sadness in his face, something like regret. "You shouldn't be able to do that!" I gasp. "You're—you're mundane!"

"I'm sorry," Alecks says softly, as if that explains anything at all.

"You don't have godmagic," I say, disbelieving the truth that I cannot deny. Because no amount of runemagic can do what Alecks just did. That was Mindchild magic. But that doesn't make any godsdamned sense, because Alecks isn't a Mindchild.

"We've wanted to tell you for some time," Orin says behind me, his hands reassuring on my shoulders. "But it wasn't safe. And now . . ."

Alecks's expression is so deeply sad, it hurts to look at him. "Now we're running out of time," he says.

"No." I pull away from Orin, tears springing from my eyes even as I wipe them away with the back of my hand. "I'm going to save you both. I'll win this competition—or I'll figure something else out—but either way *I'm going to save you.*"

Orin and Alecks pull me into their arms, and for some reason I can't stop the tears blurring my vision. "I'm going to save you," I say into Alecks's shoulder. "I promise, I promise, I *promise*," I say into Orin's arm.

"It's all right, Crow," Orin says, so gently something inside me breaks. I can't stop crying. "There's so much more we have to tell you," Orin says. "But it's all right."

"We love you, Crow," Alecks says. "No matter what. Never forget that."

"Time's up," says a deep voice behind us.

I didn't even hear the door open. Panic clambers hot out of my chest and up my throat. I cling to Orin and Alecks and I am *weeping* in ways I haven't cried since I was a child. The reality that I have to go, that I have to step out of their arms and walk away, is a physical pain in my hollow chest. I have to believe I'll see them again, but I'm terrified I won't.

What if I'm wrong? What if this, here, now, in the last whisper of a moment in their arms, is the last time I feel how much they love me? My uncles. My *fathers.*

"I can't lose you," I'm sobbing as Alecks and Orin gently, so gently, release me.

"I can't lose them!" rips through me as Chaos softly drapes his arm around me and leads me to the door.

"We love you, Crow!" Orin and Alecks call after me.

And then the door closes again, and I am on the other side. My legs give out and Chaos holds me tight, huddled against the wall, as my grief rages out of me.

CHAPTER 31

I don't know how long it takes for the tears to stop. When they slow enough for my breaths to come in something less than heaving, gasping sobs, Chaos helps me to my feet and the guard leads us out of the prison. There we stand for some time, just outside the prison holding the two people I love most in the world, until, slowly, I stop shivering in Chaos's arms.

It's raining again.

It's soothing, but it shouldn't be. Familiar. In the last thirteen days, my life has shattered in ways I fear I'll never be able to fully repair, but this rain is unchanged. I step out from beneath the small overhang that has kept us dry, blinking hard through the deluge. The prison sits on the lowest point of Midlevel, just fifty feet from the drop-off of a cliff. I step to the edge, peering into a wet smear of neon lights and flooding rainwater. I recognize it with a start, even from this strange aerial angle.

It's the Shallows.

From up here, the Shallows are sprawling fingers of light reaching out in all directions until they hit the sharp edge of the wall to the west and bleed into the encroaching ocean of the far east. We're too high up for me to make out people, but I know the streets below must be full of them, even in the rain, even at this late hour. Ghosts too.

Come to think of it, I haven't seen any ghosts up here on Midlevel.

Chaos steps next to me and whistles lowly. "Can't say I've ever seen it from this angle before."

Neither have I, but of course that's no surprise. I crouch, propping my elbows on my knees and my chin on my hands. I'm utterly drenched, but I don't care. The patter of rain on my skin is grounding. I am here, standing at the place where Midlevel meets the Shallows, overlooking my home.

"Do you miss it?" Chaos asks.

I don't know how to answer that question. I miss my family. I miss the illusion of safety, the normalcy of eating dinners together, of listening to music with Alecks while Orin whittled a block of wood into a beautifully detailed palm-sized figure. A bird. A fish. An antlered deer or moose.

I don't miss the suffering and death that were around us all the time. The mold that crept into lungs, the weekly drownings, the risk of festering infections and illness. I don't miss watching the dockside sink slowly into the ocean, every year more people losing their homes to the encroaching water.

But those problems still exist. They are still here. I've just stepped away from them temporarily. I'm a tourist in a land that has chosen to ignore the suffering of others, that has shut us away so they don't have to confront the consequences of their collective choices.

I don't know how to answer Chaos's question, so I don't.

Instead my eye catches a burbling down below, a section of water jumping over itself like a small fountain. I pull out my phone and open the camera, zooming in on the disturbance in the water.

It's just a flooded storm drain. My shoulders relax and I almost put my phone away—the storm drains in the Shallows have been useless for as long as I can remember. They flood and bubble over like an overfilled cauldron at the merest mention of rain. Even from way up here I should have recognized it—but then a flash of blue makes me pause. The runes etched onto the top of the storm drain, just barely peeking out over the floodwater. It's not a surprise to see them—the runes have always been there, as far as I know—but something about them catches in my mind. I zoom in closer until I can make out the runes glowing bright blue on my phone screen; then I take a photo.

"What's that?" Chaos peers over my shoulder, shielding his eyes from the rain with the flat of his hand.

"Flooded storm drain," I say. "Something about the runes . . ." I trail off. Something about the runes, but what? What told my mind to stop, to pay attention? Runes are on nearly everything—streets, traffic lights and signs, buildings, doors—what about *these* runes made me pause?

And then it hits me.

I snap to my feet, standing so abruptly I crash into Chaos.

"Whoa!" Chaos wheels his arms as he backs up a step. "You okay?"

"The water pumps." My mind is racing—I can barely get the words out in the right order. "The city water pumps that run during the rain. Don't the runes look like this?"

I show him my phone screen, where I've zoomed in on the runes etched into the flooded storm drain.

Chaos frowns, scratching at his absolutely soaked pink beanie. "I don't . . . Maybe? I'm not sure."

"I need to see the pumps." I'm already walking up the long hill that leads back to the Midlevel city center. "Where's the nearest one?"

Chaos jogs to catch up with me. "There's one right next to the hotel we're staying in. But what's going on? Why would it matter if the runes are the same?"

"Fine," I say, ignoring Chaos's question. "Let's head back there—we need to regroup at the hotel anyway."

Chaos follows me, the silence heavy between us for a solid minute. Then, at last, he says, "What would it mean if the runes *were* the same?"

I press my lips to a thin line. "That depends on what the runes say."

"But you must suspect something."

I do. But I won't say it. Not until I know for sure.

CHAPTER 32

The runes are the same.

It takes all of ten seconds of flipping back and forth between my photo of the storm drain and the water pump next to the hotel with Chaos, Maddox, and Lark all peering over my shoulder before we confirm the obvious.

The sequence of runes etched onto the storm drain is exactly the same as the one carved into the water pump—save for the very last rune. And I don't know what that means, not exactly, but everything inside me is itching with possibilities that feel *wrong*.

Where is all the water going? I asked.

Dread twists inside me as I stare at these nearly identical runes.

"The storm drains always flood first," Maddox says softly, confirming the dark thoughts already swirling through my mind.

"We need to figure out what these rune sequences do." Lark throws down a notebook on the counter we've huddled around.

"Does anyone have a rune encyclopedia?" I ask.

"I have an app," Maddox says, lifting his phone out of his pocket.

I shake my head. "Nothing digital. We don't want our searches traceable if we think there's some shady shit happening here."

I didn't really mean to say that so openly, but it's out and it's true. The reality sinks in, settling around us in cold silence until Chaos clears his throat.

"Uh, do we? Think that?" he asks.

Maddox bites his lip. Lark turns around and strides toward her room. "I have a rune book. Hold on."

Five minutes later we're all huddled around Lark's rune book. Mouse has fallen asleep on my lap as Lark painstakingly looks up each of the twenty or so runes in the formula. Some of them we recognize, like *water* and *motion* and *bridge*. But many of them are far more technical than anyone but a specialized Architect would recognize, and even though Maddox knows some of them, there are too many obscure runes to paint a full picture.

Too obscure, even, for Lark's rune book.

"Maybe we don't need to know all of them," I say, looking at the thirteen we've figured out so far: *water, motion, bridge, flow, intake, pull, release, push, volume, rain, threshold, displace, cycle.* I point to the last rune on the water pump and the last rune on the storm drain. "These are the only ones that don't match up. If we can find these, maybe that'll give us a better idea of what this formula does."

Lark's rune book is thick and organized by stroke. The last runes on each of the sequences are complex—whereas most runes can be made in one to three strokes, each of these is six strokes long. We go through the book meticulously, finding several runes that look similar but none that match either the rune on the pump or the one on the storm drain exactly. We spend hours going back and forth over the pages, until we're sure Lark's rune book doesn't have either.

Maddox taps my phone screen, zooming in on one of the small markings beside the rune on the storm drain. This one has a tiny plus sign and a dot to the right of the main portion of the rune.

"These look like annotations," Maddox says.

The rest of us stare at him blearily.

"They're used more frequently alongside Architectmagic," Maddox adds. "An annotation can create a variant of a rune that's unique. It can be used to add nuance, like for real precision work, or for identification, like a serial number."

Lark suddenly sits up. "So they aren't part of the larger rune?"

Maddox hesitates. "They are . . . but like, they can be used with *any* rune theoretically. They add meaning to the base rune." He points to the larger portion of the rune, to the left of the small markings.

"Then we don't need to find the exact rune in the rune book," I say, picking up on Lark's thread. "If we ignore the annotations, maybe we can find the meaning of the base rune in the book."

Lark rips open the book, moving quickly through the pages. "I thought I saw it in here without the annotations. Somewhere over . . . here." She stops flipping through the pages and points to an entry.

Lark is right. It looks exactly like the base rune, just without the annotations.

228

"Locator," she reads aloud. "Often paired with annotations, a locator rune can be used to track the location of an object. When paired with a larger formula, locator runes can also be used to direct the flow of magic from one location to another."

"'Direct the flow of magic . . .'" I whisper.

Water. Motion. Bridge. Flow. Intake. Pull. Release. Push. Volume. Rain. Threshold. Displace. Cycle. Locator.

Water. Rain. Intake. Pull. Release. Push.

It comes together all at once, so clear it's a wonder I didn't see it instantly.

"The locator runes aren't just directing the flow of magic from the pumps to the storm drains," I say. "This is where the water in the pumps is going. Midlevel is pumping their floodwater directly into the Shallows."

CHAPTER 33

We sit in silence for a long, agonizing moment with the reality of what we've just discovered. Finally, Maddox swears and stands, pacing back and forth across the room.

"What do we even do with this?" Lark asks, gripping the edge of the counter so tightly her knuckles are white. "Are we sure? Can we prove it?"

"It makes sense," Maddox says, "but if we really want to prove it, we'll need to find the storm drain that corresponds to this pump." He returns to the counter and points to the locator rune on the pump. But to do that, someone would have to go to the Shallows, and we competitors probably won't be allowed back into Midlevel."

"Or we can contact someone in the Shallows," I say. "See if they can find it for us."

"There are hundreds of storm drains in the Shallows," Maddox says. "Maybe even over a thousand. How is one person going to check them all until they find the right one?"

"We use the locator rune," Lark says. She points to the

entry in the rune book, which is still open to the page on locator runes. "It says right here locator runes can be used for tracking—that's what we need. We just need to target the rune on the corresponding storm drain instead of the one on the pump."

I stand, suddenly restless. "That could work. Have you done a tracking spell before?"

Lark grimaces. "I've . . . seen my nan do it."

I look up at Maddox, who just shakes his head with a wince. When I turn to Chaos, he smiles sheepishly. "I never did master the rune arts."

So it's on Lark and me to figure it out. I hesitate. "Maybe . . . we can video call Ravenna and have her walk us through it?"

Chaos grimaces. "You'll want to be very careful doing anything over a hackable medium. If Midlevel is truly using the water pumps to flood the Shallows, that means it's been built into the infrastructure, which means the government is involved. Trust me when I say it would not be difficult for a government agent to hack a video call without you knowing."

"Then we don't do it over a hackable medium," I say. "Maybe she can . . . write it down?" I cringe as the suggestion comes out of my mouth.

Lark looks at me like I've just suggested something ridiculous, which, to be fair, I kind of have. "And how do you suggest she get it up here in time? You know all letters and packages sent between the levels are examined."

None of us has any immediate ideas. I keep hoping

Chaos or Maddox will pipe up with the perfect solution, but instead I'm left with an itch in the back of my mind whispering that I *might* have a suggestion. It's just not one that I like.

But when no one else says anything, I push past my own resistance. "What about . . . a journo?"

Lark and Maddox look at me skeptically. "I mean, sure," Lark says, "if we knew a journo who'd want to investigate this . . ."

"I might be able to help with that," I say. Chaos's eyes widen and he grins.

Lark arches an eyebrow. "Since when do you know journos?"

I pull out my phone and open Jimena's contact card. *I've reconsidered your offer. Can you meet tomorrow morning?* It's, like, one in the morning so I don't expect a response, but to my surprise Jimena texts back immediately. *Absolutely.*

Trying to sleep is torture. Hours drag by staring at the ceiling, my mind buzzing with too many thoughts to process. The stress kicks off another autoimmune flare, and I spend half the night using Deathmagic to fight the pain spreading steadily from the top of my spine into my skull. But I must fall asleep, because I blink and tumble into a dream.

A cabin door creaking open. The cool metal of the handle slipping from my fingers. In the woods, a path blanketed in fallen pine needles, soft and warm copper beneath my feet. Ahead, a campfire, crackling in the night, casting dancing shadows on tree trunks and a warm orange glow on four log benches set around the flames.

A raven bristles its large black wings as I approach. It tilts its head and its gaze meets mine—beady black and brimming with knowledge.

It is not alone.

"Holy shit," Jimena says the next morning.

With Lark's, Maddox's, and Chaos's help I've just laid out the evidence we found and the theory we have about the pumps directly flooding the Shallows.

"I know we'll need more concrete proof if we ever want to go public, and we think Ravenna can help with that," I say, "but none of us can travel between the Shallows and Midlevel without attracting attention."

Jimena nods, pushing her red glasses up the bridge of her nose. "Which is where I come in."

"Exactly." The plan is coming together, and I can't help it—excitement is gathering in my bones. "You can meet with Ravenna and pass along our message. Then you could ask her to do the locator spell and you follow it to the storm drain linked to the pump we found."

"And in return," Jimena says, "you give me an exclusive interview if you make it to the semifinals."

I grit my teeth, but I knew this was a possibility. Of course Jimena would want to get something out of all this, even if it turns out we're wrong and there isn't a story. "If I make it to the *finals*," I counter.

"Deal."

"Okay," Lark says. "So say we find the storm drain

corresponding to the pump. We confirm what we suspect. Then what?"

I don't miss a beat. "We go public." I look at Jimena. "If you're in, that is."

Jimena leans forward. "Oh, I'm in. If what you're thinking is true and we find the evidence, you couldn't pay me *not* to go wide with it."

Maddox grimaces. "There will be riots in the Shallows if we're right."

"So be it," I say. "The government and the gods should have thought of that before trying to drown us."

When Jimena leaves, I'm feeling absolutely murderous; and judging by the dark looks on Lark's and Maddox's faces, I'm guessing they feel similarly. So I'm in exactly the wrong mood to receive the news that we have a PR outing today.

"Seriously?" comes out of my mouth before I can stop it.

Chaos grimaces. "I'm sorry. I know the timing is less than ideal—unfortunately, I don't make the schedule."

Maddox flops back on the sofa, his long limbs dangling off the end. Mouse hops onto his chest and begins kneading his belly with a low purr. He sighs, petting her gently.

"What would happen if we . . . didn't?" I ask.

Chaos sighs and runs his hand through his hair. "Technically you wouldn't be disqualified or anything, but it would look bad at a time when the three of you should be trying to make yourselves likable to Midlevel audiences. I know it's gross, but you three are giving faces to Shallowsfolk."

"Is Maddox coming with us?" I ask.

Chaos shakes his head. "He'll be coming with me to a sponsor event, where all the sponsors pretend we're best friends and not directly competing with each other. As part of Team Crow he gets backstage access."

"Lucky me," Maddox says without a drop of enthusiasm.

I frown. I don't love the idea of having to do this public event without Maddox and Chaos, but with Lark there at least I won't be alone. "I might prefer that over whatever we're stuck doing," I say. "If we have to do another panel, I'm liable to strangle someone."

At this Chaos brightens. "It's not a panel or interview or anything like that this time. It's a televised dinner for the quarterfinalists with a red carpet entry."

Maddox crinkles his nose. "People want to watch them eat?"

Chaos laughs a little. "I know it sounds weird, but it won't be live. A bunch of camera drones will record everything; then some editors will put it together in some semblance of a narrative. So you really want to be on your best behavior."

Lark actually laughs. "Good thing we learned last night that the powers that be are trying to *kill us all* in the Shallows, then. That knowledge has definitely ingratiated me to our *generous* hosts."

Chaos presses his lips into a flat line. "Like I said, I know the timing is less than ideal." He hesitates. "All right, maybe if *best behavior* isn't reachable today, you can consider a different PR strategy. You two don't have to be angels as much as you have to be likable. Snarky can be likable. Curious can be likable. Gods, even *shy* can be likable. Basically, just don't be an ass and you'll probably be fine."

235

Lark runs a fingernail over the gold ticket on her wrist. "No promises," she mutters.

⸎

After a relatively mellow morning where we become increasingly bitter at the ticking of the clock, Chaos unveils the outfits he's picked out for me and Maddox. Lark leaves to find Dez to coordinate their own eveningwear.

Until now the clothes have been *fine*—Chaos has a generally more colorful taste than I prefer, but he's respected my wishes for a more muted wardrobe.

The dark green three-piece suit he unveils for me is *fucking gorgeous*.

The lapels are embroidered with crows in a shiny silver thread, which matches the silver-embroidered black vest beneath and black tie. The boots are a combination of warm brown leather and black embroidered fabric, decorated with the same pattern and silver thread. When I put it on, it all fits perfectly. I stare at myself in the mirror, disbelieving.

I have never felt so handsome in my life.

The suit is cut to accentuate my shoulders and make my waist look slim. The pants drape perfectly, hugging my thighs before falling straight to my boots. And the depth of the deep green is *radiant* in the light.

I can't stop staring at myself. I've been adjusting my testosterone levels long enough now to generally pass for a masculine, vaguely androgynous person most people assume is a teen boy. But dressed in this suit I look like a young man.

I love it.

When I step out of my room, I look for Lark before remembering she's with Dez. Chaos asks, "What do you think?" with a small smile that tells me he already knows the answer.

"How on earth did you do this?" I ask. "It fits perfectly."

"Ah well, I can't take full credit for that. I paid extra to get it rune tailored." He grins. "It'll always fit you perfectly, even as your body shape changes as you age. Consider it a *thanks for making it this far* gift."

I can't imagine how I'll ever have another opportunity to wear this again, but it doesn't matter. I'm wearing it today, and right now it's making me feel amazing. I turn around and pull Chaos into a tight hug, which I guess takes him by surprise because he staggers into it with a laugh.

"Thank you," I say with a grin. "Seriously. This is amazing."

"You sure look amazing," he answers.

"So do you."

And he does. Chaos's suit is every bit as flamboyant as I would expect for him: slim cut and black, but from shoulders to ankles it is embroidered in bright neon purples, pinks, blues, yellows, oranges, and greens. Lightning bolts, clouds, flowers, greenery, mountains, and waves decorate the fabric save for the thin black lapels. It's stunning to look at, without a single repeated image. Beneath it all he wears a simple black button-down shirt, no tie, and black loafers. No socks. His outfit is art and it is perfect.

"If you tell me you embroidered that yourself, I might lose my mind a little," I say, shaking my head as I grin at his suit.

Chaos laughs again. "I wish I could say I did it myself, but my embroidery skills aren't ready for a suit of this caliber. But it *is* embroidered by hand, by our very own Lark."

My mouth drops open. *"Lark* did this?"

"She did." Chaos grins. "Amazing, right?"

I knew Lark did embroidery, of course, and back home she *is* a tailor, but this is next level. When did she have time to do this? Suddenly every time she retreated to her room plays back in my mind in a new light. I've been so focused on everything going on with me, I didn't even notice Lark working on this massive project. What else have I missed? "It's incredible," I breathe.

Then Maddox steps out of his room and I feel my eyebrows rising into my hairline.

He's wearing a warm burgundy suit that compliments the rich tones of his umber skin. His vest is the same maroon color with monochrome matching buttons, and his tie is a shiny black and wine-red color, with some kind of swirling design in the red. Like my suit, his fits him perfectly, accentuating his broad shoulders and cutting down to his slim hips and long legs, finished off with warm brown leather loafers. He looks incredible.

Chaos whistles. "Hello there, handsome."

Maddox shakes his head. "I think this suit might cost more than my rent back home."

Chaos's smile softens. "Well, this is all covered by the Tournament funds, so try not to worry about that."

"Hard not to," Maddox sighs.

"I know what you mean," I say. "We can't just ignore how money for these suits could pay for food for a family for a couple months, or rent, or much-needed repairs. It feels like enjoying this means forgetting where we came from."

Maddox's eyes light up. *"Yes."*

"But you haven't forgotten," Chaos says. "I hear you both, but you're here *because* of where you came from. You're fighting *for* the Shallows. You aren't erasing your past."

The reminder is fortifying. I take a deep breath and nod. Maddox puts on a small smile, though it looks a little forced. "I guess that's true," he says. "But still. That people up here have access to luxury like this while my moms have to patch up holes in my sister's clothes until they're more patches than original fabric isn't right."

Chaos nods, his face sober. "You're right. I hadn't thought of that but . . . I should have. I think there's a lot I still overlook because I'm so used to having access to . . . well, everything."

I cover a snort. Maddox raises his eyebrows at him. "You *think*?"

Chaos flushes, properly chastised. "I know."

Maddox nods and takes a deep breath, running his fingers over his silky lapels. "Well. I think my moms will be proud" seeing me in this. I mean, I *do* look amazing."

"No question." Chaos steps up to him and gently straightens his tie. "How do you feel?"

"Like I'm dreaming," Maddox says. "Except I know I'm not, because I never would have been able to dream up something so fine. You sure know what you're doing."

Chaos's face is all unabashed pride, and honestly, it's well-earned.

Chaos laughs and glances at his watch. "Speaking of which, we should get going. It won't take too long to get there, but the red carpet entrance will start soon."

I'm the first one out the door, and I stop dead in my tracks in the doorframe. Standing in the elevator, leaning against the opposite wall waiting for us, is Lark. Except . . . not Lark like I have ever seen her.

Her black hair is up in a glittering loose bun, with tendrils of curled hair framing her face. Her eyes are framed in thick dark kohl, which is fairly normal for her, and her lashes are coated in mascara. Her lips are a glossy shade of pink just slightly warmer and lighter than the natural color of her lips.

And then there's her dress. Because Lark is wearing a *dress*.

Never in my life have I seen Lark wear a skirt, let alone a full dress, and this one is stunning. All black, from high collar to the long skirt that touches the floor and emphasizes her height. But it isn't a solid piece of fabric. The front of the dress has a narrow diamond cutout covered in opaque layers of black lace beginning at the dip of her collarbones and reaching to her navel. The lace meets long points of solid fabric at the bottom of her hips, like mountains rising from the skirt. More black lace frills out around her shoulders and the tops of her arms, creating a fanlike effect over her bare arms. It's stunning. She's stunning. And I can't take my eyes off her.

"Wow, Lark," Chaos says behind me. "I guess my sister has some taste after all."

A *tsk* nearby makes me jump. Dez apparently has actually joined Lark in the elevator. This is the first time I'm seeing her up close, and she's also dressed in black—but an all-black suit, from shirt to vest to tie. Her hair is cut short on the sides and long on top, flopping over the left side of her face and showing off bright purple ends.

There are, admittedly, some similarities between her and Chaos, like their light brown skin and black hair, but what really makes their relationship undeniable is her eyes. Dez may not have heterochromia like her brother, but her eyes are the exact same shade of pale blue as Chaos's right eye.

"I don't believe my taste was ever in question," Dez says, eyeing her little brother.

"Certainly not," Chaos responds dubiously. "Anyway, Lark, if *Shadow Princess* is what you were going for, you nailed it."

Lark grins sharply. "I was envisioning *Princess Who Will Eviscerate You*, but that works."

"*Queen of Devastation*," I say before I can stop myself.

Lark quirks an eyebrow and I go hot and prickly all over. "*Queen of Devastation*," she says slowly, rolling the words in her mouth, like she's tasting it. "Hmm. I like it."

I like it too. And if I don't make myself rip my gaze off of her *now*, she's going to know it. I force myself to move out of the doorway and watch as Chaos and Maddox step into the hallway, but out of the corner of my eye I see Lark smirking in a way that makes me think I haven't escaped her notice.

Of course you haven't. You were practically drooling over her!

Oh my gods, I need to think about something else. Anything else.

"So"—Chaos claps his hands—"ready to smile for some cameras?"

CHAPTER 34

The red carpet entrance, as Chaos described it, is less of a big deal than I expected.

I don't know what I pictured, exactly, but a literal red carpet rolled out in front of fifteen feet of backdrop plastered with *Tournament of the Gods 2324* next to the dining hall wasn't it. Across from the carpet is an array of photographers—both the in-person kind and camera drones.

We're supposed to walk in with our sponsors and teams, so I cross the carpet with Chaos and Maddox, with Lark and Dez right behind us. The five of us get maybe a third of the attention of everyone ahead of us. Chaos's eye twitches with irritation at the disparity, but honestly, drawing less attention is my preference, so I can't be bothered to care.

"This is where the sponsors and competitors part," he says when we're done. "All the competitors should be gathering in the foyer right behind the door. When it's time, you'll all be escorted into the dining hall together. When it's over, we can regroup in the suite. Any questions?"

"Just one," I say. "Can I skip it?"

Chaos gives me a gentle push. "Go with Lark and watch each other's backs. You'll be fine."

Lark and I are halfway to the door before it occurs to me that *Watch each other's backs* somewhat contradicts the *You'll be fine.*

<hr />

After some awkward standing by the door, a group of servers takes all eight of us competitors to a dining room about three times the size of my entire apartment back in the Shallows, with an enormously long dining table running down the center. On either side of the table are chairs cushioned with tacky patterned fabric bordered in golden silky rope. A long table runner flows down the center of the table, with mountains of flowers and greenery piled on top and rune-spelled glass orbs filled with fire floating about a foot over the display, each about a foot apart.

Then there are the golden plates. And the handblown, flawlessly shiny glass cups. And the gold-thread-embossed cloth napkins folded in a fan shape on the center of each plate. And more silverware in one setting than I've ever seen in my life: a small fork, a regular fork, two spoons, and three knives all set out.

I'm dressed in the finest clothes I've ever worn and yet I've never felt more out of place in my life.

Someone snickers near me, and I don't even have to look to know it's Astrid. Though I don't look at her directly, her gaze is so obviously gawking that she clearly wants me to meet her eyes. So I don't. A server of some kind has approached to pull out my chair, and I hate it, but I sit. Thankfully Lark has stuck by my side.

Unfortunately, Astrid, Sergio, and a familiar blond boy sit across from us. I still make a point not to look at them.

"Do you think they know what a *fork* is?" Astrid asks Sergio, so loudly it's obvious she wants everyone to hear.

My face flares with heat at the implication that Shallowsborn wouldn't know what silverware is. But before I can think of how to respond, Lark leans over to me and stage-whispers, "Do you think she knows what a stuck-up bitch she sounds like?"

If I had started eating, I surely would have choked. Astrid gasps, her face going bright red; and I can't help it: I laugh.

"Better a stuck-up bitch than a lowtown *godkilling cultist*," Sergio hisses across the table.

The veiled accusation sends my heart galloping, but Lark seems entirely unaffected.

"So we agree," Lark says. "She *is* a stuck-up bitch."

Sergio's mouth opens and closes. Astrid looks positively murderous.

I would love to enjoy all this, but I can't help scanning the room for camera drones—were any close enough to hear what he said? Would it matter if they did? Would anyone take that accusation at face value? Oddly, I haven't seen any camera drones yet—

The rune-spelled glass orbs. I've assumed they're just decorative, but now that I look at them more closely, it hits me—*they're the camera drones.* And they were absolutely close enough to hear what Sergio just said.

To be honest, *godkiller* always struck me as kind of badass, as far as pejoratives go. But Sergio's accusation is an accusation nonetheless—he's telling us he didn't buy Lark's explanation. He's telling us he thinks I'm a Deathchild. And if I want to survive this competition, I cannot give another inch away.

So even as nausea roils through me and my body flashes with cold and heat, when the servers place a small plate of salad in front of each of us, I pick up my *fucking fork* and take a big bite. I will not let Astrid and Sergio—or these godsdamned camera drones—see how much they bother me.

I eat every last leaf, every slice of juicy tomato and shred of crunchy carrot, just to spite them.

The next course is steaming-hot bread served with salted butter. The crust of the bread is crunchy, the inside warm and just barely sweet, with a hint of honey. On top of it all, the butter absolutely melts, and I actually have to stop myself from taking a second slice, if only so I don't ruin what little appetite I have for the main course. At this point I've pretended long enough—and avoided looking at Astrid and Sergio long enough—that I can almost enjoy the full meal without the twist of anxiety in my gut.

The next course is a tiny bowl full of a creamy orange soup, sprinkled with seeds of some kind on top. They look like squash seeds. Maybe pumpkin? I dip my spoon into the soup and can't help but smile as I bring it to my lips. The soup is hot, smooth, and sweet, and the seeds add a salty bite of texture. It's delicious and does wonders to soothe my roiling nausea. Before I know it, my spoon is scraping the bottom of the porcelain bowl.

Finally comes the entree, an orange-pink grilled fish filet served on top of a bed of steaming-hot rice with carrots, peppers, onions, sprouts, and some kind of crunchy white-green vegetable I'm not familiar with. On top of it all is a sweet and salty brown sauce that smells like ginger. I dig in immediately and nearly groan aloud.

This might actually be the best meal I've had in my life.

I've devoured half the plate without even looking up when the unmistakable sound of snickering hits my ears. My face burns as it occurs to me what I must look like, bent over my plate, shoveling food into my mouth like it's my last meal.

But even though I know where the laughter is coming from, I don't look at them. I won't give them the satisfaction of seeing my expression.

"Oh my *gods*," Astrid says. "You'd think he's never *eaten* before."

"A lowtowner is a lowtowner, even in fancy clothes," Sergio responds smugly.

If I were a Mindchild with the godpower of telekinesis, I would knock their food directly onto their laps. Or maybe dump their glasses of water on their heads. Unfortunately I don't have that power, so instead I have to continue eating and ignoring them, like it doesn't bother me at all that they treat me and Lark like we're beneath them just because we're Shallowsfolk.

It's going to feel so damn good to wipe the smug expressions off their faces in the ring.

I grab my water glass and bring it to my lips, smiling as I envision kicking Astrid's ass on live tele—

Eight black eyes blink at me over my glass. A huge, pale, bristly *thing* is on my glass, right next to my fingers. A spider. A spider the size of my fist. Its soft bristles brush against my skin.

"Fuck!" I shout, dropping the glass and jerking away from the table. But the chair doesn't slide as smoothly as I would have expected, and instead my world suddenly tilts back and I hit the marble floor so hard, my teeth clack in my mouth. Something shatters near me. Pain blooms over the back of my skull, and my legs are awkwardly in the air in front of me. The water from my spilled glass is *everywhere*. All over my torso and pants and dribbling on the floor.

"Holy shit!" Lark jumps to her feet.

The glass has broken into dozens of pieces next to me, which must have been the shattering noise. I reflexively touch the back of my head, but thankfully my hair is dry. I'm not bleeding.

I roll away from the glass and scramble to my feet, searching the floor for the spider, but there's nothing there. I don't understand. Where could it have gone? And where did it come from?

"Gods above and below," Lark says. "What the fuck was that? Are you okay?"

"The spider," I say, my heart still pounding so hard in my chest that it hurts. "Did you see it?"

Lark scrunches up her nose in confusion. "Spider?"

Astrid, Sergio, and the blond boy are laughing so hard that Astrid is actually red-faced and Sergio is bent over.

"I . . . saw a huge spider on my glass . . ." I answer Lark, my voice trailing as their laughter grows. "I *felt* the bristles against my hand."

Lark looks at the hysterical trio; then her face darkens as she turns back to me. "I didn't see anything, but Astrid is a Mindchild," she says quietly. "An illusionist."

Of course she is. I didn't know illusions could feel like

physical things. Which means I just spilled my drink all over myself and smashed my head on the floor for no godsdamned reason.

"Right," I say, my voice a distant thing. "Sure."

Then I lunge toward the table.

Lark grips my shoulders hard and yanks me back, stepping between me and Astrid, who has started a fresh round of laughter.

"*No,*" Lark says firmly, grabbing my chin and forcing me to look at her. "Don't forget what Chaos told us. If you attack her outside of the ring, it's over for you. You'll be disqualified. You really want to give her that win?"

Lark is right. Of course she is, of course I don't want to give Astrid the satisfaction. But my anger is a storm and that vile bitch is *grinning* at me. She's loving every second of my discomfort, my anger, my embarrassment. She's *already* so godsdamned satisfied and I can't do shit about it.

Lark's lips are so close to my ear, her warm breath washes over my skin. "In two days you face Sergio in the ring," she reminds me in a whisper. "He's not Astrid, but he's an ass too and you get to send him home. Then you're a semifinalist. Save your anger for that."

I close my eyes and inhale deeply through my nose. When my eyes open again, I know what I have to do. "I'm going back to the hotel," I say.

Lark nods. "I'll go with you."

I never thought I'd be glad to have Lark by my side, but right now I'm grateful for her.

CHAPTER 35

We walk in companionable silence all the way back to the hotel. When we step into the elevator and the doors close quietly behind us, it's just the two of us.

I'm a muddled mess of cooling anger and embarrassment, of disappointment (in how the night ended? in myself, for nearly falling for the obvious bait?), and of something else I'm struggling to place. A softness between Lark and me that's entirely unfamiliar. A tension in the air that, for once, isn't full of anger and bitter resentment.

Lark stood up for me. Lark had my back. And when I nearly reacted in a way that would have had me disqualified, she stopped me. If she hadn't been there, I wouldn't still be here, fighting for my uncles.

A glance at her out of the corner of my eye shows me she is still flawless. I'm a sodden mess next to her, but she is every bit the queen that she was at the beginning of the evening. Her makeup pristine. Her dress stunning. Her poise perfection. She is confident and fierce. The way she fearlessly steps in when I freeze—having her by my side is everything. *Queen of Devastation was right,* I think.

"Penguin," she says suddenly, shattering the silence.

I blink, turning my gaze fully on her. She's smirking, which means she probably caught me staring at her out of the corner of my eye. Because of course she did.

"Larkness," I respond automatically.

"Is there something on my face?"

I shift my weight away from her and rip my gaze away. "Sorry," I say, though I don't really know why I'm apologizing. For looking at her? "I was just zoning out."

"Hmm," she responds. She sounds unconvinced.

The doors open with a chime and I enter the suite as quickly as possible, trying to create distance between us. Mouse, who was waiting in front of the elevator doors, immediately rubs against my legs in greeting and does the same to Lark, the little traitor.

There's too much warmth between us. Too much friendly banter. I feel pulled to Lark in a way that terrifies me. I don't understand what's changed between us. Or maybe I do: I'm not angry at her. The simmering irritation that even *thinking* of her has summoned for as long as I can remember just isn't there.

Somewhere along the way, my anger has vanished and in its place is this *pull.* This knowledge that Lark and I have orbited each other for so long that I couldn't separate myself from her if I tried.

And *that* is scary.

"You going to wear those wet clothes all night?" Lark asks.

"You dying to see me take off my clothes?" I ask before I can stop myself.

Lark raises a single immaculately shaped eyebrow.

My face is an absolute furnace now. I literally can't believe I just said that out loud. To Lark. Gods above and below, did I just *flirt* with her? I turn to my room, wondering if there are any fresh new ways I want to try humiliating myself tonight, when Lark's voice stops me dead in my tracks.

"Crow."

That's it. Just my name. My *real* name on Lark's lips. There's quiet shuffling behind me and I don't dare look back. I know she is near me like I know the ground is beneath me. I close my eyes, and the energy sparks between us so charged that I can almost taste the metallic tinge on my tongue.

And then she touches my shoulder, just a hint of fingers on the soft fabric of my suit. And I shouldn't, I *shouldn't,* but I do. I release my Deathmagic with a sigh, and though my eyes are closed I see her in my mind.

No godmagic swirls through Lark's body; instead she is pure energy and feeling, she is the beating of an electric drum in her chest and the spark of thought in her mind. She is warmth and color, blood-red particles swirling from the top of her head to her fingers and toes. Her ribs are bruised from her last match, and something itches inside me to fix it. I'd barely even have to think about it, all I have to do is reach and—

I force my eyes open. I could heal her, but I won't. Not without her consent.

"Are you all right?"

I bite my lip, then force myself to turn around and face her.

Lark is tall to begin with, and in her heels she's even taller. I tilt my chin up to meet her gaze, and I'm surprised to find warmth there. Lark has never looked at me like this.

Her hand is still on my shoulder.

"I don't know," I say, and it's the truth. "I don't know what to feel."

"Maybe that's okay," Lark says. "Normal, even. This has all been a lot, even for me, and my stakes aren't half as high as yours."

I frown. "I'm sure whatever deal you made with Dez wasn't low stakes."

She shakes her head. "Forget that—it doesn't matter. It's reasonable for you to be . . . mixed up right now."

Why do you care? I want to ask. *What are you doing?* But instead I ask, "Why did you stop me?"

Lark tilts her head. "At the dinner?"

I nod.

The sharp smile that slides over her lips is so familiar, it instantly calms me, even though it probably shouldn't. "Because, Magpie," she says, "if anyone's going to knock you out of this competition, it's going to be me."

And then she's kissing me.

It's a soft kiss. Barely a whisper of lips on my mouth. It's a question: *Is this okay?*

This is not my first kiss. But never in my wildest dreams did I imagine I would one day kiss *Lark*, of all people. Lark, the perfect daughter. Lark, the queen of irritating quips and rolling eyes. Lark, the example of everything my mother wanted me to be, everything I could never be, no matter how hard I tried.

Lark, with her lips an invitation on my mouth.

I respond in turn. Hesitant at first. Half expecting her to pull away, to remember who it is she's kissing and turn around and never speak of this again. Instead, her arms bracket either side of my shoulders against the wall, enclosing me in the clause of her affection. Instead, her body presses hard against mine, her curves against my flat chest and angled torso. Instead, she tips my chin up with two fingers, then slowly slides her hand to my tie, loosening it with a tug.

Somehow, my hands land on her hips, holding her close to me. Somehow, her deft fingers undo the buttons of my soaked vest and shirt underneath. Somehow, her hands are hot against the skin of my stomach, and *want* flashes through me like a match to kerosene. Somehow, we end up on her bed, her body pressing mine flat against the mattress.

Her kisses are the symbols of sixteen years of revolving around each other, my moon to her planet. Her touches are annotations to the spell she sends skittering across my skin. The press of her body against mine is the activation of magic between us, of sparks and heat branding my soul.

This is a chapter of our story that I did not expect. But now that we've crashed together in a flurry of movement and heat, our collision feels inevitable.

Eventually, our kisses cool to something softer. To her head against my chest, and my fingers caressing her back. Eventually, deep in the cooling night, I drift out of quiet unconsciousness to Lark rolling away from me. I reach out clumsily in the dark, my limbs heavy with sleep, and catch her shoulder.

"Don't go," I mumble.

I feel her weight shift toward me again. Her fingertips brush my temple and trace down my cheek to my jaw.

"I'm here," she whispers.

I don't know when I began searching for Lark in every empty space. I'm already drifting back to sleep, but before the heavy call of unconsciousness pulls me under, I manage three words: "Stay with me."

She does.

CHAPTER 36

The cheers of the crowd are louder than ever as the platform rises into the arena, but all I can think about is Lark. Lark's arms around me. Lark's fingers trailing down my cheek. Lark's whisper, warm against my ear: *I'm here.*

It's been two days, and I keep waiting for things to feel normal between us again. It was just making out. It didn't mean anything.

And yet.

The platform comes to a halt beneath us, jarring me back to now. Across the ring, Sergio is pacing back and forth, right behind the starting line, like a restless panther. I can almost imagine a long tail flickering behind him in irritation. As if every second before the match begins is agonizing.

It will not surprise me for a second if he turns out to be a Faunachild.

I'm just thinking that it would probably be in my best interest to start watching my competitors' prior matches when the floor *flickers* beneath me. Then, like a light switch flipped off, the floor disappears entirely.

The crowd gasps in one enormous inhale. I give a full-body flinch—but I'm not falling. This isn't like the last match, in which parts of the floor descended into the pool below. I press hesitantly with my foot, and it is solid beneath me, but my eyes are telling me there's *nothing* there but air and the pool far down below. Ahead of me is a single glowing white line—the starting line—but that's it.

The floor is completely invisible.

What's worse, though the starting lines are there, there aren't any other boundaries drawn in light. I can't see where the platform begins and ends. I can only assume it stayed the same large oval shape, but if I get too close to the edge, I could run right off without realizing.

This is, without a doubt, my least favorite arena layout yet.

Across the invisible platform, Sergio is crouching and knocking on the transparent floor beside him. Then he looks up at me with a vicious grin that I don't like at all. He stands, stretching his arms lazily over his head, then begins bouncing on his toes and rolling his shoulders.

The countdown begins.

"I hate this," I grit out between my teeth as I reach for my knives.

My first two competitors didn't use lethal force. I will not assume the same of Sergio. There isn't a single doubt in my mind that he would take pleasure in killing me in front of a crowd. But that thought is exactly what I need to banish the dizzying nausea swirling in my gut: I replace it with a flash of anger.

Sergio would love to kill me, but I will not let him. I won't let him win. I won't fail my uncles.

The siren sounding the beginning of the match screeches

through the air, and Sergio takes off running toward me, pulling two knives out of holsters by his hips and holding them out wide.

I smile. I can handle a knife fight—even one on an invisible floating platform. *Just stay away from the edges and you'll be fine.*

Sergio is still half an arena away, but he swings his arms toward me and lets out a strangled scream more animal than human. Then between one step and the next he vanishes.

I swear to the gods it's like I blinked and he disappeared.

I stay put in my starting stance, frozen as my gaze whips around. I don't understand. Is this part of the arena? Will it turn me invisible too if I cross certain points of the ring? It's not like he fell—I would have seen that. He's just . . . gone.

It doesn't make sense, but the ending bell hasn't gone off, so the match must still be on.

Burning pain rips through the skin of my left arm and I hiss, jerking away as I slap at the sting. My hand comes away bloody. I've been cut, but the wound is clean and shallow, like the graze of a knife. A knife—like Sergio's weapon of choice.

Laughter ripples around me and my blood goes cold.

"I know what you are, Deathchild," Sergio whispers, too quiet for the cameras to pick up, so close his breath washes over my ear.

I slash out with my knife and meet nothing but air. My heart is truly pounding now, but the answer is as clear as this godsdamned floor. This isn't a trick of the arena. It isn't part of the match.

Sergio is a Faunachild, all right. A descendant of Hunt if I had to guess. And his godpower is invisibility. And he's *toying* with me.

I almost let out a hysterical laugh. I'm fighting an invisible opponent in an invisible ring. And if there was any question before, it's gone now: Whether by a lucky guess or scant evidence, it doesn't matter, because he knows exactly what I am.

Somehow, I don't think Sergio intends to keep my secret.

A flash of silver slices through the air and I roll, ducking beneath the slash and crashing clumsily into invisible legs. It isn't what I was going for, but the impact lights up the part of my brain that maps out the world with Deathmagic. Sergio's orange godmagic surges through him, and I may not be able to see him with my eyes, but I can see him with my mind—a boy made of dancing orange godmagic particles.

It's all I need to avoid his arms racing down toward me, knives in hands. I block with my dagger, catching both invisible blades on their edges with a tremendous crash. Then I push myself away from him, careful to roll toward the center of the ring. Away from the invisible edges leading directly into the pool below.

This time when I spring to my feet I can see him. Or at least I can as long as I don't try to see him with my eyes. It gives me a slight headache, the contrast between the empty air that my eyes tell me is ahead of me and the swirling particles my mind knows are there. I'd close my eyes, but the last thing I need is to give Sergio another reason to accuse me of using Deathmagic. He lunges toward me and—there—just as his knives flip out to face me, they become visible.

Sergio throws one and I duck, the whir of sharp silver whizzing through the air where my shoulder was a second ago. He throws again, and this time I'm ready: My dagger knocks it out of the air and it clatters uselessly to the ground. I lunge for it, rolling as I snatch it off the ground, then spring up and throw it right back at him.

It embeds into the flesh above his knee.

He howls and staggers to a stop, red blooming in his particle form in my mind's eye. But now there's something to see—blood gathers around his right foot, and the dagger sticks solidly in the air, as if frozen in time, blood smearing the blade. Sergio rips the blade out of his leg with an agonized grunt and the blade vanishes, but his leg is still bleeding, leaving sticky red footprints where he steps.

"I'm going to kill you," he growls, a truly shocking declaration that I didn't foresee whatsoever. And then he's running toward me, his leg blooming redder, the visualization of pain spreading from his knee to his foot to his hip. He's ignoring tremendous pain right now, and I intend to make sure he can't.

Sergio's image flickers in and out in front of my eyes, his invisibility straining to keep together. I know all too well how distracting pain can be, particularly if you aren't used to tuning it out. A trail of red footsteps rushes toward me and I don't move. I think Sergio doesn't know I can see him yet. I keep him in my peripheral vision so it's not obvious I'm watching him, until, with a scream, his knives flash down.

I duck out from beneath his arms, twisting right, and plunge my dagger into his right hip, ripping it out as I twist away. Sergio screams and collapses, his leg giving out entirely. His invisibility flickers faster, like strobing lights at a rave, and his face is absolutely vicious. He glowers at me with a hatred I don't deserve. I haven't done shit to him, not really. But I suppose he expected this to be easy. He expected to be able to play with his prey, to terrify me before killing me. But now he's the one bleeding on the ground, shaking with pain and rage.

I have been here before. Countless times, looking down at an opponent who never questioned their ability to crush me under their feet. Insecure men and boys don't like being defeated by someone they see as beneath them.

I face him calmly, flipping my knives casually. "Yield."

Sergio laughs, the sound cold and hollow. Then, slowly, he pushes himself up to his feet. He's shivering from head to foot, his hold on his invisibility flickering so badly he looks transparent. Like a ghost. In my mind's eye the red of his pain has consumed his leg and hips and is spreading into his torso. But I have to give him credit, because he's standing.

"I will *never* yield to some lowtown cultist filth," he spits.

And then I suppose he pushes past the discomfort enough to focus, because he disappears. I watch his bloody footprints drag toward me as he staggers forward, barely lifting his injured leg. He evidently still hasn't figured out that I can see him even when invisible, his orange particle body lurching toward me, red mist blooming up his right side.

But then he does something I don't expect: He throws himself forward with a scream. Sergio crashes into my midsection, knocking me down, and I instantly realize I should not have let him near me, no matter how injured he is.

I move my arms before he can pin them and block his knives flashing toward me with my daggers. The blades sing against each other with a discordant crash, but even in his weakened state he is *strong,* and gravity is working in his favor.

Being on the ground in any fight is bad. But being on the

ground in a knife fight can be deadly. I can't stay here, waiting for my strength to give out or for Sergio to get a lucky strike in.

Then he leans in low, his face just inches from mine, the hatred in his eyes undeniable. "I'm going to kill you," he whispers, too quiet for the camera drones to pick up. "And then, when you're dead, I'm going to expose you. Everyone will know Crow of the Shallows was a Deathchild. They will *thank* me for exterminating you like the disease that you are."

"Go fuck yourself," I hiss back.

Then I thrust my hips up, jerking hard against his right injured hip and throwing him off-balance. He isn't ready for it, and I shove him hard, slamming my knife into his left hip. The blade hits bone so hard my arm jolts, and the sound that rips out of him is pure agony.

I pull my knife out and roll away from him, my hands slick with sweat and spattered with his blood.

Sergio does not stand. His entire midsection is the deep red of the worst kind of agony. He doesn't even bother camouflaging himself anymore—I don't think he can. He's lost a decent amount of blood, and with every second that passes, he loses more.

But blood isn't the only thing he's lost, and he knows it.

This time when I approach him, I kick the knives he's dropped out of his reach. This time when I sit on his chest, I pin his arms beneath my knees and hold my knife to his throat.

"Yield," I growl.

And somehow, still, Sergio laughs. "You don't get it," he says, his voice unexpectedly quiet. "You've lost, godkiller."

Some part of my brain knows he's said it too many times

for the cameras not to have caught it at least once. Some part of my body knows he's already painted a target on my back. Some part of my soul knows he's right, knows that even if we manage to laugh his suspicions off as ridiculous, there will always be whispers now. There will always be scrutiny. Doubt.

All because of one hateful boy who refuses to yield.

"I don't care if I've lost," Sergio continues, his voice just above a whisper. "You're dead. I'll prove to everyone what you are. You're done."

I don't know what proof he has, but it's clear: He'll never stop trying to destroy me in or out of the ring. I've robbed him of the opportunity to kill me for sport, which means all that's left is making sure I can never walk away from this.

Unless.

I have never killed. I could have many times; I faced many opponents in the Underground who wouldn't have thought twice about ending my life. And let's be clear—I am not a saint. I have maimed. I have disabled—sometimes permanently. I have made a man bleed and scream until he passed out. I have made opponents beg for mercy before yielding in pitiful sobs.

But I have never killed. I never needed to.

But then, my uncles lives have never been at stake.

Slowly, I release the pressure on Sergio's arms and stand.

I step away from him and pick up the two throwing knives he dropped—the ones I kicked out of his reach. I toss one at him, carelessly, allowing it to clatter just inches from his fingers.

I take ten long strides backward, watching as he stares, confused, at the knife I've just given him. "Get up," I say.

He looks at me, his eyes narrowed and calculating. And slowly, carefully, he pulls the knife into his grip and pushes himself up to his feet. His body is a beacon of agony—it pulses in my mind's eye like a strobe. Blood drips down his legs, pooling around his sneakers. He's already too pale, has already lost too much blood, and even as I try to make this as fair as possible, I know it isn't. He's weak. Badly injured. But I can't do anything about that without giving myself away, and that would ruin the point of all of this, wouldn't it?

Still, Sergio seems to understand what I'm trying to do, because he shakes his head with a wicked smile. "You won't kill me," he says. "Even now, when I could ruin your life, you're too much of a coward."

Scratch that. He doesn't understand, but I don't care. I'm not trying to win a moral high ground here, I'm just choosing an end to this match that I can live with.

"You have one throw," I tell him. "Go ahead."

Sergio shakes his head. "You're a fool."

Then a glint in his hand catches my eye—three shiny points catching the light just right. I have less than a second to process this before his arm whips forward like a snake and he screams, releasing not one, not two, but *three* knives.

Unprepared, I hurl myself out of the way. It's not graceful. Something slices through my leg in sharp, hot agony, and I land on the solid air on my shoulder in a way I know is going to bruise. But I don't stop. I roll out of my landing, using the momentum to twist as I let my knife fly.

My blade is a blur. Then blood bursts from Sergio's throat. He collapses first to his knees, reaching for the knife sticking out of his throat. But it's too late for that. Blood drips out of his mouth as he stares at me, wide-eyed. I have never watched someone die, not like this. And I know, instantly, instinctually, that I will never forget the shock on his face as blood bubbles out of his mouth and down his chin.

Then he falls face-first on the ground.

The crowd is roaring, but I barely hear them. The floor flickers to something solid beneath my feet. I'm literally centimeters from the edge. If I'd rolled slightly more to the left, I would have fallen right off the platform.

The announcer thunders my name to a the cheering crowd. I should feel something. I should feel anything. But it's as though I'm watching all this happen to someone else. I don't feel the ache throbbing in my leg. I don't feel the slick blood dripping down my leg.

I have won this match. I have moved on to the next round, a step closer to saving my uncles. I have silenced someone who promised to expose me. I am, unbelievably, a semifinalist.

And I don't feel anything at all.

CHAPTER 37

I just killed someone.

It's the only thought in my mind, the only reality blaring like an alarm in my skull. I just killed someone. Sergio was alive, and he was *terrible,* but he was alive and now he's—

The nausea comes on so suddenly, I have no way to prepare for it. I'm bent over somewhere in the understage, leaning against a wall, puking. I don't know when I started shaking, but I'm shivering all over and I can't stop. My teeth are chattering. My body is uncomfortably hot, a fever trying to burn away the reality of what I've done. And someone—someone is rubbing my back.

I blink blearily over my shoulder and find Lark, her expression soft and worried as she rubs circles into my back. Chaos and Maddox are next to her, arms crossed, glowering at anyone who so much as glances at me. And for some reason seeing the three of them here, watching over me, trying to offer a shield and comfort, breaks me. I stand on trembling legs, sweating and shaking and tears streaming down my cheeks.

Lark pulls me into a hug, and I press my face hard into her

shoulder. She holds me, and two pairs of strong arms join in on the hug. The pressure of their tight hold is the only thing keeping me from shaking apart. It's exactly what I need, and I'm silently crying before I can stop myself.

I just killed someone.

I didn't have a choice, I know that—Sergio all but swore to expose me, which would have meant facing my own execution the moment the competition is over. But I ended a life, and I can never undo that.

Lark murmurs something to Chaos, but I don't catch the words. Then she turns her face back to me. "C'mon," she says softly. I've never heard her voice like this. The tenderness and worry that permeate every syllable. "Let's get back to the suite."

Maddox offers me a pair of dark sunglasses. For a second I don't understand why—we're still inside, after all—but then I blink my swollen eyes and it all makes sense. I put the sunglasses on, grateful for a modicum of privacy. Not that I can expect much after puking in front of sponsors and staff.

We move through a blur of stairs and hallways, a brief walk outside, and into an elevator. I don't really register any of it. The world has become a reel of inconsequential images around me. Nothing matters. I just need to hold myself together for another minute, another second, just until we make it back to the suite. Just until that door closes behind us and we have privacy at last.

Then the elevator doors open. I step into the suite that, somehow, has begun to feel like safety. The moment the doors close behind us, I'm shivering all over again, my teeth chattering in my mouth. Lark pulls me into her arms again, and this time I let myself cry. Not the silent tears I couldn't hold back in the understage, but full-on sobs.

"I killed him," I sob into Lark's shoulder.

"I know," Lark says softly, holding me tight.

The words stumble out of me between stuttering gasps. "He said he didn't care if he won or lost, he was going to tell everyone—" It's only then, with the word on the tip of my tongue, that I remember Maddox still doesn't know I'm a Deathchild. I can't process whether it's safe to tell him, not right now when I can barely think beyond the events of the last half hour. But I don't have to. Lark holds me while Chaos and Maddox rub my back, and they don't pry. They tell me it's okay. I'll be okay.

It doesn't feel like I'll ever be okay again. The guilt gnaws deep and hot, burrowing into me relentlessly.

It doesn't feel like I deserve to be okay.

Eventually, Chaos and Maddox step away while Lark guides me to her room, Mouse chirping at my feet as she follows. It's odd, sitting on Lark's bed in a completely different context from two days ago. Unreal. I feel as though I'm floating away from my body as Lark closes the door and Mouse hops onto my lap. Lark crouches in front of me and takes my arms in her hands, squeezing gently at my wrists, then working up my forearms. It brings me back to my body. I'm here. In Lark's room. Mouse purring on my lap. And Lark is holding me.

"You're safe," she says, her voice feather soft.

"I'm a horrible person," I cry.

Lark jerks back, like I slapped her. "Look at me," she demands, the gentleness in her voice gone.

My vision is blurred and my eyelids feel heavy, but I do. She searches my eyes, her expression tinged with something like concern. "You are Crow of the Shallows. You are a survivor, because that's what this world demanded of you. Sergio tried to kill you and promised to expose you, knowing full well what it would mean. You are *not* a horrible person for defending yourself."

"But—"

"No." Lark holds my gaze, her hands squeezing my arms. "He wanted you dead. He wanted you ruined. If you hadn't killed him, I would have."

My mouth drops open before I can stop it. "You can't mean that."

Lark arches an eyebrow. "Do you doubt me?" The seriousness in her face dispels any uncertainty. I swallow hard and shake my head.

Her shoulders relax. "Good." She gently wipes my wet cheeks with her fingers, leaving my skin buzzing with warmth. "Only *I* get to antagonize you. Don't forget it."

It's only then, as she lets her hands fall into her lap, that I notice her wrists.

They're bare.

My stomach plummets, and I need to ask, but I already know the answer. Lark's last match was right before mine, but I couldn't see the result since I was up next. "Your ticket . . ." I whisper.

Lark's lips press firmly into a thin, false smile. "Don't worry about it," she says. "I'm fine."

I'm too wrung out to argue with her, but if Lark is out of the Tournament, it means she's indebted to Dez. And if Lark thinks I'm going to let that stand, she doesn't know me at all.

CHAPTER 38

The morning after next I find myself standing in the elevator outside Dez's suite. It's early—probably earlier than it's socially appropriate to knock on someone's door. But after barely sleeping the last two nights wrestling with both waves of paralyzing anxiety and joint pain that forced me to pull out the hot compresses and painkillers, it was the longest I could make myself wait.

And anyway, I want to make sure I finish my conversation with Dez before Lark wakes up.

So, even cringing while I do, I knock.

Some shuffling inside gets my heart racing, and I take a deep breath and pull my shoulders back. I have to look casual. Or at least not half as nervous as I actually am.

Then the door swings open and I'm staring up at a daughter of Discord who looks less than thrilled to see me.

"Well, this should be good," she says before turning around and walking back inside. She leaves the door open, though, so I follow her inside before it closes behind us.

Dez's suite looks identical to ours, except she's the only one in it. She flops down on the sectional in the center of the living area, her long legs taking up most of one side of it as she grabs a nearby mug, still steaming. I sit across from her as she nurses her drink. The purple ends of her black hair are strewn over her eyes, and she's wearing what appears to be a long black silk robe with matching pj pants.

"Well?" she snaps.

"Sorry," I say quickly, though I'm not sure what I'm apologizing for. "I'm here about Lark."

"Of course you are," she says, sounding utterly unsurprised. "I knew you'd come to me eventually, about either Lark or your uncles. Interesting that Lark won out."

I blink. "My . . . uncles?"

She levels me with an entirely unimpressed stare. "Surely you haven't forgotten about your imprisoned uncles."

My face goes hot. "Obviously not. I just—"

"Didn't think I knew about them?" She smirks. "Child, I know everything that goes on in the Shallows. *Especially* the lawbreaking variety. Your uncles were running a very smooth operation for years. Unfortunate that they got caught, though it was probably inevitable. Too many pieces in play. And they weren't interested in working with me, which I respect."

It honestly had never occurred to me that Dez would be aware of what my uncles were doing, let alone care about it enough to offer to work with them, but it doesn't surprise me that my uncles said no. There's always a price for working with Dez, and it's rarely worth whatever you get in return.

They would hate that I'm here. *I* hate that I'm here. But at least where Lark's concerned, Dez was already involved, so there was no getting around that.

I hesitate. "Does that mean . . . you'd be willing to help them get out of prison?"

Dez laughs. *Actually* laughs. "Absolutely not. It's far too late for that, especially now that you've made yourself so well-known up here."

My stomach sinks. I hadn't thought of that, but Dez is right.

She shakes her head. "No, your best bet in helping your uncles now is winning this thing. Which I'm assuming was the plan to begin with."

"Yeah," I say softly. "I just . . . really wanted a backup plan."

Dez snorts. "There was never going to be a way for you to get them out without putting a target on your back. Your uncles know that." She puts her mug down on the coffee table and sits up. "But enough about impossible plans. You came here for Lark, so go on. What do you want?"

I take a deep breath, pushing my uncles out of my mind, at least for now. Dez is right. I didn't come here for my uncles. I came here for Lark. I can still help Lark.

"I . . . don't know the specifics of the deal you made with Lark," I say slowly, "but I know she's probably indebted to you now that she's lost."

"Correct," Dez says nonchalantly.

"How much does she owe you?"

Dez laughs. "Much more than you'll ever be able to afford."

"Unless I win," I reply. "That's what you were counting on with Lark, isn't it? In addition to the boon, the winner gets a generous yearly stipend for the rest of their life. And you wanted—what? A chunk of it?"

"Twenty-five percent for ten years," Dez responds, picking up her mug with a smile. "That was my agreement with Lark."

My mouth nearly falls open. Twenty-five percent for *ten years*? Granted, that still leaves a person more than enough to live on very comfortably, but gods above and below, that's a lot of money.

"And . . . now that she's lost?" I ask, almost not wanting to know the answer.

"Ten years in my service." Dez smiles. "Unless of course . . . you have a counteroffer?"

This is a bad idea. Making a deal with Dez cannot work in my favor—either way, she's going to win. But if I have a chance to help Lark, shouldn't I take it? I can't just sit back and watch while Lark throws the next decade of her life away, not while I have the power to do something about it.

And anyway, if I lose this competition, what life is left for me? I'll have nothing to return to. My uncles will be dead, my home destroyed.

I've already bet my life on this competition. What's one more risk?

"I'll take on your agreement with Lark," I say. "If I win, I'll give you twenty-five percent of my stipend for ten years."

"And if you lose, both you *and* Lark will serve me for ten years," Dez says.

I bristle. "That isn't what I meant. I meant I'd take Lark's place."

"I know what you meant. No deal—I already *have* Lark; why would I give that up on the chance that *maybe* you'll take her place? My counteroffer is if you lose, I get you both. You're lucky I'm not asking for more of your winnings."

"You can have more of my winnings if you cut Lark out entirely," I counter.

Dez looks at me for an uncomfortably long time, clacking her dark purple painted nails on the steaming mug in her hand. Just when I think she's going to stare me down until I crack, she says, "Fifty percent for ten years."

It's an outrageous amount of money and it takes everything in me to keep my face neutral. "Thirty-three percent."

"Forty percent, final offer."

I grit my teeth, but it's clear Dez isn't going to budge on this. "Fine," I say reluctantly. "But Lark is free, even if I lose."

Dez's eyes gleam dangerously. "She'll be free the moment you sign the agreement."

I nod. "And don't tell Chaos about this."

She snorts. "My dealings are none of my baby brother's business." She stands and disappears into one of the bedrooms, emerging less than a minute later holding what looks like a shiny black fountain-tip pen and a small black notebook. She sits across from me again, rolls up her sleeve to just above the elbow, and presses the tip of the pen to the crook of her arm. I watch in horror as blood wells around the tip of the pen, then flows *into* the pen, like it's sucking up Dez's blood.

Which is when I realize Dez is holding a blood oath pen.

I swallow hard, forcing myself to stay. Blood oaths use rune-magic written in the mixed blood of both people in the pact to make it unbreakable. If you try to betray a blood oath, you die. Slowly. Painfully.

This is the kind of magic you run away from. The kind of magic you agree to only in the most desperate of circumstances. The kind of magic my uncles would be devastated to hear I agreed to.

And yet, when Dez leans forward and holds her hand out

for my arm, I extend my left arm. She nods and switches out the pen tip with a fresh one ("For sanitary reasons," she says), then brings the pen to just above the crook of my elbow.

"Last chance to back out," she says, looking me in the eye. "There's no shame in walking away now."

I take a deep breath and think of Lark. Lark, who has been there from the very beginning. Lark, who has defended me again and again in the competition. Lark, who has pulled me from the brink of panic more than once.

Even when we fought, even when seeing her made me furious, even when I wished she would leave, Lark has always had my back.

Now it's time I have hers.

"I'm sure," I say.

The pen bites deep. My arm jerks, but Dez has a strong grip on my forearm. I bite my lip as a stinging *pulling* sensation builds in my arm, but then Dez yanks the pen away and it's over. She offers me a wadded-up bit of tissue, which I press against the small wound. Then she switches out the pen tip one more time. Once it's attached, she shakes the pen, mixing our blood in the cartridge, and opens her notebook.

Dez flips through what must be close to a hundred pages of rusty brown writing, and I realize with a start these are all blood oaths. She finds a blank page and scrawls out some runes at the top that I recognize as binding runes. The rest she writes out plainly, laying out the terms of our agreement with two lines at the bottom. She signs one, turns the notebook around, and offers me the pen.

I look over the contract she's written one more time, just to be sure, but it's exactly what we agreed to—no more, no less. Even the runes she used to set up the binding agreement are common and easy to understand. She isn't trying to trick me.

This is what we agreed to, I remind myself.

I take the pen and sign my name in blood.

CHAPTER 39

I find myself once again in unbelievably fancy clothes. It's the same deep green suit as last time, but this time my vest and tie are black, and at my request Chaos has lined my eyes in kohl while Maddox painted my nails black. It's a quiet touch, but I still look masculine, still boyish in a way I like.

I grin at my reflection as Mouse rubs against my legs and purrs, getting her gray fur all over my pants. Chaos chuckles next to me. "Look at you, checking yourself out." My face reddens, but he throws his hands up. "No! Don't stop, it's good. You *should* check yourself out—you look hot."

"Mm-hmm," Maddox agrees in a low hum.

Hearing Chaos and Maddox confirm how I feel about my appearance makes my face warm for an entirely different reason. "Thanks," I say, picking up Mouse and scratching behind her ears. "You sure you can't come with me? If Lark hadn't been there last time, I would have broken Astrid's nose."

Chaos grimaces. "Unfortunately, sponsors aren't invited to the semifinalists' dinner. We have our own event—no guests."

"I'm fine staying here this time," Maddox says.

"You could ask Lark to keep you company," says Chaos. "You can convince her of my offer to join the team."

Chaos officially extended Lark an invitation this morning, and she said she'd think about it. Whatever that means.

It scares me a little, how badly I want her to stay. But I won't pressure her. It should be her decision.

"Are there any rules against bringing cats?" I joke, holding Mouse up.

Chaos laughs. "Like you would subject Mouse to *Astrid*."

He has me there. I smile softly, give Mouse a kiss on the head (much to her chagrin), and put her down. She trots over to Maddox and hops up on his lap, purring as she rubs against him. Maddox pets her with a smile.

Then the elevator door opens and Lark storms into the room, fury twisting her features as her gaze locks on me.

"How *dare* you?" Her voice shakes with rage. I don't think I've ever seen her this furious before, and for a moment my mind goes blank.

And then I know. I made a terrible miscalculation in not asking Dez to keep our deal from Lark too.

Lark doesn't wait for a response. "What were you thinking? Making a deal with *Dez*? There was no godsdamned reason for you to risk yourself like that, you bone-headed—"

"You did *what*?" Chaos interrupts, his eyes wide. "Crow, are you serious?"

So much for keeping it from Chaos.

"It's not a big deal if I win," I say.

Lark throws her hands up.

"And if you *don't?*" Chaos nearly yells.

"I only agreed to what Lark agreed to," I say, the heat in my face spreading to my chest. "If it wasn't a big deal for *Lark,* I don't see why it should matter that I agreed to similar terms so she'd be free from Dez."

"I don't *care* what agreement Lark had with Dez!" Chaos shouts. He glances at Lark and adds, more calmly, "No offense, Lark."

"No, go on." Lark crosses her arms over her chest.

Chaos shakes his head and turns back to me. "I didn't sponsor Lark, Crow. I sponsored *you.* I'm supposed to support *you.* What decisions Lark makes aren't my responsibility or my problem. You should have talked to me about this first. We could have found another solution!"

I feel like a reprimanded child in a way I resent. I really don't think there was going to be another way to save Lark from the consequences of her own decisions. I didn't tell Chaos *because* I didn't want him to talk me out of it.

"Well, I didn't, and I can't undo what I agreed to even if I wanted to."

Chaos frowns. "Maybe if we talk to my sister—"

"It was a blood pact," I interrupt. "Sealed with runemagic."

Chaos stares at me for a long, heavy moment. Then he shakes his head and sits next to Maddox on a nearby cushioned bench.

"Shit, Crow," Maddox says quietly, throwing his arm around Chaos.

"Yeah." Finally, I meet Lark's gaze, which is still shimmering with unspent rage. "Look, I'm sorry I went behind your back to do it, but I knew you wouldn't agree to it. You've had my back all this time, Lark, and I wanted to have yours for once. Now, no matter what happens, you're free."

Then the shine in Lark's eyes spills over onto her cheeks, and it hits me that the shimmering I assumed was anger was actually unshed tears. My breath catches. Lark is crying. Lark is *crying* and it's *my* fault.

"You absolute fool," she hisses. "Why do you think I signed up for this competition to begin with?"

This stumps me. I asked her once why she would do this, and she told me off for even asking. *What, it's only reasonable for you to risk your life to change it?*

"You said—"

"Forget what I said!" The tears are really streaming down her cheeks now, and it is absolutely breaking me. I have never seen Lark cry. Not like this. And still, I don't understand what she's trying to tell me.

"I don't know why you entered," I admit after too long a pause. "Why *did* you?"

"I *entered* because of *you*, you booby-headed—"

"You scoffed at me for even implying you were jealous!" I exclaim, outraged.

Lark laughs, actually laughs, but the sound is hollow and pained. "Gods above and below, Crow—I didn't enter because I was jealous! I entered *to look after you!*"

The admission quiets everything inside me. Every protest. Every infuriated retort. I don't have a comeback for that because I didn't see it coming at all. It never occurred to me— to *look after me?*

"What?" I gasp, and my voice cracks.

Lark wipes at her eyes furiously, shaking her head. "Is it really that unbelievable?"

"But—you don't even like me most of the time!" I protest. "Why would you need to look after me?"

I mean, sure, we had that one night . . . but you don't have to like someone to make out with them. Not that I dislike Lark, not anymore; I just—I don't understand.

Lark laughs again. "You're right, I don't like you. I've just been in love with you since I was six and resented you for that fact for just as long."

"I'm . . . starting to think Chaos and I shouldn't be here," Maddox says into the awkward silence that follows.

Lark shakes her head, wiping at her eyes again, which despite her best efforts are still steadily releasing tears. "It's fine. I'll go." She turns away.

I'm moving before I even register that's what I want to do. I catch Lark's shoulder and she looks back, a question in her eyes.

And then I'm kissing her.

I'm kissing her with years of misplaced resentment melting away. I'm kissing her with a plea for her to stay here with me. I'm kissing her with the admission that I need her with me. That I have always needed her with me, whether I wanted to admit it or not.

When I pull away, I whisper, "Stay. Please."

Lark bites her lip and wipes at her eyes one final time. "Okay." Then, softly, "I've never been very good at walking away from you anyway."

"Aww," Chaos says, to which Lark and I both give him the finger.

Chaos laughs. He knows there's no malice behind it, because Lark and I are both smiling. I don't know where we go from here. I don't know how to picture this new chapter of us.

But when Lark asks, "What do we do now?" I know the answer.

"Well," I say, "first you have to officially join my team. Then I guess we better make sure I don't lose."

CHAPTER 40

✕✕✕

A fancy car brings me to the Uppercity less than a mile from Godlevel. If downtown is a bustling city of clean streets and neon advertisements, the Uppercity is all pristine streets and marble buildings. Everything here is made to look like old money, from classical columns in front of stately buildings to large, precisely manicured gardens and enormous fountains with granite statues in the centers. Even the tiles on the sidewalk are polished stone that glitter in the warm streetlight.

It's not that it isn't nice—I mean, obviously everything is made to look beautiful. But that's just it. It all feels staged, like what I guess I'd imagine the inside of a museum to look like. (Come to think of it, there *are* probably museums up here.) Nothing here feels lived-in or used. It's like I wouldn't want to touch anything for fear of messing it up.

What adds to the eerily perfect atmosphere is the absolute silence of the car I'm in. It's self-driven and I'm completely alone in the cabin. Every drink I could possibly imagine is available to me in an enormous digital menu embedded in the divider between the passenger seats and the empty front seats, but I'm too nervous to drink anything but bottled water.

I haven't even left the car yet, and I already feel so out of place.

The car rolls up in front of a restaurant called Luxe, which sounds so pretentious I want to leave immediately. But before I can even consider skipping what is sure to be an awful night, a valet dressed in all white opens the door for me and gestures with a flourish and a bow.

"Welcome to Luxe, semifinalist Crow. May I guide you inside?"

"Uh," I say, "sure."

The moment I step out, the camera drones swarm on me, taking photos and filming my entrance. Chaos warned me about this, so I do what he suggested, which is to ignore them entirely and follow the valet inside. He opens a truly massive gold-and-glass door with a long gold handle. He bows and flourishes again, I suppose indicating I should go inside. When I step through the doors, he follows me in, closing the door behind us.

"The drones are not permitted inside, so you should have some privacy here. Unlike the last competitors' dinner, this one is not televised." He hesitates, then adds, "And you're welcome to keep your mask on if you prefer, but we do have state-of-the-art air filtration installed, so it should be safe."

"Yes," says a man behind me, and I actually jump a little. He's dressed in a tux and looks at the valet down his nose in a way that makes the valet wither and lower his head. The tuxedoed man flicks his hand at the valet like one might shoo away an annoying pest, and to my horror the valet turns and marches back outside, looking properly chastised.

So I already hate this new guy.

"You'll find this to be a more *exclusive* event," the tuxedoed man says, practically drawling his emphasis of *exclusive*. "Nothing like that pedestrian affair you suffered through four nights ago."

I consider keeping my mask on simply so I don't have to hide my disgust. But seeing as I will have to remove it to eat anyway, I reluctantly slide it off and tuck it in my pocket. The host nods and leads me inside.

The restaurant is enormous. The host leads me through the center of a three-wing dining room full of diners dressed in their finest to a huge wooden spiral staircase made of gleaming, polished oak. I follow him up to the third floor, the clamor of the patrons below falling away. Unlike the open enormous dining room of the first floor, this floor has three ornate black doors, one to the left, one directly ahead, and one to the right. The host walks up to the door in the center, his shoes echoing on the hardwood, and holds it open for me.

I step inside. My eyes go wide as I take in the enormity of the room. The domed ceiling is ridiculously high and made of glass so you can make out the stars and moon above. In the center of the room is a long dining table undoubtedly way too large for just four people. Two upholstered chairs are set out on each side, facing each other. The host brings me to the only empty space left, a chair to a blond boy's left—if I remember correctly from Lark talking about the other contestants, his name is Luka—which is a bit of a relief only because it means I don't have to sit next to Astrid.

"The first course will be out shortly," the host says after I take a seat.

I only vaguely recognize the contestant sitting across from me—a short person with light brown skin and long turquoise hair pulled back in a ponytail, showing off bleached undercut sides. I'm pretty sure their name is Lore, and like Luka and Astrid they're from the Uppercity. Which means I'm the only one left who isn't. And not only am I not from the Uppercity, I'm not even from Midlevel.

No one from the Shallows has ever made it this far.

I should be smug. I *deserve* to be smug. But all I can see are the barriers that have kept Shallowsfolk from success like this for so long. The lack of access to medical resources. To steady nutrition and education. To homes not filled with mold and rot. To an easy existence, not constantly worried about paying next month's rent or finding the resources to pay for your next meal. To *clean air.*

To a home without sewage-filled water pumped in to drown us.

There are so many reasons why we haven't made it this far before, and none of them have to do with skill.

"Congratulations," someone says, and it takes me a moment to register Lore is talking to me.

I honestly wasn't expecting anyone to even acknowledge my presence here, at least not without tormenting me for it.

"Oh," I say, doing a poor job hiding my surprise. "Thanks. You too."

Lore nods, and four servers dressed in all white emerge with silver covered platters, each unveiling a small shallow bowl with four large seared bacon-wrapped scallops plated in a pool of melted butter.

I swear to the gods my mouth actually waters.

Every course is similarly decadent: crunchy salad with some kind of rich dressing; a bowl of delicate soup that warms me pleasantly from the inside out; perfectly tender steak that may actually be the softest, juiciest cut of meat I've eaten in my life; and a chocolate mousse that melts in my mouth. To my surprise, I make it through all the courses without a single incident. I mean, Luka and Astrid don't shut up for a second, but they're easy enough to tune out, and Lore eats quietly across from me. It's almost pleasant.

Then Lore leans toward me and whispers, "The key is remembering it's not real."

My gaze shoots up from the bowl now sadly empty of chocolate mousse. They look at me and nod at my frown, as if to confirm I heard them correctly. But I don't know what on earth that's supposed to mean. Remembering *what* isn't real? This meal? The pomp and circumstance? The competition?

And that's when a huge fucking spider like the one that scared the shit out of me at the last fancy dinner scurries down the table toward me. Suddenly their words make all the sense in the world.

Lark's voice comes back to me: *Astrid is a Mindchild. An illusionist.* Which means the spider is an illusion, but as it crawls into my dessert bowl and peers over the lip with eight beady black eyes, I can't help the sweat dripping down the back of my neck. This is the largest spider I've seen in my life—the body is easily the size of my open hand, without even counting its long hairy legs.

Gods above and below, why did it have to be *spiders*?

It's not real, I remind myself. But that doesn't mean it doesn't *feel* real. I *felt* the illusion of the spider touching my hand last time. If it can touch me, does that mean it can hurt me? Can Astrid trick me into thinking I've been injured when I haven't? What are the limits to her illusions?

And why do I have to figure it out over dinner?

A server swoops in on my left and picks up the bowl with the massive spider in it. For a split second I think I'm safe because the illusion will vanish with my bowl, but then something heavy lands in my lap.

Oh gods. Oh gods.

It's not real, I chant in my mind. *It' s not real, it's not real, it's not real—*

But gods if it doesn't *feel* real. I make the mistake of glancing down, and the spider begins crawling slowly up my suit jacket, the weight of it pulling my jacket down.

Don't panic, I tell myself. *Don't give her the satisfaction of making me freak out* again. *It's not real. Just breathe.*

But the spider keeps crawling, over my belly and up to my chest. It's so close to my face. In seconds it'll touch my jaw. And if that thing touches my face, illusion or not, I don't know how I'll keep my shit together.

Which is when a gasp like a screech breaks me out of my terror. My gaze shoots up to across the table, where Lore is standing, their hands covering their mouth. And Astrid is red-faced in her fury.

"What is *wrong* with you?" Luka yells, scowling at Lore.

"Oh my gods, I'm *so* sorry!" Lore says. "I *completely forgot* my glass was right there. I'm *so embarrassed.* Here, oh my gods, I hope that doesn't ruin your dress." They grab their cloth napkin and offer it to Astrid, who is standing and glaring down at her absolutely drenched skirt. It's soaked through with some kind of red juice. I blink, trying to piece together what I missed. Lore's drink glass is knocked over. Did they . . . deliberately spill their drink on her?

"It's fucking cranberry juice!" Astrid shrieks. "What do you think? Of *course* my dress is ruined!"

It's only then that I realize the spider is gone. Lore must have broken Astrid's concentration when they spilled their drink.

"Ohh," Lore croons. "I'm so sorry about that. Complete accident, such a tragedy. It really *was* a beautiful dress. Lady Bella, right?"

I don't understand the question, but this only seems to make Astrid angrier. Her face purples as she dabs furiously at her stained dress. "Lady Bella? Are you joking? This is a Leonidas original!"

Lore gasps in a way that is absolutely exaggerated and they don't care who knows it. Astrid, somehow, doesn't seem to notice. "Not a Leonidas! Oh *no*, I'm *so* sorry." Then they look at me and wink.

I tilt my glass at them in a toast and finish my drink with a smile.

***

"So Lore seems decent," I say. I've just finished my retelling of the dinner's events, two hours after the cranberry juice incident. Lark is grinning wider than I've ever seen, Maddox is laughing, and Chaos is clapping.

"Did we just join Team Lore?" Chaos asks. "I think we just did."

I laugh. "It's too bad I might have to fight them in the final round if they survive their match with Astrid."

"They're a pretty solid mage," Lark says. "It's possible they might win. But Astrid's been adept at disorienting her opponents with her Mindmagic illusions. Whoever you face, it won't be easy."

Lark, unlike me, has actually been studying her opponents before the matches from the very beginning. I half expected her to stop after she lost last round, but she opted to join my team as the *strategist,* so now it's her entire job to be in everyone's business, I guess.

I flop onto the sofa next to her. Mouse hops onto my lap and curls up in a purring ball. I smile and run my hand down her silky-soft back. "You sure seem confident I'll beat Luka in two days."

Lark snorts. "If you *don't* beat him, I might have to kick your ass in retaliation."

"Is he a mage or godchild?" Maddox asks.

"Godchild," Lark answers without hesitation. "Specifically an elemental Architectchild. He can fly, and so far he's won by basically picking up his opponents and dropping them in the pool."

I stare at her. "Seriously?"

"Mm-hmm." Lark smirks. "But he won't be able to do that tomorrow, because the parameters of the match have been set and not to his favor. Weapons will be permitted, including rune-spelled objects, but magic won't be. Both of you will fight tomorrow wearing suppressors."

Now *that* is interesting. And unfortunately it means I won't be able to use Deathmagic to suss out Luka's weaknesses. "Damn," I say. "Too bad I couldn't fight Astrid without her illusions."

"True," Chaos says, "but maybe it'll give Lore a chance."

"Maybe." To be honest, I'm not sure who'd I'd prefer to fight in the final round. Astrid I know would be a beast to go against, but it'd also be *so satisfying* to beat her if I managed it. Lore, on the other hand, doesn't have illusion magic, but they *are* an excellent mage according to Lark, and after the way they embarrassed the shit out of Astrid tonight, I can't help but feel a small seed of affection toward them.

I suppose at the end of the day my feelings on the matter are unimportant. And anyway, I still have to get through my match with Luka.

"Okay, *strategist*," I say, scooching toward Lark to make room for Maddox and Chaos on my left. "So taking Luka's flight out of it, how does he fight?"

"Well, that's the tricky part." Lark turns on the TV and navigates to on-demand replays of the earlier matches. She pulls up Luka's first match, which was against a mage I don't recognize. Right from the beginning, Luka takes off into the air, swooping around and dodging the mage's magic attacks until he dives down, grabs his opponent, and drops him into the pool. Just like Lark said.

"He's used that same exact strategy for *every* match," Lark says.

"How about the opening round?" Chaos asks, pulling a ball of bright purple yarn out of his bag and a long hook with some sort of cord and stopper attached to it.

"I checked that," Lark said. "There's nothing earth-shattering there. Remember that tower that the three of us ended up in?"

"The one with the beetles that tried to eat us that Maddox pretended not to be able to help with?" I ask.

Lark snickers and Maddox smiles sheepishly. "I already apologized for that!"

I stick my tongue out at him.

Lark rolls her eyes. "*Anyway*, yeah, that one. Turns out Luka found a cache almost immediately, then sat on the tower the whole time. He flies up there within the first five minutes and just waits the whole thing out."

"A beacon of courage, our Luka," Maddox says, resting his head on Chaos's shoulder.

"Yeah, he's a real keeper," Lark deadpans. "Best-case scenario, that's his only trick, but I think it's in our interest to assume otherwise. We should go in assuming he's excellent at hand-to-hand combat—he just hasn't been forced to use it. Tomorrow he will be."

"Speaking of," Maddox says, "I submitted your daggers to the weapons rack for the match in two days. I took the liberty of making a small adjustment—now hold on, don't give me that look." He laughs at my narrowed eyes. "It doesn't affect the weight or use of the daggers at all. You know how you squeeze the hilt to release or retract the blade?"

I nod cautiously.

"Well, with the added rune spell, now the grips will recognize only *your* touch. So if someone else grabs your knives off you, the blades will retract and all they'll have are empty hilts." He beams, confident in his enhancement. And he should be. It's a good addition.

"Huh," I say. "Smart. Thanks, Mads."

"Awww, you used my nickname! Does this mean we're friends now?"

I gesture to Maddox's hip, which is pressed tightly against mine, even as he leans against Chaos. "I'm not usually this cozy with people I *don't* consider friends."

"I wouldn't judge you if you were, but fair enough."

"What weapon do you think Luka will pick?" Lark muses.

"He's an Uppercity kid, so I can only assume the most pompous weapon possible," I say.

Maddox grins. "Which is?"

"Saber," I say. "You know, like for fencing."

We all laugh. "I wasn't expecting you to have an answer ready," Chaos says through his snickers.

"Wait, why is fencing pompous?" Maddox asks, though he's laughing too. "It's a sword—doesn't that count for anything?"

"Have you *seen* a fencing saber?" I ask. "It's skinny as fuck—practically a needle. It, like, flops if you shake it. And anyway, it's more about the rules of fencing rather than the weapon itself—it's such a rule-oriented sport. Really impractical for an actual fight."

"Which means it's a perfect weapon for an Uppercity kid," Lark says.

"Exactly. It's the weapon of choice for someone who's never been punched in the face." I smile at the image of punching Luka in the face. It's not as satisfying as the image of punching Astrid in the face, but I'll take it.

"I don't know," Maddox says dubiously. "You *really* think no one has punched Luka in the face before? He's so . . . punchable."

"I could be wrong about what culture is like in the Upper-city, but I suspect punching people is frowned upon there."

Chaos stares at me like he isn't sure whether or not I'm joking.

"What?" I ask.

He laughs slightly. "I mean . . . is it *not* frowned upon to punch someone in the Shallows?"

We all shrug.

"I mean, sure," Maddox says, "but more because you're likely to get punched right back, immediately, and not because someone else will do something about it. Enforcers don't really care what we do to each other unless it somehow becomes a problem for *them*."

"It's not like people go around punching each other all the time in the Shallows, though," Lark clarifies. "But that's because it's a close-knit community. If you get a reputation for being an asshole, no one's going to want to help you when you need it. And you *will* eventually need it."

"So, no, I don't think Luka's been punched yet," I say with a smile. "I look forward to changing that the day after tomorrow, though."

With that, I lean against Maddox with a smile, who's still leaning against Chaos. Maddox smiles and throws his arm around me. Lark stares at all three of us with an arched eyebrow. I grin and grab her arm, pulling her against me. She squawks in protest, but it's not a real protest, and soon she's leaning against me too with a pout that tells me she doesn't actually hate it at all.

"If he *does* pick a saber, you should use the staff," Lark says.

I groan.

We've almost finished watching the rest of Luka's fights when my phone buzzes with a text from Jimena.

R and I have been working on the project throughout the city. More soon. In the meantime, you should see this.

Below the text is a clip from the news.

Chaos must notice me frowning at it, because he asks, "What's that?" I turn the phone around and he raises his eyebrows. "Can I see?"

I hand him my phone, and a few seconds later the news clip replaces the replay of Luka's match. The clip starts with some drone footage of a thick crowd amassed in front of one of the many huge screens always playing in the Shallows. Instead of endless commercials or a presidential address, the screen is playing one of the matches from the Tournament—which is normal enough. What throws me is seeing *my* face on the screen as I fight Sergio. The reminder of how that match ended is nauseating, and I look away before reliving that awful moment, but then the crowd erupts in cheers.

"Shallowsfolk are flocking to viewing centers like this one in record numbers to cheer on their last remaining competitor, Crow of the Shallows," a newscaster says over the footage. *"We have Dom on the ground to get a sense for the mood in the Shallows as Crow advances in the competition. Dom?"*

The video cuts to a trimly dressed man—Dom, presumably—standing in front of a tattoo shop I'm pretty sure is just a couple blocks from the Underground. Next to him is a man in a beanie and a black tank top showing off an arm bandaged from the top of his shoulder to his wrist.

"I'm here in front of Inked Souls, one of the many tattoo

shops that have been flooded with clients recently, like Moss here. Moss, could you tell us about your experience and your new tattoo?"

"My cousin is one of the tattoo artists; otherwise I'd have been waiting for months for an appointment. Everyone wants Crow ink." Then he peels off the bandage, showing off a tattoo sleeve smeared in clear ointment. The camera zooms in on the design and my mouth drops open.

It's crows. A flock of them overlapping the entirety of his arm, their beaks sharp and talons glistening. Their feathers are so detailed, they look like they could fly right out of his skin.

Everyone wants Crow ink.

"The Shallows loves Murder of Crows," Moss says. "We're so proud to see him fighting for us, and we've got their back."

My vision blurs with tears. The newscaster keeps talking, but I can barely hear him.

"Damn," Maddox says behind me. "Now *I* want Crow ink."

I laugh and wipe at my face as Lark gently squeezes my arm, but I can't stop smiling. Seeing their support—it means everything.

We watch the clip two more times like that, in a tangle of warm bodies and soft clothes. And as I drift off to sleep, I can't help but think that this right here, surrounded by the warmth of my friends, is exactly where I'm supposed to be.

CHAPTER 41

✕

I can't hold back my laugh when Luka selects a saber out of the weapons lineup two days later. He looks at me with an expression somewhere between disgust and confusion. I flash him a smile as I grab my two long daggers off the table, retract the blades into their hilts with a squeeze, and pocket them in the sheaths attached to my belt.

I can practically hear Lark yelling at me to grab the staff instead, and strategically she's probably right. But daggers are my best weapon, and since I'm cut off from magic, I want to use every advantage I can.

Once the weapons are selected, an attendant attaches a cold metal cuff around my ankle—the dampener. A rush of ice races up my ankle and through the rest of my body in a flash that makes me shiver. I'm still allowed to keep my numbing gloves on, which is a relief, but I won't be able to call on my godmagic or access runemagic as long as this cuff is on.

Rising into the arena for the fourth time feels familiar in a way I don't know how to feel about. The roar of the crowd as we become visible is near deafening. This time I catch my name in the screams along with Luka's. There are even small groups of people holding posters with my name on it.

It is extremely weird to think I have Midlevel fans.

Weirder still to think that if I hadn't been forced to enter the Tournament to save my uncles' lives, I might not have minded being here.

The platform slows to a halt as the pool fills up below us. I glance around, waiting for the arena to change like it has every other time. There are six glowing blue concentric circles from the center to the edge. And it's unclear what they mean.

The screens above our heads cut to a face I don't recognize at first—a man with skin like white marble and hair to match slicked neatly back. He's sitting in a VIP box in an all-white suit and tie, appearing almost bored as he gazes at the arena below with silver eyes.

It takes me a minute, but I know who this is: Glamor. As in the most influential god on the Godcouncil. As in the god who nearly all politicians descended from.

As in the god who convinced the Godcouncil to murder nearly everyone I knew. To murder *me*. As in the god with the ability to grant me my wish to pardon my uncles.

He turns to say something to a blond woman beside him wearing an elegant bright blue dress that compliments her eyes. She must be Mind, I think. Before I can get a good look at her, the camera cuts to a view of the packed stadium and I force my gaze away. I've heard some of the gods sometimes attend the later matches in the Tournament—it is, after all, the Tournament of the Gods. But I hadn't considered how off-putting it'd be to actually see them watching us.

On the far end of the arena, Luka practices a few lunges, jabbing the saber at an invisible opponent to cheers. He's fast, and he definitely knows what he's doing—his footwork seems well practiced. He may actually be a competent fencer.

It's too bad for him this isn't a fencing match.

The countdown starts and Luka bows to the cheering crowd, soaking up every ounce of attention. *Enjoy it while you can,* I think with a smile.

The siren sounds. The match begins.

I start forward, my daggers at the ready, as Luka strolls casually toward me. When I reach the first concentric circle border, where the outermost circle meets the first interior circle, I pause. While all the borders were painted in blue light when the match began, this outermost circle is now edged in green.

I glance up to check Luka's progress, but he's hesitated at the first border too—we've both experienced how dangerous the platform itself can be. Turning my attention back to the green light at my feet, I crouch and hesitantly poke at it with a dagger.

Nothing happens. I look up. Luka is watching me, but he hasn't crossed over the green line yet either. He's waiting to see what happens to me, then.

Fine. I stand, take a breath, and set one foot across the green line onto the first inner circle.

Absolutely nothing happens. I step fully into the first inner circle as the green light gradually turns more yellow. As far as I can tell, nothing else has happened, and I feel fine, so I turn back to Luka.

He crosses the now-yellow light and continues casually

toward me. I cross the blue boundaries of the other inner circles with more confidence until Luka and I meet in the center.

Luka wastes no time, lunging at me with the saber the moment I step within striking distance. I sidestep the strike easily, but he's fast and lunges again and again, stabbing the air like a pissed-off adder. My guess that he's probably a competent fencer seems to be on the mark—at the very least he knows what he's doing with that thing and how to move his feet.

I twist and slide out of the way of his attacks, waiting for the moment when I can slip in with a close strike. The key here is going to be getting close to him. The saber is most dangerous with me at a distance like now, so he can strike at me without letting me get close enough to strike back—at least not without a sword of my own. Or a staff. Not that I'll admit that to Lark.

The yellow light of the outermost circle is now a deep orange, quickly turning red. I'm still not sure what the color signifies—going from blue to green to yellow to orange to red feels like a warning sequence of some kind, but of what? What happens when it reaches the end of the cycle?

And then the light flashes bright red. Once. Twice. Three times.

And the outer ring of the platform plummets into the pool with a splash.

Luka sees it the same time I do, and his eyes go wide. He pauses, midstrike—and his distraction is exactly the moment I was waiting for. I slip past his saber and slam the butt of my knife against his sword wrist, hard. He gasps and drops the saber—I catch it before it hits the ground and spin around him, pointing his own saber at him.

Luka's mouth actually falls open. It's extremely satisfying.

I could run him through with this, I guess, but swords are really not my style, and to be honest, I'd prefer not to kill anyone else if I can avoid it. So instead I whip around and throw it as hard as I can. The saber sails through the air in a long arc, then falls into the pool.

I turn back, smiling, and very nearly take Luka's punch to the face. I jerk my head to the side and his hand grazes my ear. It throbs, but I deserve it for the sloppiness. I slash my dagger forward and catch him across the chest as he jumps back, ripping through his shirt and slicing a shallow cut across his torso.

Luka gasps and winces back, his hand flying to his cut chest. When he pulls his hand back, it comes away bloody. His shocked expression twists into something like fury.

Behind him, another circle of the ring flashes red for a third time and falls into the pool below. We started with six circles. Now we have four. And each layer seems to be dropping a little faster than the last, eating away at our fighting space.

Luka screams and races toward me, ducking low. He's going to tackle me. Frankly, it's a stupid move since I still have two knives and could very easily plunge them into his back when he smashes into me, but then I'd run a serious risk of killing him.

Does he know I'm trying not to kill him?

I don't have enough time to get out of the way, so I sheathe one knife and brace myself. He slams into me, but at the moment of impact I push back, twisting as hard as I can. I don't manage to spin us around completely, but instead of me landing on my back, we both hit the ground on our sides. My left side throbs with pain, but my gamble worked because with my right hand I bring my knife up to his neck.

"Yield," I say.

"You first," he spits.

I arch an eyebrow and he nods down to his hand, which is holding the hilt of my other dagger flush against my gut. Except he hasn't realized yet that the moment he grabbed the dagger, the blade retracted at his touch.

Thank you, Maddox.

"Oh no," I say dryly. "Not a bladeless hilt."

Luka blinks. "What?" He pulls my dagger back, and for a second time in this match his mouth falls open—this time at the lack of a blade protruding from the hilt.

"Nice try, though," I say. "Now yield."

With a growl, Luka throws the dagger as far as he can. Unfortunately, we've landed on the outermost edge of the platform, so it sails right into the pool, joining his saber and two rounds of the platform.

The next ring—now rapidly turning orange—connecting us to the platform is about a foot away from Luka's head, which means if it disconnects, we'll both go falling into the pool. I push the dagger a little harder against Luka's neck, nicking him just enough for a bead of blood to pool at the tip.

"Yield," I say again.

Luka looks me right in the eye. Then he rolls his head to the side and plunges his teeth into my gloved hand.

The yelp that comes out of my mouth is undignified even though I don't feel the pain. I squeeze the hilt of my knife, sheathing the blade before I yank my hand away so I don't accidentally slice his throat open in reflex.

The platform flashes red.

I roll off Luka toward the center of the ring, toward safety, before springing to my feet.

Second red flash.

I race over the line to the next ring of safety, Luka on my heels. I try to kick him back, but he throws himself out of the way, rolling out of my reach.

Third red flash. The outer ring drops and splashes below.

Panting, I flex my bitten hand. The numbing runes are working, and the thick leather should have blunted the worst of it, but I won't be surprised if I find a bruise I'll have to heal later.

Three circles left, including the innermost circle. We now have half the space to fight in that we had to begin with—and the new outer ring is already turning green from blue. Luka steps into the next ring, eyeing me with a hatred that feels unearned. (He's the one who bit *me*. *And* I went out of my way *not* to kill him. Twice!) I mirror his steps, slipping into the inner ring, maintaining distance between us. Reassessing him.

He's decent at fighting—the move with my knife would have actually been impressive if it hadn't been for Maddox's rune enhancement. And I'll admit I didn't expect the boy who trained in fencing of all things to lower himself to biting my hand, but I guess desperation makes animals of us all.

Then he steps into the center circle, and so do I.

The innermost circle is small, maybe seven feet across. Enough room to maneuver, but not a lot to dodge—at least not without stepping onto one of the remaining outer circles.

And the outermost circle is already orange, so that won't be an option for long.

Then Luka lifts his fists. I can't help it—I grin as I return my remaining dagger to the sheath at my hip and lift my own fists. I shift my feet seamlessly, bouncing on my toes, sinking into my fighting stance. Ready to move.

And for just a moment, standing here with the roar of the crowd surrounding me, my fists up and my focus narrowing to the opponent across from me, I'm back in the Underground. I'm home.

Then the outermost circle falls. Two left. And this time the next one takes just seconds to start to turn green.

Luka takes a few shuffling steps forward. I let him close the gap between us, staying near the edge of the inner circle. He jabs, I twist out of the way. He spins around, scowling. Annoyed.

Good.

He jabs again, and again I spin out of the way, forcing him to turn. We repeat this three more times—jab, spin, jab, spin, jab, spin—before he screams in frustration. Just behind my back foot the outer ring turns orange.

He screams and punches again. I spin out of the way, but this time I slip behind him and kick him squarely in the middle of the back. Hard. He stumbles forward, nearly falling over, but catches himself before he staggers off the far edge. Red flashes on his face as he turns around to face me, furious. I step right up to the edge of the inner circle. And this time when he punches, I don't move. I don't have to.

Because the floor drops beneath him.

Luka's eyes go wide. Then he's gone. And the crowd screams so loudly, I don't even hear the splash below.

The suppressor cuff on my ankle beeps, then falls off. The match is over.

Holy shit.

Holy *shit*.

I did it. I just became a finalist.

I stare in shock at the ripples of water below where Luka fell. I just won. I just *won*, and there's only *one* round left between me and saving my uncles. I can do this. I can actually help them.

The roar of the crowd comes to me all at once, and I can't help it—I'm beaming. They are chanting my name—*my* name—the name of a Shallowsfolk kid who they never expected to survive the opening round, let alone make it to the godsdamned finals.

The name of a Deathchild victor on thousands of tongues.

It should be terrifying, probably, but it's exhilarating. I can't wait to tell my uncles—

Two faces catch me out of the crowd and I double take so hard my neck flares with pain. The cheering of the crowd melts away. My body goes cold. Because standing at the very front of the crowd, smiling sadly at me, are my uncles.

I blink, but they're still there.

I blink again, and Uncle Orin nods at me.

"No," I whisper. "Please no."

Because I know they're not just inexplicably out of prison. They're gray from head to toe, translucent. And I know what that means.

The platform begins to descend, returning me to the

understage. Tears blur my vision, but I blink hard and my uncles are still there. At the edge of the crowd. Watching me.

I don't stop staring at them, silently pleading that I'm wrong, that this isn't what I think it is, until the ceiling of the understage closes over my head, shutting them out of sight.

Maybe for the last time.

CHAPTER 42

I can't breathe.

I rush through the understage in a haze, the pounding of my pulse throbbing in my ears and tears burning my eyes as I scan faces of sponsors and confused onlookers for my team. Chaos. Lark. Maddox. They would know if something happened, wouldn't they?

Wouldn't they?

"Crow!"

I freeze midstep, almost running directly into someone who looks at me like I've lost my mind. My reaction, I'm sure, is confusing to onlookers—after all, I just became a finalist, so why the fuck am I standing here with tears streaming down my face? But I can't be bothered to care what anyone else thinks. Not when a single truth blazes like a burn behind my eyelids.

I saw my uncles.

And I should not have.

I don't leave my room for two days.

Time is a blur of tears and emptiness and dull, throbbing pain. In my chest. In my joints. In my neck. In my hands. In my head. The stress of losing two of the people I love most in the world has triggered a flare of autoimmune-induced pain like I haven't had in years, but I don't fight it.

It feels appropriate that my body hurts as much as my soul does.

Mouse hasn't left my room either. She's sat curled up on my chest, purring, or cuddled up against my side. I think she can tell how devastated I am. I think this is her way of trying to comfort me. (I think it's helping, even if I can't stop crying.)

Sometimes Lark comes in and lies down next to me. Sometimes she holds me. Sometimes Maddox and Chaos join in too. No one tries to comfort me with words. No one knows what to say. I was supposed to use this competition to save my uncles. That was the entire point—but now, what? I've risked everything and they're dead anyway.

I just don't understand. They didn't even have their trial yet—it was pushed to after the competition, like everyone else's. So why did they die?

And why am I still here? There's nothing left that I want out of this competition. What am I risking my life for, now that my uncles are gone?

I wake up surrounded by warmth. I'm squished between Lark and Chaos, with Maddox's long arms reaching around all of us. Mouse is sleeping on my hip. I close my eyes, breathing in the warmth of being surrounded by people who care about me. I am shattered, but at least I'm not alone.

I'm not alone.

"You should eat something," Lark murmurs behind me. I jump—I hadn't realized she was awake.

"Not hungry," I mumble, pressing my face into Chaos's chest.

"We know what happened," Lark says. "But you have to eat. You can't just waste away in here."

I turn to face her. "I don't understand. They're gone, but—" My voice cracks. I close my eyes and take a trembling breath. "How?"

"They were executed in the middle of your match," Chaos says behind me. "My contact at the prison called me after it happened. I'm so sorry, Crow."

Executed. I am hollowed out by grief, my body made empty by a soul-deep sadness I've known before. Murdered like my dad. Slaughtered like my community. It is a pain woven into my marrow, made fresh by this new horror.

I meet Lark's eyes, and I don't have to say it. She knows. But I force myself to turn to Chaos and ask anyway. "I was told trials were paused until after the Tournament."

"They were," he says softly. "But the president ordered an exception due to the . . . nature of their crime."

And there it is. The president—my *mother*—had my uncles murdered. The back of my throat burns with tears. "They didn't do anything wrong."

"I know," Chaos says gently. "I'm so sorry."

I expect more tears, but instead something inside me settles. A truth that washes over me like the winter's first frost.

My mother did this.

"C'mon," Lark says, prodding my shoulder. "How about

you take a shower. By the time you're dressed, we'll have food ready."

Mouse chirps and licks my chin before standing and arching her back in a big stretch. And somehow it's this—my cat, who hasn't left my side since I shared the news, hopping off my bed and looking at me expectantly—that makes me move at last.

Freshly showered, I feel more human, though only barely. After changing, I go to my room to grab my phone and find Lark lying on my bed, arms crossed behind her head. I pause in the doorway, then slowly close the door behind me.

"Do you think she knows?" Lark asks.

There's no need to clarify who.

I sigh and lean against the door, letting my head fall back. "I don't see any other reason why she'd prioritize their case in the middle of the Tournament except to get to me," I say numbly. "So yeah, I think it's safe to assume my mother knows who I am."

Saying it aloud makes it real, and maybe that should scare me. But I am too wrung out to be scared. Too done with enduring wave after wave of living nightmares. If my mother wanted to expose me, she would have done it already. Instead, she's tried to ruin me by killing the people I love.

I wish I could say she hasn't succeeded.

"I'm dropping out of the competition," I say. "There's nothing I could win that would make risking my life again worth it."

I expect Lark to argue. To push back. To call me a coward—anything.

Instead, she sits up. "Okay," she says.

Okay.

"Mads made soup," Chaos says when we enter the living room. "Like, from scratch. Cooked the chicken bones and everything."

"Chaos was very impressed," Lark says with a smirk in her voice. "I'm pretty sure he's never seen someone make soup before."

"That's true." Chaos smiles softly. His eyes light up. "Oh! And I popped by the bakery downstairs to get us some fresh dinner rolls. Can't go wrong with soup and bread."

My stomach is a jumble of queasy knots and nauseating waves, but Lark's hand is on my shoulder and Chaos is looking at me with wide puppy-dog eyes, and then Maddox peeks over Chaos's shoulder and adds his own big pleading eyes.

"You two look ridiculous," I say, but my mouth cracks into a tiny smile.

I sit at the counter, where Maddox has placed an optimistically large bowl of steaming-hot soup in front of me and Chaos has placed two rolls on a small plate next to a tub of butter and a butter knife. Even though the thought of eating sends a nauseating pang of guilt through me, the soup *does* smell really good. Salty and comfortingly warm, with a hint of lemon.

Lark, Chaos, and Maddox are all standing on the other side of the counter, staring at me. I pick up the spoon, fill it with broth, and take a small sip just to dispel the awkwardness. The soup is warming in a way that, to my surprise, actually helps hide the queasiness a little. So I take another sip. And another.

It's not much, but I swear to gods my whole team relaxes instantly.

"You all look like very anxious parents," I say between bites.

Lark grimaces, but Maddox grins and Chaos looks thoughtful. "An anxious throuple, you might say."

"Except I'm not a baby," I respond.

"True. What's the term for four people in a throuple?"

"Polycule," Lark says without missing a beat. She grabs one of my rolls, breaks it in half, and starts spreading butter on both halves. "For any romantic or queerplatonic group of three or more."

"Is that what we are?" I ask.

Lark, Chaos, and Maddox all look at each other. Lark shrugs. "I've never been one for labels. But whatever we're doing has been . . . nice."

"And I've never been one for monogamy," Chaos says. "So I agree, it's been nice."

"I'm happy," Maddox says cheerily.

Then everyone is looking at me again. I swallow a mouthful of soup. "So am I. I mean, not right now, but . . . in general, yeah, it's been nice."

The reminder of why we're all here, huddled around me eating soup, sobers the room. My appetite withers and I put my spoon down. Lark offers me half of a buttered roll, and I almost refuse it but then she gives me a look I don't want to argue with, so I take it and nibble on the edge.

Chaos takes a deep breath. "I do have a couple updates. Firstly, Astrid unfortunately did beat Lore in their match. So the final match will be between you and Astrid."

I open my mouth to let him know I'm dropping out of the Tournament, but Lark jumps in before I can.

"Lore almost pulled it off," she says. "Astrid's prior matches have generally gone quickly, but without her illusions she had to rely on hand-to-hand combat—and she can hold her own. Unfortunately, Lore is a *very* skilled mage and a less skilled fighter, so a magicless fight was to their disadvantage."

Lore seemed like a decent person, and Astrid, of course, is garbage, so the news is disappointing. Especially since that means she's going to be the Champion now.

Lark gently touches my hand, and I relax my fist, dropping my squished roll onto my soup bowl.

"Bright side," Maddox pipes up. "I think that was the first match where Astrid *didn't* kill her opponent."

Great.

"Secondly," Chaos says, "Jimena and I have been in contact. She's been researching public works documents and says she'll be ready to meet soon. There's also something you need to see. It's not bad," he adds quickly. "But it *is* important."

I'm not sure I like where this is going, even if it isn't bad, but I nod anyway. Chaos turns on the TV, and I swivel on my stool, so I can see the screen.

Chaos opens his phone and navigates to something, then swipes to send it to the TV. An image appears on the huge screen that takes me a full minute to process.

It's the border wall, the one that separates the Shallows from Midlevel. But a huge mural interrupts the massive slab of black metal. It's an image of a crow. An enormous crow, wings out, in the process of tearing the wall down with its talons. A huge hole with scratch marks all around it has been painted so realistically, for a second I thought there *was* a hole. The crow holds a crumpled-up chunk of black metal with one foot while attacking the rest.

There aren't any words, but there don't need to be. A gods-damned *crow* tearing down the wall isn't subtle.

"How was this up long enough for anyone to get a photo?" I ask, my mouth hanging open. "Is it still up?"

"It is," Chaos says. "I actually took this photo myself when I went down there two days ago. It had only just happened when I got there, I'm pretty sure, because the Enforcers were freaking the fuck out trying to figure out how to remove it. But whoever painted it was really skilled in runemagic, because they haven't been able to so much as scratch it in two days— and they've tried."

"It's amazing," Maddox says with a smile. "They tried painting over it at first, but the paint just dripped right off— wouldn't stick at all. Then they tried scrubbing it, pressure washing it, even acid washing it—nothing. Finally, they tried putting a huge-ass tarp over it *and the tarp caught fire.*"

"And it glows in the dark," Lark adds. "So when they tried shutting off the floodlights, it didn't matter."

I really didn't think anything could make me smile today, but apparently I was wrong. Maddox is right—this *is* amazing. And also terrifying.

"I didn't do anything to earn this kind of reverence," I say.

"Crow, are you serious?" Maddox says. "You're a fucking Shallowsfolk hero and you *earned* it. Not only did the three of us make history getting past the opening round—you made it all the way to the finals. You're showing everyone on Mid-level that Shallowsfolk can't be hidden away and forgotten, and you're showing everyone in the Shallows that we are capable of so much more than society and the government says we are. You're giving people hope."

"But I didn't do it for them." My eyes blur with guilty tears. I pick at the bread roll in my bowl, my appetite vanishing entirely. "I did it to try to save my uncles and I *failed*. They're dead. I risked everything to save them, and I lost them anyway."

Then I blink and Lark, Maddox, and Chaos are wrapping me in one big group hug.

"That wasn't your fault," Chaos says. "What you tried to do was brave as fuck, but you were never responsible for what happened to them. They died because this government and the gods are greedy and scared."

I sniff and wipe at my eyes. "What do you mean?"

I can't see Lark behind me, but Chaos and Maddox look at each other. Then Chaos nods. "Crow," he says so softly, "the government didn't decide to break their own rules on judicial rulings during the competition on a whim. They opted to move forward during the competition—during *your* match—because they see you inspiring Shallowsfolk and they want to crush that hope. They need to snuff out any movement in the Shallows before it begins. And they're trying to use you to do that."

"It's *not* your fault," Lark says again. "This is the government's fault. This was an executive decision to try to guarantee a Shallowsperson doesn't win this thing."

No one is saying it, but the meaning is all too clear: An

executive decision is a decision that comes directly from the president and the gods. The president, who proposes the decision; the gods, who approve.

A new emotion blossoms around my grief. Heat fills me, swirling with determination to survive. To ensure that my uncles did not die in vain. This government, this society, from the gods at the top to the people below, have tried again and again to snuff me out.

But I am not a flame so easily extinguished.

"Then there's only one thing to do," I say.

Chaos looks at me warily. Maddox looks confused. But Lark—Lark is smiling.

"And what's that?" Chaos asks.

"I have to win this thing," I say. "And then we take down my mother and the gods responsible for the Silencing."

III

GODLEVEL

An excerpt from The Book of Deities, *first edition*

It is known that Death and his children were godkillers. A balance to the natural order; a safeguard against the seduction of greed that all beings are vulnerable to.

But here the first mistake was made: for they were the only safeguard.

Age upon age upon age passed. The gods had children, who had children, who had children. Their people grew from villages to towns to cities to countries. But the people—and the gods—forgot that Death was also Life, and the others looked upon Death's children with suspicion.

"The godkillers will destroy us all if we do not act," said Glamor, who had become the most influential of all gods.

"It is logical," said Mind, who always stood by Glamor's side, "to remove the threat."

"I do not wish to die," Architect said.

"Nor do we," said Flora and Fauna. "But we do not believe violence is the solution."

"You are forgetting," drawled Discord, "that Death cannot be killed."

"But his descendants can be," said Mind.

"Then it is settled," said Glamor. "The Deathchildren must be removed."

"You speak of the indiscriminate killing of an entire people," said Flora.

"Genocide," said Fauna.

"We will not agree to this," said the twin gods together.

"Nor will I," said Discord. "We have no reason to believe the Deathchildren mean us any harm. Simply having the potential for harm is not excuse enough for violence. Do we not all have the potential for harm? Would you argue the world is better without us?"

"That is not the same," Glamor said. "As long as the Deathchildren live, we are not truly immortal. We are not truly untouchable. We are not truly gods."

"Perhaps," said Discord, "we should not be."

"Let's put it to a vote," Glamor said. "For such a grave decision we must call upon the minor gods to vote with us. Does anyone object?"

No one did.

"As usual, Death has not been invited to this Council meeting," Discord said.

"Death has never been a part of this Council," Glamor said.

"Should Death not be permitted to speak, considering you are contemplating the murder of his children?" Discord argued.

"Absolutely not," said Mind. "Death is too emotionally entangled to make an unbiased judgment."

"I agree," Glamor said. "Death will not be permitted to speak."

And here the second mistake was made: for no one else protested Death's absence.

And so the children of Mind, Glamor, Flora, Fauna, Architect, and Discord were permitted to listen to the

Council and make their vote. But without the say-so of Death's children there was never a question where the vote would fall, even as Discord's, Flora's, and Fauna's children all voted against the measure.

"The Council has decided to remove your children," Discord said to Death once the vote was complete.

"So be it," said the eldest god, for he could not stop them alone.

So it was.

CHAPTER 43

"Go to sleep, dear one. I'll see you in the morning."

Your mother's kindness is a beautiful dream you don't want to wake from.

But you do. And when you wake, it is to smoke, and flame, and blood.

Smoke, wafting in thick through your open window. You cough, your lungs burning and your eyes stinging in the poisonous air as someone presses a generative oxygen mask to your face and cinches the ties around your head.

There is no sound. Not so much as a whisper.

Even your own coughs, as you catch your breath in the cool air blowing on your mouth and nose, emerge silently. You blink, uncomprehending, and you try to speak—but no noise emerges from your mouth.

This is when you begin to panic.

Blood. Smeared on the mask over your face. On your father's hands as he crouches in front of you, looking more serious than he ever has before. And splattered over his light brown skin and matted in his short black hair. Still wet.

You look at him wide-eyed, trembling, as he holds your shoulders with so much gentleness. Like you, he is wearing a clear oxygen mask.

He tries to say something, but like yours his voice has been stolen. He presses his lips tight and grimaces, but nods. He covers his eyes with both of his hands for a moment, then pulls his hands away and looks at you meaningfully.

Cover your eyes.

You have so many questions, but no way to ask them, not as long as you cannot speak. So you close your eyes. He lifts you into his strong arms and presses your face gently into the crook of his neck. He smells like sweat and ash and blood, but he is warm, and his arms around you are comforting. He walks for a short time, then crouches and gently places you on the floor. He taps your nose twice, and you open your eyes.

Instead of taking you out the door like you expected, he's brought you to the back of the kitchen, where there is a small walk-in pantry. His fingers brush over the tile floor, as if counting, before he traces a large square in the floor and presses his hand flat in the center.

The square he traced glows bright white. Inside the glowing shape, the floor disappears, revealing a rope ladder descending beneath your home.

He gestures to the ladder, so you take the hint and climb inside. The ladder isn't long—it deposits you in a space just beneath the floor of the pantry. You nearly trip over the electric lantern set out for you on the floor. You turn it on and look up, expecting your father to climb in after you, but instead he reaches down and hands you a folded piece of paper.

Frowning, you take the paper and unfold it, reading it in the cool light coming from the lantern at your feet.

You will be safe here. Stay here. Do not go deeper into the tunnels. I promise I will return for you. Do not leave until I return.
> *I will always love you, my child.*

Your eyes go wide and you look up, where your father is watching you from the pantry above. His mouth moves slowly behind the clear mask, and you can't hear him, but you can make out the words nevertheless: *I love you.*

He makes a large circular gesture and the floor reappears, enclosing you in just the small circle of light spilling out of the lantern.

It is so, so quiet.

You wait in the worst kind of silence.

It envelops you completely. You cannot hear your own breath. Not your own pulse. Not the settling of the house above you. When you pace the short width of the tunnel, the packed dirt moves soundlessly beneath your feet.

The silence swallows everything. Even time itself.

You sit against the wall next to the ladder and curl your knees up to your chest. You squeeze your legs tightly and press your face into your knees. And you wait.

You will wait for a long time.

But this—this is where your memory becomes fuzzy.

Eventually, light splashes onto you. You squint up at the ceiling, where three blurry faces peer down at you. Two of them are your uncles, which you did not expect—they don't even live in Homestead. The third is your father, which you did expect.

But there's something wrong with him. He's muted— gray—and not just in the soot-covered way like you. You blink and blink and try to clear the blurriness in your eyes, the fuzziness in your mind. It's not just that your father is gray; there's something else, something not quite—Ah. There it is. He's translucent—just a little. Just enough for you to know the truth.

Your uncles are here and so is your father. But your father is a ghost.

You don't remember much after that, but you know this: Your father is the first ghost you see that day, but not the last.

CHAPTER 44

No one wears masks on Godlevel and no one has to—because up here, the air is filtered clean. Illness-free. They put us on an elevated cable car as soon as we walked up the enormous, gaudy gold staircase that serves as the only entrance to Godlevel. Now in the cable car, the windows are open. It smells fresh—oddly sweet and *green* in a way I don't know how to describe. The cable car we're in is empty save for Chaos, Lark, Maddox, Mouse, and me. The inside is large enough for all five of us to spread out and walk around, and everything looks brand-new. The glass windows and doors glitter, without a single fingerprint marking the glass. The metal trim is beautifully shiny, the plush fabric seats unstained.

If you told me we were the very first to use this cable car, I would believe it. Instead I get the impression they're all this way. The rune work needed to keep something as heavily used as public transportation looking so spotless and new is complicated and expensive, but of course, up here money is an unlimited resource.

The now-familiar sensation of static washes over my skin—Chaos must have set up another disruption field, to give us some privacy. As we zip silently through the air, I peer out the window to the city below while Mouse peeks out from my hoodie and rubs against my chin. The streets are pristine and there's so much *space*—huge parks and gardens, complete with large sparkling blue lakes and rivers. The trees are colorful and healthy, the fountains are works of art, and every corner is dotted with flowers.

I thought Midlevel was ostentatious, but Godlevel makes Midlevel look overcrowded and underfunded in a way that breaks my brain a little.

"Where are all the people?" Maddox asks, peering out the window beside me. "There aren't any crowds."

He's right—this level looks almost uninhabited save for the occasional pair or family or single walker that we zip past. But there's too much space between them. People must be able to walk around down there for several minutes without passing another person in the middle of the day.

"Yeah, there isn't much in the way of population density up here," Chaos says, frowning at the outside. "I've always found it a bit creepy." He must see the look on my face out of his peripheral vision, because he looks at me and smiles slightly. "What?"

"I just . . ." I shake my head. "I forgot you must have grown up on this level."

It's a little embarrassing, to be honest—it isn't called *God-level* for nothing. The people who live up here are either gods, minor gods, or disgustingly rich godchildren.

The kind of rich that should be a crime.

Chaos smiles thinly. "Yeah, I . . . don't spend much time up here anymore. I visit a couple of times a year to see my dad, but that's about it." He hesitates, then adds, "Sorry."

I arch an eyebrow. "For what?"

He shrugs, shifting uncomfortably. "I don't know, it just . . . feels gross to have had access to all this when I know what life is like in the Shallows. I tried paying for improvements in the Shallows at first, but it was like slapping Band-Aids over leaks, you know? Sponsoring you, talking to Mads *a lot*, and working with Jimena has made me realize the problems are systemic. And I guess I wish I'd pushed for real change sooner."

I turn my gaze back to the art that is the city outside. "Better late than never."

He's uncharacteristically quiet for a few minutes. Then he clears his throat and looks at me, lowering his voice. "Can I . . . ask you something? It's kind of sensitive."

I arch an eyebrow. "Sensitive?"

"It's just . . ." He sighs and adjusts his beanie, pulling it a little lower on his head as he slips a little closer to me, his voice just above a whisper. "I've been thinking about what you said about how you knew your uncles had passed. You said you saw their ghosts."

The reminder sweeps through me, cold, and heavy, and nauseating. I take a deep breath through my nose and look out the window, ignoring the way the view goes blurry. "That's not a question."

"Right. Well, before that, you had that match where you were scared you accidentally did Deathmagic on camera, right? But that had nothing to do with ghosts."

I'm not entirely sure what he's trying to ask. I lift a shoulder. "I'm still not sure exactly how I did that."

"I've also seen you heal yourself after matches."

I frown at him. "Yeah, healing is a branch of Deathmagic. Medic is Death's child, remember?"

Chaos shakes his head. "Right, I know that, but what I'm trying to ask is . . . you don't seem surprised that you have access to more than just one branch of Deathmagic."

Oh. I guess that's a fair question—godchildren who aren't minor gods themselves generally have access to only one branch of godmagic. "Yeah, I . . . always have. I guess it's just a thing Deathchildren can do."

Chaos frowns. "I don't . . . think that's a thing."

"I've actually thought about it," I say. "I think maybe it's because of the Silencing. There are so few Deathchildren with access to Deathmagic now that I think maybe our magic has concentrated."

Chaos's frown deepens. "I guess that's . . . maybe possible. Have you met other Deathchildren with access to multiple branches of Deathmagic like you?"

"Bold to assume I've met other Deathchildren who can access Deathmagic at all," I deadpan.

Chaos winces. "Right, sorry. Of course."

I didn't really mean it as a chastisement, but Chaos doesn't add anything else for a few minutes. And I don't know what else to add. It's hard to say what's normal when everyone else like you is dead or in hiding.

"How about your parents?" he finally asks.

I glance at him. He's watching me with a frown, like this whole thing has genuinely confused him, which I guess it has.

"Well, you know who my mother is," I say. "She may think herself a god, but she's too far down the line of descendants to have inherited any magic. She's as mundane as it gets."

Chaos grimaces. "How about your dad?"

My eyes sting a little just thinking about him. I turn my gaze back to the window and take a steadying breath. "His name was Falcon. He was an . . . amazing healer. Taught me everything I know about healing."

"Could he access more than one branch of magic?"

I shake my head. "No, but that was before the Silencing."

"Could *you* before the Silencing?"

Now it's my turn to frown—because I see where Chaos's argument is going. If my theory is that Deathchildren can access more than one branch of Deathmagic because our magic got concentrated after the Silencing, then why was I able to access multiple branches as a kid before the Silencing happened?

The cable car brings us into a building before slowing to a stop and chirping as the doors open. Chaos blinks and stands up straight. "Oh! We're here."

We step into what I'd imagine the lobby of an art museum would look like—an enormous open space with art hung tastefully on every wall and sculptures dotted throughout the space. The floors are white marble streaked with gold. There's a lounge area; a clothing store; multiple booths selling delicious-smelling freshly made snacks; elevators on the far wall; an indoor waterfall; and not a single soul in sight save for the staff.

Maddox and I stare at him.

"I *know*," he says emphatically. "Believe me, I know. I won't try to justify it, but we also don't have any control over it—this is all run by the Championship-running gods themselves. Mostly Glamor, really."

"Tell us the staff at least get paid a living wage," Maddox says.

"They do," Chaos says quickly. "This is considered a cushy gig for a Midleveler."

I still don't like any of this—in fact, I hate all of it. My feelings about it don't really matter though, because at the end of the day there isn't much we can do about it. At least not yet.

"Fine," I say. "I'm assuming there's a bedroom somewhere where I can unpack my stuff and let Mouse free?"

We left our stuff at the suite—Chaos told us not to even pack, because that'd apparently be "handled" for us.

I unzip the front of my hoodie a bit so Mouse can poke her head out. She shifts in my arms and uses my chest like a springboard to launch off me and land gracefully on the floor. With a luxurious stretch, my tiny gray fluff ball trots confidently toward the elevators.

"Well," I say, "nothing left to do but take a look around this gaudy labyrinth, I guess."

Lark quickly disabuses me of the notion that there's "nothing to do" but explore. Not an hour after we've arrived, and just ten minutes after I've done my weekly testosterone ritual, she drags me downstairs. There she brings me to the indoor theater section with a plate full of snacks from a variety of food stalls on the first level—fries, spicy chicken, long skewers of roasted meat and vegetables, candy, and strips of dried fruits.

I sit in one of the plush chairs, complete with cupholders and small trays, to place my plate. A woman dressed in black directs me to the truly enormous beverage menu, and I order some sparkling apple juice while Lark gets a mug of hot ginger-and-lemon tea. Once the staff member returns with our drinks, it occurs to me I don't have any money to tip.

"I . . . think Chaos may be able to tip you?" I say awkwardly.

The woman's eyes widen. "Oh! No tips are necessary—that's all built into our salary."

"Oh," I say. "Okay. If you're sure . . ."

"Very," she responds. "It's an honor to serve you both." Then she nods and leaves the room before either of us can respond further.

That last bit makes me feel awkward, to say the least, but I don't have time to dwell on it. Lark kicks her feet up on the row in front of us and pulls up Astrid's first match on the truly enormous screen.

"Better get comfortable," Lark says. "We're not leaving this room until we've studied each of Astrid's matches."

I groan and sink a little deeper into the cushion, popping a piece of spicy chicken into my mouth. It's sweet and tender and so damn good, I can almost overlook the hours of tedium Lark and I are about to spend together.

Almost.

Four hours later we've watched each of Astrid's matches *twice* and come up with the following points:

(1) Astrid avoids physically fighting her opponents as much as possible—but when she does strike, it's usually to kill.

(2) Astrid relies on her illusion Mindmagic almost exclusively—with the exception of the last round, which was magic-free.

(3) Her illusion magic, which is visible on the screen, is *very* powerful. Best we can tell, it can't physically harm you, but judging from how some of her opponents reacted, it seems like it can make you *think* you've been injured, which seems to me almost as bad.

(4) Her strategy seems to be to terrify her opponents into near paralysis before killing them.

(5) But without her magic, Astrid defeated Lore only because Lore wasn't as skilled a fighter.

(6) Astrid's weapon of choice when she *does* have to physically fight is a spear. And she's nowhere near as skilled with it as Lark is with the staff, though she definitely knows how to use it.

"I don't suppose the final round is also going to be magic-free," I mumble, rubbing my tired eyes.

Lark snorts. "No magic in the finale? Are you joking? The audience would riot." She sips her third mug of steaming tea. "Historically, the only rule of the final round is there aren't any rules. Fighters are permitted whatever weapons they want and whatever gear they want, and they can use any kind of magic."

I groan and rub my hands over my face. "She's going to torture me with spiders, isn't she?"

Lark grimaces. "Now that she knows how much you hate them . . . probably. The important thing, I think, will be for you to remember none of it is real."

I shake my head. "How am I supposed to convince my brain that something I can see, hear, and *touch* isn't real?"

Lark pauses. "You're not gonna like this—"

I groan.

"But I think you should bring a staff."

I frown. That wasn't where I was expecting this to go. "A staff?"

Lark nods. "Her illusions can trick your brain into thinking it's feeling something, but she can't make actual physical objects. They're illusions. So theoretically, if you hit one with a staff, it won't work—you'll swipe right through the illusion. And that's how you'll be able to tell what isn't real."

I have to admit that's pretty smart. I even begrudgingly say as much out loud.

Lark smirks. "Glad to be properly appreciated for once."

I throw a cold fry at her.

CHAPTER 45

Just when I think my brain will melt out of my ears if I watch one more minute of Astrid's replayed matches, Chaos waltzes into the theater and slaps the lights on.

Considering we've been sitting in darkness for *way* too long, the flood of light means I can't see a godsdamned thing. Lark swears and slaps her hands over her eyes while I throw a blanket over my head.

"That was rude," I say through the blanket.

Chaos laughs. "Have you two not left this room at all? I'm pretty sure you were both in here when I left six hours ago."

"*Six hours?*" I groan, pulling the blanket off my face. To my surprise Chaos isn't alone. Maddox is snickering, and standing next to him, smiling awkwardly, is the red-bespectacled journo we've come to know. Jimena lifts a package wrapped in brown paper and twine out of her backpack. "I come bearing gifts."

Lark gasps. "Nan?" She perks up instantly at the thought of her grandmother. It's honestly adorable.

"Yeah. Ravenna is incredible, by the way," Jimena says, passing me the package. "It's for both of you."

I run my fingers over the rough brown paper, then glance at Lark. She's watching the package with rapt attention. I offer it to her. "Want to do the honors?"

Lark takes it with a smile. She runs her hands over it reverently, tracing the twine and her name written on the paper in black marker. She pulls a switchblade out of her pocket and runs the blade beneath the twine, snapping it. Then she rips the paper right off, like yanking a Band-Aid off.

Beneath the paper is a plain box, which she opens with more care. I grin. Inside are fresh rolled-up tortillas wrapped in cloth, small portioned steeping bags of black tea, a small jar of honey, and Lark's absolute favorite candy bar—chocolate with orange-flavored pop rocks.

Lark gasps and grabs the candy bar with glee. "Choco-pops!"

I smile and lift a tea bag to my face. It smells earthy and sweet, with a hint of something fruity. I know I'm going to love it already.

"I wasn't expecting her to make us a care package," I say with a slight laugh. "This is amazing."

"She was happy to," Jimena says. "There's more in there beneath the food, though."

I pull the honey jar, tea bags, and tortillas out and place them on a tray. At the very bottom are two folded squares of paper. I take the first one out and unfold it. It's a map of—the Shallows? I recognize the general shape and the streets crisscrossing across the paper, but there are red dots throughout the map, each marked with small runes.

Wait.

I grab the second paper and unfold that one too. It's also a map—of Midlevel, with the same red dots and runes.

And all at once I know exactly what we're looking at. Maddox looks over my shoulder and whistles.

"Holy shit," Lark says. "Is that—" She covers her mouth, then lowers her voice to a whisper. "Are those the storm drains and pumps?"

"She found *all* of them?" I gape at Jimena, who grins.

"Like I said, Lark, your nan is incredible. Once we had all the location information, she put that together in just over four hours. Done with runemagic, of course, but nevertheless, amazing."

It's been nine days since we looped Jimena in. I can't believe how much has been done already.

"This is what we need to prove what's happening in the Shallows," I whisper.

Jimena nods. "It makes the connection indisputable, but what wasn't clear was who was behind it."

"Doesn't the government oversee public works and infrastructure?" Maddox asks.

Jimena nods. "Yes, but how far up the chain does it go? The president doesn't oversee everything herself—there are hundreds of people who work for her and oversee different areas of society. So it was theoretically possible that this was approved by the Department of Infrastructure, for example, and the president never knew about it."

"Somehow," Chaos says, sitting next to me, "I doubt that's what you found."

Jimena smiles grimly. "No. It isn't." She pulls a tablet out of her backpack and begins moving her fingers over the screen. "All proposed laws, amendments, and orders are public record, even though the majority go unreported. There was a *lot* to go through, but with some persistence and a *lot* of energy rune spells . . ."

She flips the tablet around so we can see the screen, and the document she's pulled up.

BY THE ORDER OF PRESIDENT CARA:

Whereas there has been increased flooding throughout Midlevel, and

    Whereas projections by the Department of Climate indicate these floods will only increase in frequency and severity,

    Therefore an EMERGENCY ORDER from the desk of the president is hereby enacted, directing:

- *The immediate construction of rune-powered pumps throughout Midlevel to redirect excess floodwater to the Shallows, where the water will wash out harmlessly to sea.*

I stop reading after that. *"Harmlessly?"* I explode.

Lark scoffs. "Wash out to sea and take the Shallows with it."

"They don't care," Maddox says. "If they don't mention Shallowsfolk, Midlevelers can ignore it so no one has to look at the ugly truth."

He's right, of course. And it's so fucked up, I'm about ready to burn this godsdamned city to the ground.

"So this is"—I almost say *my mother's fault,* but I catch myself—"the president's fault," I finish haltingly.

"Afraid so," Jimena says. "I won't bore you with all the paperwork and hours of footage I found, but it's all documented. President Cara didn't just sign off on drowning the Shallows—it was her idea."

CHAPTER 46

After a sleepless night of glowering at the ceiling, pressing a hot compress to the base of my throbbing skull thanks to yet another flare, and imagining all the ways I'd like to deal with my murderous mother, I head for the top floor the next morning to get some air. Bright side: I'm so furious about Jimena's findings yesterday that it's overridden my anxiety about my match with Astrid later today.

The top floor is basically a massive balcony, complete with an oversized hot tub, a bar, a TV, lounge areas set up with sofas and luscious-looking giant bean bags, and so much lighting you could almost forget the sun has barely risen. When I get there, Maddox and Chaos are kissing in the hot tub, and I nearly turn around and go back inside, but Chaos calls my name.

"Crow, hold on! You don't have to go back inside—it's fine!"

I grimace, turning back to them. "Sorry, I didn't mean to interrupt. I just wanted to see the view."

Chaos waggles his eyebrows.

I roll my eyes. "Of the *city*, gods above and below."

They both laugh, and even I can't help but smile. "Please stay," Maddox says, and he seems to mean it, so I do.

I cross through the beanbag lounging area to get to the banister on the opposite side of the balcony. There's so much space between us that I can't even hear them moving around in the hot tub way behind me, especially since it's kind of windy up here.

It's nice. I lean against the rail, looking over miles of glittering lights below, and force myself to breathe deep. There's a minuscule strip of light way in the distance, barely a crescent, that I think might be the Shallows. Seeing it makes me feel hollow. Scooped out.

I am so very far from home. I wish I could forget all the things I've learned. I wish I could hug my uncles again. I wish I could complain about my history, culture, and magic classes with Ravenna. I wish I hadn't lost so much.

The view becomes a blur of smeared light, and I wipe my eyes with the back of my hand.

"I guess now it's my turn to interrupt," Chaos says awkwardly next to me.

I jump. "Gods, I didn't hear you come over."

Chaos smiles sheepishly, adjusting a towel draped over his shoulders. "Is now a bad time? I can—um, well, I guess we don't have a ton of time before we have to get you ready for the final match, but I could save it for later?"

I shake my head and take a deep, steadying breath. "No, it's okay. Is there something we need to talk about before the fight?"

"Um. Kind of." Chaos scratches his head. "I need to . . . fess up about something."

"Promising start," I say with a side-eye.

Chaos laughs weakly and leans against the railing next to me, turning his mismatched gaze to the city below. "It's nothing bad—it's just about why I sponsored you. Everything I told you before is true, but there's more to the story that I'm starting to think might be relevant."

What am I even supposed to say to that?

Eventually, Chaos grimaces, then says, "So every minor Discord god has to do a task when we come of age to prove our worthiness for our inheritance. Like, my oldest sister, Flame, literally taught the earliest godchildren how to use fire, and my sibling Panic helped create the public gardens on Midlevel. It used to be a big deal; now it's just a tradition, I guess. Ceremonial, right?"

I nod.

"Anyway, I picked sponsorship as my task. I didn't have to win, I just had to be an adequate and fair sponsor. I decided I wanted to sponsor someone from the Shallows to try to push for some kind of change by putting a face to people Midlevelers and Godlevelers are determined to ignore. My dad agreed it would count as my task, and when I told them I wanted to sponsor a fighter from the Shallows, he suggested I check out the Underground."

My mouth drops open. "Your *dad*, as in *Discord themself,* watches matches at the Underground?"

Chaos laughs. "More often than you'd think. They go in disguise, of course, so, like, no one knows it's him. But he's fond of the Shallows. And I can see the question in your face, so yes, they knew exactly who you were when I said I was going to sponsor you."

I imagined the gods all knew my name now, as a finalist, but it never once occurred to me that any of them were familiar with me *before* I entered the Tournament.

"Um," I say. "Wow. Okay."

Chaos grins, but his smile quickly slips off his face. He sighs and lowers his voice. "Yeah. Well, I didn't think much of it at first, but once I realized what god you descended from . . ." He bites his lip. "I don't know. I'm starting to think maybe my dad . . . *wanted* me to sponsor you, specifically."

I frown. "Why?"

Chaos is quiet for an uncharacteristically long time. When he finally pulls his gaze off the view and onto me, he looks as serious as I've ever seen him. "I mentioned my dad didn't support the Silencing, right? They've been Death's strongest ally essentially since the beginning of creation. My dad doesn't talk about it much, but I think they were even lovers once. And they're definitely still close."

I arch an eyebrow. "I didn't know they were . . . romantically involved."

Chaos waves his hand, like it's no big deal. "Romantic relationships between the gods aren't the same as between the rest of us. They've been alive since the beginning of creation, you know?"

That's true. I nod.

"I just keep thinking, if you win . . . and if you move forward with your plan to avenge the Deathchildren—which, to be clear, I fully support . . ." He trails off, running his hand through his hair. "It just feels like *maybe* my dad knew my sponsoring you could end with forcing the gods responsible for the Silencing to face justice."

The truth is I don't know Discord the way Chaos does, but I trust his judgment. And still, even knowing that maybe, somehow, Discord has his hands in all of this . . .

I don't think it changes anything for me.

"I can't let things go on like this," I say. "If I win, I know what I have to do. I'm not going to miss my only chance to make a difference."

"I know," Chaos says. "And I don't think you should."

"So it's settled." I roll my shoulders back. "Today I make sure *Astrid,* of all people, doesn't win the Tournament. And then I meet the gods."

Chaos leans his head against my shoulder. "I'm honored to know you, Crow."

"For a minor god," I respond, "I guess you're not so bad."

Chaos laughs.

CHAPTER 47

Unlike the stadium on Midlevel, this one sets up Astrid and me on completely different sides—as in completely different rooms. This is way preferable to the setup on Midlevel, so I don't have to look at Astrid until it's time to punch her in the face.

The other main difference, I've been told, is there won't be a pool beneath the platform. Instead, we'll be fighting on the arena floor—until one of us yields or can no longer fight.

The backstage prep room is, as expected, way larger than necessary. There are multiple rows of the plushest seats imaginable and numerous snack and beverage machines. On top of that, it's staffed with various stations: a massage therapist, weapons master, makeup artist, hairstylist, clothing stylist, and professional trainer.

At Chaos's insistence I allow the makeup artist to do my face and the hairstylist to trim up my hair. Chaos tells them my vibe is "badass androgynous rebel with a preference for dark colors," and I honestly can't even critique that description. The makeup artist and hairstylist work in tandem, and half an hour later they spin me toward the mirror.

My mouth falls open. My hair's been freshly buzzed on the sides with possibly the best fade I've ever had. The top is spiky and a little long, with a bit of fringe that I like—it has the perfectly messy balance that I've never really been able to master myself. Then there's the makeup. My skin looks flawless—and they've given me sharp black eyeliner that frames my eyes and eyebrows in shapes that look like knives. Or flames. Finally, they've given me a manicure and painted my nails black.

"Shit," I say with a laugh. "I look awesome."

Both stylists grin. Z, the makeup artist—a tall, androgynous person with a buzzed skull, gold eyeliner, and black lip paint—taps my cheek, just below the lowest part of the eyeliner. "It's smudgeproof, so even if you get hit in the face or sweat, it won't budge. Chaos can show you how to take it off after the match."

"Sure can," Chaos says with a grin. "Thanks, Z. Amazing work, as always." Then he looks at me. "See what happens when you listen to me?"

"Yeah, yeah." I wave him off with a smile. But as I look at myself in the mirror again, there's something missing.

Z must see the hesitation in my face, because they arch an eyebrow at me. "Go ahead, ask for it. Whatever it is you want to add, it's yours."

I hesitate. It's risky, but this is the final match. And I want to honor the people I've lost in the only way I know how. "Do you have charcoal paint?"

"Actually, yes. It's really useful when I want pure black." Z turns back to their kit and digs around for a minute, then pulls out a small black jar. They grab a brush, open the jar, and hand both to me. "Go ahead."

Now it's my turn to arch an eyebrow at them. "You aren't worried I'll ruin your work?"

"If you do, I'll just have to fix it." They wink at me.

I smile and almost dip the brush into the jar, then think better of it and place the brush on the table. Instead, I dip two fingers into the jar, smiling at the silky feeling of the paint on my skin. Then I face the mirror and touch my paint-drenched fingers to the center of my forehead and run them down over the ridge of my nose, over my lips and my chin, and down my neck to my collar. The paint is cool and thick and so familiar when I close my eyes that I can almost imagine my dad crouched in front of me, smiling.

I miss him so much. I wish he were here to see me fighting for us.

I take a deep breath and open my eyes. It's entirely possible that someone is going to recognize the mark for what it is—paint that Deathchildren wore during special events—but one way or the other, who I am won't remain a secret for much longer. Whether I win or lose, I can't sit back quietly knowing what I know. Not anymore.

Z nods and takes the jar back from me. "You look perfect," they say. "No touch-up necessary."

I smile.

Once that's done, I change into the outfit Chaos has picked out for me—a black bodysuit with gold trim and shiny black detailing. The detailing has the same kinds of sharp swooshes as my eyeliner design. The pattern runs up the sides of my legs and ribs and twists down my arms and over the backs of my hands. The bodysuit covers everything from the chin down, even my fingers and feet, in one sleek piece.

Looking in the mirror, I take a moment to thank my past self for my own body modification. Before I reshaped my chest, an outfit like this would have made me feel like garbage. But now I'm obsessed with how the slick material accentuates the flatness of my chest.

"It's cut resistant," Maddox explains as I look in the mirror. "But more important, I've rune-spelled it to be *very* impact absorbing. So if you get whacked with Astrid's staff, you'll bruise, but it should hopefully prevent any breakages. It's also fireproof, water resistant, and shock resistant. Oh, and I added the numbing runes you have on your gloves over the hands as well."

I stare at him. "You made this bodysuit?"

Maddox grins. "I mean, Chaos designed the aesthetic elements, but yeah, I put it together. I'm your weapons master—did you think I don't know how to make armor?"

I shake my head. "This is amazing. The attention to detail—and the numbing runes? Thank you."

"You can thank me by beating the ever-loving shit out of Astrid," Maddox says.

I grin at him. "That's the idea."

He smiles and hands me a tool belt with two sheaths for my knives, then a shiny black staff that looks like it's been dipped in molten gold. Gold tendrils drip down the top third of the staff—but it's perfectly balanced, so it must just be paint or stain or something. I twirl the staff experimentally and nod.

"How is it?" Maddox asks, watching me.

"I'm not the staff connoisseur, but I think it's perfect," I say with a wink.

"I already gave it my stamp of approval," Lark says behind

me, where she's lying across a very cushy bench. "So you know it's good."

"That's a relief," I say, only half joking as I look back at her.

She tilts her head back to look at me upside down. Her gaze rolls slowly over me before she smiles and looks back at her phone. "You should wear eyeliner more often. It suits you."

"Agree," Maddox and Chaos say together.

"Assuming you like it," Chaos adds.

"I do," I say, and it's true. I just didn't have a lot of mental space for experimenting with makeup living in the Shallows. And after this? I honestly don't know.

Whether I win or lose, life is going to be different. That at least I can ensure.

"Five minutes until entrance," says a pleasant automated voice piped through the room.

I feel lightheaded at the reminder of what I'm about to do. But as anxious as I am, I'm excited too. I've been wanting to fight Astrid since the very beginning of this competition. And though I know it's not going to be easy, I'm sure it'll be satisfying.

As long as she doesn't get the better of me with those damned illusions.

"All right." Chaos claps his hands together. "You opted not to do a grand entrance, which I think is wise. So you're gonna walk out, just like in the Underground. Except in a stadium that's, um, fifty times bigger? Something like that."

"I don't think I can even picture that," I say, and it's true. The Godlevel stadium, which is open to Midlevelers on special occasions like the Tournament, and is otherwise used for gods know what, is the largest in the world, holding 150,000 people. That's twice the size of Midlevel's monstrosity and big enough to hold, like, 10 percent of all Midlevelers. The Underground, in contrast—well. Chaos was being generous with his one-fiftieth estimate, even though the Shallows has four times Midlevel's population.

"That's fine," Chaos says. "Just walk out there and wave. Or don't. It doesn't really matter—your fans will love you regardless."

"Wave or don't," I repeat with a nervous laugh. "Okay. Any other words of wisdom?"

"Just one," Chaos says. "Win."

CHAPTER 48

"Introducing Chaos's competitor, Crow of the Shallows!"

The roar that greets me as I walk down the elevated runway to the stadium floor is so intense that my bones vibrate. Their cheers are a physical force in my chest, shaking the air in my lungs. I focus on my steps as I near the stadium floor, but the number of people packed into this space is staggering. Camera flashes burst in my eyes and camera drones whiz around me.

A strange chopping noise cuts through the cacophony, and the crowd grows even louder, which I would have thought impossible thirty seconds ago. Wind blows through my hair and I look up.

A gold helicopter is lowering itself into the stadium. Every ounce of this thing is gold and glass—from the body of the helicopter to the blades above and the rails below. It's the gaudiest thing I've ever seen take flight—and that's when I notice the thing it's carrying just below.

Astrid, it turns out, is not in the golden helicopter—which would have been bad enough. Instead, she's sitting on a solid gold throne, attached below the belly of the helicopter with gold cables.

I wish she could see me rolling my eyes down here.

The crowd, of course, eats this shit up. The audience screams in delight as the helicopter slowly lowers the throne onto the other side of the stadium floor. Astrid takes a moment soaking up the crowd's ardor as she sits casually on the throne, her legs crossed, one arm slung over the side. Then she unclips some sort of safety harness and stands, waving at the crowd and blowing kisses at the largest of the VIP booths overhanging her side of the stadium—undoubtedly where the gods are watching, though the floor-to-ceiling mirrored glass of the booth makes it impossible to confirm.

"Introducing the competitor sponsored by President Cara herself, Astrid of Midlevel!"

Wait. *What?*

The crowd's celebratory explosion is practically a sonic boom. I'm sure Astrid didn't previously mention who her sponsor was, and the reveal has the crowd losing their minds with excitement. And the buzz makes sense—I don't think my mother has sponsored a competitor before.

While Astrid is reveling in the crowd's attention, my gaze finds the massive four-way screen floating above our heads. It looks like a cube, and each side shows a close-up of what's happening here on the arena floor for the crowd sitting too far from the action to see otherwise. The camera cuts to a live feed of my mother, smiling coolly at the camera as she looks down at the arena below. At *us* below.

Apparently, she's left the Manor to make a rare public appearance.

I shiver. *It doesn't matter if she's watching,* I remind myself. *It doesn't change anything.*

It's then that I notice the crows.

Three of them, all sitting on the side of the four-way screen closest to me, peering down at me. And as odd as it is, I can't help but smile at this strange coincidence, because it is, of all things, a murder of crows. It feels like a sign from the universe, or from Death himself. A nod that I'm on the right track. That I can do this.

My mother and the gods believe they've seen me fight.

But I haven't even started.

"FIVE" begins the robotic countdown I've come to know. This time the crowd chants along. I take a deep, steadying breath, forcing my heart to slow.

"FOUR."

Across the stadium, Astrid isn't even facing me—she's still waving at the crowd.

I grab my staff out of the holster on my back and spin it slowly, reacquainting myself with its weight and movement.

"THREE."

The crowd is screaming with excitement. I squeeze the staff hard, then relax my grip. Thanks to Lark I know it well. Still, I have my knives with me too.

They're my favorite weapon, after all.

"TWO."

Astrid is still facing the crowd, her back to me. But this isn't about her. "For Orin," I whisper, resolve steeling my nerves. "For Alecks. For Dad."

"ONE."

For every suffering Shallowsperson.

For every silenced Deathchild.

I will make the gods watch.

CHAPTER 49

The starting siren blasts through the stadium. Astrid finally turns to look at me and, with a smirk, flicks her wrist.

A wall of green vegetation explodes forward like a rolling wave, racing toward me. I walk forward, bracing myself as the wave rushes into me—and *through* me. It doesn't feel like anything at all—if I'd closed my eyes, I would have missed it. Except I'm now standing in the middle of a thick rainforest.

I pause, taking it in. The ground is made of tall wild grasses shining with dew. It's soft and loamy beneath my shoes. Enormous trees tower over me in every direction, each with huge, thick leaves several feet wide and dripping with moisture. Chirps and caws of animals and birds I don't recognize fill the air, along with the rustle of leaves above me. Worryingly, I don't hear the crowd at all. It's like I've been transported somewhere else entirely.

It's not real, I tell myself. *You can walk right through it. Move.*

I take one step, then another, walking straight toward the thick trunk of a tree to test my theory with the staff. A loud crack right behind me stops me in my tracks—I spin around.

Only the dense jungle is there to greet me.

Astrid is toying with me. It's a little sadistic. And exactly her style.

I just have to figure out where the fuck she is so I can actually fight her. But how am I supposed to do that? If she were standing in front of me right now, would I even see her?

The truth is I don't know. And that scares me.

Taking a deep breath, I turn back to the tree. I'm about to take a step when the grass around my boots rustles. A thick strip of grass is trembling, like something beneath it is moving.

And then a gray spider, maybe an inch long, crawls out of the grass and onto my boot. Followed by another. And another. I blink and there are dozens scurrying up my boots.

I stumble back with a yelp. I try to shake the spiders from my boots. A few fall off, but they're quickly replaced by more—there's an entire swarm in the grasses gunning right for me. I take off running in the opposite direction, praying my steps will jostle the spiders already climbing up my boots and legs, swearing. Grasses and low-hanging palm fronds slap at my legs and face and arms, and I swear to the gods if the real jungle is anything like this, I *never* want to see it—

Wait. The real jungle.

It's not real. *It's not real.* I force myself to slow to a stop, looking down at the spiders that are now crawling over my knees.

It's not real. It's not real. It's not real.

But it *feels* real. Their weight on my pants, the skittering of tiny legs over the fabric—I don't know how to convince my brain it's not real. Unless—

I grit my teeth and swipe at a spider on my thigh with my

hand. My skin meets something soft and fuzzy and I nearly scream—but then the motion pulls my hand *through* it like a ghost.

Or like an illusion.

"I hate this illusion." I grit my teeth, but I've been distracted long enough. I need to find Astrid, and I need to find her *now*.

Which is when a massive white spider bursts through the trees just twenty feet ahead of me.

When I say massive, I don't mean the fist-sized thing that Astrid made me think was sitting on my glass. That was huge for a spider, but this—this is the size of a shack. Or a bus. My mouth hangs open as I stare at the nightmare racing toward me on eight hairy legs that are each twice as long as my entire body.

"You're not real," I say, forcing myself to stand my ground as my grip tightens on my staff. "You're not—"

One of those eight hairy legs whips toward me, catching the center of my staff and ramming it into my midsection. I'm airborne, my ribs throbbing; then my back hits the ground hard.

That felt real. But that doesn't make any sense—Astrid can't create physical creatures. Her godpower is illusion, not conjuring. Unless she used runemagic?

Or unless she's actually there and hit me with her spear.

I push myself onto my feet, ignoring the throbbing in my ribs as I readjust my grip on the staff. I squint hard at the enormous spider, trying to ignore its large, shiny black eyes fixed on me, unblinking. I don't see Astrid—not even a hint of the girl beneath—but that doesn't mean anything.

The spider must be masking her physical movements. So if

I can track the appendage the spider tries to hit me with, I can estimate where she's attacking from. In theory.

The spider charges me, lifts two legs, and swipes at me. This time I throw my staff out, blocking it like I would a hit from a staff. Metal clashes against metal with a clang—very much *not* the sound of a metal staff hitting a giant furry spider leg. I grin and press forward, whipping my staff fast, focusing on the two legs that just attacked me. The legs move quickly to block me, but the movements are disjointed and weird—and I'm fairly certain not remotely the way a real spider fights.

I can't see her at all, but I'm sure Astrid must be right in front of me. I push hard, striking out aggressively, imagining her behind the two spider legs moving together in tandem.

The spider *screams* with a grating noise that rakes against my eardrums. I cringe. The next slash digs deep into my right shoulder. I stumble back with a gasp, throwing my staff out to block the next strike. The impact reverberates up to my burning shoulder. Blood, hot and slick, streams down my arm, but I can't let the pain distract me.

I push harder, striking faster. Every hit connects with her spear behind the illusion with a *clack,* and I move faster and faster on the rebound, pushing past burning muscles, the thick smell of iron, and—

Crack!

The spider, the jungle, the sounds of a tropical rainforest and dew gathering on my boots—it all disappears in a blink, like a switch has been flipped. The roar of the crowd rushes over me so fast it's disorienting.

I'm back in the stadium. Not that I ever left, but now I can see it—over a hundred thousand spectators, and flashes of cameras, and the rumble of music, and the hard, cold floor beneath my feet.

And Astrid. Lying on the ground just a few feet ahead of me. She's dropped her spear. Blood is trickling from her mouth, and a red welt across the side of her face marks where I must have hit her.

My stomach drops out from under me. I was not holding back. I was moving quickly, fighting hard—and I *hit her in the face*. With a metal staff.

Oh fuck. Is she dead?

She groans and rolls over, and I have never been so relieved to see an opponent still moving. Even one as vile as Astrid. As hard as I was fighting, I was not trying to kill her. I don't *need* to kill her. I just need her to yield or reach a point where she physically can't continue fighting.

I wait as Astrid slowly gets up on all fours, her limbs shaking with effort. She spits, and two teeth clatter on the floor in a glob of pink-and-red spit. She's still conscious, so I kick her spear far out of her reach, just in case. Then I walk carefully around her and crouch in front of her, my staff resting on my knees.

"Yield," I say.

A scream behind me turns me cold. Astrid grins, her mouth full of needlelike fangs. An illusion. Which means the spear I kicked—

I throw myself sideways. My sliced shoulder hits the ground hard, the pain biting bone-deep as I slip on my own blood. I roll onto my back and throw my staff up, just in time to block the thrust of Astrid's spear. But instead of the motion being stopped entirely, the spearpoint glances off the curve of my staff and plummets right into the meat of my already bleeding shoulder.

This time the scream is my own.

The pain is blinding. For a second my vision goes black, and I think I'm going to pass out. But I can't. I won't. I didn't come this far to lose it all now.

And especially not to fucking Astrid.

I move quickly, shutting off the nerve endings in my impaled shoulder. I can't heal it here in front of an entire stadium, but that doesn't mean I have to suffer. My whole arm goes numb, which isn't ideal, but my vision clears as I gasp in a lungful of air. Astrid is standing over me, smiling viciously as she twists the spear. The welt she gave her illusion was apparently real, because there's a puffy pink stripe where my staff connected with the side of her face.

Just not hard enough, apparently.

"This," Astrid seethes, twisting the spear and pushing down harder, "is where you belong. At the feet of your betters, you filthy lowto—"

I slam my knife through the center of her sneaker. Right down to the hilt.

The howl that comes out of her is nearly inhuman—and so very satisfying. She drops the spear, collapsing into a crouch to grab at the knife I'm still pressing through her foot. The blade shudders as it scrapes the metal tile beneath the sole of her shoe—and unlike me, she can feel the knife tearing through skin, tendon, and muscle.

Astrid claws at my hand. I release the knife, leaving it in her foot, and yank the spear out of my arm. As I stagger to my feet, throwing her *real* spear out of reach this time, my arm feels like dead weight. I'm going to need both arms to finish this. And it's going to hurt.

Astrid is sobbing over her foot now, but she hasn't pulled the knife out yet. I have maybe seconds before she pulls herself together enough to yank it out. I take a deep breath. Pick up my staff. And brace myself for the pain.

Flipping my nerve endings back to life feels like setting my arm on fire, from shoulder to fingertips. But I grip my staff, step toward Astrid, and swing.

She crumples like a discarded doll.

I stand over her, panting hard. Bleeding so much my grip on the staff slips. But I don't relax. I won't let my guard down again. Not until I'm sure it's not an illusion.

I prod Astrid with the staff. She's solid. Unmoving. But breathing.

It's really her. Which means—

"Honored audiences of Escal!" roars a voice over the speakers. "Please join me in welcoming our newest Champion, Crow of the Shallows!"

CHAPTER 50

I won.

I can barely think over the thunderous applause and screams that make up the crowd. Their celebration rumbles in my chest and sets my bones vibrating. My vision blurs with tears, and I wipe at my eyes with the back of my hand.

Ridiculous amounts of shiny gold and silver confetti fall all around me, landing in my hair and on my shoulders, followed by a wave of gold and silver balloons.

I actually did it. Me, a Deathchild from the Shallows, someone who, by this government's laws, shouldn't even exist. Champion of the very gods who wanted me dead as a child. I could laugh at the absurdity of it all.

And I did it with Deathchild paint on my face.

Something rams into my back so hard I nearly fall over before I register Lark, Maddox, and Chaos wrapping me in a tight group hug. "Arm!" I shout with a pained groan, and they quickly readjust. They're laughing and crying. I press my face into Lark's shoulder and hold her tightly with my good arm.

"You did it!" Chaos shouts.

I can hardly believe it, but he's right. Maddox takes my wrist and throws my uninjured arm up in the air. "Champion!"

The crowd loses their shit.

Maddox lets my arm fall and we laugh. Lark catches my eye and smirks. "You're welcome for forcing you to learn how to use the staff."

I groan. "You're never going to let that one go, are you?"

Lark's eyes twinkle with mischief. "Never."

"In that case I'm never shutting up about how I saved us both from Dez." Saying that aloud fills my chest with lightness— I didn't realize how heavy it felt having that threat looming over us both.

Lark rolls her eyes, but she's smiling.

"What now?" Maddox asks, pulling away and shouting over the booming celebration music.

"Crow gets to collect their boon," Chaos says. "It's time to meet the gods."

Suddenly I'm nervous.

A Godcouncil secretary leads Chaos and me to a glass elevator. I turn to the wall facing outside and watch the city's upper level shrink to miniature size below me. I don't know how long—or how far—we rise, but when we stop, I can see everything: Godlevel, Midlevel, and even the Shallows far in the distance—a strip of darkness and flashes of muddled neon colors.

"Right this way," the secretary says behind me.

Chaos touches my shoulder. It's wrapped up—though just

for show. It took only a couple minutes backstage to heal my arm entirely. I force myself to turn away from the view and follow them both out of the elevator.

The secretary takes us down a long hallway full of enormous white marble columns and black stone floors so shiny I can see my reflection in them. At the end of the hallway are two of the largest doors I've ever seen in my life.

The doors are solid gold and must be at least three stories high. They're impractically tall, and there's no way a human could ever open them without serious magic or machinery. But I suppose that's probably the point. These are doors for godchildren and gods alone.

"The gods are waiting for you. Chaos must wait outside." The secretary turns to Chaos. "Though I've been told your father does want to speak to you, so they've asked that you not leave yet."

Chaos and I exchange a glance.

Chaos nods. "I won't go anywhere without Crow anyway." He pauses, then looks at the Council secretary. "Can I have a word with Crow in private before he goes in?"

The secretary nods. "When you're ready to enter, Crow, just speak your name at the door." The secretary turns away, then pauses and looks back at me, their face eerily blank. "Oh. And congratulations."

Chaos waits until the Council secretary boards the elevator down the hall. Once the elevator doors close, he takes a deep breath and looks at me.

"You can still go in there and ask for a normal boon."

I shake my head. "You know me better than that, Chay. I didn't come all this way to back out now."

He nods, unsurprised, but his face is grim. "That's what I thought you'd say." He sighs. "Well, I can't go in there with you, but I have your back. I'll fight for you however I can."

Then he gives me a tight squeeze, pressing his face into the crook of my neck. I smile and squeeze him back, closing my eyes to enjoy this.

"You know this isn't goodbye," I say.

"I know," Chaos says. "I'm just really proud of you. I hope you know that."

I smile, squeeze him one more time, and let go. "I know. I'll see you soon."

Chaos takes another deep breath and wipes at his eyes, which have gone misty. "Go on," he says, nodding at the doors. "The gods are waiting for you."

I smile. "Don't worry. You'll always be my second-favorite god."

Chaos scoffs. "*Second* favorite?" I arch an eyebrow and he laughs.

I smile and turn to the door, shaking the nerves out of my hands before I step up to the massive gold structure.

"I am Crow of the Shallows," I say. "And I'm here to see the gods."

CHAPTER 51

※

The doors open silently.

Frictionlessly. It's eerie.

I step inside. Like the massive hall that led to these doors, yet another long aisle lies ahead of me. I follow it, trying not to ogle at the pure white room around me. The walls and columns seem to be made of the same pure white marble. The aisle has a carpet runner—also pure white—that muffles my steps. About halfway down the aisle, the columns become tall partial walls made of the same white stone. Up ahead, the aisle ends abruptly before a long dais, where six people are seated on elaborate thrones.

No, not people. Gods.

I stop at the end of the aisle, not sure who I'm supposed to look at. Or maybe I'm not supposed to look at any of them? I've never learned the etiquette for interacting with a major god, probably because it never occurred to anyone that such a thing would ever be possible for me. Meeting the gods, after all, is extraordinarily rare—even for Uppercity folks.

The god in the center is on a raised dais, his throne made

of some kind of opalescent white stone that shimmers with a rainbow of colors. He's so pale he nearly blends in with all the bleached rock of this room, and his hair is pure white. His eyes, caught on me, are the pale gray of a winter sky, and his immaculate suit, tie, and shoes are all white.

It's a bit much, to be honest, which is how I know I'm looking at Glamor.

The god who convinced the rest to kill the Deathchildren.

He gapes at me still proudly bearing the mark of a Deathchild. "You're a bold one, aren't you?" he says. "Foolish, but bold."

"*Foolish but bold* since childhood," says a voice behind me.

I spin around. Standing just a couple feet back and to the left is *my mother,* which shouldn't surprise me, but what she just said sure as shit does. *Foolish but bold since childhood.*

My heart leaps into my throat. I'd suspected as much, but here it is: the confirmation. She knows.

"Hmm," says Glamor. "Then this is the child you warned us about."

My mother looks directly at me and says, "Unfortunately."

It seems unfair that her callousness still stings even all these years later, long after I've accepted she was a terrible mother. Long after I've accepted that I could never be the perfect mundane daughter she wanted me to be. That the moment I told her I was her *son,* the moment I showed her my prowess with Deathmagic, I was useless to her. That she never wanted a child at all, so much as she wanted a perfect doll she could parade around as her own.

But somehow, even after accepting all that, seeing the disdain written so plainly on her face as she looks at me still hurts.

How did she figure out who I am? Has she known from the

very beginning? I have so many questions, but the one that I ask is "Why are you here?"

President Cara arches an eyebrow. "Surely it doesn't surprise you that the liaison between the gods and humanity would be present during such an event."

I roll my eyes. I suppose when she puts it that way, no.

"Granted, I usually take more of a symbolic role," she continues. "An observer, you might say. But your presence adds a complication that requires my participation."

I open my mouth to answer, but suddenly Glamor is standing in front of me. Like *right* in front of me. I stumble a step back, but Glamor doesn't seem to mind. He tilts his head as his gaze rolls over me, from head to toe, before turning back to my mother.

"It doesn't look anything like you, but its features are certainly of its father."

My mouth curls with disgust. "My pronouns are he/they, not *it*."

Glamor doesn't even glance at me.

I'm so grossed out by the blatant dehumanization that I almost miss what he said. It's true that I don't look anything like my mother—and as I've gotten older, I don't have much of my dad's features either. I have his coloring—his black hair and light brown skin—but that's about it. I've never really questioned it much—genetics are weird, and I figured some cross between my mother's and father's features might not really look like either of them.

"If I hadn't birthed he—"

"His pronouns," one of the gods interrupts, their voice thunderous, "are he/they."

Hearing a god advocate for me fills me with unexpected

warmth. They have brown skin and long black hair, and he's dressed in an all-black suit, with gold chain earrings dotting their ears. But it's his eyes—mismatched light and dark blue—that confirm this is Discord, Chaos's father.

Cara purses her lips, but even she doesn't dare argue with Discord.

"If I hadn't birthed them," my mother starts again, not even attempting to hide her displeasure, "I would have questioned whether they were my child at all. ██████████ is certainly their father's child."

My face goes hot. The use of my deadname is deliberate—a rejection of who I am. After all these years, even in front of two trans gods, she still can't accept me as her *son*. She's always been the variety of bigot that was fine with trans people existing—as long as there weren't any trans people in her family. Some things never change, I guess.

"*That* is not my name."

She rolls her eyes.

Discord stands, glowering at Cara. "I will not tolerate dead-naming and misgendering before this Council. Speak of Crow *respectfully*, or do not speak at all."

My mother's face goes pink. It is *so* satisfying. But the matter is settled, and Discord sits again, his face stormy.

Into the quiet of the room, I mutter, "And I don't look *that* much like Dad."

Cara looks at me. Then she blinks, her eyebrows rising high. And she laughs—though the sound is forced. "Oh no," she says. "Do you mean Falcon? Did your uncles really never tell you?"

I'm not sure how to respond to that, so I don't.

"Crow," she says, in the most patronizing tone possible, "*Falcon* isn't your father. Not biologically, anyway."

My mouth opens and closes. Is this a joke? If Falcon isn't my father, then—

Cara tuts and shakes her head. "Haven't you ever wondered why you're able to access so much godmagic? Deathchildren aren't special. Tell me, what are the only beings you know of able to access multiple branches of godmagic?"

I shake my head. "Major and minor gods, but . . ."

Her eyebrows rise higher. I hate how she's looking at me— like I should have understood this impossible thing she's implying long ago. Like there's something wrong with me for never jumping to such an outlandish conclusion.

"But that's—that's not possible," I stammer. Because surely she isn't implying that *I'm*—

"That's enough," Discord says. "We aren't here to toy with the Champion. Crow has won the right to ask for a boon, and we must respect the rules of the contest and grant it to them."

Glamor's face contorts into a snarl as he turns on Discord. "*Respect the rules of the contest?* This *vermin's* participation in the contest has thrown the rules out the window! Not only is it illegal for any Deathchild to participate—"

"Actually," I interrupt, scrambling to pull my whirring thoughts back to the conversation at hand, "there isn't any rule in the contest about Deathchildren being prohibited from participating. There isn't even any rule in the contest about using Deathmagic—I checked."

Discord smirks.

Glamor turns on me with a glower. "Regardless of whether it's against the *Tournament* rules, the existence of Deathchildren is *illegal* in Escal. And I won't spend one moment arguing with a person who should not exist. Crow of the Deathchildren, you are hereby found guilty of being a Deathchild. All who agree say aye."

"As the elected human representative," says my mother, "aye."

"Aye," says Mind.

"Aye," says Architect.

"Nay," says Discord. "Crow is a Deathchild, but as I have maintained from the beginning, that should not be illegal."

"We vote with Discord," say Flora and Fauna.

"Well, I say aye," says Glamor. "So the majority agrees."

Sudden pain bursts through my chest, hot and wet, and I gasp, but I can't move—something cold and hard is holding me in place. There's a blade. A long, pointed blade, pressed to the hilt into my chest. Glamor releases the hilt and lifts his chin, satisfied.

I can't breathe. Black spots cloud my vision. This isn't— I don't want to—

"Crow," Glamor says, "you are hereby sentenced to death."

My legs fold beneath me. I hit the ground, but I don't feel it. There is shouting, somewhere far away. I blink up at a cold white ceiling as my vision dims, as hot rust fills my mouth.

My mother is crouched over me. She brushes the hair out of my eyes. And she does not look sorry. "Goodbye, ██████████," she says. "You can join your father now."

Deadnaming me now as I lay dying is the ultimate insult. *That's not my name!* I want to scream, but blood chokes out my voice. I blink and blink, trying so hard to clear my dimming vision, but it doesn't work. The darkness comes for me no matter how hard I fight. And though I am not ready, I sink into black.

CHAPTER 52

My eyes open.

I'm sitting in an oversized chair, plush with pillows, a fur blanket draped over my torso. In front of me is a crackling fireplace, filling the cabin with warmth. The cabin is small but cozy—to my left is an empty love seat that looks just as plush as the oversized chair I'm sitting in, and to the right a large window overlooks a beautiful snowy day. Evergreens heavy with snow droop in the wintry light, and beyond the trees is a completely frozen lake covered in snow.

It's gorgeous. And I have no idea where I am or how I got here. Normally that would worry me, but I've never felt so relaxed in my life. Everything is okay. I'm safe.

I close my eyes and press my cheek against the soft blanket. The plush, warm fabric is so comforting against my skin. I could stay here forever, snuggling in this blanket in front of this fireplace. What a perfect morning.

"Hello, Crow."

My eyes snap open. "Dad?" My voice breaks, but I'd know

his voice anywhere. And there he is, crouched right in front of me, holding his hands out to me.

Any composure I briefly had is gone. I burst into tears, throwing myself into his arms. His slightly smoky scent, the scratchiness of his short beard against my cheek, the softness of his midsection—it's all exactly the way I remember it. He hasn't aged a day.

That's the thought that forces me to pull away, wiping at my teary eyes. "I don't understand," I say through tears. "You're dead."

"I am," Falcon says. "As are your uncles."

I look up—and there they are. Orin and Alecks, smiling gently at me.

"What are you doing standing there?" I demand with a sob. "Come here!"

They laugh and join in on the hug.

I don't know how long I stay there, wrapped up in the arms of the people who loved me most in the world. The men who raised me. Who looked out for me and did everything they could to keep me safe, to the very end of their lives.

The men who went to the place I couldn't follow and left me with empty grief that I could never fill.

And slowly, slowly, it dawns on me. My dad, Uncle Orin, Uncle Alecks—they *died*. And if they're here now . . .

"Ah," my dad says, seeing the change in my face. "You've realized."

"I'm dead," I say. The words are hollow. Tasteless.

Orin grimaces. "At the moment, yes."

I arch an eyebrow. *"At the moment?"*

"There's someone you need to meet," Dad says. "We'll explain everything together." He and my uncles all stand, and my dad offers me his hand. He helps me up, wrapping me in the fur blanket. I'm wearing the same clothes I wore in the arena, but where a bloody mess should be in the center of my chest is smooth skin and fabric.

I wrap the blanket tighter around myself.

Orin opens the cabin door, and the three of them lead me outside into the woods. What I couldn't see inside was a small path between the trees that leads to a campfire. Four log benches have been set up around the fire, many of them occupied by ravens and crows.

I stop in my tracks so abruptly, my dad bumps into me. I've been here before, in my dreams. There's a man sitting on one of the log benches, dressed in a black cloak. He has golden brown skin; loose, wavy black hair; and deep brown near-black eyes that glint with warmth. A raven sits on his shoulder and tilts its head at me as I approach. A trim beard frames the stranger's angled jaw, and he smiles as he gestures to the log nearest him.

"Go on," my dad says softly behind me. "We're right behind you. It's okay."

My heart thuds heavily in my chest as I step forward. Snow crunches beneath my boots as I approach the log, and some ravens hop aside to make room for me.

"Do you know who I am?" the man asks with a gentle smile. I cannot pull my gaze away from his warm eyes. They are so familiar. Too familiar for me to deny who he must be, but I can't—

"Death," I whisper. I swallow hard and try again. "You're the god of life and death."

The man smiles. "Ravenna taught you well. Good. Do you know why you're here?"

I glance up at my dad, then at my uncles, who are now settling across the campfire on the unoccupied logs. Some crows rustle their feathers, but none seem overly concerned by my uncles' intrusion.

My dad sits on the log next to me and nods with an encouraging smile. This is Death's realm. It's tranquil in a way I'm not sure I've ever really experienced in the living world.

I bite my lip and meet Death's familiar gaze again. "The crows and ravens," I say instead of an answer. "In the living world. Did you send them?"

Death smiles. "I did. I've been keeping an eye on you from the moment you were born."

"Why?" Death doesn't answer—he just watches me with those warm, dark eyes. So I answer his question at last. The question of why I'm here. "I'm dead."

"You are," Death says. "But not for the first time. We've met before—do you remember?"

I frown. "I think I would have remembered dying. Or meeting Death." I hesitate. "Wouldn't I?"

"I'm afraid I'm to blame for that," Alecks says. "Orin and I thought it best to shield you from the trauma, at least while you were young. We were planning to restore your memory after you became a legal adult, but . . ." His lips thin.

"But we died," Orin finishes for him.

"Yeah," Alecks sighs. "That was inconvenient. I'm sorry, Crow. We thought we had more time."

"We assumed we had at least until the end of the Tournament," Orin adds. "We were wrong."

"About that," I say. "When were you going to tell me Alecks is a Mindchild?"

Alecks lets out a long breath.

"I was worried that if you knew, you might rightfully question the gaps in your memory. It was never something I was proud of, so I rarely used it anyway—and even less so after Mind sided with Glamor in their decision to murder the Deathchildren. I'm sorry we lied to you, Crow."

I'm almost afraid to ask, but now I need to know. "What memories did you alter?"

"Just one," Alecks says quickly. "From . . . the Silencing. You remember waking up just as your father came to get you." He bites his lip, reticent to continue.

"The way you remember it," Death says, "Falcon found you before the Enforcers did. But in reality, he found you too late. The Enforcers entered your room while you were sleeping and shot you."

My eyes go wide. "I don't remember being injured at all. Did I heal myself?"

My father touches my shoulder, and when I look at him, his eyes are filled with tears.

"You were dead when I found you," he says, his voice tight with pain. "They'd used bullets—shot you multiple times in the chest. There was so much blood, Crow. It was awful, the worst moment of my life."

"That doesn't make sense," I whisper. "I can't have died."

Falcon shakes his head. "I checked if you were breathing first—you weren't. Then I checked your pulse—nothing. You were gone, Crow. I was inconsolable, weeping like I've never cried in my life, and then—you woke up and began coughing on the smoke. You were absolutely covered in blood, but when I checked your chest again, the wounds had closed without so much as a scar. Like it never happened."

"I altered the blood and your clothes in your memory," Alecks says softly. "You were covered in it when we found you, and your shirt was torn from the bullet holes. You'd sat in that safe room for a long time, and you'd put together that the blood was yours and you'd been shot. You were panicked about it when we found you. So I made you sleep. I altered your memory so you wouldn't remember what had happened to you or your meeting with Death." He looks at Death. "I'm sorry. We thought it'd be safest if they didn't know about you, especially after the Silencing."

Death nods.

I have so many questions, but one is loudest of all—one that I can't understand. I look at Death, meeting his familiar dark eyes, and ask, "But why did you bring me back? Out of all the Deathchildren—so many died that night. Why bring me back and no one else?"

A ghost of a smile whispers over Death's lips. "I didn't bring you back, Crow. You did that yourself."

"That doesn't make any sense," I say. "Deathchildren aren't immortal. Even the minor gods aren't immortal."

But then something Orin said the first time I visited them in prison comes back to me: *The minor Death gods can't die. They're Death's direct children—the only truly immortal beings. Deathless.*

My breath catches in my throat. "Except for the minor Death gods," I whisper.

Death nods. "My direct children cannot die. At least not for long."

Death looks at me, and his gaze is so warm, so familiar, because it's my own.

"You're my father," I whisper.

"You are my child." Death smiles.

My mouth is open, but I don't know what to say. What to think. If Death is my *literal father,* that means I'm a—

"Holy shit," I say.

My uncles laugh. Death's smile widens. Then I blurt out my first question before I can stop myself. "Wait. Then *my mother* had a child with *Death?*"

Death's smile fades. "The pregnancy wasn't intentional. But your mother was always an ambitious woman, and when she learned she was pregnant with a minor god, she thought she could leverage you in her quest for political influence." He nods at Falcon. "That's why she went on to marry a Deathchild."

"Public opinion about Deathchildren hadn't soured so dangerously when you were born," Falcon adds. "But that changed a few years after your birth—and so Deathchildren were no longer useful to her. I think your mother began to resent you when she realized her connection to Deathchildren wouldn't help her political dreams, even though she birthed a minor god. Not long after that, you shared that you weren't a girl, and . . . she didn't like that."

I snort. "That's an understatement." I frown. "But . . . did you know I wasn't your kid?"

Falcon's face goes serious in a way I rarely saw from him. He takes my hands in his and squeezes lightly. "Son," he says, and that word alone fills me with so much warmth, my vision goes blurry with tears, "I knew you weren't my blood—your mother didn't hide that—but I never cared. You were, and always will be, my son. My only child. And I'm so, so proud of you."

I can't stop the tears streaking down my face, and I don't try. Instead, I press my face into his shoulder and hug him tightly. His arms wrap around me, and he presses his face into my hair, just like he used to do when I was little. I never want to let go, but eventually I do, wiping at my face as my uncles, Falcon, and Death watch me with nothing but warmth and love in their eyes.

Leaving this place, this sanctuary full of so many of the people I love most in the world, is going to be excruciating. But something in me senses my time left here is slipping away like a fistful of sand.

Death must sense it too, because his dark eyes meet mine, and he nods. "You've done well, my child," he says. "You are Vengeance. And it's time for you to accept your inheritance."

An excerpt from The Book of Deities, *fourth edition*

THE GODS

Creators of godmagics. Ancestors of all. Keepers of civilization.

Glamor (he/him): the benevolent god of influence; the father of Beauty, Charisma, Love, and Lust

Architect (he/him): the sculptor of the world; the father of Earth, Skies, Ocean, Space, Industry, and Textiles

Mind (she/her): the strategic thinker; the mother of Logic, Telepathy, Empathy, Foresight, Illusion, and Telekinesis

Flora (she/her) and **Fauna** (they/them): the twin gods; the parents of Harvest, Vegetation, Animalia, and Hunt

Discord (he/they): the unknowable god; the father of Flame, War, Panic, Disaster, Deception, Destruction, and Chaos

Life/Death (he/him): the god of the beginning and end; the father of Herald, Medic, Malady, Shade, and Vengeance

CHAPTER 53

✕

For the second time in my life I wake from death to chaos. This time surrounded by screams. But these are not the screams of the devastated, of the terrified, the dying. These are the shouts of the furious, the conflicted, the outraged.

"What are you *thinking*?" Discord thunders. "You just murdered the Champion! They earned the right of an audience with us, the right to a *prize*, and you killed them!"

Glamor tsks. "What choice did we have? Can you imagine how it would look if we allowed a *Deathchild*, whose existence is *illegal*, to become Champion?"

"Oh, because I'm sure it'll look *much* better that we've started killing Champions," Discord shoots back.

"Only *illegal* Champions," Mind retorts. "That *godkiller* never should have been permitted to compete to begin with!"

I'm unsure if I died with my eyes open, but no one seems to notice when I blink. I'm lying just behind Glamor, his shiny white shoes less than an arm's length to my left. Beside him, Mind is also facing away from me, arguing with Discord. I relax and let my eyes unfocus, allowing my view of godmagic to form in my mind's eye. Where most people have particles of magic coursing through them like blood through veins, the gods are brilliant beacons of power. Glamor is pure gold light, so bright it's nearly blinding. Mind, beside him, glows similarly in blue.

I blink again and allow a slow, full breath—wincing at stiffness in my chest. Glamor's dagger is still buried between my ribs, angled up and digging into my heart. I focus my magic around the blade, dulling the nerves and preparing to rapidly stitch up the deep wound I'm about to have.

Then, gritting my teeth, I grab the hilt with both of my hands and yank it out. The pain is hot but distant thanks to the way I dulled the nerves first. Once it's out, my sinews, muscles, and skin stitch rapidly closed. The blade drips with my blood as I sit up and push myself to my feet.

Discord, Mind, and Glamor are still yelling at each other. Discord has absolutely seen me—they're facing me directly, so there's no way he hasn't noticed me getting up—but they seem unfazed. Glamor and Mind are still facing away from me.

Flora and Fauna, on the other hand, leap to their feet.

There's no time to think. No time to reconsider. I know what I came here to do, and nothing will stop me. Not even death.

I move fast. Taking one step to close the gap between myself and Glamor, I plunge his dagger into his back.

Everything happens very quickly from there.

Glamor chokes midsentence and drops to his knees. He tries to grasp the blade in his back, but he can't reach. Gold light bursts from the wound.

I rip the dagger out of his back and throw it at Mind just as she turns to me.

"No!" Mind screams, but before she can properly react, the blade plunges deep beneath her collarbone, near her shoulder. Blue light explodes from the wound. Mind rips the dagger out of her chest. It shouldn't be a killing blow—the blade landed too close to her shoulder for that—but the color is draining out of her nevertheless. Blue light spills down her cheeks like tears as Glamor collapses to his hands and knees, molten gold pouring out of his mouth and puddling on the floor beneath his hands.

"Godkiller!" Architect cries, nearly falling off his throne in haste to get away from me.

I flip my knife out of its sheath and send it flying. It hits Architect square between the shoulders.

"Hmm," I hear myself say. "I guess that's finally true."

Maybe I should be happy, watching the masterminds behind the destruction of my people bleed out every ounce of their power. Maybe I should feel triumphant. Or maybe I should be horrified.

Instead I am numb.

I turn to my mother, but she's already reached the massive doors. I flick my last knife into my hand. She heaves the door open and shrieks, "Guards!"

I let my knife fly. Enforcers burst into the room. My knife clatters uselessly against a helmet as my mother stumbles into the hallway, out of sight. I lunge toward her, swearing under my breath, but there's no time. Two Enforcers tackle me to the ground and roughly yank my arms behind my back. My fury at my mother's escape clashes with my satisfaction. I did what I needed to do. The gods behind my people's devastation are dead. There's only one person left to answer for her crimes, but I'll have to find another way to ensure she doesn't escape justice.

The Enforcers drag me to my feet, but I don't struggle. Discord catches my gaze and nods at me, his face grim.

Then the Enforcers shove me out of the room.

As soon as we step out of the elevator, cameras are in my face. Flashes of photographers and drones alike, making the space feel unreal. The Enforcers struggle to hold a crowd of journos back while moving me forward.

"Champion Crow!" someone yells. "What happened? Why are you being arrested?"

It feels like an out-of-body experience. Like none of this is real. Like I didn't just kill a bunch of gods. Like my hands aren't slick with their cooling blood.

But there's no sense in hiding it. So I don't.

"I am Death's youngest child!" I yell over the crowd. "And I will not rest until my siblings are free!"

Something slams against the back of my skull, and my legs give out from under me. I'm crouching on concrete and blinking through shadows. There are boots and legs and screaming all around me. My head is throbbing, but it barely takes a pulse of magic to stem the bleeding from my scalp and melt the pain away.

"Get up!" an Enforcer screams before leveling a kick at my ribs. The pain is dull and distant thanks to Maddox's armor, and once again my magic works quickly to heal any damage. When he pulls his boot back again, I stagger to my feet. I want so badly to spit in his face, but I don't.

I don't hide from the cameras—I keep my head held high.

I don't fight—I let them shove me into a van.

And only when the van doors shut, closing me into a compartment with six Enforcers, do I sit down, close my eyes, and let the gravity of what just happened, of what I just did and what I am, sink in.

Minor god.

Deathless.

Godkiller.

Me.

I did what I set out to do. The Deathchildren are avenged. The gods behind our annihilation are dead. Because of me.

As reality settles over me, I can't stop shivering. My teeth are chattering in my mouth. But I don't regret the chaos I just unleashed. I am forcing much-needed change.

And I am not sorry.

CHAPTER 54

It is finally true what they say about you, my child. My Vengeance.

You are a godkiller.

Your arrest does not go quietly. While they register you and imprison you with your siblings, the media is in a frenzy. Your name is repeated on every channel. *Crow of the Death-children*, they say. *Crow the Godkiller. Crow the Champion. Crow of the Shallows.*

Crow of the Dead.

And just as the news of an imprisoned Champion breaks, your friend the journalist publishes her interview with you, taken before your final match. Together you discuss the wide gap of inequality between the upper levels of the city and the Shallows. You call out the exorbitant levels of wealth on display on Godlevel and Midlevel while people starve and drown and die of infection in the Shallows.

Then you discuss the pumps. The way the upper levels of the city dump their floodwater into the Shallows. Together you detail the evidence: the maps, the translated runes on the pumps, the president's signature on the order directing the creation of pumps to flood the Shallows.

The reaction might have been quieter had you set off a bomb.

In the Shallows, over a hundred thousand people gather at the wall. It is a mass protest the likes of which Escal has never seen. It is solidarity in pain and righteous anger.

The lawmakers panic and activate martial law. The Enforcers gather before the wall and demand that the people return home. They point guns and water cannons and throw smoke grenades, but the people push forward. They will not turn back.

Out of an alley emerges a god dressed in a plain black hoodie and dark jeans. They slip soundlessly between people, bumping shoulders and weaving around protesters until he reaches the center of the crowd. And as water cannons bruise the front of the crowd and smoke wafts thick and burning in the air, the god Discord breathes generations of pent-up rage into the crowd and whispers, *Now is the time to fight*.

It is a match to kindling.

It is an explosion.

CHAPTER 55

The air is heavy with magic suppression.

I sit with my back against the wall on a hard white floor. The entire cell is white—the floors, walls, and single door are all coated in some kind of shiny reflective material, like ceramic. A small bench made of the same cold material is on the opposite side of my small cell, with a thin white sheet thrown over it. The sheet is as soft as sandpaper—I guess it's supposed to pass as a blanket. In the corner a small metal toilet and sink. Above me are blindingly bright lights, all white, save for a thin strip of green light outlining the rectangular ceiling.

The strip indicating the suppressor is on. As if the weight of the room didn't give it away.

The active suppressor makes the air feel as heavy as lead. My muscles ache with the strain of holding myself up, like I've been lifting weights for hours. My joints, already aching from my furious immune system, are near to the point of screaming without my Deathmagic to divert the inflammation. The space where my skull meets my spine is throbbing so badly I can feel it in my temples, and moving my fingers or knees at all is agony.

At least the pain distracts me from the silence. I hum just to prove I can make noise. Tap my foot against the wall, even though it sends twinges of pain through my knees. Anything to break the quiet. Anything to prove that I can.

I don't know how long I sit there. I don't know how long they intend to keep me here. I only hope my godsiblings haven't been kept in isolation like this for the last ten years. That kind of isolation, for that long, can break a person.

I try not to think about an eternity imprisoned in a cell like this.

I try not to think about what they will do to a godkiller who can't die.

I breathe deeply into my belly and squeeze my forearms, gritting my teeth at the ache in my fingers. But every squeeze and every breath gives me something to focus on that isn't the void of terror threatening to swallow me whole.

And then the lights flip off.

I blink in the sudden red-tinted darkness. At the lightness in the air. At the strip of red now outlining the ceiling. I grin. The lights didn't just turn off—the *power* did.

And so did the suppressor.

My Deathmagic floods back in all at once, and I redirect it toward my neck, hands, and knees, soothing the inflammation that has my joints throbbing. It isn't enough to erase the pain entirely, but it makes it bearable.

Then, wincing as I stretch my stiff knees, I stand and face the door. Without electricity keeping the room magically suppressed, it's just a locked door. And when you have magic, you have all the keys you could possibly need.

I step up to the door, lick my finger, and trace a single small rune in the center. *Open.* I press my palm against the rune, activating the magic. A rush of warmth bursts down my arm, followed by a quiet *click.*

Just because there isn't power doesn't mean there aren't Enforcers. So I push open the door, just a bit. Nothing. Carefully, I open it all the way.

The hallway is lit with the same eerie red light. I half expect to find guards and guns, but instead I find four people, all in matching gray prisoner uniforms, speaking quietly among themselves. When I step into the hallway, they stop and look at me. They all look related, with varying lengths of black hair, dark eyes, and shades of similar golden-brown skin. They don't just look related to each other; they look related to *me.*

The four minor gods of Death are watching me.

"Well," says the thinnest of the bunch—a man who is little more than skin and bones. Malady, I think. "That answers that question."

The tallest of them—a woman with long hair woven into a simple three-strand braid—smiles at me and steps forward. "You must be Crow—Vengeance now, right? I'm Herald. These are our siblings, Mal"—she gestures to the man who's just spoken—"Medic"—she nods to a short, curvy woman beside her—"and Shade"—she gestures to a tall person with a freshly shaved head leaning against the wall.

"Oh," I say. "I didn't expect any of you to know about me."

"Dad kept us up-to-date," Shade says, crossing their arms over their flat chest.

"Does that mean you know where the Deathchildren are being kept?" I ask.

Shade smiles.

⸻

Fifty-seven Deathchildren brimming with Deathmagic and five Death gods meet a wall of Enforcers at the prison's exit. Blazing red lights flash through the darkness while a panic alarm screams, but it's far too late for that. The Enforcers are spaced out just enough to create a wall-to-wall barrier of glowing shields. Their helmets are down, full-body armor donned, and heavy guns pointed in our direction.

I don't know how many Enforcers are supposed to guard a high-security prison, but the thirty or so standing between us and the exit seem like nowhere near enough.

"You do realize," I say, stepping forward, "that there are at least two of us for each of you."

"Stay where you are or we'll shoot!" an Enforcer screams.

"Why don't you see how that goes for you?" I call back.

A *pop* like a firecracker and the world is noise. But I don't flinch. With a flick of Shade's fingers, a wall of solid shadow flies up in front of us all, shielding us from the bullets.

Shade steps next to me, their expression wholly unimpressed. "Mind if I . . . ?"

I step aside. "All yours."

They crack their fingers. Smile with the expression of someone who has been dreaming of this moment for a decade. Then they move their long fingers like plucking the cords of an instrument—or manipulating puppet strings. With a sharp yank they pull their hands up, and the shadows explode in a writhing mass of ravens trailing darkness. The ravens screech, forming two flocks so thick we can see nothing but darkness and feathers and sharp beaks and talons. They descend on the screaming, shooting Enforcers, creating an aisle for us down the center.

Shade nods at me, gesturing down the aisle with their chin. I wave at the others, and we walk right through, past the beat of wings and rip of flesh and blasts of gunfire and wet screams. Past the clattering rifles falling to the floor. Out the front door of a prison that has held my siblings for far too long.

CHAPTER 56

The last time I stood outside this Midlevel prison, the rain was coming down like the end of the world. Tonight the only clouds in the sky are smoke.

I walk up to the edge of the cliff, peering into what should be the neon lights of the Shallows below. Instead there's only darkness. The city of Midlevel is dark too, which explains the power outage in the prison.

Well, I know exactly how Shallowsfolk reacted to my interview.

A raven flies down and perches on the ground next to me. It blinks up at me with unfathomably dark eyes.

Now that I know the truth, it feels like Death—my father, I guess—telling me he's with me. I smile.

Herald approaches me. "Medic and I are going to take the Deathchildren to safety outside the city. I understand you likely have unfinished business here, but when you're done, you should meet us so we can discuss next steps."

I nod. "I will."

"Good." She looks over my shoulder, and I turn to find Shade and Mal watching us with wide smiles. "I know it's not in your nature for either of you to turn down a fight, but the invitation to join us is open nevertheless," she says.

Shade stretches their arms over their head. "And miss out on all the fun?"

"*Someone* has to look out for them," Mal says, rubbing Shade's bare head, which earns him a slap on the hand. "I'll make sure they make it to the haven when we're done."

Shade rolls their eyes. "Okay, *Dad*." They look at me. "Hey, I know you haven't had much chance to practice, but everything we can do? You can do. We each have our own areas of expertise, so you'll have to figure yours out eventually. But in the meantime . . . don't hold back."

Suddenly Chaos's skepticism about my ability to access more than one branch of Deathmagic makes a lot more sense.

"Crow!"

Chaos, Lark, and Maddox come running down the hill leading out of the city.

"We're here," Chaos pants out between breaths, "to rescue you."

Lark rolls her eyes. "I told you both they'd be fine."

The three of them notice the gods standing all around me and stop in their tracks.

"Whoa," Maddox says.

"Awww," says Chaos. "I love a good family reunion."

While Shade and Mal go wreak havoc on the city center, Chaos, Lark, Maddox, and I head for the wall separating Midlevel from Godlevel while we all catch each other up.

"The people have taken over the lower wall," Maddox tells me with a grin. "The Enforcers were badly outnumbered, so they retreated to Midlevel. They tried to shut the whole thing down, but they were overrun. People got control of the elevator and a bunch more set up ladders and ropes so people are just *climbing* the thing."

"Turns out," Lark says, "telling everyone the rich are deliberately drowning the general public while they live in luxury kind of pissed the public off. And arresting the first Shallowsfolk Champion didn't help." She pauses. "Though you *did* kill a bunch of gods, so . . . fair?"

"I'm pretty sure my family helped move things along," Chaos adds with a smirk. He gestures to the flaming buildings, flipped-over cars, and broken glass all around us. "This is all very Discord."

"Are Ravenna and Mouse safe?" I ask. "And Maddox's family?"

"I left Mouse in a rune-warded room in the hotel," Chaos says. "It's possible the people will trash the place, but no one will be able to get into that room but me. I promise."

"And Nan is going to meet us outside the city with Maddox's family," Lark says, lifting her cell. "We've been in contact with her."

I nod. "Okay. Good."

We reach the border wall separating Midlevel from Godlevel, where a crowd of people has amassed, throwing rocks and whatever other junk they can find at the barrier. Unlike the one in the Shallows, *wall* here is a misnomer—it's more of a force field artificially walling off the only entrance to Godlevel: the staircase made of gold. Now there's another wall made of Enforcers, keeping everyone at least fifty feet away from the staircase.

We make our way to the front of the crowd, where Enforcers are sitting in a line of armored trucks. It's the trucks, specifically, that make my stomach curl with disgust, because even with the water cannons they're preparing and the guns at the ready, I wouldn't put it past the Enforcers to run over people to protect the obscenely wealthy.

I look at Chaos. "Do you think you can handle the trucks?"

He grins. "I was hoping you'd ask."

Chaos crouches and touches the ground, smiling as he closes his eyes. For a long moment nothing happens, and I realize that beyond the disruption fields, I don't actually know what Chaos can do. Discord's children are all about, well, *destruction,* but that can look like a lot of things.

Then the ground begins to shake.

An earsplitting crack rips through the air so loud that I jump. Then the entire line of trucks falls a foot straight down into the earth. Enforcers scream and scramble to get out of the way— and out of the trucks—as the ground breaks like a cracked egg beneath them. The void grows wider, opening up beneath the barrier separating us from Godlevel until the barrier crackles with static, then blinks out. The trucks sink deeper and deeper into the chasm until they topple over entirely and tumble into the rapidly deepening crack fifty feet from us. Then, once the trucks are gone, the ground snaps shut like the closing jaws of a giant, and a *boom* thunders around us.

The crowd surges forward with a cry, meeting the Enforcers head-on.

"Damn," Maddox says with a low whistle as Chaos stands. "I thought only Architects could move the earth like that."

"Architects can *make* stuff out of the earth," Chaos corrects. "I can't do that. But I sure as hell can rip things apart."

"That's useful," I say. "Think you can help me destroy a bunker?"

Chaos grins. "Sure. What bunker?"

The genocidal gods are dead. But there's still someone in a position of power who knew the annihilation of Deathchildren was coming and did nothing to warn us. Who has spent the last decade demonizing Deathchildren. Who has turned her back on all of us in the Shallows and left us to drown.

I step into the wave of people streaming into Godlevel. "It's time to pay my mother a visit."

CHAPTER 57

The Manor is the most heavily guarded building in all of Escal, so none of us are surprised to find an electrified force field gate erected around the presidential grounds.

By the time we arrive, a huge crowd of people who have forced their way into Godlevel have already found the Manor public entrance, and they're throwing sticks, planks, tires—literally anything they can find—at the gate, only to watch their ammunition largely burning up on contact. One group of people is even trying to roll a car up the hill. Their presence has warranted a large group of guards standing just inside the barrier in case they make it through, so Lark, Maddox, Chaos, and I walk quietly to the other side of the grounds, far from the entrance.

There are significantly fewer people the farther toward the back of the property we go. The grounds are actually several miles long, and after about half a mile we stop, near the tall, picturesque rows of a vineyard. As we near the barrier, it buzzes lowly, like a quiet growl.

A distant *boom* that shakes the ground makes us all pause.

We look toward the sound—the front of the Manor—where there's now a plume of dark smoke. Still, smoke from Midlevel has been rising, so hard to say if that's really new.

"I think," Maddox says, "that might have been the car." He frowns at the barrier. "But it didn't even flicker."

"I don't think blowing it up is going to be the answer," Chaos says. "Not unless you want to meet whatever's left of the army."

"I was hoping for a stealthier approach while the Enforcers are distracted with the crowd out front," I say.

"I imagine a gate meant to protect the president isn't going to succumb to mundane magic," Lark says thoughtfully. "At least, not the easily accessible kind."

I look at Maddox. "I know your thing is weapons and armor, but is this something you can finesse?"

Maddox bites his lip thoughtfully. "This *is* armor, technically." He pauses, then nods. "I think our best bet is interrupting the flow of the charge to create a gap we can enter through. But if *I* were the creator of this barrier, I'd make sure an alert was in place to let me know if that happened."

"I bet this thing kills squirrels and birds all the time, though," I say. "Even if we set off an alert, the Enforcers are stretched pretty thin. I'm willing to bet they won't send a whole army over here to check it out."

Maddox nods. "I agree."

"Great," Lark says. "So how do we interrupt the flow?"

Maddox crouches in front of the barrier, frowning deeply. "I need metal. Preferably something high-quality, like steel or cast iron."

"Damn," Chaos says, "I forgot to bring my frying pan to the riot."

Maddox smiles, just a little.

"They took my knives at the prison, but I'm assuming you guys didn't come empty-handed," I say.

Lark hesitates. "Is this going to destroy the metal item?"

"Yeah." Maddox grimaces. "Sorry."

Chaos gasps. "Wait! How much do you need?"

"Enough to make a wide enough hole for us to crawl through," Maddox says.

Chaos drops his backpack and begins digging inside. Then he pulls out a metal ruler, of all things, and a folded leather case. He opens the case to reveal a set of sleek black metal knitting needles.

I arch an eyebrow. "You thought you were going to have time to knit during a riot?"

Chaos blushes. "I didn't bring them intentionally—I forgot to take my supplies out of my bag. But they're steel—will it be enough?"

Maddox reaches toward the case, then hesitates. "Yes but . . . are you sure? I won't be able to restore it when we're done."

Chaos looks sadly at his needles but then bites his lip and nods. "They're my favorite set, but I can buy more. And I have, like, five other sets anyway. I'm sure."

Maddox kisses Chaos's cheek. "I'll make you another set."

"Oh, you don't—"

"I'll make you another set," he says, more firmly. Then he takes the leather case and reverently pulls the knitting needles out, lining them up in pairs to create a long line in the grass.

He frowns, rearranging them so the thickest needles are no longer in pairs and the thinnest needles are arranged in triplicate to create a somewhat even width. Then, apparently satisfied, he nods and brings his hands over the lined-up needles.

Maddox moves his fingers fluidly, and the needles vibrate hard, then press together into a long strip of liquid metal in the air. His fingers move like a sculptor working clay, stretching and pinching and pushing together and shaping. The metal strip forms into a circular frame about two feet across and several inches wide.

Maddox tilts his head, gaze fixed on the floating frame. "Think everyone can climb through that without touching the metal?"

"Why without touching the metal?" Chaos asks cautiously.

Maddox nods to the barrier a foot ahead of us. "Because once I shove this in there and hold it in place, it's going to get really hot."

"I'm pretty sure you have the widest shoulders," I say. "So if you can fit in there while holding it in place, the rest of us will manage."

"All right." Maddox positions himself in front of the barrier, the frame just inches away from the pulsing energy. "Once it's in, we should move as quickly as possible. I don't know how long I'll be able to keep it in place, but I'll go through last."

"And I'll go first," I say.

No one argues with that.

Maddox throws his hands out and the frame shoots forward, slamming hard into the barrier. Blue energy pulses from the impact, and the frame shivers as it presses harder against the barrier. Huge sparks fly off the metal, but then—it's in. A gap in the barrier appears within the frame, energy hissing around the metal.

"Go!" Maddox says, his voice strained.

I dive right through, landing in a roll and scrambling out of the way. Lark follows after me the same way—but much more gracefully. Chaos shakes his head and crawls awkwardly through, wincing as the heat of the metal gets close to his skin—but then he's through. Maddox moves slowly, sliding one leg in before ducking through and pulling his second leg through. Then he drops his hands as he collapses back in the grass. The frame *flies* straight out of the barrier like a rocket, flipping end over end before it lands, smoking, between two rows of grape vines.

"Holy shit," Maddox says with a laugh. "Holy shit, that actually worked."

"Because you're a *genius*." Chaos grabs his hands and helps him up, grinning widely.

Maddox beams and jogs over to the smoking hunk of metal, turning it into a balled-up lump with a swipe of his hand before depositing it in his pocket. "Just in case."

"Great," Lark says. "Now for the hard part."

We turn toward the Manor.

Heavily armed guards patrol the grounds wearing night-vision helmets, so I cloak the four of us in shadow and lead the way through the world draped in gray. Under the shadow, the air is thick and cold, and the darkness sits tangibly on our shoulders.

"Will anyone hear us if we talk under here while someone's nearby?" Chaos whispers from somewhere behind me.

"Not if we whisper," I respond quietly. "Just keep your voices down."

We slip past half a dozen guards in this fashion, beyond the vineyard, and past the private gardens. We weave around lounging chairs and slip between hedges and topiary before pausing in the shadow of a large bush just around the corner from the back door.

The back door is guarded by no less than four Enforcers.

"I don't think we'll be able to slip past them," I say. "They're blocking off the entrance, and even if we could, the lights are on inside, which would make our shadow cover a lot more obvious."

"Then we forget the stealth plan?" Chaos asks.

I frown. "I'm not sure it's going to be possible to get to my mother with a hundred Enforcers chasing us. Especially since we don't know exactly where in the Manor she is."

"We could try taking them down quietly," Maddox suggests.

"Or," says Lark, "we go in through this window."

I blink and look back. Lark is pointing to a first-floor window just above her head. The room behind the window is dark.

"That can't possibly be unlocked," I say.

Lark pulls an oil flask out of her pocket with a grin. "That won't be hard to fix."

"Won't it set off an alarm?" Maddox asks.

"Probably." Lark shrugs. "But as long as the Enforcers don't find anything when they come to check it out, I don't think they'll be able to do much."

One rune and three minutes later, Lark is wiping off the oil from the window as she closes and locks it again behind us. We then crouch beneath a desk, where I keep the shadows cinched tight around us. Moments later, the beat of boots against hardwood fills the room as the lights slap on. The overhead light casts shadows beneath the desk we're hiding under, so our shadow coverage blends right in.

We watch in silence as several pairs of legs walk past us and the Enforcers search the small room. It seems to be a private office of some kind, with a nice view out onto the garden. On the left side of the room are bookshelves and a huge map hung on the wall, with a lounge and coffee table in the center of the room, and of course the desk we're under on the right. An Enforcer pulls the desk chair out and crouches, staring directly at us.

This is where we'd be in trouble if we were using runemagic to make ourselves invisible. I stare back into the visor equipped with heat vision and night vision, but unlike typical runemagic invisibility, the shadows I've pulled around us cloak our temperature as well. I hold my breath for what feels like the longest five seconds of my life before the Enforcer stands and turns to their colleagues.

"Clear."

"Clear," someone else responds. "Do you think it was a malfunction? The window isn't even unlocked."

"Who knows?" a third person says. "Those lowtowners are still messing with the barrier, and even Godlevel residences and businesses are losing power."

The lights turn off. The boots march out of the room.

"That was awesome," Chaos whispers. "I love Deathmagic."

I smile and let out a slow, shaky breath. "We should move on."

We climb out from under the desk, and I start toward the door, but Lark grabs my arm. "Hold on." She nods to a computer propped up on the desk. "Whose computer do you think that is?"

I shrug. "If it's in here . . ." I glance around the room, and the map tacked up on the opposite side of the office catches my eye. Even from over here I can tell it's of the Shallows, which seems . . odd. I cross the room, frowning. It's a pretty up-to-date map, but there are buildings x-ed out in red, and there's a second map on translucent paper draped over the first that looks almost like a map of pipes beneath the Shallows.

I look at the Xs again, but I don't recognize what they're marking—they just seem to be random residences.

Residences like mine.

My finger hovers over the red X on my uncles' home. The one that is now little more than a burned skeleton.

"Are these . . . people who were helping Deathchildren?" I ask.

"What?" Lark looks up from the other side of the room, where she's bent over the computer with Maddox. "Is my nan's house marked?"

I check and breathe a sigh of relief. "No."

Lark nods and turns back to her work. I press the translucent map down again. There's a pipe leading out from the red X of my home, but not every home has a pipe—in fact, most don't. So not pipes, then.

The answer hits me with a pang that makes my heart stop. "They're mapping out the tunnels."

"Hey, these aren't books," Chaos says somewhere behind me.

I turn and find him standing in front of the nearest bookshelf, holding open what looks like a book. When I walk over and look at it in his hands, my frown only deepens. The "book" is actually just a case made to look like a book. Inside are pages of data chips.

I grab another "book" off the shelf at random—same thing. Closing the case, I find the title printed on the front cover and go cold: *Known Cultist Sympathizers*. My heart in my throat, I close one Chaos is holding: *Record of Cultists, A–B*.

I can't hide the horror from my voice. "Are these *all* about Deathchildren?"

Chaos frowns and starts pulling more cases from the shelf. I walk over to the next bookshelf and grab two more cases: *Cultist Magic: Herald Branch* and *Cultist Magic: Shade Branch*.

"The computer's full of that shit too," Lark says grimly across the room.

The panic is rearing up inside me, making it hard to think. Hard to breathe. I close my eyes and force myself to take a slow, deep breath, filling up my belly and letting it out. I can't lose my shit. Not now. Not here.

Later. I can freak out later.

I shove the cases back onto the shelf. "We have to destroy it. All of it. Everything in this room."

What if we hadn't come in through this room? I never would have known this was here. I would have *left it here* for any rogue Enforcer to use to hunt the rest of us down. I would have walked right—

Lark is in front of me, and she is holding my arms and squeezing lightly. "Come back," she says softly. "You're here with me. I'm here. Chaos is here. Maddox is here."

I squeeze back and take another deep breath through my belly. Focus. I have to focus.

Chaos gently touches my shoulder. "It's going to be okay, Crow. If there's one thing I'm good at, it's destroying shit." He grins. "How about you let me handle turning everything in here to ash while the rest of you go find the godsdamned president?"

I bite my lip and nod. "I won't be able to keep cloaking you if we split up."

Chaos's grin only widens. "I know this baby face is deceiving, but I'm not a kid, I'm a *god*. I'm not afraid of some Enforcers. And you shouldn't be either."

I nod again, my body buzzing with anxious hooks. "Okay."

"Say it."

I hesitate, but Chaos is serious, and even Lark is nodding along. So as silly as it feels, I force the words off my tongue. "I'm not afraid of some Enforcers. I'm a god."

"Again."

This time the words come out easily. Forcefully. "I'm a *god*. I'm not afraid of some godsdamned Enforcers."

Chaos smiles and snaps his fingers, conjuring a ball of flame in his hand. "You're ready. Go."

CHAPTER 58

We've barely stepped into the bright light of the hallways before the fire alarm goes off in the room we've left behind.

Now in a brightly lit space, our shadow coverage—which currently resembles three large blobs of inexplicable shadow—is a lot more conspicuous. Out here, the floors are a rich dark hardwood made up of thick, expensive planks, and the walls are painted a deep burgundy, which at least makes the stark contrast of our shadows a little less obvious. I crouch and keep close to the walls to try to keep out of anyone's immediate line of sight as much as possible. Behind me, Lark and Maddox follow my example.

We've traveled about halfway down the hall before six Enforcers race past us to the office now spewing smoke into the air. I worry about Chaos for about half a second before a loud *whoosh* and a burst of heat explodes from the office door, followed by a massive wall of flames.

So, yeah, he's fine.

We round the corner and more Enforcers run by, some carrying fire extinguishers, but it is way too late for that. The hallway has opened up into a massive room, to the side of a grand staircase that branches off in three directions at the top. A group of Enforcers are descending the stairs in a tight formation as the three of us step to the end of the staircase.

A familiar woman's voice cries out, "Stop!"

The Enforcers stop in the middle of the staircase. I freeze, looking more closely at the group now that they've stopped moving. And there she is, right in the center, flanked on all sides by heavily armed men.

And she's looking directly at me.

"Gods above and below," she hisses. "Don't you see that? Right there?" She points at the blob of shadow the three of us are standing in. "It's *the cultists*! They're here!"

For one long, satisfying moment the guards squint at us, then look at each other, clearly confused. But at the end of the day, it doesn't really matter if the Enforcers see us now that I've located my mother.

I throw the shadow off us, enjoying the way the guards go stiff with shock at us materializing seemingly out of thin air. All but one guard rushes toward us, while the remaining guard ushers the president out the front door.

"We'll handle the guards," Lark says, giving me a shove. "Go get her."

So I do.

CHAPTER 59

I don't realize how smoky the air inside the Manor has gotten until I burst out into the cool outdoors. The Enforcer escorting the president spins around to face us, gun ready. I throw my arm up, thickening the night into a solid wall of shadow like Shade did; then I push it forward, imagining it wrapping around the Enforcer like a cocoon. The shadow wall shoots forward, engulfing the Enforcer and sending him sprawling to the ground in a writhing mass of shadow.

Which leaves just President Cara.

She stares at me, wide-eyed, as I approach her. She stumbles back, her arms out defensively. "Please!" she cries. "My child. I'm your *mother*!"

"Any attachment I had to that label evaporated when you left me for dead," I say coolly.

"I—I'm sorry," Cara stammers, eyes wide and filling with tears. "I didn't want to leave you behind, but I didn't have a choice! You are *a child of Death*. I couldn't shield you from what was coming." She staggers backward, and her foot catches on the shadow-encased Enforcer's leg. Cara sprawls onto the ground with a cry and begins crawling backward, trying to keep distance between us. "If you weren't a god, I would have tried to save you!"

"No," I say flatly. "You wouldn't have."

"If I could do it again—"

This actually makes me laugh, though the sound is hollow. Cold. "It hasn't even been a day since you stood aside and watched Glamor *kill* me. You've had your chances."

"Please don't kill me," she whimpers.

"I won't."

Her eyes go wide, confused. Hopeful.

"Get up," I say. "Hands behind your back."

She stands, trembling. I glance back at Maddox and Lark, who have just stepped outside. "Mads, do you still have that metal in your pocket?"

His eyes go wide, which is all the warning I have before hot agony cuts deep into my chest. A scream catches in my throat, wetness slicking my shirt. I look back at my mother, who's holding a knife to the hilt in my chest.

She's smiling. Victorious. The performance of a regretful mother wiped clean from her triumphant face.

"I think," I say through gritted teeth, even as my mouth fills with hot rust, "you've forgotten I'm a *Death god*."

███████████████

"To you," I say, "my name is Vengeance."

I grab the hilt of the dagger. She jerks her hand back, like my touch has burned her. Then, with a yank that makes my vision go white with pain, I slide the knife out of my chest and throw it to the side.

"Maddox," I say stiffly as I direct a flow of magic to healing the wound in my chest, "I'd appreciate it if you'd cuff President Cara with that metal in your pocket."

She runs. I throw up a wall of solid shadow that she crashes right into. She sinks to her knees with a wail as Maddox and Lark approach her.

"Don't *touch* me!" she screeches as Lark pulls her hands behind her back. Then she must recognize Lark, because her eyes go wide. "Lark! Don't do this to me—I tried to save you, you know—"

"I think," Lark responds icily, "it'd be best if you stopped talking."

"You won't walk out of here alive!" she screeches as Maddox approaches her. "You're dead! All of you! *Dead!*"

Maddox works quickly, forming the metal over her wrists into thick cuffs connected at the center.

"Thanks," I say to my friends when it's done.

Maddox nods at my bloodied shirt. "You okay?"

"I'm fine." I take my mother's shoulder firmly. "Let's go."

<hr/>

We've just crested the hill looking onto the grand entrance—and the barrier below—when an explosion behind us sets the rest of the Manor aflame. Bursts of static shower over the barrier; then that too blinks out, all at once.

"Hmm," I say. "Looks like the fire has reached the power generator."

Cara's eyes go wide. "No."

The crowd surges forward, slamming into the sparse wall of Enforcers left. It doesn't take long for the sheer mass of people to push through the Enforcers' weakened defenses, and soon they're racing up the hill toward us.

Cara digs her heels into the stone pathway. "No!" she screams. "No, no, no! The people—"

"Aren't thrilled to see you, I agree," I say. "Do you think it's because you're living in luxury while they starve? Or maybe it's because you've been deliberately drowning them. Hard to say."

She turns around, her eyes wide, staggering as I continue pushing her toward the crowd. "You can't do this to me. They'll *kill* me!"

"Yes," I say, steeling my voice. "I imagine they will."

"I'm your *mother*! I *gave birth* to you!"

"You stabbed me five minutes ago. You can't possibly expect me to feel bad for you."

The crowd is upon us now, but they pause, giving us a wide berth.

"Lark, please!" My mother lurches toward her. "You were always like a daughter to me. I never wanted any harm to come to you—"

"I was never your daughter," Lark seethes. She points to me. "*Crow* was your child. And you left them behind to die with the rest of us."

"I didn't have a choice!" Cara insists.

"You always have a choice," I say. "You just chose to abandon your family and save yourself. So be it."

She turns to Maddox. "You seem like a nice young man—"

He throws his hands up and takes a step back. "Don't look at me—I don't even know you."

I shove her toward the crowd and take several steps back. "She's all yours."

President Cara tries to run, but she barely makes it a foot before the crowd descends on her, swarming around her so quickly that in seconds I can't see her anymore. A scream rips out of her, one long note before it abruptly cuts off.

I turn away, facing Lark and Maddox, who are watching me with sad, grim expressions. "Let's find Chaos and go," I say. "We're done here."

CHAPTER 60

Standing on a cliffside, I watch for the second time as a place I called home burns. But this time it's different. This time the upper two levels of Escal were never really my home, not really. While the Shallows took me in and called me their own, Mid-level and Godlevel ground us into dust. They shut us away so they wouldn't have to look at the suffering of their own making.

So now we're making them look.

Mouse purrs beneath my chin, and I gently pet between her ears. After we found Chaos, he brought us to the rune-warded room in the Godlevel hotel so we could retrieve her, along with bags of packed clothes, food, and water for each of us.

I don't know what will happen from here. The Godcouncil will need restructuring. The minor gods and godchildren will argue about how to move forward. Maybe the elected president after this one will work to repair the damage done to the Shallowsfolk. Or maybe the president will be worse than the last and try to wipe the Shallows from the map entirely. I don't know. But I know this time we aren't going to sit around waiting for it to happen.

Someone touches my shoulder—Ravenna. I turn away from the flaming mass of city below, from smoky skies and blackened buildings, to my friends. To Lark, and Chaos, and Maddox, and Ravenna, all watching me with concern in their eyes. To Shade, and Mal, and Herald, and Medic, and the crowd of Deathchildren congregated behind them along with Maddox's family, watching the city burn with something like satisfaction in their expressions.

"Are you all right?" Chaos asks me.

Lark tsks. "Of course they aren't."

Chaos winces. "Sorry, I just mean—"

"It's okay," I say. "I'm not okay, but I will be."

Ravenna nods. "Together, we will survive, and we will rebuild. Starting with Homestead."

It was Ravenna's idea to rebuild Homestead to house the escaped Deathchildren now that the engineers of our destruction are dead. While Chaos works with his dad to re-form the Godcouncil with the remaining gods, Ravenna, Maddox, Medic, and Mal will stay behind to begin rebuilding the first Deathchild village in over a decade. Maddox's moms have said they want to stay close to Maddox and help the Shallows recover. The rest of my siblings, Lark, and I are going to find the other Deathchildren survivors to return to Homestead.

Herald meets my gaze. "You said you know how to get to the Deathchild haven?"

I nod. The directions Alecks gave me, all those nights ago, are etched into my brain forever. The haven where they've been sending Deathchildren for years. "It'll be a long journey on foot, but we can do it."

"Better get going, then," Shade says, stretching their arms

over their head. They heft up a truly enormous backpack and sling it over their shoulder.

I take one last look at the burning city behind me. At a place soon reduced to rubble. At a place I've left undeniably broken, that I can only hope will be rebuilt into something better than it's ever been before. A place with little left but ash.

But we Deathchildren are nothing if not resilient.

Lark takes my hand and squeezes tight. I squeeze back. Mouse chirps and rubs her tiny head against my chin.

"C'mon," I say, turning away from the city one last time. "Let's bring everyone home."

ACKNOWLEDGMENTS

Wow. Another book complete. They say it takes a village to raise a child, but the same is also true of releasing a book into the world. And I'm so grateful for my incredible publishing village.

To Louise, for having my back through the world's longest contract negotiations (I exaggerate, but only slightly) and persevering through a very weird and rocky time in publishing—thank you.

To Jenna and Jasmine, for latching on to Crow, Chaos, and Lark's story and helping me pull the very best version of this story out of every draft; for your hilarious comments, brilliant ideas, and absolutely vital suggestions; and for cheering me on while I plotted a book/planned a wedding/wrote a book/got married all within a few months—seriously, thank you both so very much! To Rebecca and Clare for your excellent attention to detail—thank you. And to Aishwarya and Clarence, I can't thank you enough for taking the time to share your absolutely vital feedback. What you do isn't easy, and I hope you both know how appreciated you are.

To the design team for creating a truly badass and aesthetically beautiful book across multiple formats, including Leo, Angela, Liz, Michelle, and Jinna—thank you. Book design remains one of my favorite parts of watching my books come to print, and I am so grateful for all your work!

To the Random House Children's Books team for working tirelessly to get Crow, Chaos, and Lark's story out into the world, including Caroline, CJ, Josh, Stephania, Katie, Erica, and Nichole—thank you. Walking into a bookstore and seeing my books on the shelves will always be so special, and I so appreciate every one of you for helping to make that dream a reality.

To Kit and Genie for always being ready to cheer along for my secret victories and flip virtual tables for my publishing rants—your support means the world to me. And to Molly, for giving me the very tools that Crow and Lark use to tackle Crow's anxiety—I can't emphasize enough how much what you've taught me has improved my day-to-day.

To my readers—I may not always be able to answer your messages, but I read them, and they make all the harder publishing days worth it. Readers like you are the reason I get to keep writing books, and I am so grateful for your excitement and support. Thank you.

Finally, Jay. My love. My heart. My husband. I'm so damn grateful for you every day. Marrying you was the easiest and best decision I've ever made, and I'm so excited for the adventures that lie ahead of us. I'm delighted I get to share all of this with you. I love you so much.

ABOUT THE AUTHOR

GABE COLE NOVOA (he/him) is a Latinx transmasculine author who writes speculative fiction featuring marginalized characters grappling with identity. He is the award-winning and *New York Times* bestselling author of *The Wicked Bargain, The Diablo's Curse,* and *Most Ardently*. He also wrote the Beyond the Red trilogy under a former pseudonym.

GabeColeNovoa.com